From across the room, Gabriel closed his eyes and imagined touching Eden's soft, tender skin. Mentally he concentrated on arousing her.

He imagined his hand on the fullness of her breast, felt the weight and the texture. Jesus . . . he gritted his teeth, his own arousal profound and painful as he teased her nipple to a sharp point. Lips parted, a hectic pink bloomed in her cheeks. She was close. Damn close.

Jesus. This was killing him. Letting his mind touch her as he wanted to do, Gabriel eased her jean-clad thighs apart. Almost there.

Glass shattered, breaking the moment, and there was a yell from the kitchen. "Sorry!"

Eden moaned. Dazed and disoriented, she opened her eyes. "What the hell was *that*?!" she whispered, shaken.

EDGE
of
DANGER

A Novel

CHERRY
ADAIR

BALLANTINE BOOKS • NEW YORK

A Ballantine Books Mass Market Original

Copyright © 2006 by Cherry Adair
Excerpt of *Edge of Fear* copyright © 2006 by Cherry Adair

Published in the United States by Ballantine Books, an imprint of The Random House Publishing Group, a division of Random House, Inc., New York.

BALLANTINE and colophon are registered trademarks of Random House, Inc.

This book contains an excerpt from the forthcoming book *Edge of Fear* by Cherry Adair. This excerpt has been set for this edition only and may not reflect the final content of the forthcoming edition.

ISBN 0-345-48520-3

Printed in the United States of America

www.ballantinebooks.com

OPM   9 8 7 6 5 4 3 2 1

I have been given this day to use as I will.
I can waste it or use it for good.
Whatever I choose to do is important,
because I am exchanging a day of
my life for it.
—ANONYMOUS

In loving memory of my father, Ralph Campbell
October 4, 1915–September 18, 2005

From curtain rise to curtain fall
He lived life to the fullest and with great gusto

Gone, but in my heart always.

Duty o'er love was the choice you did make
My love you did spurn, my heart you did break

Your penance to pay, no pride you shall gain
Three sons on three sons find nothing but pain

I gift you my powers in memory of me
The joy of love no son shall ever see

When a Lifemate is chosen by the heart of a son
No protection can be given, again I have won

His pain will be deep, her death will be swift,
Inside his heart a terrible rift

Only freely given will this curse be done
To break the spell, three must work as one

EDGE
of
DANGER

CHAPTER ONE

"I don't give a damn if it's a matter of national security or not," Gabriel Edge savagely told the man he held at sword point. "I am *not* having sex with that woman."

The two men could have been sword fighting in medieval Scotland instead of twenty-first-century Montana. But both the castle and the heavy claymores the two T-FLAC operatives so expertly wielded were the real deal.

For several minutes the only sounds in the Great Hall were their breathing, the clash of ancient steel, and the soft sibilant shush of bare feet on stone. Swordplay was a well-choreographed dance, and they knew how to keep it interesting.

Their blades slid against each other ritually as the men circled each other, feinting, testing for weakness, waiting for a split-second opening. Slightly better conditioned for a sport that required both strength and dexterity, Gabriel intentionally moved off balance to fool his opponent. Then, keeping his swift curse mental instead of verbal, sidestepped Sebastian Tremayne's lightning-fast return thrust.

Pleased with himself, Sebastian shot him a triumphant glance. "Your country nee—"

"Same tune." From a high guard Gabriel made a strong downward cut, the blade of his broadsword flashing silver in the early morning sunlight streaming through the high arched windows. He moved with a feline grace and speed that had Sebastian backing up. Fast.

The first time Gabriel had set eyes on Dr. Eden Cahill he'd felt this same cold clench in his gut. It was getting worse.

"I'll find another way," he assured his friend grimly. And he would. As soon as he damn well came up with something that would work just as quickly, and just as well, as having sex with her.

Sebastian almost took off Gabriel's hand because he was so distracted. He'd taught his friend well. "Good one." He brought his attention back to the task at hand. Cutting back on the inhale, he halted his own strike an inch from his friend's heart. Again. "You're dead," he said with satisfaction.

They straightened and parted, each pausing to wipe the sweat from their eyes with their forearms. They were in hour two of practicing cuts and strikes. They'd stop soon. But not yet.

"Ready?" Gabriel asked after a few moments' rest, replacing both hands on the leather hilt of his sword.

"Yeah." Tremayne stepped back, sword raised.

Agile and fast on his feet, Gabriel circled. The longer they practiced, the heavier the claymore seemed to become. That ten pounds felt more like fifty after wielding it for an hour. A good workout. Both for his body and his mind.

"Been at it longer than you," he pointed out, reading the familiar I'm-going-to-beat-the-shit-out-of-you-this-time glimmer in his friend's eyes. They watched each other like hawks, slowly circling each other.

Waiting for an opportunity. Waiting for an opening.

From a hanging guard, Sebastian brought down a strong diagonal thrust. "Faster on my feet than you."

Knuckles white, Gabriel blocked. "You'll have to be."

Tremayne was a little out of breath, Gabriel noticed with satisfaction. They were evenly matched; he was just better at hiding his uneven breathing than his friend was.

Buttery light streamed through the leaded glass windows embedded in the thirteen-foot-deep walls. The Great Hall was constructed of rough-hewn stone the color of a good wine cork, and hung with enormous, priceless, centuries-old tapestries, coats of armor, ancient weaponry, and other *objets d'art*.

One of Gabriel's distant ancestors had built the castle in the Scottish Highlands for his young bride, Janet, in the first part of the fourteenth century. Hadn't worked out too well for *him,* but Gabriel wanted to live in the castle that had housed seven hundred years of the Edridge family. They might no longer use the old Scottish name, but the castle would always be home.

A man with his abilities could always get what he wanted.

As a boy he'd wanted the castle, and he'd gotten it. Using his wizard skills, he'd teleported his ancestral home stone by bloody stone until it stood, stark and proud, hundreds of miles from civilization. Somewhere inside that foolish boy had lived the naive hope that, with the ancestral home in Montana, his father would venture from his native Scotland to be with his family more often.

Magnus, unable to resist the lure of his Lifemate, had wanted Cait badly enough to ignore the Curse. Thinking he could change it, he married her. The first year had apparently been idyllic. Then things had turned to shit.

Terrified that she would die due to his close proximity, Magnus had spent the next twenty years in exile from his beloved wife and their three sons. Once a year he'd visit, but a series of near fatal accidents, or Cait's failing health, would always compel him to leave.

Their mother had been in ill health all their lives. She'd wasted away, pining for the husband who had married her and then lived to regret it. Their parents' frustration and unhappiness had been a stark lesson for Magnus's three sons.

Gabriel and his brothers were certain their parents had died of broken hearts. In five hundred years, no Edge had ever broken Nairne's Curse. None ever would.

Okay. He *got* it.

He could marry someone he didn't love, but could never love the woman he married. Hell, he could never *love*. Period.

No Lifemate.

No three sons on three sons.

No such fucking thing as happily ever after.

Screw it.

He had his work with T-FLAC. The counterterrorist organization was his life. His passion. It was enough.

Between missions he relished the isolation, the ancient history, and the drafty halls of Edridge Castle. In a world filled with death and betrayal, the connection to his past kept him centered.

In his daily life as a T-FLAC operative in the psi or paranormal branch, he used the most sophisticated high-tech military hardware coupled with ancient magic. When he was in his ancestral home he used the weapons hanging on the walls. Weapons his family had collected and used for centuries.

His weapon of choice for today's exercise was the claymore.

Weighing close to ten pounds, and with an overall length of more than four and a half feet, the claymore was a formidable weapon. Despite its antiquity, the lethal sword could deliver great sweeping slashes or powerful thrusts. Just what he was in the mood for this morning. He'd slept like shit last night, thinking about the good doctor. Or rather—trying *not* to think about her.

Narrow-eyed, Gabriel choked up on the leather-covered hilt with both hands as he anticipated his opponent's next move.

"If I could read minds," Sebastian said, clearly flagging, "*I'd* sleep with her."

"I'm sure you would." He used Sebastian's distracted focus to springboard his riposte off his blade. And the game was back on. "But you can't," he told his friend, who was T-FLAC but not part of the special "psychic phenomena" branch. The psi division was considered, by some, to be the elite group of the counterterrorist organization. By others it was the whoo-hoo division that they didn't understand. None were permitted to acknowledge the group outside the organization.

While there were still a few hundred known wizards in the world, the general population—normal people—were totally unaware that they even existed. And Gabriel and his brothers wouldn't even *be* wizards if not for that long-ago Curse.

Jesus. Talk about a woman scorned. The witch Nairne had laid one on his cheating great, great, how ever many greats, grandfather, Magnus Edridge, several hundred years ago.

The Edge family had changed their name, and had paid for the slight ever since.

Thank God he and his brothers had decided that the Curse, like the proverbial buck, stopped with them.

Not that any of them believed there was such a thing as a "Lifemate." But they weren't taking any chances. It wasn't difficult to keep women at arm's length, not in their business. The hours were long, their whereabouts frequently top secret.

The three of them had long ago agreed that they'd keep their relationships with the opposite sex casual. And if one of them should veer off the straight and narrow, the other two would pull him back from the abyss.

In thirty-four years, Gabriel had never met a woman who tempted him to change the "casual" rule, not even a little.

Until he'd laid eyes on the gorgeous doctor Eden Cahill.

He'd been near her that once. It had been enough. He'd taken one look. One. And been consumed by an unspeakable lust. It had been instantaneous, overwhelming, and dangerous as hell. He'd wanted to breathe her breath, to absorb her distinctive scent, to learn her textures. He'd hungered to taste her soft mouth, and run his hands over her silken skin.

For the last three days he'd been able to think of little else.

He blocked Sebastian's parry, edge on edge, with the *incrosada,* the crossing of the blades, bringing both weapons to a bone-jarring, shuddering stop. The vibration shimmied up his arm. The very air reverberated with the sharp scraping sound of steel on steel echoing off the ancient stone walls.

Their eyes met. Held. *Not sleeping with her,* he telegraphed as he gave a sharp twist of his wrist to indicate that his opponent should step back. Bloodlust raced through Gabriel's body.

Don't think about her, he told himself, feeling feral and slightly out of control at the memory of Dr. Cahill's glossy dark curls and her big brown eyes—

Jesus. He had to put a stop to his thoughts. He'd give anything right now to have a tango opposite him rather than a trusted friend and fellow operative. He'd trained Tremayne well enough to know that his friend could most certainly block a full force blow from him if he lost control enough to deliver it. But this was supposed to be merely an exercise, not a fight to the death.

"Why not—"

"I'm not discussing my sex life with you, Tremayne," he said coolly when inside he was anything but. He felt—annoyed. Hot. Twisted. And, if he didn't know better, scared as hell.

His friend raised a brow at his vehemence. "But it doesn't have to be sex *per se*. Does it?"

"At the risk of repeating myself: I will categorically *not* have sex with that woman. I made that crystal clear at the onset. When will Stone be back from Prague?" This wasn't the first time that Gabriel wished to hell he lived in the fifteenth century, when lopping off a man's head with the sharp blade of his broadsword wouldn't have the local cops inconveniently pounding on his door.

"After the Terrorism Summit." Sebastian parried another blow, grinning as he made a lunge of his own. "Another three weeks. I don't believe his presence would make this situation any less onerous for you, Edge."

Gabriel swept the claymore in a wide arc that had Sebastian dancing back a step or two. "Perhaps not. But having you breathing down my neck isn't improving my disposition any."

"Easily resolved. Extract the necessary data from Dr. Cahill's memory banks, and you may paint me gone." He advanced again, clearly determined to impress Gabriel with his prowess with the blade. "Until such time as you've accomplished your mission, I shall remain a guest in your . . . home."

"Guest my ass. You needed another lesson. You've gotten lazy."

"You could always do what other operatives do—use the damned telephone." Sebastian ignored the sweat running into his eyes, his concentration just as fierce as Gabriel's. "A castle, appropriated from the Highlands of Scotland and incongruously placed in the middle of Montana, isn't my idea of a vacation hot spot. The halls are drafty, it's two miles to my room, and the electricity is iffy."

"Edridge Castle isn't a hotel, Tremayne." Gabriel circled him, holding his gaze as intently as a cobra did a mongoose. Right now it was a toss-up as to which of them was which. "You're at liberty to fuck off any time you like. Now would be a good time."

"It's big enough to be a hotel." Sebastian's incoming attack was lethally fast. Gabriel moved faster. "Let's expedite this situation as rapidly as possible," he said, breathing heavily. They both were. Unfortunately, they were each ferociously competitive. Neither would back down until Gabriel's majordomo, MacBain, stepped in and had their half-dead bodies hauled upstairs.

"Get over your aversion," Sebastian rasped. "Have sex with the doctor. Close your eyes and think of Scotland if it'll help you stomach it. Just get it done."

If only it were an aversion, Gabriel thought furiously, slicing down his opponent's diagonal sweep with a descending cut, knocking his friend's sword away. "I'm going to say this for the last time." To control the other man's weapon Gabriel needed a lever. He stepped in closer. Tighter. Met his friend's predatory eyes.

"I. Will. Not. Have. Sex. With. Dr. Cahill. I'll get what we need from her in my own way. Is that clear?"

"Abundantly." The point of contact between the two shiny blades was halfway. There were no knucklebows on their broadswords and there was a very real possibility of cutting off a finger or two.

Steel clashed against steel, and the whisper of the men's feet moving across the stone floor echoed in the vast room.

They parted and Sebastian recovered quickly as Gabriel forced him to sidestep inside the cut, meeting his blade with a solid blow. "Good one."

His friend paused to draw in a ragged breath. "I'm just saying. We need that intel. It's the means to an end. Could save the lives of millions of people."

Gabriel knew that, God help him. The Edridge family Curse hung over his head like the sword of Damocles and he felt the swish of that heavy blade nearly parting his hair.

"It hasn't come to that." He aimed his cut at the midpoint of the incoming blade. "Yet. If and when it does, I'll take action."

"See that you do. When will you attempt it again? She doesn't need to be asleep for you to bring her to orgasm, does she?"

Gabriel allowed Sebastian's blade to travel to his crossguard, then struck with the edge of his own blade so their faces were inches apart. "Listen to yourself, for Christ's sake!"

Lightning fast, Gabriel attacked, swinging his sword into *posta frontal* as he sidestepped, meeting the other man's blade in a clash of metal and flying sparks. "Does anything about this conversation strike you as off limits?"

Sebastian, quick as always, met him with *mezza spada*. Gabriel's blade slid down to his friend's crossguard again.

Hilts and eyes locked.

"I'll tell you how it strikes me. It strikes me that Dr. Cahill has all the information about the robot in her freaking *head*. It strikes me that the only way to get said information is to read her mind, and that you can't read this particular mind because of some ancient and ridiculous curse. It bites, that's how all of this strikes me."

"You don't think I know that?"

"You are first and foremost a T-FLAC operative, Edge. A wizard in the psi division *second*. If you can't extract the information we need from Dr. Cahill in the usual manner, then you'll use whatever mumbo-jumbo re—"

Gabriel gave a savage thrust and disarmed his opponent.

"Ow! Shit! That stings like a son of a bitch!" Sebastian's sword skittered across the stone floor as he nursed his hand.

"Want MacBain to kiss it better?" Gabriel knew everything Sebastian was saying was only the truth. But hell, it didn't make it any easier to take, did it? "Jesus. I miss Stone."

Sebastian dropped his hands to his knees, hanging his head as he tried to catch his breath. "Don't we all."

Gabriel had tried *again* to probe Dr. Cahill's mind for the vital information he needed. He'd failed. Goddamn it. He *hated* to fail.

He'd cloaked himself, gone to her computer lab in Tempe, Arizona, three days ago. All he needed was a few seconds to retrieve the data and then get the hell out. Easy. She'd never even know he'd trespassed.

She'd been alone. Perfect timing. But much to his surprise, he hadn't been able to penetrate the hot, soft darkness of her mind. Something he could usually do with ease when he wanted to. And damn it to frigging hell. He *wanted* to.

He'd also wanted to shake her and demand how the hell this could happen. But he knew instinctively why he couldn't extract the secrets he needed from her mind. Somehow, God only knew how, she had him blocked.

He'd tried to get her to lower her defenses—even a few seconds would have done it—but he'd found his every attempt unsuccessful.

He had to get her to lower her guard. One of the quickest, easiest ways was if she had a climax. Her mind would be unprotected by her usual defenses. One quick climax and he'd be in and gone before she knew it. A few seconds with her emotional shields down, and he'd have everything he needed.

Now he was going to have to go back to damned Arizona, and try again. He knew if it didn't work this time, he was going to have to bring her back here to a more controlled environment. As much as he didn't want her anywhere near him, or the castle, he was running out of viable options.

He'd skip the preliminaries, and take her to a fast, unexpected climax. Surprise was going to be his weapon against Dr. Cahill's strong will.

Sebastian straightened to look at his friend. "She's not safe in Tempe." He accepted a bottle of water and a fresh white towel from Gabriel's butler, MacBain, who gave every appearance of being a deaf-mute. The wily bastard was anything but. The man had ears like a bat, eyes like a hawk—despite his glasses—and the organizational skills of Attila the Hun.

Gabriel knew without it having been said that Sebastian was giving him an inch more wiggle room on this because of their long-standing friendship. As his temporary control, Tremayne had every right to demand Gabriel extract the information from Dr. Cahill in the most expedient way possible.

"I know. Do you think I'd leave her there unprotected?" Gabriel had dispatched two T-FLAC operatives to watch her 24/7. They could not, however, get into the lab. And that was a problem that deeply concerned him.

Concerned him enough that he'd placed a protective spell on her.

"You'd trust someone else to keep her safe?"

"I'd trust myself to keep her alive."

"Really? And how do you propose doing that if you won't even touch the woman?" Tremayne took a long pull from the bottle, then upended it over his head, sluicing water over his sweat-soaked hair and face. "The good doctor scares the shit out of you. Doesn't she?"

Towel up to his face, Gabriel stopped what he was doing to stare at his friend. "Are you *insane*?"

"You've seen her once. Yet just thinking about the woman makes you screw up your face like a monkey's ass, Edge. Admit it. And the reason you're whining for Alex Stone is because he buys into this whole Edridge Curse bullshit. What happens if you touch her? Your dick turns black and falls off?"

MacBain cleared his throat. " 'When a Lifemate is chosen by the heart of a son, no protection can be given, again I have won. His pain will be deep, her death will be swift, Inside his heart a terrible rift.' It's Nairne's Curse, sir. The witch made no mention of anything turning black or falling off."

As a close friend, Sebastian was aware of the content of the Curse, and Gabriel knew the other man thought it was so much bullshit. Frankly, Gabriel wished like hell *he* was as certain. But it was damned hard to refute five hundred years of history to the contrary.

"Since Dr. Cahill isn't my Lifemate, if such a thing existed, which I seriously doubt, I can protect her just fine, thank you very much." Gabriel shot a cool glance at MacBain. "Don't you have butling duties to perform?"

Small and wiry, snow white hair immaculate, the butler drew himself up to his full five feet four and a quarter inches and peered at Gabriel through the thick, black-rimmed glasses perched on his beak of a nose. As always he was immaculately dressed in a natty black suit, crisp white shirt, and a tie in the Edridge plaid. "It is my *great* fortune to attend ye at every opportunity, sir," he said, the burr of Scotland in his voice, his expression as innocent as a babe.

"If only," Gabriel muttered. MacBain pretty much did as he pleased.

"Why do you bother working for this Philistine?" Sebastian asked with a grin. "My offer is still open, MacBain."

MacBain's bushy white brows dipped in a frown behind his glasses. "Ye live in a *condominium*, sir."

"Less dusting. Big screen television. No Curse."

"Enormous incentives, but I'm afraid I must decline yer tempting offer. I made a promise to the lad's father that I'd keep an eye on him. And here's where I'm needed."

"Why don't you hie yourself off to keep an eye on Duncan or Caleb?" Gabriel demanded, making the decision he had to make. He'd try one more time with Dr. Cahill. But he suspected he'd have no chance of breaking through her barriers while she was in Arizona and in her own little safety zone.

"While I ponder that intriguing question," MacBain told him facetiously, "might one inquire as to what yer intentions might be regarding this Dr. Cahill?"

His intention was to do what he had to do as fast as humanly possible. And then keep out of Arizona until hell froze over. "I'll give this one more shot," Gabriel told Sebastian and MacBain, his tone downright grim. "If that doesn't work, I'll bring her here, and *make* it work." Here on his turf. Where he was strongest.

Tremayne raised a brow. "You'll kidnap her?" Not a question.

Still looking at Sebastian, Gabriel tossed his claymore

to MacBain who, braced for the weight, deftly caught it. He was damn strong for a wiry old guy. "If I have to."

His friend gave him a mild look. "When are you going?"

"Now," Gabriel said grimly.

The air swirled, his image blurred. And he was gone.

Sebastian glanced at MacBain. "I freaking *hate* when he does that."

Gabriel's majordomo cleared his throat. "*Och*, aye. As do I, sir. As do I."

"Damn it to hell. She's *naked*!"

The man's harsh, disgruntled whisper cut through the blackness of Dr. Eden Cahill's bedroom. Despite yesterday's heat still trapped in the room, the voice chilled her to the bone. Her eyes sprang open as her brain leapt from deep sleep to total awareness between one heartbeat and the next.

A myoclonic jerk? No. She was sure she'd fallen asleep hours ago. Was it the stifling heat that had woken her? More likely it was her subconscious reliving what was going on in her life.

Feigning sleep, she held her breath, waiting. Had she actually heard the voice? Or dreamed it? She strained to listen. She couldn't hear anyth—No . . . There was *definitely* someone there. Barely breathing. Certainly not moving. But *there*. Close. She sensed the heat and power of the intruder as he loomed over her bed. The faint scent of his skin—soap—male—seemed to envelop her with a strange yearning she couldn't begin to decipher.

Sharp prickles of fear danced across Eden's bare skin as her heart raced and her mind went into overdrive. There was unquestionably someone in the room. She could feel his presence. Were there two of them, or had he been talking to himself? Hard as she tried, now all she could hear was the soft hum of the struggling air conditioner in the other room.

She realized with surprise that she *was* naked. Normally she *did* sleep this way. But for the last couple of weeks she'd worn pajamas because of the security people in the other room. She frowned. She was positive she'd put on her ladybug jammies before she'd crawled into bed last night . . . Hadn't she?

Obviously not, since she was bare-butt naked under the sheet.

She didn't waste time wondering how or why, or what he/they were doing in her apartment, or how he'd managed to get through the locks on her doors and windows, and then past several company security guys sitting in her living room just feet beyond the closed and locked bedroom door. She didn't waste time anticipating what he might do to her, either. With any luck she'd have time to ponder those questions—later.

Barely breathing herself, she surreptitiously slid her hand beneath her pillow. *There.* Her fingers closed around the cool butt of a small LadySmith.

Why hadn't her bodyguards stopped him? The chilling answer was: Because they were dead. She clicked off the safety as she said coolly, "I have a gun and it's pointed at whatever body part is at my eye level. Back off." She was surprised her voice wasn't a feeble croak. Not only was she naked, protected by nothing more substantial than a thin sheet, but she was on her back. The only way she'd feel more vulnerable was if he was holding the gun and the lights were on.

The image of Dr. Kirchner sprawled on the stark white floor of the lab, the horrifying memory of glistening red blood pooled beneath his head made Eden's hand steady as a rock.

Terrified? Yes.

Determined to pull the trigger. Absolutely.

Her finger squeezed—

"You don't want to shoot me, Dr. Cahill." There was something unsettling, something hinting at a different kind of danger beneath the almost casual caution in the man's voice. The iron fist in a velvet glove method of intimidation.

Eden readjusted the short barrel of the gun in his direction without letting up on the trigger. "Don't bet on it, pal." Another little squeeze and he'd be dead. "You're close enough that I can't possibly miss."

Where the freaking hell *was* he so she could make sure of that? She noticed vaguely that there wasn't even the faint glow from the red LCD numbers on the bedside clock to help her see where exactly he was. The realization that he'd managed to unplug her clock before she was even aware of his presence creeped her out even more.

What else had he had time to do?

She wished the light was on—No. She didn't. Whoever this guy was, he wasn't going to see her naked before he died. Not if she could help it.

She was banking on helping it.

For the past couple of weeks, thanks to her boss, and sometimes date, Jason Verdine, she'd had four beefy bodyguards with her at all times. If they hadn't stopped the man from entering, they were most likely incapable of stopping him from leaving. And the only logical explanation for the intruder to be in her apartment was that he'd killed the guards, just as he'd killed Theo.

Now he's going to kill me.

"Step away from the bed. And keep walking. I'll even give you a head start before I call nine-one-one." *Not.* He couldn't know the bedside phone had 911 on speed dial.

She who hesitates is lost. She didn't wait to see if he

started to retreat. Bracing for the loud retort, and the killer's death scream, Eden pulled the trigger.

No big bang. No flash of light.

"What happened to my head start?" His voice was dry and very much alive.

"I lied." Eden squeezed off another shot.

CHAPTER TWO

It didn't make a freaking sound.

Oh shit! Eden's heartbeat skittered and jumped. Bad time for the gun to jam.

Refusing to panic, she ignored the buzz of terror dulling her hearing. Mentally she choreographed getting out of bed, picking up the bedside lamp—the only thing close to hand that could be used as a weapon—and hitting him. All before he killed her.

She didn't stand a snowball's chance in hell of pulling that off. He was too close.

"This is a dream, Dr. Cahill," he said gently into the thick darkness, his husky voice almost hypnotic.

"Oh, for heaven's sake. How lame is that?!" she said indignantly, struggling up on one elbow while trying to hold the malfunctioning gun steady and anchor the edge of the sheet over her chest at the same time. *Come closer, asshole. I'll beat you bloody with this useless damn gun.*

It wouldn't kill him, but it might give her enough time to get away. "Look," she told him reasonably. "I have nothing but a few bits of costume jewelry." *And if you've come for anything else, you won't find it in a drawer.*

As she talked she shifted the gun so she could use the barrel as a handle and hit him with the wooden grip. "Take what you want and get o—Oh." A brush of air, barely felt, and the small gun vanished from her hand. Just like that.

Poof. Gone.

Cocking her head—*damn it, where* was *he?*—she scowled. Smoke and mirrors. "Who are you? What do you want?"

It was unnerving having a stranger in her bedroom in the pitch dark. Hell, he'd probably scare the hell out of her in broad daylight too. "Are you alone?"

There was a thoughtful silence before he answered the last question. "Why?"

"I heard you talking to someone when I—woke up." Nightmare or fact, Eden considered how to get out of the room and make it to the front door without being killed in the process. If the guy had come in that way, he'd probably left the door unlocked. Her tattooed and pierced neighbor was a big guy with chronic insomnia. If she could just make it out into the hallway . . .

The head of her bed was closest to the door. Lie here and die, or die trying. She voted for trying. She slid her right leg carefully, inch by inch, across the cool, smooth sheet.

She felt odd. Breathless and tingly. Fear, of course.

"I'm alone."

Eden brought her left leg slowly across the mattress. Too damn slowly. At this rate she'd still be slithering across the sheets come December, for God's sake.

She inched her bare bottom across the sheet that no longer felt cool. The fabric seemed to caress her naked skin, and she stopped moving, puzzled by the odd manifestation of sexual heat her body was experiencing. Fear-induced lust? Nonsense.

Fear frequently masquerades as another emotion, she told herself firmly. She wasn't experiencing lust, she was experiencing justifiable fear.

She moved another inch. "Where are the security guys? Did you kill them?"

"*Jesu*—No, I didn't. Lie back and relax."

Relax?! As if. From the sound of his voice he was no longer standing beside the bed, but she still wasn't sure where he was in the room. His voice came from farther away, although she hadn't heard him walking across the hardwood floor.

Her Grandma Rose's old chair squeaked. "You're dreaming," he murmured, settling into the cane back. His voice, a whisper of smoke, curled around her.

She remembered a poem her father used to quote. *The other day upon the stair, I saw a man who wasn't there. He wasn't there again today. I wish that man would go away.*

It didn't feel anything like a dream. His voice was real. *He* was real. She might not be able to see him, but he was *there*. She knew he was there.

She moved another inch across the bed. Closer to the door. This was pretty freaking bizarre. "Are you my subconscious trying to make sense of why Theo was killed?" She demanded an answer, caught between the hope that this was indeed a dream, and the fear that it wasn't.

Dr. Kirchner's murder had shaken her to the core. Clearly she was under considerable stress to be hallucinating this vividly. But could a hallucination take her gun from her?

The mind was a powerful thing.

"Leave the killer to the authorities."

She would. Of course she would. But she had plenty of questions of her own. And Theo's cryptic warning to process. Not to mention a major case of guilt for her inability to save him.

"Who are you, and what do you want?" Eden demanded with more heat. She didn't understand her body's behavior. Her skin felt hot and tight, her lips swollen. Her heart was thudding arrhythmically. She was conscious of the smooth fabric of the sheet rubbing

maddeningly over her nipples as she shifted, and the un-
relieved throbbing between her thighs.

She ached with a nameless longing—No, she thought,
appalled and half embarrassed. Not nameless.

She was turned on.

Sexually aroused by a man who wasn't touching her.
A man who wasn't there.

"Who would you like me to be?"

Her heart was galloping uncomfortably, and it was
hard to keep her tone even. "Not the invisible man,
that's for sure."

"I told you, this is a dream."

"If this is a dream I get to ask you questions." She
realized she still felt antsy—not very scientific, but—
antsy. Respiration up. Heart racing, skin tingling, body
parts that had no business making themselves known,
on high alert.

Sexually aware. And becoming more so by the minute.

Freaking bizarre all right. Telling herself not to be
ridiculous didn't help.

"What kind of questions?" he asked impatiently. The
chair creaked as he shifted.

"That depends on who you are," she pointed out, lick-
ing her dry lips. "Since this is my dream I suppose I can
make you anyone. How about Albert Einstein?" *How
about* . . . Her mind went blank as she tried to come up
with some fantasy man to ease the flutter of arousal she
was feeling. Nobody came to mind. How sad was that?

"How about not?"

"Well, that's unreasonable since it's my—" she broke
off as she suddenly noticed the drag of the sheet sliding
down her body toward her feet. The cool silkiness of the
fabric skimming her skin made her shiver, and her respiration and heart rate jumped alarmingly as her breath
snagged in her throat.

"Hey! Dream or no dream. *No touching.*" She made

a useless grab for the rapidly retreating material. It, like her gun, disappeared.

Look Ma, no hands.

The chair hadn't creaked. He hadn't moved. Either the guy was a magician, or it really was a bona fide, stress-induced, break-with-reality kind of dream. And if it *was* a dream, she had no reason to be scared.

Like hell she wasn't scared.

She knew her own body like . . . the back of her hand, she thought wryly. And this was turned on. Big time turned on. Hot to trot turned on. Ready for hard fast sex turned on. Moisture pooled between her legs and her nipples ached to be touched turned on.

Dream or no dream, it *felt* real.

Moving made it worse, and she forced herself to lie still, hoping to God the sensation would pass so she could leap out of bed and make a run for it. She lay back against the pillows, forcing herself to breathe slowly and deeply. In. Out. In. Out.

"How about—" Intimate pulse points started to throb maddeningly, joining all her other symptoms. "Ah . . . Dr. Betsy Ancker-Johnson?"

Lying still wasn't helping. Not at all. There wasn't a breath of air in the room, yet her nipples peaked, hard and painfully, and goosebumps roughened her skin. Goosebumps she always got when she was sexually aroused. "Yes. Ancker-Johnson." Her voice was thick, husky.

She cleared her throat. "I'd love to ask her about her observations of microwave emission without the presence of an external field. Or Steven Spielberg? He'd be fascinating to talk to."

"I'm going to make love to you now, Eden," he cut off her nervous ramblings.

That spiked her heart rate even more, and made the nerves under her skin jump. *"Jason?!"* The dream suddenly made some sort of crazy sense. There were many empirical findings about dreams that didn't fit with any problem-solving theory that she knew of. Still—

"Ja—? Yes. *Jason*." He didn't sound particularly pleased. "Close your eyes."

She closed them. It was a strain trying to peer through the darkness anyway. "That doesn't sound very lover-like," she told him crossly. Really, if she wasn't ready to have sex with Jason Verdine in real time, she highly doubted she'd be ready in a dream.

"Listen to the music, Eden."

"There isn't any mus—Oh. That's pretty." Something with flutes that made her think of splashing water and soaring birds. Instead of relaxing, she found herself tensing, feeling a crazy—make that *insane*—urge to invite him into her bed. That, if nothing else, convinced her this was a dream.

Captivated by the way her body was behaving, Eden tried to look at this scientifically. But, oh, God. She was on fire. Her skin felt sensitized. *Fascinating*. But how could this be? It took more than a suggestion of intimacy to make her hot. She was a girl who needed foreplay. Clearly her brain was her largest erogenous zone.

She relaxed into the overwhelming sensation. The anticipation of his touch, the breathless, knife-edge of expectation had her lifting her hips.

"I know this is just my subconscious trying to help me sort out the violence, or what to do about Jason, or . . . some—Oh, God what are you doing to m-me . . . But I don't think it's w-working."

It wasn't working because she was suddenly consumed with the need for sex. Hard and fast and *now*. Her skin burned. Hell, she felt hot all over, and it had nothing to do with the warm Arizona night. She shifted restively on the sheet, her breasts, her thighs, her belly, every throbbing, needy part of her demanding physical contact.

Relief was in the bedside drawer. But dream or no dream, she wasn't masturbating with some strange, disembodied invisible guy in the room watching her. No matter how much her body begged for release, or how sexy he sounded. She moistened suddenly dry lips with the tip of her tongue. Wanting—Needing—

"I am not touching you." He said it, not as though he was assuring her, but as though he refused to do so.

"You can't, Sparky. You're a dream. An illusion." The smooth bluesy music filled the room, but did nothing to slow the thud of her heart as adrenaline raced through her veins in a white-hot tide of desire.

Eden's body felt like a gathering storm, drawing tighter and tighter. Her knees moved apart without her conscious thought.

He might be sitting ten feet away from her in her granny's boudoir chair, but Eden's nipples suddenly responded as if they *were* being stroked. The sensation was nothing short of electrifying, and her stomach seemed to drop as though she were freefalling. She gritted her teeth, trying to shut off the sensations spiraling through her.

She waved a hand over her breasts, sure that someone was physically touching her. Her hand passed through air before dropping back to clutch at the sheet beneath her hips.

Holy cow! When I have a break with reality, I do a really, really good job.

This is one hell of an adept apparition.

She swore she felt the heat of his skin. But he wasn't anywhere near her. Good Lord. The scientist in her didn't believe in ghosts. On the other hand, she didn't believe in telekinesis either and he'd made both gun and sheet vanish into thin air.

"Don't fight it," he said, clearly exasperated. "Just feel."

"I'm feeling plenty," she muttered, still not sure why she was feeling *anything*. She shivered as the hair on her neck was brushed aside. The tightness in her stomach grew stronger as she imagined cool lips moving over the hot, damp skin of her nape. A shiver went through her, and she couldn't help the little moan that escaped her parted lips as warm air fanned her skin.

"Ah. You like that." Her hair seemed to fall, sifting to tickle her neck. Eden squeezed her eyes tightly closed, knowing only pure sensation. She wanted to crawl completely into the dark, sweet fantasy that was wiping everything out of her mind but what he was doing to her. The heat and scent of the man's skin—a man who wasn't there—became etched on her memory.

Not satisfied with this ethereal phantom lover, Eden craved the physical touch of his body like a drug. The pulse in her throat beat wildly as a trail of moist heat seemed to move from the base of her neck to her right breast.

Her pulse went into overdrive as an inextricable pressure around her nipple drew it into a tight, almost painful nub. Her nipple was manipulated into an aching peak, but she had no idea how. She didn't care. Ultra-sensitive, her skin burned, and a deep pulse of expectation made her hips arch up off the mattress.

She moaned. Instinctively she reached out her arms to hold him. There was nothing there. She dug her fingers into the sheet on either side of her hips to anchor herself again.

"Let yourself go," he whispered, that voice as deep and arousing as the whisper of sensation on her skin. "Just . . . let . . . yourself . . . go."

The cunning stroke of an invisible hand trailed a fiery path from her breasts across her tummy. Eden bit her lip as need ratcheted up and up unbearably. She couldn't quite catch her breath. She wanted—she needed—

She opened herself, yielding to the craving, desperate for sweet relief, her body as tightly coiled as a spring.

But there was something—something on the periphery of her consciousness that kept that final release at bay.

"Come for me, Doctor," he said urgently.

"No," she told him with spurious calm, breath coming in short choppy bursts as she tried to regulate it. By crossing her legs tightly she could send herself into orbit in about three seconds if she wanted to.

"No?" he asked, sounding annoyed. "Why the hell not?"

"Because, even in a freaking bizarre dream like this I want more than a quickie orgasm, that's why." Her jaw ached from gritting her teeth to try to counteract the insistent pulse of her body readying itself to climax.

"God, I'm arguing with an imaginary man." Eden pushed herself up against the pillows very carefully. At this point her body had a hair trigger. "When—*if* I eventually do make love with Jason, we'll do it together. Not in my imagination. Until then I have Richard for that."

She used iron control of mind over matter. Her body started to cool, very much like water having boiled in her kettle. A twinge here, a ping there.

The chair creaked. "Who," he asked disinterestedly, "is Richard?"

"None of your business. Look, this is my dream. And I'm ending it. So get lost. I can have sex—good sex I might add—by myself any time I like. I don't need some figment of my imagination manipulating me."

"You're wet. On the brink—"

"Yes. And yes. Most uncomfortable. But not fatal. Don't you have some other dreamer to annoy?"

She sensed rather than heard him sigh, then jumped

at the unexpected brush of his hand across her eyes when he'd been safely across the room. "Close your eyes, Eden," he said softly.

She flinched at the brilliant flash of light beyond her closed lids. *Well, shit,* she thought indignantly, *the son of a bitch killed me after all.*

CHAPTER THREE

"This still feels too weird. Does it still feel too weird to you?" Marshall Davis, Eden's assistant, demanded as the inner door opened.

"It's bound to feel odd without them," Eden answered, preceding him into Verdine Industries' computer lab in the Tempe, Arizona, head office. High, narrow windows flooded the stark room with morning sunlight.

Marshall was a tall, almost gaunt young man, who looked, and frequently behaved, years younger than his actual age of twenty-two. Like Eden, he'd been on an accelerated learning curve. His black hair always looked as though it had been chewed off instead of cut. Choppy and uneven was made worse because Marshall tugged at his hair when he was concentrating, so it usually stood straight up in ragged steps around his face. The bane of his existence was his acne, which usually translated into a debilitating shyness around women.

He didn't exactly consider Eden a woman. She was his idol. His leader. His mentor.

"Weird," he repeated, looking around.

"Weird" summed up the bizarre dream that had wakened her in the early hours of that morning. Sex and violence. Crazy dreams and brutal reality. Each profoundly disturbing in its own way.

It had been just over two weeks since her mentor, Dr. Theo Kirchner, had been murdered, and the prototype of their top secret Rx793 robot stolen. There was no evidence now of either crime. The trashed computers and equipment had all been replaced with dizzying speed. The crime scene people were long gone. There was no taped outline in the small kitchen where Eden had discovered Theo's body that night, no smudges of black fingerprint powder dusting every surface.

She'd been told to take two weeks off. She'd reluctantly done so. After spending two days cleaning her apartment she'd been out of her mind with boredom. Bored enough that she'd hopped a flight to Sacramento and gone to see her mother.

The visit had been better than expected. Of course, Eden thought wryly, her mother was interested in the murder, something that wasn't about her daughter's work. They loved each other, but they were so dissimilar that it was hard to sit down and have a real conversation, although they always tried.

Eden was pathetically grateful to be back at work.

The lab was once again pristine. No wonder her subconscious was freaking out. How could she pretend that things were normal when they were anything but?

Theo wasn't just "gone"; her eighty-six-year-old mentor had been murdered in cold blood. He should have died in his own bed. Peacefully. Instead, he'd been shot and filled with terror, his last words to her: *"Destroy everything. Trust no one. Promise me."*

Though Jason Verdine had provided round-the-clock bodyguards to ensure her and Marshall's safety, Eden was nervous as hell. She had wiped all the data from the computers, as Theo had instructed. But 80 percent of their work was in her head.

If anyone ever discovered *that* . . .

She'd worked for Verdine Industries for more than a

decade. This, the Elite Team lab, was the nucleus of VI's long-term projects in core areas of artificial intelligence. Supposedly headed by Dr. Kirchner, but really overseen by Eden.

The R&D department next door consisted of a hundred and fifty-some people, and their support staff. The rest of the employees in the building were admin, sales, and manufacturing. Verdine Industries was a multibillion-dollar corporation. They manufactured everything from home robots that cleaned and vacuumed floors, to innovative items for NASA, to high-tech robotic toys.

The Elite Team had consisted of the three of them. Herself, Theo, and Marshall. Now there were two.

The authorities suspected one of Verdine Industries' rivals of the theft, but so far had no proof. The police had to be right on target; the killer, the thief, must be a competitor.

But no one knew how they'd been able to bypass the security systems in order to get into the lab. No one, not even the United States government, could penetrate the complicated, sophisticated access system at the lab. Particularly this smaller lab.

Yet, somehow, someone had.

Theo's death and the theft were an active case. Every now and then another alphabet soup government official would show up with more of the same questions. Eden and Marshall had no answers. She wished they did.

She glanced around the brightly lit lab. She'd designed it herself and every aspect of the room usually brought a thrill of pride. This was normally the time of day she enjoyed most. When the day was just beginning and ripe with possibilities. When hours stretched before her, each one conceivably holding the key to something she hadn't known the hour before.

But Jason had been told to halt any further develop-

ment of a replacement for Rex, pending the outcome of
the investigation.

Eden felt lost. Dr. Kirchner's murder, and the theft of
a decade's worth of work, had changed her fundamen-
tally, and nothing would ever be the same again. The *lab*
would never be the same. She'd never again feel the
peace and joy walking in here as she had done every
morning for the past ten years.

There had been breakthroughs made in this lab that
no one but the three of them had known. Not even
Jason himself knew the extent of their advances. And
even Theo and Marshall didn't know how much further
Eden had gone on her own.

The ramifications of such advanced robotic technology falling into the wrong hands were terrifying. She'd
known pushing the AI envelope that far was dangerous.
Known it, but kept on going past the point of no return.
Because her damn curiosity had compelled her to keep
striving for the holy grail of AI.

The Rx793 robot they called "Rex" now had the capability of reasoning abstractly. Which allowed him to
reason analogically and hierarchically. Rex was capable
of interacting without benefit of communication.

Marshall, a mechanical engineer, had designed the au-
tomated parts of Rex with 3-D geometry, and had spent
hundreds upon hundreds of hours "playing" with the
robot, teaching it human behaviors.

Even he had no idea just how far she'd taken their
creation, Eden thought, pressing a hand to her stomach.
Forget about butterflies. She had pterodactyls swarming
and dive-bombing inside her.

And now someone else had Rex.

All that someone needed to do was ask Rex the right
questions. Oh, God—She felt sick to her stomach. No
scientific advancement was worth a human's life. She
knew with every fiber of her being that Theo had died

trying to protect the robot's technology from falling into the wrong hands. He'd tried to warn her that the world wasn't ready for such advancements. But she hadn't listened.

Her eyes stung. She'd already cried buckets. She didn't have a drop left. "Theo practically shoved me out that damn door that night. If I'd stayed another half hour—"

"*You'd* be dead too." Marshall reached out and gave her a hesitant, awkward hug. Bless his heart, he smelled strongly of Clearasil and Brut cologne. In all the years they'd worked together, he'd never touched her. Embarrassed, he let her go immediately and shot her a self-conscious smile as he stepped back, his face pink.

"I don't want you to be dead, Eden. Losing Dr. Kirchner was bad enough. I *really* don't want you to be dead."

"That makes two of us." She was thankful for Arizona's open carry law that allowed her the LadySmith .357 Magnum, five-shot revolver she now had in her purse. The gun had been under her pillow when she'd woken this morning. She'd been wearing her ladybug pajamas as well. Which proved, no matter how realistic it might have been, her dream had been just that. A dream.

Perhaps her body was trying to let her know subconsciously that it was time to find a lover. Jason?

He was charming, and nice looking, and wealthy, and—

Not him, she thought, puzzled by her own reticence.

Marshall pulled out his chair and sat at his workstation, picking up a small red ball. "I have no idea why I'm holding on to this stuff. It's not as if we'll need it again."

They'd used dozens of toys as learning tools for the robot. Balls, mechanical insects, colored blocks. Flash cards. Items that to untrained eyes were just clutter.

Apparently whoever had killed Theo hadn't taken any chances of leaving anything behind. They'd taken every disk, every scrap of paper, everything except an overlooked red ball.

"Hey, you never know." Eden sat down in her ergonomic, five-thousand-dollar chair, booted her computer, and tried to sound cheerful. "Maybe Jason will give us the go-ahead to rebuild him."

And if I could do it again? she asked herself. *Honestly? In a heartbeat.* It had been the most exhilarating, fulfilling event in her career.

But realistically? Now that I know someone can just walk in and take the technology? Absolutely not.

"Not with every government agency breathing down his neck, he won't," Marshall said with disgust.

Eden looked at the preliminary designs for the voice-tech band and wanted to hit delete. Who cared? Yes, she grudgingly acknowledged, the concept had military as well as practical applications. The skeletal line-drawing rotated in virtual 3-D on her computer. The unit was no larger than an average wristwatch, but this design would allow the embedded computer portability as well as incorporating basic AI. Once built, it could process, analyze, and mimic everything from the commands of a seasoned general in battle to the mundane dictates of a babysitter. Eden thought it was an unambitious project. A freaking micro-nanny. It wasn't Rex, damn it.

Marshall gave her a cautious look. "Maybe you shouldn't have been so evasive about Rex to that Homeland Security guy."

"I didn't lie to Special Agent Dixon." *She'd lied by omission though.* Once the authorities realized the extent of the technology unleashed, the shit would hit the proverbial fan.

The pterodactyls went kamikaze, and she pressed her hand to her midriff. *They don't know half of what he's capable of. And please God, let's hope they never need to find out.*

"To give Jason his due," she said, striving for calm she was in no way feeling, "they probably gave him no choice but to shut down the program." She was torn. Admit the full extent of her research. Or pray that whoever had Rex never discovered all his capabilities.

Marshall snorted. "I hate to be cynical, but Mr. Verdine will make a mint from the insurance claim. Without having to go to the trouble of putting Rex into production."

"That's ridiculous. He was the one who told us to come up with a humanlike robot they could use as a medic in war zones in the first place."

"True . . . Radio on or off?" He asked absently, already focused on his computer.

He'd been about to say something else, Eden knew. Marshall didn't much like Jason Verdine. "On."

He turned on the state-of-the-art stereo system, and the too quiet lab filled with quiet jazz.

She was going to have to come clean to the authorities. She knew it. She had no choice. She'd already waited too long. Guilt was burning a hole in her brain, and in her poor, abused stomach.

She'd honored Theo's dying last words as promised. But she was going to have to break that promise. Because the longer she kept these secrets the worse the possibilities became. She couldn't in good conscience not forewarn the authorities, even if the bad guys never figured out what they had.

The authorities might or might not find the perpetrator and retrieve Rex, but Dr. Kirchner would still be dead. She could at least give him the credit for her work—

Oh for God's sake. Eden thought, furious with herself. And then they'd blame *Dr. Theo Kirchner* for being an overreaching, overachieving, overeducated . . . *moron* for unleashing Rex on the world.

She wouldn't do that to Theo.

He'd been more family than her own. He'd shared her frustrations. He'd celebrated her successes. He'd understood her. Something that couldn't be said for pretty much anyone she now knew. She'd loved her professor like a grandfather. She would miss his gentle humor, his sharp intellect before age had diminished it. She'd miss their shared experience, miss his joy and pride at each new discovery she made. God. She missed *him*. Desperately.

She'd felt more alone, more *separate* than ever, standing at his graveside. He'd had no family there. The closest "family" had been her and Marshall. How sad was that? And who would stand wet-eyed beside *her* grave? It was a sobering thought.

Having no interest or excitement in this new project, Eden's gaze kept returning to the other end of the room and the doorway to the kitchenette where she'd discovered Theo barely alive that night two weeks ago.

"Destroy everything. Trust no one. Promise me."

Well, she'd destroyed what was left, and God only knew, she had trust issues by the bushel already.

She wished she could share her guilt with Marshall. Wished she could confess that she'd been an egotistical idiot to push so far and so fast with the technology. Marshall would certainly understand. Hell, he'd be ecstatic to learn just how far she'd been able to go. But as strongly as she wanted to tell him, Eden knew she would never put Marshall in the position of knowing something that could get him at best arrested, at worst, killed.

God, what a mess she'd made.

And how could she drag Marshall into the abyss with her? She knew without looking that his brow would be furrowed like a sharpei as he concentrated. He was cute and geeky, with no social skills, little self-confidence, and a brain few people understood. He reminded Eden of herself at the same age.

Like herself, Marshall had a few body image issues. She'd been a plump, shy misfit until she'd gotten rid of two hundred and forty some pounds. Fifty excess pounds of her own, and a hundred and ninety of ex-husband.

She missed neither her ex, nor the weight she'd lost through mind-numbing diligence, discipline, and sheer determination.

Marshall would come into his own. He was only twenty-two, a mishmash of disproportionate body parts. Not that Eden gave a damn what he looked like. He was funny and dear, and the best lab assistant she'd ever had. He'd worked with her for three years, and she trusted him implicitly. Something she couldn't say about most men of her acquaintance.

She could hear Marshall typing behind her, clicking away as his fingers flew over his keyboard. It didn't take much to get Marshall deeply involved.

Eden glared at her monitor and lightly tapped a short nail on the delete key.

She felt burned out. Guilt ridden. Stressed as well. She hated that she had those bodyguards with her 24/7. They'd gone with her to Sacramento, and camped out at her mom's while she slept. Not that she'd been sleeping well lately.

Which brought her full circle to the bizarre dream she couldn't forget.

Suddenly her heart started pounding erratically and she felt hot. Fever hot. She scowled. A hell of a dream if just the memory of it got her all hot and bothered.

She related the sensations she was experiencing to a surge of adrenaline. No—more like *anticipation*. Of what she had no idea. She had the sense that, somehow, she was on the brink of something . . . life altering.

Fanciful nonsense, she told herself. She was a scientist. Her elevated heart rate and respiration were directly correlated to her thoughts about everything that had happened in the last few weeks. Her fear was justified. Under the circumstances, she'd be a damn fool *not* to be scared. The ramifications of what had been stolen were far-reaching and of monumental proportions in the wrong hands. And she was almost wholly responsible.

Guilt was a heavy burden.

CHAPTER FOUR

She doesn't look happy, Gabriel thought, not too fucking happy himself. Invisible, he stood unnoticed twenty feet away from her, yet he still felt the same pull he'd felt in her bedroom earlier. He let his gaze slide down her lush body as she sat at her computer.

He closed his eyes briefly as her fragrance filled his senses, hoping, praying that the unbearable tension inside him would ease. His attraction to her was powerful. Good sense clanged a loud warning to get as far away from this woman as possible before it was too late.

Stunned by the strength of the blinding physical awareness he felt just *looking* at her, Gabriel wanted to be anywhere but here. Wanted to feel anything but the raw longing scorching him deep inside.

The fact that he'd *imagined* her naked before he'd entered her bedroom in the early hours of this morning, and she had *become* naked, concerned him a great deal. How was his subconscious suddenly capable of performing magic tasks not commanded by his conscious thought?

That had never happened before.

He'd have to be a damn sight more vigilant about what the hell he was thinking when he was around Dr. Cahill.

Thank God he wouldn't have to be around her for long.

Unfortunately he was near her *now*.

He remembered the sight of her beautiful plump breasts with the peaks of her aroused nipples begging for his touch. He pictured her parted lips, and the sounds she made as her arousal built, and gritted his teeth hard enough for his jaw to ache, willing away the vivid pictures in his brain.

What would happen if he gave in to the powerful temptation? Just to *touch* her? How dangerous could a touch be? Lust wasn't love. And God only knew, this was lust to the nth power.

It was useless trying to resist the compulsion to stare at her. Impossible. He'd proved *that* to himself the last time he'd watched her here in the lab several days ago, and again early this morning before the sun was up.

It was even worse this morning. He'd known—*known*—that seeing this woman again would be dangerous. But what choice had he had?

The Curse.

The fucking, goddamned Curse was alive and well and already biting him in the ass. He'd felt the pull the very first time he'd laid eyes on this woman. A pull he'd never felt before in his life, but one he recognized immediately. Scared the living bejesus out of him.

When a Lifemate is chosen by the heart of a son: No protection can be given, again I have won.

Not that he'd let it get *that* far. Hell no. He'd do what he had to do and get the hell out of Dodge. Besides, it wasn't his *heart* that was turned on by Dr. Eden Cahill.

Close enough to reach out and touch her, he watched her work. Her hair gleamed, beckoning to be stroked. The curly, chin-length strands bared the vulnerable curve of her neck as she leaned over the keyboard. He wanted to put his mouth there. Her dark lashes cast shadows on her cheeks; he wanted to feel the brush of them on his skin. He wanted to run his mouth lightly across the smooth skin beneath her stubborn jaw, and then taste the lobe of her ear. She was oblivious to his presence as she concentrated. He wanted her to be that focused, that intense as she became familiar with his body.

Strictly speaking, she wasn't beautiful, merely pretty, he thought desperately. Her mouth was full, and clearly used to smiling, although right now she was frowning, and looked very serious. Her eyelashes were thick and naturally dark, long enough to cast shadows on her cheekbones. Her large, chocolate brown eyes were pensive as she stared into space. Something was worrying Dr. Cahill. Something that had her combing her fingers through her dark hair. He almost groaned; he wanted to push her hands aside and do that himself. He didn't wonder how it would feel—he could *see* how soft and silky her hair would be, tangled between his fingers.

Resisting her was like trying not to breathe. He could manage it for slightly longer than he could hold his breath on a deep sea dive, but eventually the clawing need had him again.

Every muscle in his body was tight. The magnetism was undoubtedly sexual. But it was more than that.

Stronger even than lust.

The knowledge that this was beyond lust terrified him right down to his marrow.

He'd felt sexual attraction to plenty of women in his thirty-four years. Lust at first sight a time or two. But never like this. Never a slam in the gut so powerful he grew hard.

Every hunter's instinct in him demanded he go to her. Claim her. Right now. Right there in her chair. And to hell with her assistant. To hell with the consequences.

He'd slide the zipper down on her jeans, yank them off and spread her legs—Ah, Jesus—He crushed the thought, because if he let himself finish it, the tenuous hold he had on his control would shatter.

Today she was wearing jeans and a plain red T-shirt with a little pocket over the swell of her right breast. Gabriel's hungry gaze traveled greedily down her body, all the way to her pretty feet with their bright pink polish and little black ring on the pinkie toe of her right foot. His gut tightened just looking at her sexy toes in those high-heeled sandals that showed off her slender ankles.

He wanted to hold her in his arms for real. Hold her and touch her silky skin. His hands hurt from wanting to touch her. His breathing had to be shallow, because he could smell her heady, womanly fragrance, and it made him dizzy with longing. She liked perfume, different ones. He'd seen the fancy bottles lined up in her bathroom. Today she had on something intensely feminine, smelling of flowers and sunshine. The fragrance mingled with the scent of her skin in a way that made Gabriel feel drunk just inhaling it.

He knew she'd taste as delicious as she smelled.

Don't go there. He wished to God he could do this to her from a distance. About five thousand miles might do it. But to do what he needed to do, he had to be within sight of her. Frigging hell, he thought, so frustrated he wanted to chew glass.

It hadn't worked six hours ago.

He was desperate enough to try again. He couldn't take her back to the castle. He just fucking *couldn't*. She was seductive and succulent enough as it was, sitting here in a sterile white lab. What in God's name would he do if he ever saw her naked again? Just the memory almost made him swallow his tongue.

He liked that she was womanly. Not fat by any stretch of the imagination, but magnificently curvy. She had a spectacular ass, long gorgeous legs, and fantasy-worthy breasts.

He hungered to see her naked again. He wanted to mold the thin cotton to her breasts with his hands. He wanted to slide his fingers beneath the shirt and feel her smooth, bare skin. It would be warm. Silky smooth. Responsive—

Half expecting her to look up, he thought it inconceivable that she wasn't just as aware of him as he was of her. His own elevated heartbeat threatened to choke him. All his senses were so sharply attuned to hers.

Indeed, he'd noticed that within moments of his appearance her heart rate *had* shot up, and her respiration *had* changed. So she felt the same inescapable pull he did, even though she couldn't possibly know that he was watching her.

She was clearly thinking, her eyes as large and trusting as a child's as she stared into space. *What's going on in that clever brain of yours, Doctor?* She chewed on her lush lower lip, and Gabriel bit back a groan. Damn it. He had to make this quick. But first he needed to get Marshall Davis out of the room. He considered just vaporizing the guy, but dismissed the idea as medieval. Fast, expedient, but unduly harsh.

A woman as strong-willed as Eden Cahill wasn't suddenly going to allow herself to let go to the extent he needed her to let go. Not with someone else in the room.

He placed a suggestion in Davis's mind.

The younger man swiveled in his chair. "Hey, you didn't have your tea yet, did you? Want me to get it for you?"

She blinked, and her eyes came slowly back into focus. "That's okay, I'll get it in a minute."

Get her the fucking tea.

"No prob. Be right back." Davis darted to the back of

the lab and the kitchenette. He started opening and closing cabinet doors in his search for the tea bags. That would take a while, since Gabriel added an oldie but goodie to his mental messaging to Marshall, blanking the definition of a tea bag from the kid's brain.

Gabriel closed his eyes and imagined touching the soft, tender skin of Eden's nape where, he'd discovered last night, she was extremely sensitive. Mentally he brushed her hair aside, then ran his lips from her hairline to the first vertebra of her spine. She tilted her head and shivered.

He concentrated on arousing her. No matter how much of a hurry he was in—and God help him, he wanted to get the hell out of there P-fucking-DQ—he needed her to climax for at least twelve seconds. He'd have to have that much time to get into her mind and retrieve the data.

He imagined his hand on the fullness of her breast, felt the weight and the texture. Jesus . . . He was swimming in shark-infested waters here. His own arousal profound and painful, he teased her nipple to a sharp point. Then made the mistake of opening his eyes to watch her.

Head resting against the back of her chair, eyes closed, she'd sunk her teeth into her lower lip. Gabriel almost fell to his knees, he wanted her so badly.

This was as close as he could get to the good doctor, he reminded himself.

The tight buds of her nipples pressed against the thin cotton of her T-shirt and her breathing become increasingly erratic. Lips parted, a hectic pink bloomed in her cheeks. She was close. Damn close.

Jesus. This was killing him. Letting his mind touch her as he wanted to do, Gabriel eased her jean-clad thighs apart. Picturing the heel of his hand on her mound, he pressed firmly. Almost there.

Glass shattered, breaking the moment, and Marshall yelled from the kitchen. "Sorry!"

Eden moaned. Dazed and disoriented, she opened her eyes. "What the hell was *that*?!" she whispered, shaken.

"That what?" Marshall asked coming up beside her. "Sorry it took me so long. I had one of those things, you know? When you walk into a room and completely forget why you're there? Anyway, here you go." He placed a steaming cup of coffee beside her. "It's hot, so be careful."

I'm hot, too, Eden thought, picking up the jumbo cup with both hands. The heat bled through to her palms as she lifted it to take a sip. "Perfect." Other than it being coffee, which she never drank, not tea. She hoped he didn't put her into a diabetic coma after apparently dumping the entire box of sugar into the cup when the most she allowed herself was half a pack of Sweet'N Low.

She sipped anyway as she considered the possibility that she might have a brain tumor. What else could explain these hallucinations and inappropriate sexual behaviors?

Or, maybe she was just on the brink of a good, old-fashioned nervous breakdown. Clearly the stress of her moral dilemma was taking its toll. Taking another small swallow of too sweet coffee, she glanced up at the man beside her. "Do I look normal to you?"

Marshall's lips twitched. "Define normal?"

Eden reached out and swatted his arm. "Seriously. How do I look?"

With his sharpei frown, he stepped back, then scanned her from top to toe and back again. "Normal. A little flushed. But normal."

She blushed harder because she was blushing. "How have I been behaving lately?"

He gave her a bewildered look. "Like a person who

found the murdered body of a friend should behave? Sad, angry, frustrated. And sometimes like a woman whose favorite toy was taken away. Pissed off." He shrugged his bony shoulders. "I don't know, Eden. You've been behaving like . . . a *girl,* I guess."

She narrowed her eyes. "Guys don't get sad and angry and frustrated?"

"Oh, yeah, sure we do. A lot." Marshall flushed. "It's—well, it's *you* who usually doesn't."

"I don't?" *She didn't?*

"Eden. You're always so . . . *focused.* Ninety-eight point seven percent of the time you don't notice anything that goes on around you when you're in here."

"I notice things that go on around me."

"In *this* lab?"

"Yes. Sometimes."

"As I said. Normal." He wandered back to his desk.

"Talk about the pot calling the kettle black." She shot at his back. He was already pounding his keyboard.

The truth was, she wasn't very good with people. Give her a computer any day. Not only was a computer logical, it wasn't judgmental either. She'd always been a misfit because of her high IQ. She'd never really fit in anywhere but in an academic setting and the lab. Was it any wonder she felt emotionally safest, *happiest* here?

Theo's violent death had taken some of that away from her. Not being able to continue their work on the robot was contributing to her enormous feeling of loss. She liked her life ordered. Regulated. Predictable. Right now it was none of that.

Getting back to work, miring herself in a project, would, she hoped, get her back on track. And get her emotions back on an even keel where she could deal with them in a rational manner. She'd rather spend the day with her computer than a person.

God, she thought with self-deprecating humor, *no wonder I can't get laid.*

A focused hour later, Marshall swiveled his chair around. "Can I ask you a hypothetical question?"

"Hmmm?"

"Could we maybe rebuild Rex?"

Eden's head snapped up as she realized just how dangerous that information could be. "Even if we could, that's something we'll keep to ourselves." *God.* He'd just voiced her worst fears. "Imagine what the wrong people could do with Rex. Imagine it—multiply that grim possibility only a hundred times worse, and then tell me, should we rebuild him?"

His face went blank with disappointment. "Damn. What a waste of brilliant technology."

"Yes. It is. But that's the way it has to be." Once the killer discovered that Dr. Theo Kirchner was merely a figurehead in the lab, and that he'd known very little, that whatever schematics and data they'd stolen from her computer were pretty much useless window dressing, she was positive they'd come looking for *her*.

In fact, she couldn't understand why they hadn't already.

She rubbed a hand absently around the back of her neck. She had the uncomfortable sensation that someone was watching her. Silly of course. Only she and Marshall were in the lab. The problem was she had been waiting for the other shoe to drop for weeks. Everything was creeping her out right now.

"We shouldn't even be talking about this," she warned, dropping her hand. The sensation of being watched persisted, but this time she ignored it.

Marshall's eyes brightened and grew large. "But you could? Right?" He tapped his forefinger to his temple. "You've got it all stored in your head, don't you, Eden?

You remember everything down to the smallest detail. We could rebuild Rex. It would be way cool. Give me schematics to work from, and—"

"Forget it," Eden said harshly, then modulated her tone because it wasn't Marshall's fault that she'd done something terminally stupid. "Schematics take time, and most of them were on the hard drives. The computers were wiped clean, remember?" She gave him a pointed look, which he returned with a blank look of his own.

"Oh, yeah." He rolled his eyes. "Mr. Verdine was totally pissed that the data was wiped from the hard drives."

They shared a glance. She didn't give a damn if she was acting paranoid, and as if the walls had ears. There were anomalies happening that she couldn't explain. She wasn't willing to put either her own life, or Marshall's, in danger by saying anything about . . . *anything*.

Marshall knew she and Jason Verdine had shared a few dinners and must be wondering why she'd left out the part that she had total recall of the data. "Of course."

His brow furrowed and he lowered his voice to barely a whisper. "Are you ever going to tell him that everything *wasn't* lost because you have it all in your head? What about that Homeland Security guy? The cops? *Any* of them?"

"Marshall, my friend," Eden said just as quietly. "Right now there are only two people I trust in the world. You would be the other one."

"Who . . . Oh, you mean *you*. Yes, of course. Sorry. You're right. Excellent. Don't tell anyone. Right. Got it." But he clearly couldn't understand why something so incredible was being kept under wraps. He'd never understood why Eden didn't share with people the fact that she had a photographic memory.

He just didn't get it.

And that was fine with her. Ignorance, in Marshall's case, could very well save his life. And hers.

"Don't freak on me now, Marshall."

"I don't want to freak *you* out, Eden. But I keep telling you. You need more than those four muscleheads as bodyguards. You need—an army maybe. If not, somebody—a *bad* somebody—could get that information out of you. Easy."

They probably could. She hated pain. A hangnail required an Advil. Okay, not quite. But close enough. On the other hand, if she knew someone wanted what she had in her head, she would use every fiber of her being to make sure they couldn't access it. It was a case of mind over matter. She took pride in her willpower. A woman who had lost fifty pounds through sheer determination, and then *kept* it off for years, could achieve anything.

"Uh-oh! You've got that look on your face. I'm not putting money on it!"

"Marshall. Listen to me. Nobody can know that I have a photographic memory. Swear to me."

"I do. But you *are* scaring the crap outta me, Eden."

"That makes two of us," she told him grimly, wishing the eerie feeling of being watched would go away. She was spooked enough as it was without being paranoid as well. "From now on I don't even want it discussed. Not even between the two of us, do you understand?" She waited for his emphatic nod.

"It wouldn't have taken the killer long to realize that Dr. Kirchner wasn't the one who made Rex. You know that, Eden. You must know that."

Eden frowned fiercely. Bless his heart, she'd adored Theo, but Marshall was right. Theo had become vague and forgetful by the time he'd slid into his early eighties. At one time he'd been a brilliant mathematician and scientist. A pioneer in the field of artificial intelligence. Proving to his peers—and teaching her—that truly autonomous robotic behavior was feasible long before anyone else thought it was much more than an idea on the drawing board.

His first AI project, many years ago, had put his expertise and skill above everyone else in the field. Five years later, he'd groomed a seventeen-year-old student straight out of MIT to follow in his footsteps. But for years, it had been Eden, his former student, who'd made startling findings in the artificial intelligence field.

Her brilliant mind, coupled with a photographic memory and—as Theo used to put it—the retentive skills of a pachyderm, had allowed Eden to catapult artificial intelligence to an entirely new level.

She'd allowed her mentor to accept all the accolades and credits. He deserved them.

But now he was dead.

She straightened her shoulders. "I can't *know* anything," she told Marshall. More to calm herself down than to pacify him.

"Let's get out o—" She spun around to look at the door as the buzzer sounded, alerting them that someone had entered.

The inner door swung open. "Jason?"

"Good morning," he said, his handsome face showing concern as he strode toward her, hands outstretched. "I called your apartment to see if you'd like to join me for breakfast, and was told you'd left for work. I couldn't believe it."

She gave him a blank look. "Who could tell you that? I live alone. And why couldn't you believe it? I work here."

"Of course you do. But I told you to ease back into your routine slowly. You've been traumatized. And the answer to that is that I have my security people there watching your place. Dr. Kirchner was brutally murdered thirteen days ago," he reminded her unnecessarily. "I'm not taking any chances with you."

He looked genuinely concerned, and Eden was touched. "But I'm here. Behind a locked door with your whole security detail posted inside and outside the building. No one can get to me, Jason, thanks to you."

"I still wish you'd take me up on that cruise I offered you. Take a few months off. Regain your equilibrium. Let the authorities put Theo's killer behind bars."

"That would be a pretty long cruise," Eden said mildly. Jason might be offering her time off, but they both knew the only place he wanted her right now was here in the lab. Jason was good at saying what he believed the person he was talking to wanted to hear. But Eden never mistook the subtext. He was all about the bottom line.

"You know what I mean. I care about you deeply, Eden. I'd hate for anything to happen to you."

That made two of them, Eden thought rather bemused as Jason pulled her into his arms. She wondered if he even noticed Marshall sitting ten feet away. Probably not.

As kisses went, Jason's were pretty good. But even a full lip lock with Jason Verdine didn't come close, not even marginally, to the sensations evoked by a dream man who hadn't ever touched her. Eden almost smiled. Imagination was an amazing thing.

As pleasant as the kiss was, she wondered, not for the first time, why she felt not even a spark of sexual interest in Jason. And, just as puzzling considering his amorous and frequent attempts to get her into his bed, she suspected he felt none for her.

Whatever the motivation, this was neither the time nor the place. He wore some sort of necklace or medallion beneath his shirt that always jabbed into her chest when he embraced her, as it did now. She didn't like jewelry of any kind on a man so that was a demerit—a small one, but a demerit anyway.

Gently she extricated herself from his arms and smiled. "Good morning."

Jason had a lean, clever face, with laugh lines beside his attractive blue eyes, although he wasn't laughing now. He looked serious and intense. His hair was dark blond, thick and expertly cut and styled. He dressed well. Always wore very nice suits, silk shirts, expensive shoes.

He ran his multibillion-dollar R&D company like a well-oiled machine. And he looked like exactly what he was: wealthy, handsome, used to having his own way, and as though he'd stepped straight from the pages of a magazine.

Which was only slightly problematic for Eden. She usually looked as though she'd gotten dressed in the dark. And the only time she combed her hair was when she got out of the shower. It curled and waved no matter what she did to it, and since doing anything to it took far too much time, she left it alone to do whatever it wanted to do.

Her two concessions to fashion were killer shoes and great perfume. The best she could say about her clothing was that it was—usually—clean. Today she'd tossed on her usual uniform of jeans and T-shirt, and wore her favorite FM scarlet Jimmy Choos in an attempt to lighten her mood. The only jewelry she ever wore was Grandma Rose's lucky ring on her baby toe.

"What's up?" she asked her boss. Not elegantly put, but it saved time.

"Special Agent Dixon from Homeland Security is here again." Jason started walking around the lab. Observing, but not touching. She wondered if he was thinking as he looked around the lab, "This is mine. This is mine. This is mine."

And did he think the same thing when he put his hands on her? *This is mine?*

The thought annoyed her a little. Which didn't bode well, she supposed, for their budding relationship.

Jason glanced over at Marshall, who was watching the two of them like an attendee at a tennis match. "They're waiting for you in conference room seven. Go ahead."

Marshall blinked several times as if getting his bearings. "Oh, but—Eden—She needs me to—" Jason gave him an uncompromising look. Marshall turned scarlet. His Adam's apple rose and fell in his throat as he swallowed. "Okay. Sorry. I'll go now."

Eden waited until the door closed behind her assistant. "You intimidate him."

"I barely spoke to the man."

"My point exactly. You make him feel worthless."

"He *is* worthless," Jason said, standing a little too close for Eden's comfort level. His eyes held hers. His breath smelled faintly of licorice from the Sen-Sen he was always eating. "I've been aware of the inequity in this department for years," he told her gently. "We all know who generates the most products for the company. And Kirchner and Davis aren't two of them."

"Oh. Please! That is absolutely not true." She and Marshall had worked on dozens of Verdine Industries' top-selling AI products together.

Jason brushed her lower lip with his fingertip. She shifted her face out of reach.

"I don't want to argue with you, babe."

Oh, yeah? Then why did you malign both my friend and my mentor? And don't call me babe *in that annoying, condescending way either.* "Dr. Kirchner has been—

was my mentor for a huge chunk of my career. Everything I know I learned from him," she told him stiffly.

"And," she added, "Marshall Davis is one of the smartest people I know. He's invaluable to this company and to me." Eden wasn't subtle about her steps out of range. "Not only does he work with me, I consider myself fortunate to call him my friend." Another demerit for Mr. Verdine. He was racking them up fast. How could she have ever thought of him as her fantasy man last night? "I'd appreciate it if you'd grant him the same respect you grant me. I'm serious, Jason."

He gave her an assessing look. "I intimidate a lot of people. But not you."

"Not in the least," she told him, trying to keep her voice calm. What was he referring to? Her refusal to his frequent requests that they sleep together? Or the fact that he'd been pressuring her into taking the development of Rex into a military application for more than two years?

As yet she was undecided about the former, but it wasn't looking good, and she refused do the latter. She wasn't prepared to budge on either stance. She'd already gone further than she'd wanted to. Just for her own curiosity. But Jason, no matter how much he paid her, wasn't privy to that information.

"I understand that you were devastated by Dr. Kirchner's death. But since you refuse to take any more time off, I want you to reconstruct your research on the Rx793 as quickly as possible. I don't have to remind you that the government has a sizable contract with us. We've already been paid ten million dollars for the prototype. Just because the robot was stolen doesn't mean we don't have to give them what they paid for."

He held up his hand when she wanted to speak. "Hear me out, would you, please? We've gone over this a dozen times, Eden. You know damn well it's a practical, and in the end, *humane* application of something you've already developed. A humanlike robot going into war zones to treat and retrieve wounded soldiers will save thousands of lives. A machine won't cut it in this application. I don't understand your reticence now, when you've already done most of the work already. I know you've experimented with a flexible silicone skin and can make it look human. A few more tweaks is all it would take. They've already paid us to produce a dozen adult-sized humanoid androids."

"Money isn't the issue," Eden told him, wishing that her damn ego hadn't been so eager to invent something so potentially open to misuse. "We already *have* a model of motion perception utilizing the output of motion-sensitive spatiotemporal filters with Rex."

Jason frowned.

"The power spectrum occupies a tilted plane in the spatiotemporal-frequency domain," Eden explained, noting the glazed look in his eyes. She laid it on a little thicker. "The Rx uses 3-D Gabor filters to sample his power spectrum for a fixed 3-D rigid-body motion, depth values parameterize a line through image-velocity space . . ." He had that blank expression she was accustomed to seeing on people's faces when she started expounding on her passion. Jason wasn't a scientist, and she usually attempted to put what she was doing in layman's terms for him. But not today.

Her research had been directed at the electrical circuit domain, but she'd branched out. *Way* out. It was a damn good thing Jason didn't understand one word in a dozen of what she was telling him.

Artificial intelligence was a primordial soup of computer and cognitive sciences, psychology, mathematics, linguistics, and computer sciences. The field had been just waiting for that bolt of genius that would bring it all together in a new life-form.

Eden, God help her, had made that life-form.

"Never mind," she told him, wishing he'd go away and stop insisting on something she had absolutely no intention of doing. Ever. "What I'm saying is we almost had what you want in Rex. Now Rex and all the notes and files are *gone*. To replicate what we had would take another six or seven years."

"And what I'm saying, Doctor," Jason stated flatly, the lover gone, "is that you've done it once, and you can not only do it again, but this time make it bigger and better. My God, you got accolades for the mobile robot they're using in Afghanistan to remotely explore caves and remove bombs. People said it couldn't be done. But *you* did it. A machine that does reconnaissance and bomb retrieval. An amazing and brilliant feat."

The problem, Eden thought, was that she was damn proud of her accomplishments. *Damn* proud. The government had requested a versatile payload carrier. She'd added reconnaissance payloads with a pan/tilt head and night vision. Chem/gas/radiation payloads, and bomb disposal. That bot was doing good.

Jason stepped into her space, forcing Eden to take a step back. "Doing this would save countless field medics from endangering themselves. An AI doctor, if you will," he told her, sounding reasonable as he dangled the challenge like a carrot. "Think about it, Eden. This is exactly what you've been working toward for *years*."

"We've had this conversation ad nauseam," Eden told him flatly. She'd already done what he was asking. With Rex. And fresh, exciting new ideas and solutions kept her awake at night.

But in light of Theo's murder, she was going to forget everything she knew, everything she'd learned. She had to.

She'd known that proceeding, giving in to the curiosity, was going to get her into trouble. Hell, forging ahead had most likely gotten Theo killed. Damn, she just hadn't expected anyone, least of all *Theo,* to pay the price for her intellectual curiosity.

Artificial intelligence needed three things. Intelligence. Reasoning. And strategy. Strategy was the only element that had been missing. Eden was pretty damn sure she now had that one nailed as well.

She gave Jason a level look. "As tempting as the idea is, I can't do it. We just haven't reached that level yet." This was one lie she hated telling. But she was determined to tell it well, and often.

She was going to an AI symposium in Berlin the following week as their featured speaker. According to statistics and her peers, she was now the leading expert in the field of AI.

She was going to stand up there and flat out lie.

Once machines became more intelligent than a human there would be no way to control them. So no matter how much she wanted to lead the AI revolution, she refused to cross that line. At least publicly.

If an AI somehow gained *consciousness,* it could very well start making its own decisions. In theory, it could turn on its creators and the danger in *that* was too horrible to contemplate.

"You won't do it."

"Same thing," she said flatly. "You can always fire me and get someone else to try."

His mouth tightened, and his pale eyes hardened. "There is no one else. You're the top of your field."

"True." And that burden was giving her a hell of a headache.

He sighed. "I'm sorry I annoyed you." He touched her cheek with two fingers, his eyes softening. "Forgive me?" He removed an envelope from his inside pocket with beautifully manicured hands. "We'll shelve this conversation for now. This should please you." He handed it to her. "I've made a list of things already ordered to proceed with the robot. If there's anything, anything at all, that you want or need, let me know."

Whatever else he was, Jason had charm in abundance. It had taken him more than a year to chip away at Eden's firm resolve not to date the boss. He'd surprised her with his persistence. But what Eden, like droves of other women, *really* liked about Jason were his millions, and what his money could buy for her. Unlike other women, Eden didn't want jewels or furs or cars or houses. Eden wanted carte blanche for her lab work. Easy access to the incredibly expensive equipment required for her work. She took a closely typed piece of paper out of the envelope and unfolded it to rapidly scan the list.

Okay. She'd give him back a few of the demerits she'd subtracted. Her lab, and all the bells and whistles she could possibly want, were worth a little easing of her standards.

"You've thought of everything." And then some.

"I believe so." He shot his cuff to glance at his Rolex. "I don't have time for breakfast now. I have a ten o'clock meeting. Would you like to go somewhere for lunch later? You should be done with your security interview by then, too."

"No thanks. I think I'll go home and take a nap. It's been a long day."

"It's nine fifteen in the morning," he pointed out.

"Feels later."

He bent his head to brush his lips to hers. "I'll call you."

Clutching the paper, Eden watched him leave. "I'm not going to sleep with you, Jason Verdine," she said out loud after both doors had opened, closed, and locked automatically behind him. "No matter how many lovely new toys you offer me."

She shook her head, smiling ruefully. "I must have

holes in my head for not *wanting* to, but there you go."
She turned back to her desk.

Eden's steps faltered, and then she stopped dead and
froze.

There, leaning against her desk, was a strange man.

CHAPTER FIVE

The blood drained out of her head, and her heart started racing painfully in her chest as she stared at him, mouth suddenly dry. The man's hot blue gaze raked over her from head to toe, as possessive as if he were physically touching her.

He radiated sex appeal. Not so much his looks, but something innate, primitive. Compelling. Just looking at him made Eden think of hot, sweaty skin and tangled sheets.

God. He made her think about her early morning erotic dream. Heat scorched her cheeks, and her breath quickened in time with her rapid heartbeat.

He was—*big*, was her first bewildered thought. No, not big, although he was at least six three, he gave the appearance of being bigger somehow. The man radiated danger. Who the hell *was* he? And how had he managed to breach Verdine Industries' tight security? Her heart thudded and she felt sweaty and hot despite the air conditioning in the lab.

She also felt shaky and disoriented, as though she'd walked onstage without a script.

It was almost as if he'd materialized out of nowhere.

She should be running for her life, but her shoes seemed glued in place. And she would run, as soon as she could move, as soon as she could think coherently.

Light-headed and dry-mouthed, she just stood there staring at him.

She was a sensible woman. But, God. He was *gorgeous*. Even if it was far from sensible to notice his hard, lean, muscled body, or the way he watched her with an intensity that was unnerving. Tightly leashed power hummed around him.

He was an intruder. And by the look of him, a dangerous one at that. So why was her body drawing her toward him, instead of away?

Dark blue eyes, mocking and enigmatic, watched her with the focus of an animal on its prey. His slightly shaggy, midnight dark hair was a little too long, hanging almost to his shoulders, and the angle of his head made the dark strands cast a sinister half shadow across his face.

He was casually dressed in worn, nicely fitting—*really* nicely fitting—faded blue jeans, and a navy T-shirt. The jeans loved his hips and long legs, the T-shirt showed off an impressive chest and the muscles in his tanned arms.

Oddly, he was barefoot. He gave her the unnerving feeling that he was crowding her space, but he was a good fifteen feet away and hadn't moved.

Eden, all five feet seven sturdy inches of her, suddenly felt petite and more *female* than she'd ever felt in her life. Dear God, who *was* he?

For God's sake, she gave herself a mental shake, *one* of them should say something. "Who are you?" she said, taking control of the situation. "Where did you come fr—"

His silence, his uncanny stillness, was more unnerving than if he'd physically, or even verbally, threatened her. *Fine, buddy. Go ahead and look your fill. Twenty seconds after I press the emergency buzzer, this lab will be filled with security people. I'll stand right here staring*

back at you as long as it takes me to get to that buzzer.
Then you'll be toast.

The lab seemed to fade away. Her entire focus and awareness were on this man watching her. She could hear her own pulse in her ears, feel the frantic rush of blood through her veins. She was ultra aware of her hair tickling her neck, and the press of her breasts against the inside of her bra. She even felt the brush of her eyelashes against her too-long bangs.

She was shaken to the core by her own powerful, all-consuming reaction to this man. This stranger. It was as if she knew him on some deep primitive level she'd never experienced before. She was aware of danger. Of longing. Of need and of fear. Fear, not of him, which was insane, but of the power of her own reaction to him.

She'd never felt such a visceral response to a man in her life. She wanted to run into his arms and bury her head against his broad chest.

Involuntarily, she took a small backward step as he pushed himself off the edge of her desk and silently started walking toward her on large, bare feet. Feeling stalked, panic welled up inside her.

Run, for God's sake. Run!

If she'd found his disconcerting stillness unsettling, she was even more panicky as he approached. Her heart thumped harder and harder. All the little hairs on her body stood to attention as if electrified.

"Close your mouth, Dr. Cahill," he said mildly enough, but his nostrils flared like a stallion scenting a mare as he came closer and closer. His voice resonated inside her like a tuning fork. Incapable of dragging her gaze from his mouth, she thought vaguely, *I know that voice . . .* Then she pulled herself up short. *Get a grip here, Eden,* she warned herself, forcing her attention away from his mouth. But seeing the strange intensity in his narrowed eyes was almost as unnerving.

His gaze fell, drifting like a physical touch, over her shirt, down her jean-clad legs, lingering on her bare toes in the strappy red sandals, then just as slowly, meandered back to her face.

Her eyes widened at the warmth suffusing her body. The sexual chemistry between them startled the hell out of her. It was so hot, so fast, so unexpected, it stole her breath.

Horrified, she felt her nipples peak and her body throb as though she were being touched. Snapping her mouth shut, Eden narrowed her eyes right back at him. Tension stretched between them, heavy and thick.

The only way he could possibly have come in was to have passed Jason as he exited. He hadn't.

"How the *hell* did you get in here?" And that was only one of many questions that demanded answers. Damn him. Was he performing some sort of hypnosis? She couldn't figure out how, or why, she was suddenly feeling aroused. It was as inappropriate as it was unlikely. And the second time today.

Stop that, she told her body. *Just damn well stop that.* The rise of her jeans caused a friction she didn't need, and she wasn't moving so much as an eyelash. Her heart rate was so elevated she was scared she'd pass out at any minute. Her core temperature seemed to rise the closer he came.

She shot him a suspicious glare.

His lips twitched. His predatory smile was that of a male intensely physically aware of a female. Or a jungle cat about to have lunch. "If you think that smile will allay my fears," she told him coolly, "it doesn't."

Over two thousand people worked in the building. The computer lab right next door held several hundred of them. Just a—soundproof, damn it—wall away. Not only that, but even after several weeks, the building was crawling with Jason's security people, uniformed officers, detectives, FBI, and a fruit salad of other agencies.

"How did I get in? Magic." His gravelly baritone was ironic.

That voice again. The one she'd heard in her erotic dream. The one that had haunted her since.

Which was, of course, ridiculous. The room was flooded with sunlight, yet to Eden it felt as though it were filled with shadows. This man's presence seemed larger than life. She could ponder his method of gaining entrance later. The fact that he was ten feet away from her, that she was alone with him behind three locked high-security doors, that somehow he was raising her body temperature and heartbeat without touching her, all bothered her a great deal.

She had to lick her lips before she could push the words out. "You're wasting your time." Her voice was steady, but she stuffed her shaking fingers into the front pockets of her jeans so neither of them would know just how damn scared she really was. He didn't move, but his heated gaze was on her mouth as she spoke. Slowly he lifted his eyes to meet hers. The nonphysical contact jolted Eden right to her bones.

Oh, God. She *had* to get to that buzzer. Theo had been shot. Did this guy have a gun secreted somewhere on him? Probably.

Her little gun was in her purse, which unfortunately was directly behind him in her desk drawer. Her only hope was hitting that silent alarm. And the odds of her doing that before he reached her were slim to none.

"You'll get no more from me than you got from Theo. How could you kill a defenseless, harmless old man?"

"Who said I did?"

Eden rolled her eyes. "Well, it defies logic to think more than one person has managed to break the Verdine security system in such a short window of time. It's called deductive reasoning. If you're here now, you must have killed Theo. But this stealthy little visit is a waste of your time."

"Why is that?" he asked softly.

He stood between her and the emergency security button under her desk. But Theo's desk was about five feet to her right. She held his gaze as she took a casual step closer to the desk. "Because you've already killed Dr. Kirchner and taken everything of value. Killing *me* would be—redundant."

"Is that right?"

When she didn't respond he asked softly, "Stupid or brave, Doctor?"

She met his eyes. They weren't black, but a dark, fathomless, deep blue. "If you're referring to me not running like hell—*neither*. I'm paralyzed with terror."

His expression darkened. "Are you always this honest?"

"No. Yes."

"Which is it?"

"What difference does it make?"

"Close your eyes, Dr. Cahill."

With him scowling at her like that? Not a freaking chance. "Don't be ridiculous. I want to see what you're doing." Marshall would be back soon, she thought with rising panic. But soon enough to prevent her death?

"Are you going to scream?"

Hell, yes. She could feel it building deep in her diaphragm as he approached as silently as a large, predatory cat. "What's the point? This is a soundproof room."

He frowned. "That is a dumb-ass thing to tell a man you believe is a killer."

"I'm not going to waste oxygen screaming." No matter how logical that response might be, the tightness in her chest ratcheted up another notch as the scream gathered inside her.

"Close your eyes."

"Go to hell."

The sudden flash of blinding white light seemed to pierce her brain. Eden screamed, and kept on screaming as she fell through space.

The moment they arrived in the castle's vast dining room Gabriel waited for her screams to peter out.

"Jesus. Fuck. What the hell did you do to her?" Sebastian demanded.

Gabriel leaned against the long, carved mahogany sideboard, arms crossed. Dr. Eden Cahill, she of the curly dark hair and snapping brown eyes, was curled in a tight little ball on the Aubusson carpet in his dining room. At least she'd stopped screaming. The scent of tuberose, warm female skin, and obstinacy filled his senses.

He'd been too close to her for those few seconds before they'd teleported, and his heart was still racing and sweat dampened his forehead. Even his goddamned *skin* felt too tight. He dragged in a deep breath, held it, let it out slowly, but his self-control didn't extend to his thoughts.

Sebastian snapped his fingers to get his attention. "Yo. Up here."

He dragged his attention away from Dr. Cahill to glance at Sebastian. "She refused to close her eyes." Plucking a lemon from the filled blue-and-gold Murano glass bowl beside him, Gabriel brought the fruit to his nose. His pulse was throbbing through his veins like a freight train, but he made sure neither his impassive expression nor his posture betrayed his thoughts to his friend.

Desire, sharp and strong, continued surging through his body. The hunger clawing at him was invasive, blinding. Dangerous as hell because the temptation to put his hands on her was almost overwhelming and damned hard to resist.

He wasn't sure how he knew that by *touching* Eden Cahill he'd be lost. He just—*knew.*

How fast could he do this?

Right now she was disoriented, weak, vulnerable. Desperately he tried again. A quick hard push at her mind.

Soft, fragrant, and still fucking *closed* to him.

Her eyes were squeezed shut, her white teeth embedded in her lower lip as she lay without moving. Twisting the small lemon between his long, elegant fingers, Gabriel inhaled the sharp citrus smell, but it did little to blot out the fragrance of her.

Jesus. He was insane to have brought her here. He'd never felt such lust in his life and he had a pretty good idea of why. Which only made a bad situation a whole shitload worse.

"You can open your eyes now, Doctor." He'd tried bringing her to orgasm one last time in the lab earlier. As frightened as she'd been, as confused as her rising libido had made her, she'd still managed to deny herself. And him.

He was out of choices.

Gabriel loathed having his hand forced. He didn't want her here. He didn't want this woman any-fucking-where *near* him. Yet here she was. Sprawled out on his carpet. Easily within reach. Everything about her was profoundly sensual, calling to him on every level.

He'd be fine, he assured himself, as long as he didn't touch her. Unfortunately, that was what his beleaguered brain was insisting he do. "I know you're conscious, Doctor. Open your eyes or I'll have my friend here tip a jug of ice water over you."

"Christ, Gabriel. Is this really necessary?"

He sent a warning glance in Sebastian's general direction. "My question exactly. Eyes, Doctor. Now."

Both eyes shot open to spear him at ankle level. Still dazed, she frowned, letting her gaze climb his legs and continue all the way up to his face. "What did you do to me, you sick bastard?"

"Much as I relish nicknames," Gabriel told her dryly, "my real name is Gabriel Edge."

"Sick bastard works for me." She struggled to sit up, but her eyes lost focus and she slumped back to the carpet. He knew the room was spinning for her. Reentry could take its toll.

"Stay put. I wouldn't get up too fast if I were you," he warned, a day late and a dollar short.

Interesting how she fought the dizziness and nausea, rejected it, used her will to overcome it. Reluctantly fascinated, he watched her forcibly relax her body as she concentrated on deep breathing to regain her equilibrium, using all her concentration to accomplish it.

That damned willpower of hers had landed her here in Montana, miles away from her lab and inches from him. The sooner she gave in, the sooner he'd send her back home.

The sooner the better.

Foolishly tenacious, she started up for a second time, then realized she wasn't going to make it, and rested her head back on the carpet as she tried to stop the room from spinning.

"Jesus," Sebastian rose from his seat on the other side of the long refectory table, which ran the length of the room. "Help the poor woman up off the damn floor why don't you?"

"She's fine where she is for now. If you want her up, feel free to help her yourself." Gabriel tossed the lemon from hand to hand. "My recommendation is for her to lie there for about half an hour and then take a nice long nap. She'll feel better in a couple of hours." With any luck, an hour after that she'd be sick again because he'd have teleported her back to her lab. Mission accomplished.

"Man, that's cold."

Her breathing was a little erratic, and her eyes were closed again. She was listening to every word. "May I remind you," he told Sebastian tersely, "this is not a situation of my own choosing?"

"And may I remind *you,* T-FLAC operatives rarely get to pick and choose their own missions. Especially you guys in the psycho unit."

"*Psi.* And I'm neither."

"Excuse me. You psi/spec ops guys are all touchy."

"Deal with it."

Gabriel might have known she wasn't going to lie there as instructed. She managed to sit up, her jean-clad legs curled beside her curvy ass for ballast. She looked like a mermaid. Lorelei calling some dimwitted suitor to his death. He shook his head at his own idiocy.

If he could make her climax, get the intel she was storing in that agile little brain of hers *out* of that brain, he could have her back at the lab before she could cry uncle. He shot Sebastian a hard look. "Get lost."

Oblivious to his motivation for getting rid of his only witness, Dr. Cahill cradled her head in both hands. "You drugged me," her voice was muffled. She lowered her hands to shoot him a venomous look over her fingers. "Didn't you?"

He should tell her yes. A pat answer that would require no explanation, unlike teleportation, which would. "No."

"Liar."

Sebastian, who hadn't moved from his seat, grinned. "Wait till you hear the truth. That'll really make your head spin," he told her helpfully.

Big brown eyes narrowed, but she didn't turn to look

at Sebastian. She had her gaze fixed on Gabriel. "Who's your accomplice?"

"Sebastian Tremayne. Don't try getting u—Damn it, woman. I told you to *stay put*." Gabriel sidestepped her grasping hands as she tried to use his legs for purchase. The thousands of hours of swordplay paid off in many ways, he thought, well out of reach. His quick footwork was legend. But despite the extra few feet he'd put between them, his heart raced and his pulse beat a frantic rhythm at her nearness. The overwhelming urgency to touch her, to claim her, might well drive him insane.

It was as if, by bringing her here to Edridge Castle, he'd unleashed a form of powerful magnetic current that drew him to her no matter how hard he resisted. The only way to get rid of this need, this fucking—pun intended—urgency, was to get the intel he required and get her out of his sight.

He knew, bone-deep, that if he so much as touched this woman he'd never want to stop. He couldn't permit his compulsion to possess her to overcome his good sense. He didn't need to touch her to get what he needed.

Unfortunately, common sense was being overridden by his libido. As he had in the lab, he wondered if her fine skin was soft to the touch. Not that he'd ever know. He was never going to feel it. Never get that close. Sunlight slanted through the stained-glass windows, gilding her flesh as she used the edge of the sideboard as leverage and wobbled to her feet.

Her gaze was slightly unfocused as she struggled to find her equilibrium. Sebastian, who'd come around the table, stepped in and grabbed her arm to steady her as she swayed on those ridiculously sexy, foolishly high, "fuck me yesterday, today, and tomorrow" red sandals.

"It's okay. I've got you." He wrapped an arm about her slender shoulders, supporting most of her weight with his body, and shot Gabriel a hard look. "You really are a bastard, Edge. What do you want me to do with her?"

Oh, Gabriel had a raft of ideas concerning things *he'd* like to do to Eden Cahill. The stronger the temptation to touch her, the stronger his resolve. He wasn't going to do any of them. *Ever.* The family curse was just that. A curse.

"Take her upstairs for now."

"Two flights? No way in hell. She's your guest. Beam her up or something."

"The correct term is teleport," Gabriel informed him. And doing it so soon again would likely kill her. He didn't want her dead. "This isn't the Starship *Enterprise.* If you don't want to take her upstairs, prop her against something. Leave her right there. She'll feel better soon enough. Then she can take herself upstairs."

"E-excuse me?" If her voice hadn't been quite so reedy she would have sounded indignant. "I'm right he—oh!" Big brown eyes lost their focus. Her knees buckled. And while Sebastian fumbled with her dead weight, she threw up.

Gabriel gave his friend an evil smile. "No good deed goes unpunished."

Chapter Six

MacBain came up beside Gabriel, barely sparing a glance at Sebastian and his problem. "I've prepared a chamber for Dr. Cahill on the second floor."

He shot his butler a look of horror. *His* floor? No frigging way. "Here." He turned to toss a priceless, sixteenth-century tapestry table runner at Sebastian. Beside him MacBain whimpered. "Use this to clean up, then give her a few sips of whiskey. Put her in the east wing," he addressed MacBain, his eyes on Dr. Cahill.

Christ, her face was pale. Eyes closed, she was sitting on the floor again, back propped up against the far end of the sideboard while Sebastian dealt with the mess.

She still had on her shoes. Sandals. Fire engine red. Mere straps across her pale slender feet with her bright pink polished toes and sexy little black toe ring. His jaw hurt with the burning desire to lavish attention on her extremely pretty toes.

The woman had just ignominiously thrown up. He should feel sympathy, aversion, something, *anything*, other than lust, shouldn't he? Apparently it didn't matter. Christ. He scrubbed a hand roughly across his jaw.

God. How soon could he get rid of her?

Soon enough to allay the maddening sexual intensity that was clouding his judgment?

Beside him, MacBain cleared his throat. His white hair, mustache, and eyebrows made him look stately. He had the temperament necessary to run a large household with a steel hand, and the slyness of a weasel when it came to manipulating people for their own good.

He was a gentleman's gentleman, and had been with Gabriel for more than twenty years, after first being in the service of Gabriel's father. There was little he didn't know, and didn't interfere with, in the Edge family. Sometimes that was great, other times, like now, it was a pain in Gabriel's ass.

The old man cleared his throat again. Loudly.

Gabriel shot him a brief glance. "Now what?" A few more sips of his prized whiskey should put the roses back in her cheeks.

"There is nothing *in* the east wing, sir."

Gabriel frowned. Was she pulling that face at his aged single malt? "Then I suggest you *put* something there," he told MacPain. Yes, by damn. She *was* shoving the glass away.

"Certainly, sir, I shall have a tradesman come and install air conditioning. That should be done by next Thursday. If I put a rush on it. The furnishings will be moved later this morning. It's the plumbing that might prove problematic, however."

Sebastian had his hand resting on the top of her head, his fingers tangled in her dark glossy curls. What for? What was the man going to do? Shove her face in the glass even if she didn't want it? "What's wrong with the goddamned plumbing, MacBain?"

"There isna any, sir."

No, by God. He was stroking her curls and talking to her softly. *Son of a bitch*—

Gabriel's jaw was starting to ache from gritting his teeth. "What room do you want to put her in then?"

"The chamber Mr. Tremayne just vacated."

Fucking hell. Right across the hall from *his* bedroom? "I *am* cursed."

"Aye, I know, sir. Excuse me. I shall go and fetch warm water and clothes for our guests."

"Yeah, you do that," he muttered, watching as Sebastian crouched beside Eden, tilting the glass to her lips again. She grimaced, but drank. The bastard knew his way around women, Gabriel thought sourly. His friend had hands like ham hocks, but they were gentle on her skin. How dare Sebastian touch her, when he couldn't?

There was no need for Tremayne to hold her face while he was pouring liquor down her throat, he thought, irritated. No need to crowd her like that either. *Give the woman some air, why don't you?*

Big brown eyes met his over the rim of the glass. Pushing Sebastian's hand away, she ran her fingers through her hair in a nervous gesture that was at odds with her murderous expression. Her dark hair went every which way and looked charmingly disheveled and as silky as mink. Damn it to hell.

Sebastian had touched it. Had touched *her*. His friend had felt the warm satin texture of her skin beneath his fingers. He'd been close enough to feel the sigh of her breath on his skin. Close enough to feel the brush of her hand against his.

Sebastian had been close enough to be puked on, Gabriel reminded himself with marginal satisfaction. Resting his ass on the sideboard behind him, he crossed his legs at the ankles. "Feel better?" he asked politely, tossing the lemon back into the bowl and sticking his fingers into his front pockets.

"I'd feel better if you told me where I am, and why you kidnapped me."

It actually took all of Gabriel's concentration to hear her words, he was so *fucking* busy watching her mouth. Soft. Pink. Damp with his smoky whiskey. He could almost taste it on his own tongue. Her mouth tightened, and her chin came up. Stubborn, he thought as he pushed away from the sideboard. He crossed to an ornate mahogany chair at the far end of the table. Yanking it out, he sat down. "Help her into that chair next to—"

"I'm going to wash up," Sebastian told him with a grin. "Don't get to anything interesting until I get back."

Eden ignored the wink from her kidnapper's smiling accomplice as he dashed from the room, leaving her and her abductor alone.

"Damn it," he snarled. "Couldn't you wait for him to help you?"

"Why would I trust any of you to *help* me?" Still a little dizzy, she'd managed to stand, stagger, and immediately plopped her butt into the closest high-backed, heavily carved antique chair. Everything looked authentic, although Eden wouldn't know if they were the real deal or fake. She glared at him over the straight row of candles in pewter holders evenly spaced down the gleaming length of the table.

In fact, looking around at the dark paneled room hung with tapestries and filled with dark, highly polished antiques, she'd swear she was sitting in the middle of a museum replica of a medieval castle.

An elaborate coat of arms, silver with a red lion rampant and a black eagle—it looked vaguely familiar—hung over a stone canopied fireplace big enough to roast a herd of cows. Monstrously huge oil paintings, depicting dour men and pained women in period costume lined the walls, interspersed with some fearsome-looking weaponry.

The narrow room had to be at least sixty feet long and forty feet wide, she thought with awe. The table alone would seat thirty. Eden didn't even *know* thirty people.

If she wanted mourners at her funeral she was going to have to get out more, she thought a little hysterically.

"Better?" he asked, seated at the far end of the

table as though she were contaminated with the bubonic plague. She had the most ridiculous urge to walk the walk and go and plop herself down right next to him. Breathe on him, and see if he'd run. She didn't think so. He looked big and mean enough to take on the Marines, the Navy, and the Air Force. *Combined*.

And where did that leave her?

She didn't have the brawn. She looked him over. She'd bet she could run circles around his brain with her eyes closed and one hand tied behind her back. "I'm fine," she lied, folding her hands on top of the table. The wood was smoothly weathered and scratched and gouged from age. She traced her thumbnail around one of the nicks as her mind whirled and her stomach settled. First she had to find out where she was.

"No you're not. You're still sick to your stomach and you have vertigo."

True, unfortunately. She tilted her chin and gave him the evil eye. "You don't know anything about me."

"T-FLAC has a crack research team who came up with a profile of one Eden Elizabeth Cahill, age twenty-seven," he told her flatly. "Want me to continue?"

She waved a hand in a "go for it" gesture. While he told her where she'd been born, the names of her parents, and where she'd gone to nursery school or whatever, she considered how many people there might be in residence. One or one hundred. She wasn't going anywhere until the nausea passed and she knew exactly what she was dealing with.

"Married to Dr. Adam Burnett, who was what? Twenty-five years older than you?"

She presumed the question was rhetorical and kept her mouth shut. She did her best not to think about either Adam or their marriage. As short a time as it had lasted, they'd both gotten what they wanted, or deserved, she sometimes thought. Adam had attached himself to her accomplishments, and she'd learned that she'd rather be lonely by herself.

"Divorced at twenty-one." He had a great voice. Smooth and mellow. Under normal circumstances she'd quite enjoy listening to him. But he was reciting her life as though it were scrolling in front of him on a TelePrompTer.

"Dr. Burnett took credit for most of your work while you were married. After the divorce and MIT, you went to work for Jason Verdine at Verdine Industries." He was tapping his index finger on the edge of the table as he talked. An annoying habit that on anyone else Eden would've read as nerves. But not this guy. She'd be willing to bet nothing fazed him.

"You've been called one of the most brilliant scientists in America by *Popular Science* magazine. You were what? Sixteen?"

"You tell me. You seem to know it all." The finger-tapping was as annoying as jiggling change in a pocket. She glanced from his face to the offending finger, and back again. "In a hurry? Or do I make you nervous?"

He flattened his hand on the table. "Honored by *Technical Review Magazine* as 'Innovator for the Next Century.' Ten years' experience in robotic technology—including the year when Verdine Industries loaned you to NASA's Jet Propulsion Laboratories. BS in Mechanical Engineering, and an MS in Computer Science, both at MIT. Nobel Prize for computer language processing for dialogue and translation—"

"Very thorough," she interrupted. Very thorough, and freaking *creepy* to know that *anyone* was interested enough in her life to bother digging all that up.

"You're a woman who's used to being alone. A woman comfortable with her own brilliance, but modest about her contribution to both the scientific and commercial inventions. A woman who spends more every

month on shoes—size seven and a half—and perfume—
you favor florals—than she does on rent. An honest
woman who told the biggest lie of the century and now
regrets it. More?"

"That pretty much covers it," Eden said briskly. The
only thing he hadn't mentioned was how many pounds
she'd been overweight. "Who did you say dug all of this
up?" Her stomach was settling. A few more minutes and
she'd ask for the bathroom. The second she was out of
this room, and away from him, she'd run like hell.

"T-FLAC."

She had no idea what that was. Nor did she care.
Everything he'd just said by rote was true.

But he couldn't possibly know about the lie. Could
he? Why the hell not? She still didn't understand how
she'd gotten here.

Stay calm, she cautioned herself. *Don't let him see
me panic. Don't let him think he can bully me into
admitting—anything.*

Giving her rapid heart rate time to return to some
semblance of normalcy, Eden spared a glance through
the leaded-glass windows. Evergreens. Shrubs. Mountains in the distance. None of it looked familiar. "Where
are we?"

"Montana."

Eden stared at him, wide-eyed. "Montana? My God,
what did you give me that could keep me out for so
long?" She, who loathed exercise, felt her body vibrate
with unspent energy. She felt the need to run. To jog five
miles, to swim laps or leap tall buildings. She had to escape this kidnapper with his dark eyes and bad disposition, *tout de suite.*

"I didn't—never mind that."

He didn't—*what?* Drug her? "What do you want
from me?" *Because as hunky as you are, weasel dog,
you are* not *going to get it.* "Kidnapping is a felony, and

I assure you, I'll prosecute you to the full extent of the law."

"They'll have to find you first, won't they?"

She gave him a stony look. "A threat layered over a kidnapping is just overkill."

The man who she'd thrown up on earlier walked back into the room and shot her a smile as he walked the length of the table toward her. "He kidnapped you to protect you, Dr. Cahill." He took a chair a few feet away from her.

No fair, she thought, that he's had a shower. She shot him a quick glance. He was a nice-looking guy. Tall, dark, light blue eyes, dimple. But her heart didn't accelerate when she looked at him. *He* didn't worry her, or make her feel threatened. Eden looked back at her kidnapper. "Really?" My God, the man had a scowl like nothing she'd ever seen. "How kind of you. But I have all the protection I need back in Tempe. I'd like to go home now."

"Your prototype for the Rx793 robot was stolen," Gabriel said unnecessarily. "Know who has it?"

Eden reached for a glass and the crystal decanter of whiskey on a nearby silver tray. She rarely drank, and certainly not at this time of the morning. However, these were definitely extenuating circumstances. She needed time to come up with a good answer. If he was toying with her to find out how much she knew, she'd have to be on guard.

She poured half a glass, then drank most of it down in one gulp. It was vile and hit her stomach like a tsunami. It tasted just as bad now as it had when the other guy had poured it down her throat. She swallowed it like medicine, grimaced, then set the glass down. "You should know. You trashed the place."

"No, Dr. Cahill. I didn't. Neither did I kill Dr. Kirchner. So let me answer my previous question. The person or persons responsible for murdering Dr. Kirchner, and stealing the robot, most assuredly, are *terrorists*."

The pterodactyls rose inside her, clamoring for immediate attention. "Or a Verdine Industries competitor," she pointed out in a voice that didn't betray her fear. *Please God,* she prayed, not for the first time. *Please let it be SpaceCo, or Hazlet Toy Company that has Rex. Please.* Theo was gone, but she had to hold on to the belief that Rex wasn't going to be used in some dreadful terrorist act.

"I want every one of your backup files, Dr. Cahill. Where are they?"

Eden laughed without humor. "You want my backup files? You say you didn't kill Dr. Kirchner, but you did take me against my will. Think I'm going to hand anything over to a kidnapper? Just like that? What have you been smoking?"

"There *are* backup files."

"Are you telling me or asking me? When will you get it that I'm here under duress, and I'm not telling . . . you . . ." She felt a familiar wash of warmth travel through her body and glanced down. "A—a th-thing." Her erect nipples showed through her bra and T-shirt.

Horrified, furious, *baffled,* her head shot up. "Damn it! Are you *hypnotizing* me?"

"Why? Feel like clucking like a chicken? Of course I'm not hypnotizing you. Tell me where the data can be found, and I'll have you home in a flash."

She didn't believe him.

"Do you have a backup for the robot that was stolen, Dr. Cahill?" Sebastian asked. "Is there a second one?"

Eden had seen enough television to wonder if these two were pulling the good cop, bad cop routine on her. Well, she wasn't buying it. Just because he was polite didn't mean he wasn't as culpable for this crime as the other one. She'd see justice served on both of them. As soon as she got away.

Eden took another large gulp of whiskey.

Without a shadow of a doubt, despite his manners, she knew this was not a man to cross. "What was the question?"

"The robot?"

Right. "Rex was a prototype. The data was destroyed by Dr. Kirchner's killer."

Keeping her gaze steady with effort, she said flatly, "There was only one Rex." She checked her watch. Nine twenty-three. My God. How long had he held her here? "What day is it?"

"Monday."

It couldn't still be Monday, barely enough time had elapsed for him to get her out to the company parking lot, let alone more than a thousand miles from Arizona to Montana. "Oh, for heaven's sake! I'm still having that ridiculous dream, aren't I?"

"If this is a dream," the other man said dryly, "I've been having it for fifteen years."

"Shut up, Sebastian," Gabriel said coolly. "Don't you have to be somewhere?"

"Nowhere half this entertaining."

"Well, aren't you two just the sweetest couple?" Eden rose, a little shaky yet. Chugging all that whiskey hadn't helped her equilibrium any, but she was on her feet and blessed with a sudden surplus of bravado. "Not only don't I care who you are, I can't give you what you want. So if you're going to kill me, give it your best shot. If not, I'm out of here."

"It's a hell of a long walk back to Tempe," Gabriel said in a neutral tone.

Eden gave him a cool look. "Then I'd better get going, hadn't I?"

"Antagonizing her isn't going to get you what you

want, Gabriel." Sebastian seemed to be enjoying himself. "Let the poor woman sit down and get her bearings. MacBain? How about a spot of t—Oh, there you go. Tea for the lady."

The old man deposited a tea tray almost bigger than he was on the table close to Eden. "I took the liberty of providing a few delicacies, madam. I'm sure you must be hungry after your . . . trip."

Her lips twitched. She was dying for a cup of tea amidst this madness. How could she refuse the offer from a crusty Scottish butler with a sense of humor? Come to think of it, what was a butler, Scottish or otherwise, doing in Montana?

But she wasn't here to be amused, and she wasn't here to drink tea from a cup with little purple pansies on it. And without a doubt those scones would sit like lead in her jumpy stomach. Eden considered her limited options. "As delicious as that looks, I'm afraid I have to pass." For all she knew the tea was drugged.

Her host rose from his end of the table. Lord, he was big. And broad. And surly looking. "Any one of a dozen terrorist groups could have stolen your robot, Dr. Cahill. It's a given that they'll use it for something nefarious. *Soon.* Yes, I see by the look on your face that you've considered the ramifications of the theft.

"So tell us, Doctor. Exactly what can this super robot of yours do? Exactly how far has research taken you?"

So far, Eden thought, nausea rising again, *that if you knew, you'd torture me to get the information you want.* "Are you the terrorists that stole it?"

"We're *counter*terrorist operatives, Doctor," Sebastian said, snagging her attention as he removed the tapestry tea cozy from the plump teapot. He poured two cups of steaming tea into the translucent cups, then used silver tongs to pick up a cube of sugar and cocked a brow.

Eden nodded. What the hell. This wasn't the time to look around for Sweet'N Low. And if this guy was drinking it, too, it was probably safe. He pushed a cup and saucer in her direction. She glanced from one man to the other, but it was Gabriel Edge she wanted to keep in her sights.

"You work for the government?" Eden sat down and started stirring her tea. No they didn't. She'd been interviewed, hell, *interrogated,* for hours, days, *weeks* by Homeland Security, FBI, and whatever. Not one of those men looked anything like this man.

Oh, God. Why hadn't she been brave enough, *smart* enough to tell all those government people the truth? She'd known, of course, she'd known the second she'd seen Theo lying there in the kitchen, that the bad guys had Rex.

There'd been so much blood. How could there be so much blood? A human body only contained 5.6 liters. Six quarts. It had looked like gallons. It was only later that she'd been told he'd been shot five times. At the time she'd been frantic. The blood was everywhere and nothing she'd done had stanched the flow. Nothing she'd done had been enough to save Theo's life.

She'd cradled his head on her lap as she listened for the sirens. *Comeoncomeoncomeon.* Hurryhurryhurry. "I love you," she told him, forcing her voice steady although she had a boulder clogging her throat. "Please—Oh, God. *Please* don't leave me."

"E-den."

She'd cupped his papery cheek, her eyes hot and burning with unshed tears. The sirens wailed in the distance. Too late. Too damn late. She could barely swallow, as she said calmly, "I'm right here."

Theo's rheumy eyes flickered up to her face. "Destroy—*everything.* Trust no one. P-promise me."

Sebastian touched the back of her hand. "Dr. Cahill?"

Eden blinked the two men back into focus. She wanted to go home. She wanted to do what she should have done the first time she'd been interviewed. She had to tell the authorities what it was they'd be up against. These two men *weren't* the authorities. They were possibly crazy, and absolutely dangerous. They wanted information from her. She'd get information from them. "What exactly do you do for our government?"

"Freelance work."

Eden set down her spoon, hiding the tremble in her hand. "Mercenaries."

"Counterterrorist operatives," he corrected, still scowling.

Rude bastard. She glanced at Sebastian. "Does that mean I threw up on your shoe phone?" she asked sweetly.

"Look, lady," Gabriel snarled, clearly at the end of his very short rope. "Cut the crap. Take my word for it. We're the good guys. Exactly what the hell will your robotic pal do for the *bad* guys, Doctor?"

She was tempted, God, was she tempted to tell them she'd invented a robot that did excellent pedicures. They'd let her go. Or kill her. She might be scared, but she damn well refused to be intimidated. "Anything."

A muscle ticked in his jaw. "Give us an example of 'anything.' "

Rx793, Rex, was Eden's pride and joy. She'd worked on the robot for more than ten years. "I hadn't finished running the variables," she told the two men reluctantly. "He wasn't nearly finished yet. I still had at least six months, maybe more—"

Gabriel wound his hand indicating she get on with it.

"When he's completed he'll be impervious . . . to just about anything. Heat. Cold. Chemicals. Toxins. Rex will have the ability to go into the most intense burning building to perform rescues impossible for a human. He can be used to clean up chemical spills, go into any toxic environment and bring back samples."

"What the *fuck* was Verdine thinking?" Gabriel pushed away from the table to pace. "Anyone with half a goddamned brain cell would know that having something this sophisticated would appeal to every damned terrorist on the planet."

She pressed a hand to her stomach and said almost desperately, "The marketing people at Verdine Industries have been talking to firefighters, law enforcement agencies, and the CDC. He's an enormous breakthrough in AI. I'm doing a symposium on him in Berlin nex—"

The two men made eye contact, and Eden felt a premonition-type shiver run up her spine. She had to tell the right people just how much more advanced she'd made the robot. She'd done everything she was telling her kidnappers. And more. If the American government didn't put her in front of a firing squad on the spot, they'd probably throw her in jail for sixty lifetimes. She hadn't known how far she could go. Was that defendable?

"Tell us how to destroy it, and we'll let you go."

Her mouth was dry, but she couldn't make herself pick up the cup in front of her to take a sip of tea. "I can't."

"Can't, doctor? Or won't?"

"The Rx793 can't *be* destroyed. It was made to be indestructible."

"Nothing's indestructible," he said grimly. "We don't have all day here, Doctor. What will annihilate your robot?"

"Nothing." Nothing but another Rex just like it. But since she was never going to let that happen, it wasn't worth mentioning.

"How about a duplicate?" he demanded.

My God, was he a mind reader? Eden thought, horrified. She debated for a few seconds whether to lie or tell him the truth. "Possibly," she said reluctantly. "If there was another such bot. There isn't."

"There will be," he said grimly.

Eden didn't bother correcting him.

"What's its fuel source?"

"An extremely inexpensive thirty-two-processor distributed control system. It runs asynchronously with no central locus of control." No. Worse. *Much* worse. She'd given Rex an easily renewable hydrogen fuel cell. All he needed to run for three hours was a cup of water.

"Does the arm need a parallel processor?"

"No. All computing is done onboard." She'd thought herself so clever to make Rex almost autonomous. Now she was scared stupid. Oh, God. She should have stopped last year when her gut and conscience told her to. She'd never considered herself vain before. But damn it, she'd wanted to prove to herself that all those accolades, all those prestigious science awards, all the fawning and flattery, were as valid today as they'd been ten years ago.

Which proved that she wasn't nearly as evolved as she thought she was.

No matter what veneer she'd assumed over the years, no matter what she wore, or how many acclaimed papers she wrote, no matter how brilliant her inventions— that fat, geeky, insecure kid still lived inside her. And even though she'd known she could never tell anyone the incredible advances she'd made, *she* would always know how far ahead of the pack she really was. That vanity was about to bite her in the ass.

"How big is it?"

Eden held her hand up over the floor. "He's the size of a five-year-old." An almost perfect humanoid robot who could catch a ball and knew his left from his right. Who could consume a glass of water and keep on going like the Energizer Bunny.

Her hand shook as she picked up the delicate bone china teacup. The tea was cold, but she sipped it anyway. English Breakfast. She looked from one man to the other. "The prototype was stolen. There are no backup files. I don't see how I can help you."

"How long will it take for you to rebuild the robot?" *Never.* "I can't."

"You built it before. You can build it again."

She shook her head. "No, I can't. All m—*our* notes were stolen."

"But you don't *require* notes, do you, Dr. Cahill?" Gabriel Edge said, his voice cold and hard as he watched her, his hands gripping the high back of the chair. His direct gaze was unnerving. "You have it all up here." He tapped his hard head with his finger, and Eden felt a chill rush through her body like ice water. He couldn't know that. He couldn't possibly know that.

"*You* have a photographic memory, Doctor. And *I* have a fully outfitted computer lab right here. You can reconstruct what was taken."

Eden laughed. And she made sure it sounded sincere. "You must be kidding! Photographic memory is fiction. I have a *good* memory. A very good memory. But reconstruct, from scratch, *thousands* of man-hours' worth of intricate and complicated equations and schematics? From memory? Not possible."

Very possible, unfortunately, and exactly what she was best at. She was the one in one billion people who actually *could* retain everything she read. She refrained from fiddling with the delicate cup in her hands, and kept her gaze steady. If she hadn't already emptied her stomach she'd be throwing up again.

Destroy everything. Trust no one. Promise me.

Eden felt like a very small rat in a very complicated maze.

Gabriel Edge was the extremely large cat lying in wait for her at the other end.

"Anything's possible, Doctor," he told her. "If you put your *mind* to it."

Eden looked directly into Gabriel's eyes. Just why had he put so much emphasis on that one word? Another thing he'd said slammed into her head. Teleport. Cold permeated her insides, and sweat dotted her brow. These men were crazy, and she was damned if she would give them what they wanted. She'd given them as much of the truth as she was prepared to give them. The rest would remain a secret.

She owed Theo that much.

CHAPTER SEVEN

Dr. Cahill had reluctantly allowed MacBain to escort her upstairs to freshen up. Gabriel was grateful that she was out of his range so that he could draw an unrestricted breath for the first time in what felt like months. Christ. He didn't need this kind of complication in his life. Who could have anticipated this kind of magnetism?

His parents, he thought grimly. If they'd been alive they'd have tried everything in their considerable power to prevent so much as the first encounter between himself and Dr. Eden Cahill.

They, better than anyone else, would have known the ramifications of bringing his Lifemate here. Especially now.

They would have been appalled—*terrified* for him. Hadn't they experienced exactly what he was experiencing now? And look where their great love had ended. Not even together in death, but buried apart for all eternity. His father on a wind-tossed knoll in his beloved Scottish Highlands, his mother here in Montana, in the rose garden she'd planted as a shrine to lost love.

He was the oldest. He *did* know better than to tempt the Fates this way. If his brothers, Caleb and Duncan, heard about this, they'd be here before he made it to the front door with Sebastian, Gabriel thought grimly.

They'd insist on whisking him out of harm's way. But even they would have to admit that he was out of choices.

Wouldn't you just know his damn Lifemate would be the one woman who could help him through this latest T-FLAC crisis?

"Think she was telling the truth?" Sebastian's shoes scraped on the worn stone floor.

The vast entry hall, with its sweeping staircase and unusual and spectacular fan-vaulted, umbrella design ceiling, was hung with thirty-foot-tall tapestries of battles covering the ages. Polished suits of armor lined the walls. The castle was more than Gabriel's ancestral home. He remembered his parents here. How brief their reunions were. He remembered meals in the dining room, cozy evenings by the fire in the book-lined library. Normally this house, these rooms, the very stones it was built from, gave Gabriel the kind of solace men like him didn't usually find. But today, the old castle felt like a cage.

"I think she's lying through her pretty white teeth," he told his friend grimly, mentally opening the front door when they were twenty feet away. Sunlight flooded the worn ancient stone floor ahead of them, but he still felt a chill.

"Neat trick," Sebastian murmured. "You psi/spec ops guys have all the cool toys."

And the burden and responsibilities that came *with* those special powers. Gabriel had never questioned who and what he was. Until today. "From what I observed in the lab earlier, Dr. Cahill has a photographic memory like nothing I've seen before. Despite her protestations, I believe she's mentally retained all her notes and files for the bot. She hasn't forgotten a damn thing."

"But the development has taken her years—"

"Six."

"And you think she was able to retain every step?" Sebastian demanded, "Every zig and zag necessary to re-build the damn thing? From *memory.*"

Gabriel nodded "Yeah. I do. Dollars to doughnuts, T-FLAC is going to get a call. And we're going to have our asses in a sling if we can't destroy the Rx793 the second we know where the damn thing is."

"But will she tell us how to do it?"

Gabriel thought of her flashing dark eyes, large and expressive, and speaking volumes. He thought of her white teeth biting into her mutinous soft lips. He thought about how desperately he wanted her. And he thought about how, stubborn woman that she was, she was fighting him on every front.

"Yeah." God help him. "I'll make sure she does. I also want to know exactly what it was she *didn't* report to the authorities."

Sebastian gave a mock shudder. "Give the poor woman a look like that and she'll tell you anything."

"Not this woman." Gabriel stepped through the open door, walking out into the midmorning sunshine. Sebastian hitched his duffel bag over his shoulder as they stopped next to his car, a low-slung black Lamborghini Murciélago parked in the shadow of the east turret.

"My way would be faster," Gabriel pointed out as his friend slung his bag into the backseat, then vaulted the door. Nice car.

"Maybe," Sebastian smiled as he put on his sunglasses. "But I'm scared shitless one day I'll come back looking like something Picasso painted. I'll pass."

"Nothing scares you." Gabriel stroked the glossy black paint on the door absently. He was going to have to go upstairs and talk to her.

Scared didn't begin to cover it.

The engine started up with an expensive purr. "That brainy woman of yours inside does. What's coming down the pike does. Yeah. I scare."

That woman of yours.

If I don't claim her, Gabriel wondered, feeling a familiar race of panic, *is she still mine?* He was afraid he knew the answer to his own question. "Ditto." Any man in their line of work would be a fool not to be afraid. Fear kept them sharp. Fear let them know they were alive. But this—this was different. Way different.

Sebastian put the car in gear. "I'm twenty minutes away. Call if you need me." T-FLAC headquarters was sixty miles south.

Gabriel slapped his shoulder, a little harder than necessary. "Make sure the highway patrol doesn't see you."

"Have to catch me first."

The sun beat down on his head as Gabriel watched the car until it was nothing more than a speck down the road. He couldn't delay this any longer. He had to face her again.

Alone.

He broke out in a cold sweat.

As soon as MacBain left the bedroom, Eden dashed into the exquisitely appointed en suite bathroom. Oh, God. She half laughed at her appearance in the well-lit mirror over the sink and vanity. Her face was white. Her hair, as usual, had a life of its own—a cartoon life apparently, as she looked like a woman who'd stuck a finger in an electrical outlet. Once again, she'd only remembered to apply mascara to one eye—her left, by the look of the black half circle beneath it. She washed her face with French-milled, rose-scented soap, dried her face on a handy towel, and appreciated MacBain's attention to detail when she saw the new toothbrush and her favorite brand of toothpaste next to a row of perfume bottles.

She cleaned her teeth and drank three glasses of water.

Her hair she left to its own devices. Then she went into the bedroom to wait.

The bedroom was richly appointed with velvets, silks, and brocades in varying shades of gold and sapphire blue. Not her colors, but very pretty all the same. If she could sit still and admire pretty, Eden thought, pacing to the door and back to the window. The portraits on the walls were huge and probably valuable. The canopied, heavily posted, cherry wood bed could sleep the entire population of a third-world country.

Why had she never heard of this place? Surely, when something of *this* magnitude was being built it would have had a ton of press? She'd never heard of a castle being reproduced in the wilds of Montana. She'd have to Google it. Perhaps it had been built for a movie, or it was a hotel. Although she hadn't seen anyone other than the three men around since she'd been there. Come to think of it, she also hadn't seen a phone.

Either way, she had no intention of remaining here. Wherever here *was* exactly. There must be a town reasonably nearby. There was certainly a major highway. Cars. People.

Jason and Marshall must be frantic by now. It helped that all those lettered agencies had already been on the premises investigating Theo's death when she disappeared. They'd have started looking for her almost immediately.

Someone must have seen Gabriel take her out of the building. There must be an eyewitness at Verdine Industries who'd seen *something,* and she had absolutely no intention of hanging around here while they tried to find her. She'd help from her end.

Eden rubbed her arms, feeling both hot and cold at the same time. And antsy. Anticipatory.

Standing at the arched, leaded-glass window, she observed Gabriel and Sebastian talking down below on the gravel driveway. She'd love to be a fly on the wall for *that* conversation. After a few minutes Sebastian drove away. Other than a long stretch of surprisingly well-maintained road, there was nothing but dense, lush, rolling forest as far as the eye could see.

The rosy stone of the castle walls soared at least four stories into the clear blue sky, turrets and all. Everything in it looked authentic, although Eden wouldn't know a genuine antique from Ikea. If the windowsill was any indication, the walls were twelve feet thick. The date 1324 had been carved in the stone lintel above the window.

Who *was* this guy?

It would be cold at night. She'd just follow the road until she hit civilization. She'd need water. She'd also require proper shoes. She wouldn't get five feet out there in these high-heeled sandals, much as she loved them. She'd also need sunblock in case she was out there longer than anticipated, and if she could find one, a cell phone.

Sure. She could do this.

The size of the castle notwithstanding, Gabriel and his butler had to sleep sometime.

With at least the start of a plan made, she leaned against the warm stone of the windowsill. Shading her eyes against the sunlight streaming into the room through the open window, she turned her head to look back outside at the lush landscape painted a million shades of green.

In the distance, the Rocky Mountains were hazed lavender by the heat. Eden inhaled a calming, deep breath of evergreens-scented air—Her breath stopped.

The road was—gone.

She blinked.

She considered what she was and was not seeing. Nothing else had changed. Not the wind nor the angle of the sun. One minute there had been a two-lane black-top cutting through the trees. Now there was not.

She knew by the sudden increase in her respiration and heart rate that he was in the room without turning around. She hugged her arms around her body as she stared outside. The sun was still shining, a bird's sweet song soared overhead.

She didn't like the way her body responded to his presence. She hated not understanding what the hell was going on. And she was bewildered by her visceral reaction to her kidnapper.

Not having answers, and being out of her element, scared the crap out of her.

She was pretty used to being out of her element in a social setting, not that this was social, but she hated being scared. She rubbed her arms without turning around. "What kind of hallucinogenic did you give me?"

"No drugs."

She turned slowly.

Heat rapidly spread through her. God. There was no scientific explanation to her reaction to this man. Potently masculine, Gabriel Edge stood beside the bed. Twenty feet away. Yet she could almost feel the heat of his body and smell the sun-washed fragrance of his hair from clear across the room.

She frowned as she looked at his mouth. With a raw hunger, she wondered what it would feel like touching hers. What his muscular arms would feel like wrapped around her. He was tall, muscular, strong . . . How would that animal-like strength translate in bed?

And how freaking illogical that she wanted him to hold her when he was the very man she was half terrified of, and knew she must run from? With an inner groan she jerked her thoughts away from how he would taste and back to the view outside the window.

Yes, he was good-looking. But she'd encountered

dozens of good-looking men over the years. The sense of euphoria when he was near, the racing pulse and elevated breathing, were physical manifestations associated with falling in love. She felt as giddy as a teenager. But she'd never *been* a giddy teenager.

She'd been a brain with legs. A plump, too smart, lonely geek that no one understood, and colleagues mocked behind her back. She'd never fit in anywhere. It was no wonder Adam had been able to sweep her off her feet so easily.

And she hadn't felt one particle of the sexual awareness for Adam Burnett she felt for this man.

Eden's skin felt as if it were on fire, and feverish shivers danced across her nerve endings. This was insane. Everything in her was responding to him, totally independent of her control.

She wasn't a teenager. And this wasn't the junior prom. This son of a bitch had kidnapped her and was keeping her prisoner. She'd do well to remember that.

She let her gaze drift over him. Lord, he was potent. His navy T-shirt showed off his chest to perfection, and bared his tanned arms lightly furred with dark hair. Would his chest be hairy or smooth? Eden ached to find out. His long legs were encased in faded jeans and bluntly showed he was male.

All *aroused* male, she thought, finding it hard to swallow. She looked down at her short, unpolished nails and pale hands, and wondered if Gabriel liked his women to have long, red fingernails to score his skin when they made love. He probably liked them skinny and lean. *Bastard.* She gave him a hot look.

An almost wary expression hardened his features for a moment as their eyes met across the room. Then even that glimpse was gone as he continued to watch her with remote, unreadable eyes.

She rubbed her upper arms. "Can you explain what I just saw?"

He lifted a brow. "What did you see, Dr. Cahill?" he asked in a lazy and somehow remote tone. The calmness of his voice, when she was feeling rising agitation, annoyed the hell out of her.

"The fact that one second there was a road out there," she said tightly, pointing through the window, "And now—*look,* there isn't—"

A stripe of black again cut a swath through the trees.

"You were saying?"

She spun away from the window to shoot him a puzzled glance. "Either you're causing me to hallucinate or I'm losing my mind."

"Come with me. I want you to see the lab so you can let me know if there's anything else you'll need before you get started."

Eden frowned at the non sequitur. "Are you going to give me some answers?"

"Apparently not. Come on. The bad guys already have a head start."

"That's right. Six years' worth." Jason must have considered this possibility as well. Of course he must have. And while he himself didn't know *all* of Rex's skills, he had to have considered the ramifications if the robot fell into the wrong hands. Eden felt a little easing in her stomach. Not much. Just a tiny spurt of hope. She wasn't alone.

If she and Jason went to the FBI and Homeland Security together . . .

"Let's go. We're wasting time."

She didn't want to have anything to do with this guy. She didn't like the swirling emotions she felt whenever he was around. He made her feel like a rabbit faced with a rattler; terrified, but fascinated at the same time.

Even though his expression was impassive when he

spoke to her, she could read the hunger in his dark eyes. He wanted her, and for some reason it pissed him off that he did.

Eden knew exactly how he felt.

She was bewildered by the strength of her attraction to a man who had taken her against her will. Her safest bet was to ignore the sensation for the duration. She wouldn't be here long enough to have to figure it out.

Pleased that she'd regained her composure and shored up her defenses, and since she knew she wouldn't be making her escape down the sheer side of the stone walls, Eden followed him out of the room.

Any escape opportunity presenting itself, she would take. If she ended up walking out of here barefoot, so be it.

CHAPTER EIGHT

The walls on either side of the wide upper corridor were paneled in mahogany with intricate carved moldings. Arched windows ran down the entire length of the right-hand wall, the wide expanse of glass interspersed with enormous family portraits in ornate gilded wood frames that must have weighed a hundred pounds apiece.

Curious about the "lab he'd prepared for her," Eden glanced about to get her bearings for her escape later. Everything about Edridge Castle was made on a massive scale.

Including her host.

His long legs and big feet ate up yardage in the black, gold, and red swirls of the carpet as he forged ahead of her. *Way* ahead. That whole contamination thing again.

What was the bastard using on her? Hypnosis? Drugs? She'd drunk at least half a glass of whiskey and a cup of tea. She felt physically fine, better than fine actually. She was filled with energy and clarity of thought. And was acutely aware of him no matter how far apart they were.

She'd never noticed a man's butt before, but his was prime, and did excellent things for those jeans.

He had an interesting loose-limbed walk, light on his bare feet. Her heels sank into the thick carpet as they walked, and she had to do a little two-step to catch up. As soon as she got closer, he seemed to speed up.

Eden spotted what could very well be a Fabergé egg, or an excellent replica, on a table beneath a gruesome painting of a guy in a kilt killing a boar. The artist had used an excessive amount of red paint. She paused to look more closely at the jeweled egg caught in the sunlight streaming through the window.

Would anyone display the real thing this casually? Probably not. Still, it was very pretty.

"You have some beautiful things in your home." And if they weren't walking at warp speed she might have liked to look at some of the artifacts and paintings on their safari.

She had dozens of questions that had nothing to do with the freaking decor, but he'd have dozens of slippery replies, so why bother? The authorities could interrogate him—torture him for all she cared. After she was gone.

"It's home." There was pride in the simple words.

"When was it built?" she asked curiously, before reminding herself that she wasn't a guest. "More to the point, how long did it take to build?"

Sunlight, in dusty motes, streamed through the arched, leaded-glass windows on their right in a striped pattern down the entire length of the corridor. She walked through a shadow, then back through sunlight.

"It was built in the Highlands of Scotland in 1321. Edridge Castle was the original seat of my family. Edridges have lived in it for eight hundred years."

She frowned. "I thought your name was Edge?" Boy, was *that* a name that personified the man. Hard. Sharp. Cutting.

"Changed from Edridge to Edge by a distant relative in the mid sixteen hundreds."

"One step ahead of the law, was he?"

"Magnus was cursed."

She knew the feeling. Her own marriage had been cursed too. Cursed by her own naïveté and stupidity. She'd actually convinced herself that she'd learned and grown from the experience. That she'd left those insecurities behind with the divorce. Apparently not.

She walked faster to catch up, intrigued in spite of herself. The man must have eyes in the back of his head, because he sped up just enough to keep the distance between them exactly the same at all times. "Why was he cursed?"

"Because he fell in love with the wrong woman."

"Was she married?"

"No."

Eden sped up. Not that it made a jot of difference. The man must have a built-in radar. "Too young? Too old?"

"No and no."

"Too pretty, too ugly? What? If she was single, then she would have been appropriate marriage material, right?"

"He was betrothed."

"Betrothed?" Eden cut in with a smile she couldn't help. "I don't think I've ever heard anyone use that word."

He glanced over his shoulder. "Engaged. Happy now?"

"Sure," Eden replied somberly. "Who was he engaged to?"

"The chieftain's oldest daughter."

"I would've cursed him too," Eden told his back. He sounded just somber enough to give the story verisimilitude, which surprised her. She would never have pegged him as a storyteller. He seemed too prosaic. Too intense and serious.

Live and learn.

"So he was fooling around on *both* women." She

would've preferred a husband who had a girlfriend rather than the one who stole her inventions and patented them under his own name. But that was water under the bridge.

Like her ex, this guy's ancestor would have wanted to make the most advantageous alliance. In her case, she'd been the chieftain's daughter and her credentials had been the village girl he'd loved. He hadn't married her for herself. Adam had married her just to advance his career.

Dr. Adam Burnett was a competent scientist who wanted to be brilliant. Once he'd realized that he'd reached his full, mediocre potential, he'd married her and set about taking credit for her early ideas and work.

"Did he marry the chieftain's daughter and dump the girlfriend?"

"Nairne—the village girl—was pregnant. She was also a witch. She showed up at the kirk on his wedding day."

"Ouch. Both women probably cursed him."

"One curse was enough for a lifetime. Several lifetimes, in fact."

"True. Must've been a pretty powerful curse to last— what? four hundred years?"

"Five hundred."

"Really?" Eden said to his broad back, fascinated by that kind of unbroken history, and intrigued that this man, who appeared to be capable of kidnapping and all manner of other unsavory deeds, sounded as though he actually believed in witches and that said witch had put a curse on the entire family. She wondered how she could play into that to make her escape.

"So, what kind of curse was it? Damned for all time or run-of-the-mill turned into a frog?"

"The sons have to choose duty over love for all time."

"Payback for all eternity for being jilted? That's pretty intense. Do you believe it?"

"I don't have to believe. It just is."

Uh huh. "Is that so? Who el—"

"Subject closed."

In effect, door slammed in her face. Intriguing. Eden backed off, but saved the knowledge that he was superstitious for later when she could figure out how to use it against him.

The irony was, for all her scientific background, she was a little superstitious as well. She never walked under ladders, and crossed the street if she saw a black cat.

And even though she knew it didn't have any basis in actual fact, she truly believed that wearing her Grandma Rose's ring on her toe had brought her luck for most of her life.

"Tell me about this place," she said easily, glancing at the portraits as she passed them. All of the women were surrounded by varying size groups of boy and girl children. They all looked uncomfortable, no matter what period clothing they wore. Each woman wore the same three pieces of heart-shaped jewelry. A silver necklace, bracelet, and ring. Not particularly attractive or valuable. Must be something handed down to each new wife, Eden guessed. "What did you do? Have the original castle dismantled in Scotland, and brought here? Did you know Robert McCulloch bought London Bridge in 1962, dismantled it, and had it rebuilt in Lake Havasu City, Arizona? That engineering project took three years. But this . . . this must've taken three times that at least." She imagined every stone with a number on it. One giant Erector set. She'd love to get her hands on the blueprint . . .

"It didn't take that long," Gabriel told her dismissively.

"Why Montana? Seems an odd place to stick a medieval castle."

"My mother's folks had a ranch on this land, it was hers to do with as she pleased. She wanted to have the castle here. Enough personal questions."

Conversation closed, apparently.

"Do you have a large family? People who'll chip in to pay your bail when they arrest you for my kidnapping?"

"No."

She stopped dead, and shot a glare, which of course he couldn't see, at his back. "Give me a break here. I'm the prisoner, remember? I'm sure the Geneva Convention allows for polite conversation."

"It doesn't, actually."

Behind his back Eden rolled her eyes before speeding up, trying to catch up with him.

No go.

As she walked she glanced at the portraits of men and women, all dressed in stiff, formal clothing, that lined the walls.

"Are all these portraits your ancestors, or are they actors hired by your decorator?" Eden asked mildly, pretty damn sure that Gabriel Edge hadn't hired a decorator for his castle, but she was not opposed to needling him. Just because she could.

If he didn't like it he could always take her back to Tempe.

Gabriel nodded toward a portrait as he passed. "The first is Magnus's mother, Finola. He's the kid on the right. And the portrait to the left is Magnus's bride, Janet."

Curious, Eden stopped while he, of course, moved a little farther down the hall before he stopped too.

She went to stand under the portrait of a dour-faced woman holding a little white dog with bulging black eyes. Both woman and dog wore matching powder-blue satin dresses. Nestled in the many folds of the woman's skirts sat three stair-stepped little boys with black hair, midnight dark blue eyes, and Stepford expressions.

"Triplets?"

"Nine months apart."

Eden rubbed a sudden chill from her upper arms. "No wonder she doesn't look like a happy camper." She glanced at the other portrait. A horse-faced girl clutching a pearl-studded fan in a death grip, also with three young boys clustered around her. This new bride wore no jewelry. Her neck, wrist, and fingers looked conspicuously bare without the twists of silver. "Doesn't look as though Magnus made either his mother *or* his wife happy."

"Apparently not."

"Well, hopefully Janet's children fulfilled her. Didn't they have dozens of kids in those days?" Eden couldn't imagine how hard life had been in medieval times. Particularly for the women.

"Only the three sons shown in the portrait. All Edge couples have three sons."

She had no idea why the closer he got, the harder her heart thumped. Eden turned to look at him. He was standing at least fifteen feet away. It was as though her body had a Gabriel antenna to let her know when he was approaching.

"Really?" Improbable, but she'd let it pass for the moment.

When she got back home she'd pull the research on pheromones to see if the antenna thing was documented, or if, instead, she was already suffering some form of Stockholm syndrome. She didn't need to place two fingers on a pulse point to know it was going wild.

Fascinating.

"Three sons? That's a genetic anomaly if ever I've heard one," she murmured, distracted by the speed of her heart rate and the flush of her skin. Because he was watching her mouth she had to swallow before she managed to speak. "H-how far back?"

Sunlight tangled in his dark hair and made his eyes molten and intense. Her stomach felt all jittery and her pulse fluttered wildly. God, the attraction was powerful. The sooner she got the hell out of here, the better.

"Five hundred years."

Her lips tilted, because he sounded not only serious, but—*beleaguered*. By what, she had no idea. But anything that could annoy Gabriel Edge, even a far-fetched family fable, was fine by her.

"I think someone is pulling your leg," she told him dryly. "Five hundred years of only boys? No daughters?"

"Not just boys. *Three* boys."

She glanced back at Janet's mother-in-law. "Is that why—what was Magnus's mother's name again?"

"Finola."

Eden stepped closer to the portrait of the older woman, eyes narrowed. "Is that why she's wearing three pieces of jewelry? I noticed the same three pieces in other portraits as we were walking. One to give each son to pass down?"

"The jewelry was given to the oldest son. Magnus. The story goes that he first gave the ring, the bracelet, and the necklace to Nairne. The village girl. When he told her he was to marry the chieftain's daughter instead, she threw them back at him."

"And he took the same pieces and gave them to his new fiancée? Boy, talk about some tacky regifting. That was callous and unfeeling. No wonder the wife isn't wearing them."

"It was customary in those times to give your betrothed jewelry. According to the stories passed down, he'd given the pieces to Nairne and when she—*returned* them, in keeping with tradition he gave them to Janet. There was no sentiment attached. The jewelry was valuable."

Eden stepped closer to better see the detail on Finola's portrait. "Weird, my lucky ring looks a bit similar." She glanced down the hall to where Gabriel had moved back into the shadows.

"Mine's just costume, and probably of no worth in dollars and cents, but for me, the sentimental value is priceless." She glanced down fondly at the little black ring on the pinkie toe of her left foot.

"My Grandma Rose gave it to me years ago." She smiled. God, she'd adored her Grandma Rose. Her maternal grandmother had always been . . . *happy*. And bless her heart, Eden thought fondly, she hadn't given a damn that her only grandchild was a little butterball of a misfit. A square peg in a round hole.

Rose had died when Eden was fifteen. She still missed her.

Gabriel walked toward her through the stripes of sunlight and shadow. He stopped about six feet from her, making Eden wonder what kind of problem he had that he couldn't get near a woman.

Not that she cared. And really, she didn't want him anywhere near her anyway.

Liar.

"Where'd she get it?"

"What? The ring? She bought it, or so she told me, from a gypsy at a carnival in Italy on her honeymoon."

He gave her a strangely intent look. "Do you still have it?"

Eden held up her foot.

He glanced down, then back up. "That's your lucky ring? Doesn't look anything like the ones in the portraits," he said dismissively, and walked off.

"I didn't say it was *identical*." God, the man was

testy. Grandma Rose had told her the ring was silver, but really it just looked like a blackened twist of metal with two hearts on it to Eden. Not that she cared. She never took it off. Whether it was lucky or not wasn't the point. The point was her grandmother whom she'd adored had given it to her, and she believed it was lucky.

Her host meanwhile had put more distance between them. She shook her head at his rudeness, and since she was standing there, and he was already twenty paces ahead, slipped off her shoes before following him. Much as she loved these sandals, they were meant for looking pretty as she sat at her computer, not for cross-country hiking. If push came to shove she could use them as lethal weapons.

The thought brought her up short. She had never— *never*—in her entire life *ever* thought of striking someone. Oh, she'd wanted to put fire ants in Adam's shorts every time he told her she was packing on the pounds. She'd fantasized about supergluing his eyelids, lips, and fingers together when she first discovered he'd stolen credit for the mainframe reconfiguration she'd spent her last year at MIT perfecting. But the thought of physical combat had never occurred to her.

Right now, though, she was having some pretty violent thoughts about Gabriel Edge. The sooner the authorities figured out where she was, the safer he'd be.

The plush carpet cushioned her bare feet, but the corridor went on forever. More dark paneling, more gilt-framed paintings, more interesting-looking objects on tables and in glass-fronted cabinets. More stripes of sunlight and shadow.

And every woman in the portraits now had only three little boys with her. Eden backtracked a few portraits. How weird was that? From a certain point on, every woman with children had three almost identical sons. No wonder this guy believed in the family curse, looking at these family portraits every day. She turned around to see Gabriel turning a corner. She had to run to catch up with him. "Where's this lab? Tibet?"

"Opposite wing."

"Tibet it is." Eden wondered darkly how hard it would be to get blood and brain matter out of fine-grained leather.

He walked faster. It was that or touch her, and touching her would be a bad move. An incredibly *stupid,* bad move. Unfortunately for him, the longer he resisted touching her, the more powerful the need became. Gabriel wasn't a tactile man. Neither was he prone to obsessing, brooding, or fixating.

He was doing all that and more. And God! He wanted to *touch* her. Hell, yeah, he wanted to have sex with Eden Cahill. Hard and fast. Long and slow. Standing. Lying down—hell—sitting. Any way, any how, any time.

He enjoyed sex. Damn it, he *loved* sex. But if the opportunity didn't present itself he was fine going it alone. His sexual appetite had never concerned him overly much. There were frequently ops that required months of undercover work, when sticking his dick anywhere but behind a closed zipper could prove fatal.

He was not going to have sex with the lovely Dr. Cahill. That was a given. As all-consuming as that imagery was, he was disciplined enough, strong enough, hell, *motivated* enough not to give in to the hunger. So all he could think about, all he *fixated* on, was *touching* her.

What harm could just one touch bring? He found himself desperate for a crumb, since he couldn't have the whole meal.

Christ. Now he was making up excuses. One touch of Eden would never be enough.

That's it, dickhead. Heart rate normal. Respiration

normal. Keep it that way. Gabriel closed his eyes. *Fat fucking chance.*

Feeling grim, he turned down a side corridor, Eden close on his heels. While they walked, he conjured the lab she'd need to do her job in a distant suite of rooms. He'd made note of everything in her Tempe lab and duplicated it, right down to her ergonomic chair and oversized teacup with "IQ Matters" on it.

As she followed him, making her wry observations every now and then, Gabriel could smell the warm, heady fragrance of her skin, kissed with tuberose. She'd fallen silent about midway, and God, he was grateful. Every step he'd taken had ratcheted up the temptation to let her to catch up with him.

He wanted to turn, back her against a wall, a table, anything, and sink his fingers into those glossy dark curls. He wanted to feel the texture, he needed to stroke the softness of her skin, he craved inhaling her fragrance. Up close and personal.

He wanted to kiss her. Desperately.

He was a starving man presented with a banquet and then told to step away from the table.

The Fates must be laughing their collective asses off. They'd presented him with his perfect temptation. *Every*thing about Eden Cahill enticed him. From the lush look of her, to her wit, to her stubbornness.

Goddamn it!

Step away from the table.

"This is it." He shoved open the door and preceded her, by a good ten feet, into the state-of-the-art computer lab. He glanced around. He did nice work.

The lab was a means to an end. He watched her openly as she walked in behind him, then did a slow circuit, seemingly oblivious to his presence in the room.

"Impressive."

Gabriel heard the excitement in her voice, but he was

distracted by her bare feet. He dragged his attention back to her face. She'd shown less interest as they'd passed priceless Fabergé eggs and Rembrandts.

Her eyes, those glorious big brown eyes, glowed with temptation as she walked around the room, touching objects as she went. "Who usually works here?"

"As of now, you do."

If he could get her to lose control—twelve seconds was all the time he needed—he could extract the information she held in her subconscious. With that information he could conjure her robot with little difficulty. If he could do that, Gabriel thought grimly, watching the sunlight tangle in her hair, then damn it, he wouldn't need her here.

Why did *she* have to be his Lifemate, the only person whose mind he couldn't read? Hell, she wouldn't feel him trespassing. She'd never even know he'd been there.

Extracting the data wouldn't hurt her.

But if she stayed, it just might kill her.

CHAPTER NINE

There was a phone in the library. If either Gabriel or MacButler caught her skulking, Eden decided, she'd say she couldn't sleep, and had gone down for a book.

"What am I thinking?!" She stopped pacing a path in the bedroom carpet. "No, I won't! I'm a *prisoner,* for God's sake! I don't have to make excuses for a freaking prison break."

The "couldn't sleep" part would've been true even if she wasn't determined to put as many miles between herself and her kidnapper as humanly possible.

Guilt weighed heavily on her mind. As did the attraction she felt for the man who'd kidnapped her. And how sick was that? Opting to put the Stockholm syndrome thing out of her mind, she concentrated on what was *important.* Getting to the authorities with all haste.

After MacBain had escorted her back upstairs several hours ago, Eden had explored the room they'd given her. Just for something to do while she tried to formulate a viable escape plan. A basket on the bathroom sink held all of her usual brands of toiletries. She glanced at the row of familiar perfume bottles with a frown. "A full-service kidnapping, how lucky can I get?"

She was also suitably freaked out to find the armoire she thought held a TV was actually filled with clothing in her size. Her taste, too. Until she realized they were not just her size and taste, but damn him to hell and back—they were her own clothes. Pilfered right out of her closet at home.

How, and when he'd had time, was a mystery. He was pretty damn sure of himself if he imagined she'd be here long enough to need this many clothes, she thought with annoyance as she ran her hand over the row of colored T-shirts and jeans. She actually got excited when she realized if he'd brought her clothes, he must have also brought shoes.

She had a dozen or more pairs of tennis shoes tossed into the back of her closet. Tennies she'd bought every time she'd gotten motivated about a new exercise class. Most of them had hardly been worn.

But no. The son of a bitch had *only* brought her Jimmys and her Manolos. *Thirteen pairs* of high heels. There wasn't a pair of flats in the bunch.

"Officer: 'How did he keep you prisoner, ma'am?' Kidnap victim: 'Oh, officer. He forced me to wear my high heels and oh! I just couldn't *run* in them.' "

Eden paced as she pictured the conversation. "Nice try, Mr. Edge, but no cigar," she told her absent host. "Shoes or no shoes, I'm out of here."

After what felt like years, she decided she'd waited long enough for the household to be asleep. Feeling like a cat burglar, she changed into black jeans and pulled on a practical, long-sleeved black hoodie over several of her pocket T's.

A drawer held her panties and bras—the bastard—but there wasn't a sock to be found.

Barefoot it was.

Even though it was midsummer, the air was decidedly chilly here in the mountains when she opened the window to check. She wasn't in any danger of hypothermia. She wasn't in the Antarctic, she reminded herself when she shivered. Cold and uncomfortable, definitely. But a brisk walk would take care of that pretty fast.

She didn't relish a long trek on an unfamiliar highway in the dark, *barefoot*, but she was going to do it anyway.

Of course there was always the possibility of stealing some sort of vehicle. She'd have to see what she could find, within a time limit, of course. The longer she skulked, the better the odds that someone would catch her.

She gave herself a mental pep talk. Get away from this castle. That was probably, relatively speaking, the easy part. Once she was back in civilization she'd call Jason. It didn't matter where she was—Jason *would* send someone to get her. She might not find their personal relationship filled with bells and whistles, but she knew she was too valuable to him as a scientist for him not to race to her rescue.

He'd have contact information for the right people for her to talk to at Homeland Security. Eden was sure he'd want to go with her when she confessed. If not to back her up, then to make sure she didn't implicate him in any wrongdoing. Either way, she'd tell the authorities what to watch for, and fill them in on *all* of Rex's capabilities.

Then maybe she'd take Jason up on the offer of a monthlong cruise. If she wasn't in jail for withholding evidence.

She glanced at her watch. Almost eleven. Opening the bedroom door in small increments, she prayed it didn't creak. It didn't. She closed it just as quietly and carefully behind her. She almost expected the flicker of oil lamps or candles, but the lights were electric. All the modern conveniences of home, she thought as she paused to listen. Not a peep.

Dimly lit wrought-iron sconces lined the upstairs hallway, illuminating the way. Good. She wasn't fond of the dark, which was why she'd opted to find the phone before forging outside into the great unknown. There was a sliver, a very *small* sliver of moon. She'd prefer the headlights of a cab to take her where she was going.

All she had to do was go right, walk down the hall, take a left down the stairs and she'd be in the entryway. Straight ahead was the front door and freedom, left was the library and a call to the cavalry.

The place was dead quiet. Not a rafter to creak, not a floorboard to squeak. Every time she stood still, the silence of the enormous spaces throbbed against her eardrums. While the upstairs corridors and rooms were carpeted in plush wool, the floors downstairs were comprised of large worn stone slabs that were icy under her bare feet.

Totally Gothic, and she wondered what secrets this castle harbored, what ghosts haunted the halls. She shivered as she remembered Gabriel and his talk of a curse.

More sconces along the wall provided muted light as she ran lightly down the sweeping staircase, and across the ridiculously large entry hall.

By the time she darted into the book-lined library she was out of breath and her heart was pounding as if the Hounds of Hell were after her, fangs bared.

Closing the door quietly behind her, she leaned against it and waited for her heartbeat to settle down and her breathing to even out. She really needed to make use of one of her gym memberships when this was all over.

The room was dead quiet and softly lit. And, thank God, empty. She half anticipated running into Gabriel—somewhere. Not seeing him was a huge relief.

The room smelled faintly of musty paper, leather, old fires in the blackened fireplace, and the fresh flowers placed on the mantel and on several tables about the room.

Two-story-tall, built-in, ornately hand-carved mahogany bookcases lined three walls; the fourth was taken up by the huge stone fireplace. There must have been several thousand leather-bound books with faded gold titles housed on the shelves, she thought, and wondered if her kidnapper had read *any* of them. Probably not. He didn't strike her as particularly cerebral. He was more the Me: Tarzan, you: Jane, kind of guy.

He certainly hadn't attempted any conversation, scintillating or otherwise, at dinner earlier.

Waited on by MacBain, she and Gabriel had eaten dinner in here several hours ago. Of all the rooms in the incongruously and inexplicably placed castle, Eden liked this one the most. The dark brown leather chairs and sofas looked old and comfortable. All the furniture in here was probably antique, but it didn't have that highly polished "do not touch" look to it. It all had the patina of use, as though people had placed their feet on the coffee tables, and taken long naps on the deep cushions of the two sofas flanking the fireplace.

Yeah, well, no naps for her for a while, she thought, crossing the room to the desk placed beneath a window.

She'd seen the phone on the desk, and then forced herself not to look at it again for the duration of the meal. Not a simple task, since once she'd seen it, that was all Eden could think about.

The conversation, what there was of it, had been strained. They were two strangers. One a kidnapper and one a kidnappee. She didn't see that they had anything *to* discuss. She'd eaten what was placed in front of her, refused wine, and sipped on a glass of water. And as soon as the meal was over had requested that she be allowed to go to her room.

MacBain had escorted her up hours ago.

Nice to know *he* wouldn't be chasing her down. It had taken them twice the time to mount the stairs it would have taken her alone, because: He. Walked. Very. Slow. Ly.

The marble game table, which had served as their dining table, had been cleared. The room smelled faintly of oranges, which were heaped in a large copper bowl on a sofa table. She'd noticed a similar bowl of lemons in the dining room this morning. A lifetime ago. Either he had a thing for citrus, or they were a decorator element she didn't understand.

Shooting a nervous glance at the closed door, heart lodged in her throat, Eden snatched up the phone and punched out 911. If ever there was an emergency, this was it.

An extension somewhere in the castle was picked up midway through the first ring. "How may I be of assistance, Doctor?"

MacBain. *Shit.*

At exactly the same time the operator came on the line. "Nine-one-one. What is the nature of your emerg—"

"Good evening to ye, Dorie. This is Alfred MacBain at the Edge ranch. I'm afraid a guest misdialed."

"No problem, sugar."

The emergency operator clicked off the line. *Shit. Shit. Shit.*

"I need a cab," Eden told the unseen MacBain.

"It is ten fifty-seven P.M., madam."

"Thank you," she said dryly. "I have the time. What I want is a taxi."

"If one is required, I shall be happy to procure it for you in the morning. Would you like my assistance in returning to your chamber?"

He wouldn't procure anything for her that Gabriel didn't sanction first. "No thanks. I can navigate on my own. I'll just find something to read before I go up."

"Shall I bring a glass of warm milk to your room to assist you in sleeping?"

"No thanks."

"Very well. Good night, Doctor."

Foolishly, her heart started to gallop and her palms

felt damp as she replaced the receiver. "Stupid. Stupid. Stupid! What's the bet five seconds after he puts down the phone he wakes up his boss?"

"Actually," Gabriel drawled from behind her, "I was already awake."

"Jesus, Mary, and Joseph!" Eden slapped a hand to her heart and spun around.

He was stretched out on one of the sofas, hands stacked under his head. He cocked a brow. "Catholic?"

Mutely she shook her head. How had her body known he was in the room before she did? It was as though her reaction to him were stamped on her DNA. When Gabriel Edge was anywhere *near* her, whether she saw him or not, she felt almost giddy. Euphoric.

Ridiculous. Because not only didn't she *know* the man, she didn't even *like* him. "Where did you come from?" she asked crossly.

"Originally?" He swung his big, bare feet to the floor and sat up. His eyes were heavy-lidded, and his hair mussed as if he'd climbed out of bed. "I'm a Montana native. On my mother's side. Scotland on my father's— didn't I mention this before?"

His strong jaw was stubbled. Unfortunately he was one of those men who looked even sexier and more appealing when they were . . . rumpled.

He looked disreputable. Dangerous. Sexy.

He looked, Eden thought, like the kind of man mothers warned their daughters about. Except for her mother. Her mother would probably like him. She preferred them big, dumb, and interested. "Are you being particularly obtuse," she asked him coolly, "or are you playing with me?"

"Are those my only two options?" He still wore jeans, but he'd changed his T-shirt since dinner. This one was a dark purple.

He had about as much fashion sense as she did, Eden

thought, leaning against the desk behind her and trying to appear unaffected by his close proximity.

She saw the sensuality darken his eyes as he watched her. The temptation to walk across the room and press her mouth to his was overwhelming. *I'll die if you don't kiss me.* She was stunned by how strongly she yearned for this man's touch.

She'd never craved a man's body as she craved Gabriel's. Curiosity and passion rose in a dizzying cloud of desire. What if she gave in to the clawing hunger? What if she said to hell with her principles, morals, and intentions? She'd never wanted to know a man as intimately as she wanted to know him.

He looked so hard. Both physically and emotionally. Would he allow her to touch him gently? Would he have the patience to allow her to learn? Would he give her the time so that she could explore his body with her hands, and her mouth, her fingertips? Would his neck be as sensitive as hers?

Would she be able to bring him to the peak, and then have the power to hold him there while she climbed to the same level of need?

Anger and sexual hunger warred inside her. She'd known more conventionally handsome men, men with charm. Like Jason Verdine. But no man, not even Jason, had ever called to her mind and body the way Gabriel did.

Trying to talk herself out of even going down this slippery slope *mentally,* she straightened and gave him a hard look. "You know this is absolutely ridiculous, don't you? You can't *force* me to stay here."

"Of course I can."

"Why? I can't give you what you want."

"You can give me one of the things I want."

"Don't *do* that," Eden said crossly, irritated at his innuendo. "Why are you playing this game? Shooting me looks that melt my insides, yet you stay as far out of reach as you can. What do you really want?"

She was taken by surprise when he answered, almost angrily, "You. Bad. Every time you speak I have to force myself to concentrate on what you're saying and not focus on the way your mouth moves. I've been walking around with a woody for days."

"Charming," Eden said dryly, her heart racing. Did she dare answer her body's need for this one man? She took a deep, fortifying breath, aware of the rise and fall of her breasts and the fact that Gabriel couldn't look away. "Nothing's stopping you, least of all me." *Which probably makes me certifiable,* she thought, as the color of his eyes changed from deep blue to hot black and a flush rode his cheekbones. He was watching her with an intensity that should have made her back off, but instead made her yearn to get as close as she could.

"Believe me," he said in a low voice, "I have the deterrent of all deterrents."

Eden felt the sting of rejection all the way down to her bare toes. She was immediately thrust back into the time when her brain was the only thing a man would lust after. She wasn't the type of woman to make a man forget about "deterrents."

She'd imagined she'd read desire in his eyes, but if she had, it was his desire for what she knew, not who she was. Been there, done that. Cheeks scorched with humiliation, she pushed thoughts of hot, steamy sex out of her head. *Thank God* he hadn't taken her up on her offer. Hadn't she already learned this lesson? She lifted her chin and gave him a cool, hopefully sophisticated look. He was still talking duty, while *she'd* let thoughts of *him* push duty to the side. She felt a grudging respect. "So you're refusing me, even though you want me? Not that I care, one way or the other. But I like to understand my rejections."

"Once I have what I want you'll be gone, and we'll never see each other again."

"And you have a moral, general, or specific objection to one-night stands?"

"Specific."

"And that is?" She hated herself for insisting. But, damn it, she wanted to know—hated *not* knowing—what was going on between them. Illogically, his rejection was as sharp as a knife in her chest.

"Doesn't matter," he said dismissively. "I'm not taking you up on your offer."

Eden exhaled, glancing away; she reached deep for the control she needed to stay where she was and not run. She'd made a fool of herself. It was no wonder he wasn't leaping the furniture to take her up on her bold offer. Well, she was a brilliant scientist, and if he wanted her mind, he'd have to work hard to get it.

She glanced back at him. "You're right. The reason isn't important. It's no wonder I'm off kilter. You've kidnapped me and you're holding me hostage in a medieval castle."

"That can be resolved—"

"By me bending to your will. No."

"The lab upstairs is crying your name."

She'd rather *he* were crying her name. "The answer's still N.O." She cocked her head. "Has anyone ever told you no and you've listened?"

"Rarely." He leaned back, relaxed—almost. No, he wasn't relaxed at all, she realized, watching his eyes. He was alert, like a big, sleek cat, ready to pounce at any second. Tension stretched between them, heavy and dark. "Let me be the first of many, then." She felt a tickle up her nape, and twitched her shoulders. The sensation didn't go away and she rubbed a hand across the back of her neck as she tried to figure out what he was up to.

Pulses throbbing, she felt as though her entire body were expanding from the inside.

He was . . . *doing* something to her, she realized. Something that made her body react as though he were touching her, playing with her hair, stroking a gentle finger up and down her nape. Her dazed eyes met his.

Fierce, blatant lust burned and glittered in his eyes.

Her nipples tingled and hardened, and she couldn't look away. "Whatever the hell you're doing," she told him hoarsely. "Stop it! Right now."

They faced each other like gunfighters across the library carpet. He was watching her with barely any expression on his face, but the heat of his gaze was as strong as if he'd reached out and touched her. *Just breathe normally,* she coached herself. *Don't let him make a fool of you twice.*

Her breathing evened out. A little. *Good for me. Knew I could do it.* She tunneled the fingers of both hands through her hair and rubbed her scalp where a headache brewed.

"Jesus," Gabriel snarled. "Stop doing that."

She gave him a blank look. "Doing what?"

"Running your fingers through your hair, all sleepy-eyed, like you've just gotten out of bed. And you weren't alone."

She dropped her hands. What was she missing here? He sounded turned on, yet he'd refused her offer.

"Look," he sounded beleaguered. "There's a way for you to get out of here in a matter of minutes."

"Good." The tickle on the back of her neck stopped. She felt disturbed, shaken. "I'll take that option. I don't even need to go up and get my things. Let's go."

"If you'd just let down your mental defenses for a few seconds, I could extract the data from your subconscious."

Eden waited for him to qualify the bizarre statement.

He didn't. She mulled over what he'd just said. "Are you saying you're *telepathic*? You can read my mind? Because, buddy, if you're stomping all over my mind looking in corners you've got no business looking in, you'd better get the hell out!"

"I can't read *your* mind."

He sounded pissed and that was an enormous relief. There were things in there even Eden didn't want to scrutinize too closely. "Are you implying that you *can* read other people's minds?" she asked with some skepticism. "What is this? A party trick?"

"I could read your mind if you weren't throwing up a block. Let me in, and I'll . . . download, if you will, the data we need to build another bot."

"How about if I *won't*? If a door is closed to you it's for a reason. And it can stay closed as far as I'm con— Damn it to hell! *That's* what you've been doing, isn't it? Knocking at my mental door trying to get into the data for Rex?! You son of a bitch." Feeling betrayed, she backed up a step. None of this was sexual. He was trying to manipulate her. Using her own attraction for him to get what he wanted. Information on the bot.

"A sexual climax would open that door," His voice was deeper than normal. Husky. Thick. His eyes smoldered with hunger. "I need to get in."

"A sexual . . . *climax*?" The words, and the intensity of his midnight dark eyes made her feel decidedly hot. *Edgy,* she thought, *hungry.* Still, damn it.

Clearly her own mental pep talk had gone by the wayside the second he made any kind of advancement. God, she was an idiot.

"You're crazy if you think I'm going to fall for that crap." She knew she was about to babble. But it was babble or do something really stupid. Like grab him and kiss him until he forgot all about, what had he said? Deterrents. "Do you *hear* yourself?" *Good God,* Eden thought with some alarm at the directions her thoughts were taking her. *Do I hear myself?*

"I'll do whatever is necessary to build another Rex before the terrorists use the one they stole."

"And you think you can read my mind, extract six years' worth of data, and *build* one. Yourself?"

"If you let me in. Yes."

"Speaking of minds, you're out of yours." Unfortunately, he believed what he was saying, which in Eden's opinion made him even more dangerous. "I thought this place might be a hotel. But now I realize it's a *psych* hospital. The telepathy thing should have tipped me off." He stood clear across the room, yet Eden felt as though he were standing too close. As though he were invading her space, but he hadn't moved. Oh, God. Was she going nuts? She reminded herself that this was just a case of compatible pheromones. Nothing more than chemistry. Science.

This man had a power to disturb her on a level she hadn't even known existed until she'd met him. Was it only this morning? "One person can't *let* another person into their minds, okay? It just can't be done."

"Yes." His dark eyes watched her with an unnerving intensity. "It can. I'm a wizard, Eden."

She was so busy looking at his mouth and fantasizing about what it would taste like that she wasn't really listening. "A—lizard? What does *that* mean?"

"Oh, for—A *wizard*."

"Oh. Okay. I'll bite. A wizard at what exactly?" Eden asked, keeping her tone even. She had absolutely no experience with mental illness and wasn't sure what to do.

"Jesus." He rubbed his jaw, clearly exasperated. "I haven't had to prove myself in—I don't remember when." He extended his hand. A melon-sized ball of fire materialized out of thin air to dance just above his palm.

She hoped he wasn't burning himself. "That's . . . very

nice." She glanced toward the closed door, hoping someone, *anyone*, would get in here. Soon. "Impressive. Really."

She presumed he had some sort of propane device strapped to his palm, an ignition source, and voilà, magic. It *was* impressive, although she wasn't sure someone like him should be allowed to play with incendiary devices inside the house-castle.

"I'll just go up to my room, we can talk tomorrow, okay?" A left outside the library door and a fast race across the entry hall and she'd be at the front doors. Outside in minutes. And while clearly, Gabriel would know the grounds better than she could, she was smaller and a hell of a lot more motivated.

All she needed was opportunity.

The fire on his outstretched palm blinked off.

"Well, shit. That was stupid. That didn't convince you of a damn thing, did it?" He paused. "Remember I told you about Nairne's curse?"

Eden nodded.

"She was a witch. When she cursed Magnus Edridge for all time, she made his three sons wizards."

Where the hell was MacBain when she needed him? "*Magical*—er . . . wizards?" she asked carefully.

"Yeah. Magical."

Good Lord. He actually sounded as if he believed his own delusion. "What exactly did the curse entail?"

He motioned to the two leather sofas. "Want to sit down?"

"I'm fine where I am, thanks." Clear across the room.

" '*Duty o'er love was the choice you did make,*' " Gabriel quoted flatly, as if by rote as he sat on the sofa facing her. " '*My love you did spurn, my heart you did break.*' Magnus's rejection cut her deep," he inserted, crossing his ankle over the opposite knee. "She was one pissed off witch."

" 'Your penance to pay, no pride you shall gain. Three sons on three sons find nothing but pain. I gift you my powers in memory of me—' She passed her powers on to us, making every Edge a wizard from that time forward. 'The joy of love no son shall ever see. When a Lifemate is chosen by the heart of a son, No protection can be given, again I have won. His pain will be deep, her death will be swift, Inside his heart a terrible rift. Only freely given will this curse be done. To break the spell, three must work as one.' "

The little hairs on the back of Eden's neck were standing on end, and she rubbed at the sudden chill on her bare arms. "And you believe this . . . curse?"

"It just is."

"Is what?"

"Unequivocally, irrevocably—true."

"So you all have to choose duty over love?"

"Yeah."

"And if you don't? What happens if one of you falls in love?"

"The woman will die."

"Come on. You can't *possibly* believe that. It's a fairy tale. A parable."

He rose, then strode over to the bookshelf and pulled out an enormous, leather-bound book. A Bible. "Come and take a look at this." He placed the Bible on a coffee table and sat down on the sofa again before opening it.

Eden came and knelt on the floor opposite where he was sitting. Her attraction hadn't faded just because she'd discovered the man was delusional. Unfortunately. But she wasn't going to sit next to him. "What am I looking at?"

The Bible was at least nine inches thick, and musty with age. Gabriel turned it around to face her, and opened it to the first gilt-edged page. Eden peered down at the spidery handwriting, faded by age. She glanced up at him.

"Every Edridge and Edge—Marriages and births for the past six hundred years. Check out the notations down the left side."

For half an hour Eden read the entries in the family Bible. For the first five minutes she was aware of nothing but Gabriel's gaze resting on her bowed head. But he faded from her consciousness as she absorbed the family's history.

Three hundred years of Edridges had apparently led happy, fulfilled lives with the men or women they'd loved. They'd prospered and had large families.

In 1503, there was a notation that Magnus Edge had married Finola. She'd borne him three sons. The next Edridge had changed his name to Edge—in the hope of dodging the curse? He'd married later in life. Thirty-two. His wife had died in childbirth. Not unheard of in that day and age.

She went on to the next entry, and the next, and the next. If the couple had married for love, a small double heart, a luckenbooth, had been drawn alongside their names. At first those hearts were clustered close together. But over the years the "love" hearts became farther and farther apart.

"Well?"

Eden looked up. "From Finola and Magnus on, every woman bore three sons."

"And?"

"If what the double hearts indicate was true—then every time one of those sons married for love, the woman died. Most of the deaths unexplained."

"The Curse."

"People died from a hangnail in those days." Eden pointed out mildly.

"Not *these* people. Not my mother. She just went to sleep one night and didn't wake up."

"But they were married for—How long?"

"Eighteen years."

"So her death wasn't 'swift,' was it?" Eden said gently.

"Swift is relative. And perhaps it took longer because she and my father lived apart their entire marriage."

"They must've got together at least three times," she said dryly.

"They spent a week every year together in Scotland. But they were afraid every second of that time together. My father wasn't going to risk her life."

"But she died anyway."

"She'd been with him for three months that time. The longest they'd ever spent together." His voice was grim. "She died the morning after her return."

She shivered. Crazy as it sounded, she believed him. And if she believed that the Edridge family had been cursed, then was it such a leap to believe that the witch had imbued the sons of the man who had jilted her with her powers?

But a *wizard*? "I'm a scientist. I don't believe in magic."

"My parents were living thousands of miles apart," Gabriel told her flatly. "I wanted them to be together. God, they loved one another. My mother had us kids on this property. Living in the ranch her grandfather had built, while my father, terrified his love would kill her, lived in Scotland.

"I thought—" He rubbed a large hand on the back of his neck. "Hell, I thought if I brought this castle here, my father would be drawn to it, and come and stay. Stay with her. Stay with us."

Gabriel met her eyes. "Eden, I *teleported* this castle, all one hundred and ninety-five thousand square feet of stone. Teleported it here one afternoon after school."

Little waves of excitement rippled through her body. Just because she couldn't understand something didn't mean it wasn't true. But this . . .

"I went to your apartment the other day to make you climax so I could find out how to destroy the bot. I was in your lab while you and Marshall Davis talked. I was there when Verdine came in. I was there the whole time. Invisible."

"You've mastered *invisibility*?" Oh, my God. She had to get him to her lab. She wanted to run tests, feasibility studies—If what he was telling her was true, this was amazing, incredible.

"Among other things."

"Like what?" She pulled herself up short. For heaven's sake, she was buying into his delusions.

"It doesn't matter. Listen to me. It's imperative we have a Rex robot to counter what is, without a doubt, going to be done with the one stolen from your lab. We can do this easy, or we can do this hard. No more bull-shit. The next time I'm required to prove who and what I am, it won't be with a party trick.

"The reality is a terrorist group stole your technology, and they won't be manufacturing children's toys based on your prototype. Do you get that? From what you told me, this robot of yours, especially in the wrong hands, could feasibly be an almost indestructible killing machine. It could run suicide missions and not die. Am I right?"

Yes. God, yes. He was absolutely right. For a crazy man.

"Building another Rex would cost close to three hundred million dollars," Eden informed him, grateful to be on solid ground once more. People confused the hell out of her. Particularly Gabriel Edge, she thought wryly, closing the heavy leather cover of the Bible on the table in front of her. But she knew everything there was to know about robots.

"Terrorist or not, it's cheaper to use a human being to do what you're suggesting." She was grasping at any straw she could. Eden knew she was trying to convince herself, not Edge, who was clearly already anticipating the worst. "Terrorists consider human life expendable, don't they? For that price they could have *thousands* of killers. Why build a robot?"

"Because they can. Money isn't an issue with most of these groups. They'll mass-produce the Rex and they'll be unstoppable. Is that what you want your technology used for?"

"No." She pressed her palm to her stomach where birds of prey swarmed. "Of course not."

Was he telling the truth?

Was he a counterterrorist operative who worked for their own government? Or was he a terrorist trying to get a leg up on technology that some other terrorist group had stolen? Or maybe just an eccentric loony escaped from the bin?

She had no idea.

There were people who dealt with this sort of thing, Eden thought, feeling sick with fear and tension. She had to get to someone qualified to sort this mess out.

She was a scientist, and people skills weren't her forte. He sat between her and freedom. There wasn't enough room between the furniture for her to pass him. All he'd need to do was stretch out his arm. Eden didn't think she could bear it right now if he touched her.

She'd never been so afraid in her life.

"For God's sake, let me retrieve the data the easy way. It won't hurt—hell, you won't feel a thing, other than sexual satisfaction. The other way, the hard and time-consuming way, is for you to rebuild Rex upstairs in the lab I prepared for you. Your choice. Because, I assure you, Doctor. An accurate duplicate *will* be produced."

"I guess we'll just have to see who has the most patience, won't we?" she told him, feeling a chill of premonition slither up her spine. No matter how much she hoped that it had been a Verdine Industries competitor who had stolen Rex, on a gut level, she believed what Gabriel was telling her.

Some terrorist group had her brainchild, and they would do exactly what he said they'd do. They'd mass-produce her technology, and they wouldn't be able to be stopped.

"I have infinite patience. I could outwait you. But that's unacceptable. We don't have the luxury of that kind of time."

"Then let me contact Homeland Security," Eden said as calmly as she could, but a tremor crept into her voice. "Please? If they tell me you people are who you say you are, I'll help you develop a duplicate Rex."

She had a perfectly good lab in Tempe. A lab well away from this man with his intense burning eyes, who aroused some kind of strange yearning inside her that she neither understood nor welcomed. He'd offered her an orgasm in exchange for Rex. God help her, she was almost tempted. Almost.

"You're going to have to take my word for it."

"Your word? And if I don't?"

"We go back to the easy way or the hard way."

"That's rape."

"Jesus, woman!" He looked horrified at the suggestion. "I can't touch you."

His curse made no mention of no touching. He'd made that one up to suit himself. A curse for all seasons, she thought with annoyance. "Can't, or won't?"

"Same thing."

It wasn't. But if *he* felt it was, that was fine with her.

She rose to her feet, and stared at him lounging on the sofa, his arms outstretched on the back cushions on either side of him, ankle crossed over the opposite knee. "Ever?"

"Ever."

"Good." She broke eye contact, and ran flat out for the door. She heard his oath behind her, but kept going, dodging furniture, sure he was fast on her heels but prepared to risk it. She had to, had to, *had to* get away from him. From *here*.

Panting, more with fear than the exertion of doing the one-minute mile across the library, Eden grabbed the ornate wrought-iron handle with both hands, and yanked the door open.

Chest heaving, she stopped dead in her tracks.

A large black panther crouched on the other side of the partially open door. It bared big white teeth, growling low in its throat as it watched her with acid yellow eyes. *God*. Eden slammed the door in its face, then fell back against the heavily carved wood, heart twisted in fear, then stopped cold.

"Oh, my God, Gabriel. There's a—" She was talking to herself.

The room was empty.

CHAPTER TEN

Gabriel shimmered back into the library where Eden was backed against the door. Her eyes went even wider with alarm when he materialized directly in front of her.

The long muscles in his cat's body stretched and bunched as he crouched, watching fear leach what little color she had left in her cheeks. The smell of her skin, the heat of her body was amplified a hundredfold in this form. He snarled, baring his teeth as he inched closer.

He couldn't mate with her like this. Not in this form. But the fact that he *wanted* to put the fear of God into him.

"Nice kitty," she said, not moving. "Oh, God. *Nice kitty*? If you're here, you're a pet, right?" Her fingers fumbled for the handle behind her. "Attacking me would be a very, very bad idea."

Her pulse beat a staccato tattoo at the base of her throat as she watched him unblinkingly. Gabriel felt the overpowering desire to lick her there.

In the blink of her eye, he morphed back into his human form. Showy, but effective.

Her hand covered her mouth and her eyes went wider still as he rose to his feet.

Even in human form he wanted to taste her. *Step away from the table.* "Convinced, Doctor?"

"My God!" She dropped her hand limply to her side. "How—? Who—?"

"I told you what I am." He made no apologies. His special talents were an asset to T-FLAC. Another tool in his arsenal. Just like his Glock. He was who he was. She didn't have to like it.

"You told me what you *think* you are. There are no such things as wizards. There aren't."

"My brothers would be surprised to hear that," he told her dryly. When she listened intently, she had a way of looking at him under her lashes, a small frown between those gorgeous big brown eyes, that made his heart lurch and his blood roar through his veins.

For a moment she was distracted. "You have brothers?"

"Two. Both wizards. I told you. There have always been three sons in our family. It's a trait passed down through the generations. Since the sixteen hundreds. I come from a long line of wizards."

"You are so full of crap."

He watched her, wishing like hell things could be different. The fact that they couldn't should have negated his attraction for her. He couldn't have her, so wanting, craving, didn't make a fucking jot of difference. He should be capable of turning off that particular switch. With her, he couldn't.

She moved smoothly on bare feet. And while there was nothing overtly sexy about Dr. Eden Cahill, her glossy hair beckoned his fingers, her too loose jeans cried out to be stripped from her long legs. Her stubborn mouth just begged to be kissed. He cursed the quickening of his body, and got back to business.

He stepped closer, and told himself he wouldn't inhale. The thought made him want to laugh. Or howl at the moon. "One of our most popular presidents was a wizard."

"If you're doing this to scare the hell out of me, you're succeeding. I fail to see the point, however. So I'm terrified of you. So what? What the hell does my fear get you, Gabriel Edge? Do you really think that you can scare me into doing what you want?"

"Calm down."

"Don't tell me to damn well calm down! I can do whatever the hell I *feel* like doing, including scream at the top of my lungs if *want* to."

"You're hysterical."

"Gee. Do you think so? In the space of one day, I've been kidnapped, mind . . . *probed,* coerced, bullied, threatened, and almost freaking *eaten*. So yeah. I'm just a tad on edge."

"Eden—"

"Don't *Eden* me, godd-damn it."

His face a mask, Gabriel hid his abject terror. If she cried now he'd be fucking lost. She was genuinely terrified, and he felt like the asshole he was for being responsible. Jesus. *Just give me what I want and save us both.*

He wanted to go to her and pull her into his arms. He wanted to hold her and comfort her and tell her he was sorry for putting that look on her face.

He wanted to touch his mouth to hers and feel the soft brush of her breath as she welcomed him inside. To accept that brave offer she'd made and take away her embarrassment when he'd had to turn her down. He wanted to touch her petal-smooth skin, and tangle his fingers in her hair.

He wanted to strip off her clothes, cup her bottom in both hands and slide her body up his so he could taste her breasts. He wanted to lay her down on the three-hundred-year-old carpet beneath their feet and sheath himself so deep inside her that they wouldn't know where one of them began and the other ended.

The irony wasn't lost on him that comforting her might very well be the death of her.

"Is this how you handle peer challenges at those symposia you attend?" he asked, keeping his voice cold. He saw her breath hitch as she tried to suck back the tears. "Pull the girl card? All big glistening brown eyes and a quivering lower lip?"

"Is this *your* version of charm?" she demanded, dashing the moisture from her eyes with the back of her hand. "Because if it is, you *suck* at it." She narrowed her eyes at him. "You find this amusing?" She started walking toward him, a glint of fury showing between her lashes.

The urge to swing her up in his arms and carry her upstairs—if he could even wait that long—made a mockery of his self-control. He took a step back, clenching his fists to keep his hands from reaching for her. "What are you doing?"

"I want to see if it feels as good as my fantasies when I hit you."

He saw her fist coming toward his face—Jesus, if she punched him that way she'd break every bone in her hand—and did the only thing he could do.

He sent her back to her room before she made contact.

Eden didn't throw up the second time Gabriel did whatever he'd done to transport her from one place to another. For one thing she was so completely furious, she could barely pace the bedroom she'd left half an hour before. Too furious to consider her mode of transportation.

Pressing a hand to the agitation in her stomach, she walked. Back and forth, back and forth.

She didn't know what to believe.

She didn't know who she could trust.

Shaken by what had just transpired in the library, she finally wore herself out and climbed into bed fully clothed, and pulled the covers up. She knew she'd never sleep. Too much data was swirling around in her brain.

The fire he'd produced on his palm could have been a magician's trick. Seeing a panther materialize into Gabriel, even if it was an illusion, was pretty damned effective, though. There was nothing wrong with her eyesight. She'd seen what she'd seen. Gabriel had been behind the closed doors of the library with her, but when she'd slammed the door behind her just seconds later, he was gone.

The panther had metamorphosed into Gabriel while she watched.

As a scientist she wasn't prepared to dismiss out of hand the possibility, no matter how preposterous, that he *was* a wizard. Anything was in the realm of possibility. In fact, even the smallest chance that he had spoken the truth was intriguing to her.

Intriguing, but she wasn't a fool. She'd watch him like the proverbial hawk. As long as she was here.

After that she didn't give a fig if he turned himself into a three-horned toad by real magic or sleight of hand.

She closed her eyes against the glare from the bedside lamp. Was magic involved in the way she responded to him physically? Was he putting some sort of spell on her so that he could stomp all over her brain to get the data for Rex?

The idea was preposterous.

Yet here she was. In a medieval castle slap-bang in the middle of Montana, with a man who had transported her here—how? Teleportation? She'd heard him and Sebastian talking about it, but she hadn't believed what she was hearing.

Now? The possibility seemed quite likely, and the scientist in her felt a leap of excitement. If she could study what made Gabriel tick, it could further her work.

She drifted off to sleep formulating questions to ask her mysterious host.

Eden had dozens of questions buzzing around in her head by morning. She didn't know what to make of last night, she thought, walking carefully down the sweeping staircase in search of food and escape, not necessarily in that order. She kept her eye out for Gabriel, the man, the big cat, the whatever the hell he was.

Dressed in another natty black suit, white shirt, and red-and-black tartan tie, MacBain stood at the foot of the stairs as if he'd been expecting her. "Good morning, Doctor. Breakfast is being served in the conservatory. If ye'll come this way?"

Holding on to the ornate newel post, she stepped down beside him. "Thanks. I'll take a table for one."

His lips twitched. "He's out riding."

Her heels clicked on the stone as she followed him. "What? A broom?"

"That would be a witch."

They crossed the vast entry hall. Both front doors were open wide, letting in a wide swath of brilliant sunshine and the smell of pine. Eden followed MacButler, but she kept an eye on the scenery. Pinkish beige gravel covered a circular driveway, beyond which were towering evergreens, a hazy blur of mountains, and freedom.

The road she'd seen and then not seen, then seen again—wasn't there again this morning. *The other day upon the stair . . .*

If escape was as easy as strolling through those doors, he wouldn't have left them open, Eden knew. Fine. A *sunroom* must have windows.

A shiver traveled up her spine as they passed the doors to the library. What had he meant last night when he said he couldn't touch her? She couldn't imagine a man like Gabriel Edge wasting time reassuring a prisoner.

And while he said he wouldn't touch her, if the heat in his eyes was any indication he wasn't going to keep that vow long. Not long at all. Curse or no curse.

Especially, Eden admitted to herself, when she felt exactly the same way. How could she have made herself so available? Something about him drew her like a moth to flame. Even knowing he could shape-shift didn't dampen her desire. He overrode her common sense.

She'd only slept with two men in her life. Once, at sixteen, out of curiosity, and once for love.

And look how well those turned out, she thought wryly, following close on MacBain's polished heels. The first had slept with her on a bet, the second had married her for career advancement.

Of course she wasn't going to have sex with Gabriel Edge. For one thing she wouldn't be here an hour from now if she could help it, and for another she was pretty sure sleeping with him would in some way change her irreparably. With Gabriel, it wouldn't be just sex.

And Eden was just fine with the way her life was right now. She'd be even finer once she talked to the authorities.

She bit her lip. Okay. Right now her life *wasn't* fine.

Her life was in crisis.

She'd built a robot that very possibly had been stolen by a lunatic terrorist group that could potentially use him for harm. She'd been kidnapped by a madman who either kept a black panther as a pet or was a bona fide wizard of the magic variety.

And she was so turned on physically by her kidnapper that she felt hot and cold every time he was in the same room.

Okay, she thought semihysterically. My life is a hundred and eighty degrees from fine.

Perhaps if they did have sex, it would be out of both their systems and they could move on. Because right now she could think of only two things to do with Gabriel: Either make love with him or kill him.

Of course she reminded herself, she wasn't going to do either because she wouldn't *be* here. But it was nice to fantasize.

MacBain showed her to a lovely room overlooking a small, tree-ringed lake where two black swans circled each other like combatants. Like all the other rooms in the castle, this was huge. A curved glass ceiling soared at least three stories above her head, and both the ceiling and the glass walls were supported by intricate, white wrought-iron framing that looked as delicate as lace.

The room was filled with trees and flowers, and smelled delectably of orange blossoms. A round table, large enough to seat four, was spread with a pale green linen tablecloth, and set for one. It had been placed in the spill of sunlight coming through the open French doors at the far end of the room.

The doors led out to a gravel path that meandered around the blue water of the small lake.

MacBain pulled out a white wrought-iron chair for her, and Eden sank down on the plump floral cushion, accepting the napkin he handed her. "Coffee or tea?"

She tossed the fine linen napkin onto her lap. "Tea, please."

She suspected Gabriel was expecting her to make a run for it. So she'd just sit right here, enjoying the sun on her face, sipping her tea as MacBain served her breakfast. Then she'd find a window or door that hadn't been deliberately left open to tempt her.

MacBain brought her a familiar tray with a covered teapot, cup, and saucer, setting each item on the table near at hand. "I took the liberty of making several breakfast selections for ye, Dr. Cahill."

Good, because astonishingly, Eden realized she was

hungry. She stared outside as he butled, or whatever, her breakfast.

Looking at the open French doors three feet from where she sat, she wondered darkly what Gabriel had done to prevent her from just walking through them. Something. Of that she was absolutely positive.

She thanked MacBain as he placed a plate precisely so in front of her. The fragrant, golden omelet oozed cheese, and seeing the small mountain of crisp bacon made her mouth water. He returned to the table with a rack of toast and small dishes of jams and jellies, which he took his time arranging to suit whatever pattern he had in his head.

"You feed prisoners very well," Eden commented, inhaling the savory steam as she picked up her fork.

"Only the pretty female scientists. I'm afraid the lesser prisoners must subsist on gruel and brackish water in the dungeons."

Eden smiled at his droll tone. "Have many prisoners, do you?"

"None but yerself at this time. But we live in hope."

Eden laughed. "Can you keep me company while I eat?"

"Aye. I'd be most honored to be interrogated by ye, Miss Eden. I happen to have brought me own cup."

They smiled at each other in perfect accord.

"Are there really dungeons in the castle?" she asked curiously as he pulled out a chair and lowered himself into it carefully. Arthritis, she thought. Grandma Rose had had it too.

"Och, aye," he said with relish, drawing the tray closer. "In the mid sixteen hundreds, Cromwell himself ordered Lord Edridge to vacate the castle. Which of course, he didna do."

"Of course not," Eden said dryly. If Gabriel's ancestors were anything like he was they'd have fought the enemy at the gate tooth and nail. "What happened?"

MacBain filled a cup with fragrant black tea, and handed it to her. "Milk? Sugar? I did bring a spot of lemon if ye'd prefer?"

"Black's fine." Eden set the saucer on the table, and took a sip from the translucent cup. The tea was steaming hot, strong enough to grow hair on her chest, and deliciously fragrant. She took another small sip before deciding it needed to cool a bit and set it down. "Go on."

"Lord Edridge proved that the castle walls were impregnable. If one goes around back to the north side of the castle, one can still see the artillery damage that mars the walls."

MacBain poured himself a cup of tea, added a splash of milk, and six teaspoons of sugar before stirring his cup vigorously.

"I'm sure Gabriel would take ye on a tour. I doubt ye'd enjoy the dungeons. Claustrophobic and damp. Most unpleasant. The small cells honeycomb the basement, and they still house the iron manacles used on prisoners. Quite grim, really. Remainders of the cruelties from medieval life."

"I'll take the tour without the side trip to the basement, thank you very much," Eden said with a small shudder. *Modern day* small dark places bothered her; the idea of a medieval basement was enough to give her hives. "How long have you worked for Gabriel?"

"Almost twenty-one years, now. And forty for his father before him. Both Cait and Magnus died when the boys were in their teens," MacBain told her, pinching off a corner of toast and putting it in his mouth. He chewed for several seconds. "Broken hearts, I always said. Couldna be together, couldna bear to live apart. Cait passed here at Edridge Castle, and is buried out there in her beloved rose garden, beneath her favorite Peace rose."

"Died a week apart, Cait and Magnus did. Magnus now, he's buried 'neath the ancient foundation of Castle Edridge in his beloved Scotland. Even in death they are torn apart."

"How old was Gabriel?"

"Not yet seventeen. A hard age for a lad to lose both his parents."

"And his brothers?"

"Caleb was sixteen. He turned wild after. Duncan, he's the serious one, was but a lad of fifteen. Quieter and more sober, was our Duncan."

"And what was Gabriel at almost seventeen?"

"Responsibility weighed heavy on the lad. He learned the lessons of the past too well, did Gabriel Edge. What his parents tried to deny, he knew to be the truth."

"Do Duncan and Caleb live here too?"

The old man shook his head. "They canna be together, lass. They cancel each other out."

"Cancel each other out?"

"They lose all but their most basic powers when they are within a mile of one another." His white brows met in the middle as he frowned. "Not that they don't get together now and then, but in their line of work it's best not to be without their special skills for long."

"Are you telling me you believe that Gabriel, and I presume his brothers, are really wizards?"

"Do ye doubt your own eyes then, lass? He told ye of Nairne's Curse, did he no'?"

"Yes he did. *He* certainly seems to believe it."

"Dinna doubt it, lass. Nairne's Curse is very real."

Despite the warmth of the sun, Eden rubbed the sudden chill on her arms with both hands. "What has to be given freely? Love?"

"Love is always given freely, is it no'? Magnus and Cait loved fiercely and freely, but they couldna ever be together. She wasted away before our very eyes, and when he heard of her death, Magnus couldna take it. No Edge has ever managed to escape Nairne's Curse, lass. No' one. And we have yet to discover what it is that must be given."

"Telling her where we hide the silver, old man?"

Eden merely blinked when Gabriel suddenly appeared at the table. No. She couldn't doubt her own eyes. One moment she was enjoying a peaceful view of the gardens and the lake beyond, the next, his large body took all her attention. Slouched back in his chair as though he'd been sitting there the entire time, Gabriel looked mouthwateringly disreputable.

He brought with him the fragrance of the outdoors and the pleasant farmy smell of horse. Unaccountably, but not unexpectedly, her heart rate zoomed out of control.

"Is there a way for you to warn me when you plan on doing that? Maybe a bell around your neck?" she asked with asperity as MacBain rose and started clearing the table. "Something?" The way he was watching her made her pulse kick. The heat in his eyes made her clothes feel too tight. Every time she thought she had him pigeonholed, he surprised her. Behind those evasive dark eyes was a first-class brain. She'd do well to remember that.

"What have you decided?" he demanded.

She felt trapped, frightened, God help her, *excited* by him. "My decision hasn't changed." Her eyes were steady as she regarded him over her teacup. "I'll talk to Homeland Security to see if they agree with what you suggested."

She'd talk to them. Confess was more like it. But she

had no intention of building a Rex 2. For anyone. The potential for disaster was just too great.

"As far as I know, right now one of Verdine Industries' competitors could be hard at work fabricating Rex. Teams going at it twenty-four seven. With the right amount of qualified people on it, they could probably have it on the market next week." Impossible, of course. Even with everything they needed, even with the Rex itself, it would probably be a year before the robot could be put into production.

"Denial is not just a river in Egypt. And have the Feebs and HS on their asses before they shipped the first unit? For God's sake, surely you can't be this naive. What the hell did you expect, working for a company that handles so many government contracts? Verdine has always been ripe for espionage. Either from the inside, secrets sold to foreign governments, or from outside terrorist groups."

She bristled at his accusing tone. "We make highly sophisticated household appliances, advanced robotics for industry. Toys . . ."

"What do you think Rex was for?"

"Not *think*. I know *exactly* what it was for. A tireless health care worker. An adjunct to firefighters, to be used in earthquake rescues . . ."

"An indestructible soldier."

Oh, God. Yes. "No."

"Absolutely. And you know it. A *toy* manufacturer doesn't require the level of security they have at Verdine."

"People would sell their firstborn for the schematics on our self-propelled vacuum cleaner alone. Not to mention all our other products. Verdine is so far ahead of the pack, industry observers can only speculate what we're working on. It's a multibillion-dollar corporation. Of *course* we have high-level security."

He just looked at her.

Eden couldn't hold his gaze a moment longer. "Oh, God."

"Who do you want to talk to at Homeland Security?" She was pale, but resolute. "Special Agent Dixon."

"You trust him?"

Eden bit the corner of her lower lip. "Yes."

He watched her for a moment, his eyes on her mouth. Stubborn woman. Cautious and stubborn. In her line of work he suspected she'd had to be both to get where she was today. He'd take what he could get. If Dixon could motivate her, then Dixon it would be. Whatever it took.

"I'll contact him, but it's going to waste precious time getting him out here."

She shrugged. Clearly not giving a shit. "I'll catch up if he vouches for you."

Dixon would vouch for him. For T-FLAC. And Gabriel hoped to hell she *could* make up time. She'd have to.

Gabriel was surprised she hadn't immediately launched into a request for an explanation of last night. He'd been prepared to listen to her questions and demands for proof of what she'd witnessed.

Every movement she made was unaffected but seductive. His blood heated and his pulse raced. It was becoming more and more difficult to keep his hands off her. Close enough to touch her, he kept his hands in his pockets, and made sure to take shallow breaths. Made no damn difference. He could still smell her skin.

She wore jeans, and one of a dozen identical, plain, pocketed T-shirts. Today's was grass green. The color looked good on her, Gabriel thought absently, acutely aware of her in every cell of his body. He should have sat across from her instead of this close. But it wouldn't have made any difference. She might be a pain in his ass,

but his desire for this woman hadn't diminished over-
night. Unfortunately, it never would.

He looked away from the distracting way her hair
shone in the sunlight streaming through the windows.
She'd crossed her legs while she'd been talking to
MacBain, and now he realized he was fixated on her
swinging foot. Today's shoes consisted of three slender
apple green straps that crossed her pretty toes, then
wound around her instep and ankle. A tiny red ladybug
adorned the section where the straps crossed on her high
instep, and clashed with the bright pink polish on her
toenails. The dark metal of the "lucky" ring made her
skin seem more creamy in contrast.

"They left you alone for years," he said flatly, his
breathing deliberately shallow. God almighty. She smelled
of jasmine. The fragrance, mixed with the familiar scent
of her warm skin, was swimming in his bloodstream like
a fine wine.

"Left you alone," he repeated harshly, shoving his
chair back a foot or two to put a little distance between
them. "*Knowing* what you were working on. Waiting
for you to perfect the prototype. Then they walked in
and took it."

"You believe that the person who killed Dr. Kirchner,
and stole Rex, worked for Jason Verdine?"

"Don't you?"

Eden nodded. "I do. But only because of the top-level
security on the project. Theo and I were separated from
the rest of the R and D teams. Given our own lab to
work independently on Rx793 six years ago. Besides the
team that drew up the noncompete agreement and did
the repeat background checks, there were only a handful of people that even knew what we were working
on."

"How many is a handful?"

"Jason Verdine. His president of marketing, Tom

Reece, his president of sales, Steven Absalom, Hector Gonzales, vice president of R and D, and, of course, Marshall Davis, our assistant."

"All of whom had a hell of a lot to gain by stealing your prototype."

"I doubt it. I don't see any of those men walking in and killing Theo in cold blood. And frankly, whoever has Rex wouldn't be able to spend the money they made from the sale for twenty years or more, because it would just be too obvious. Not to mention the capital outlay to go into production. It would be prohibitive to the average person. I told you, Rex cost over three hundred million dollars to create. So whoever has him has to have enormous start-up capital to afford to manufacture even one unit, let alone several.

"And without my working notes, my data, and schematics . . ."

"Anyone with half a brain looking at your notes and your program would realize like I did that you have a photographic memory, Eden. They tried to take you next."

"Now, *that's* not true. Honestly. No one came near me."

"They came near you," he said grimly. "Too damn near you. Or rather, they tried. In the past twenty-eight days, there were two kidnap attempts. The only reason they didn't succeed was because I put a protective spell on you the night Dr. Kirchner was killed."

"But as it turns out *you* were the lucky winner in the kidnap Dr. Cahill sweepstakes."

"They didn't want to protect you."

"Right. 'They' just wanted to suck information out of my brain. Oh, wait. That's exactly what you want to do, isn't it?"

CHAPTER ELEVEN

Gabriel observed Eden as she completed her third lap walking around the pond. She'd kicked off her shoes by the door, then stuffed her hands into the pockets of her jeans. Head up, she kept to the softness of the grass rather than walk barefoot on the gravel path rimming the water's edge. It was close to midday, and no shade was cast by the thick hedge of natural scrub and twenty-year-old Douglas firs ringing the glade.

Gabriel's mother had been an avid gardener, and in an attempt to make her husband feel at ease here, had the clearing planted, and the small pond chiseled out of the land. The original had sat just as this one did, beyond the doors of the castle's solarium in Scotland. She'd wanted her husband to feel at home.

Magnus Edge had never seen it.

Living here fatherless, Gabriel and his brothers had watched their beautiful mother fade away, day by day, as she waited in vain.

"She'll do the right thing," MacBain said, standing beside Gabriel's chair. Both men watched Eden's long strides on the unfamiliar landscape, yet she didn't look down. She looked ahead at possibilities, Gabriel realized, almost hearing her mind racing with each pensive step.

A large part of him admired her for her vision. And the mind and talent she possessed to bring that vision to reality. But the cold, hard truth was, from everything he'd gleaned, she'd perfected something that could get millions of people killed. Today.

It didn't matter how brilliant her invention was. It didn't matter a jot *what* altruistic functions her Rex bot was capable of. As valuable as it was for good, its value for just the opposite would have many more far-reaching and devastating consequences.

T-FLAC operatives all over the world were on high alert for any lead on who had stolen the prototype, and what it was going to be used for.

Gabriel's job, his only job here, was to retrieve the necessary data to duplicate the robot. T-FLAC had scientists on staff, a superior think tank with some of the best minds in the world, but none of them could do what he could do. Build a fully functioning robot, within minutes, from Eden's thoughts alone.

When—not if—the original was located, it had to be destroyed.

Like against like.

How long did he have before she either relented and allowed him in, or he had to use a form of coercion? There was a lot to be said for self-discipline, he thought, stretching his legs out beneath the table. He was proud of his ability to control his raging appetite for her. Proud of his iron will, and downright fucking thrilled by his restraint. "I won't touch her."

"And I see the strain that's putting on yer face, lad. Yer options are running out."

Gabriel shot the old man a fulsome look. "Do you think I'm not *aware* of it? She'll give more freely if no force is used."

He thought about what he'd learned of her life: the string of degrees before she was even sixteen; the early marriage; the rapid divorce after the son of a bitch husband had stolen her life's work. She was still singularly unused to the kind of deceit Gabriel was familiar with. Despite all she'd gone through, Eden Cahill was straightforward, honest, and honorable.

He could overwhelm her doubts and objections to extracting the data from her mind, but that would take time, and a finesse he didn't feel when he was anywhere near her.

"All of us give more freely if no force is used," MacBain said quietly beside him. "That curse of yers is a form of coercion, is it no'?"

"It is what it is." Gabriel watched Eden pause near the rose garden. If she walked around the low wall behind her, she'd find a small stone bench tucked into a shady corner. It was where his mother had sat, for hours, talking to his father on the phone. Montana to Scotland. More than fifteen hours of air travel had separated his parents.

Five hundred years of Edge men had tried to break the curse.

It could not be done.

It didn't matter, he told himself, watching Eden cup a pale yellow rose in her hand. It didn't matter because unlike his father before him, he wasn't stupid enough to buck the inevitable. Gabriel had learned by experience.

Had he ever seen his father smile? Had he ever heard his mother laugh?

Hell no.

Because they'd foolishly believed that what they had was strong enough, *powerful enough,* for God's sake, to turn five hundred years of cold hard fact into fiction.

Eden bent to smell his mother's Peace rose. Her green T-shirt pulled out of the back of her jeans as she leaned over, exposing a smile of pale skin, and the indentation of her spine on the small of her back.

Gabriel wanted to put his mouth there.

He wanted her. So much so that it scared him in

ways bullets and bombs never had. "She's a smart lass," MacBain rested a gnarled hand on Gabriel's shoulder. "I'm guessing she's almost as stubborn as ye are. Note I said *almost*. She'll work through her conscience and do what needs doing. But ye, my fine lad, are playing with fire, keeping her here, and ye know it. I see the way she watches ye, with a hunger that should be singeing yer hair follicles." His fingers tightened warningly. "Use caution with the lass. It is already beginning."

"Where would she be safer, old man?" Gabriel glanced up at MacBain. "Tell me that?"

"Where could she be in more peril? Tell *me* that?"

The answer, Gabriel thought grimly, to both questions was: Here. Here at Edridge Castle. With him.

God help them both.

"She's no match for ye, lad. She's led a sheltered, sterile kind of life there in her insular scientific world. Yer offering her danger and excitement. To a lass like Dr. Cahill that could be seductive indeed. 'Tis fortunate Nairne's Curse prevents ye from playing with her, my lad. There's a lass who'll believe herself in love with one kind word."

Gabriel gave a snort of disbelief. "Don't fool yourself, old man. Eden Cahill is nobody's fool. She dislikes me intensely. As she should. She wouldn't trust a kind word from me if I had it notarized, believe me."

"She's a wilted flower with her face turned up for a drop of rain. Ye better watch yerself, ye hear me? The wee lass has had precious little love in her life from what I can gather, so don't ye be doing any more with that sweet girl than is absolutely necessary."

"You're flogging a dead horse, MacBain. She's just a means to an end."

"Keep reminding yerself of that."

Gabriel didn't even pretend to himself that he wasn't observing every graceful move she made. He watched her hips move beneath those baggy jeans, and tried to imagine her heavy. Instead he conjured up an image of her even more lush, more desirable, if possible. He pictured a younger Eden, self-conscious as any teenage girl would be at that age, overweight, out of her depth trying to relate to students years ahead of her in age and experience.

A light breeze teased her hair, causing the glossy curls to shine chocolate in the brilliant sunlight. He gripped the metal arms of his chair to hold himself back from charging outside and pulling her to him. The more he was around her, the stronger the hungry yearning to touch and be touched by her. Hell, he thought, just observing how the wind lifted her hair from her slender neck made him harden uncomfortably. The depth of his response to the stimuli that was Dr. Eden Cahill scared the hell out of him. It was too strong. Too tempting. Too dangerous.

Idiot.

He was like a dog chasing a car. He couldn't catch her, and even if he did, there was absolutely nothing he could do with her once he did. Yet the hunger inside him was building and building like a gathering storm, tearing at him, driving him insane, blinding him to reason.

Get a grip, dickhead. A man in his line of work who wasn't in control of himself made mistakes. Fatal mistakes. Wanting and taking are vastly different things, he reminded himself. *Acknowledge the want, then deal with abstinence and move on.* "She's wearing a ditch in the fucking path."

MacBain smacked Gabriel on the back of the head. It was no light tap. "Mind that mouth, my lad."

The Edge boys hadn't grown up without a father figure, Gabriel thought, wryly watching as Eden, deep in thought, started on her fourth lap.

He frowned.

Years ago, while on assignment in Johannesburg, Gabriel had reason to be at the zoo. He'd watched a polar bear circle the too-small confines of its cage. Clockwise. Then counterclockwise.

The animal had kept up this ritual for hours. He'd gone back the next day, and the next, compelled to see if the animal had eventually resigned itself to its fate. Each day was exactly the same. A continuous loop. When he'd sought out the keeper, he'd been told that eventually the magnificent animal would die, because she wouldn't stop looking for a way out of the confined space.

Gabriel had offered to buy the animal. What the fuck he'd thought he'd do with a six-hundred-pound polar bear he had no idea. Bring it back to the States on the T-FLAC jet? But by God, if they'd let him, he would have figured out that minor detail in a heartbeat.

"Hot out there on that pretty fair skin. She needs a hat," MacBain moved away to straighten a fold in the pristine tablecloth.

"She's a big girl. If she's too hot she'll come in."

"Aye, but then maybe she thinks it's hotter in here."

"It *is* hotter in here," Gabriel told him. Which was a ridiculous lie, since the old castle walls were a foot thick and kept out both heat and cold. He stood. "I'll be in the library if you need me."

In the library doing my job, not thinking about a caged polar bear walking herself to death. Gabriel considered asking Sebastian to come back when he talked to him next. He'd really like to get out the claymores and do an intense round of swordplay. Maybe it would get rid of some of this pent-up sexual tension.

And maybe not.

MacBain had a way with those white eyebrows that said it all. He verbalized the brow wiggle. "And why would I be needing ye?"

"If *anyone* needs me," Gabriel told him tightly. He strode out of the solarium, shoulders stiff, temper hanging on by a thread.

"Ah."

"Ah?" Eden asked, walking back into the sunroom, blinking to adjust her eyes from brilliant sunlight to the dimness inside. She knew instantly that Gabriel wasn't there anymore. The disappointment she felt was disproportionate. But there she was. She'd just made the hardest decision she'd ever made in her life. And that decision was based on nothing more concrete than a gut reaction to a man she didn't know, and probably shouldn't trust.

The other day upon the stair, I saw a man who wasn't there.

She smiled as MacBain handed her a frosted glass of orange juice, partially wrapped in one of the pale green napkins.

"Thanks." She took a sip of freshly squeezed juice; it was tart and sweet, the flavor bursting on her tongue. "Are you talking to yourself?"

"It would appear so. He said to tell ye he's in the library."

Eden raised her eyebrows. "He did?"

"He'd surely enjoy a cold glass of fruit juice," MacBain poured a second glass, expertly folded a napkin around the lower half, and handed it to her. "He mentioned he was overly warm."

Yeah. She could understand the sentiment. But perhaps not in quite the same way. "It is a hot day."

"And getting hotter by the moment," he told her. With that parting salvo, he turned, back erect in his natty black suit, and shuffled off at the speed of snail.

Setting down the two glasses, Eden grabbed her shoes, and with a smile sat down to put them on as she watched him go. "What a funny, dear old guy."

"Eighty-three isna old!" MacBain shouted from the other side of the room without turning. He disappeared from view behind a giant broad-leafed tree in a terracotta pot the size of a small car.

She grinned as a door slammed shut out of sight. "And he has ears like a bat."

Shoes on, she rose, picked up the glasses of juice and headed to the library to tell Gabriel that as long as he could assure her of two things, she'd agree to work with him on Rex 2. One: She wanted assurances and confirmation from Homeland Security that he was who he claimed to be. Two: Once Rex 2 found Rex 1, both bots would be destroyed. This time she'd build in a self-destruct mechanism to the bot. She didn't want one particle of them to remain.

As she came to the slightly ajar door of the library, she noticed that the front doors were still standing wide open.

Turn left. Talk to Gabriel.

Run like hell, and go through those doors. Possibly to freedom.

Decisions. Decisions. Life-altering decisions.

"I have her," Gabriel said quietly from inside the room. He was on the phone.

"I agree. Whatever it takes." His cold grim voice sounded impersonal. Businesslike. Matter-of-fact. "No. As I suspected, nothing useful on the hard drive. I took care of the little I did find. Yeah. I used mumbo-jumbo," he responded dryly.

"She has a photographic memory for Christ's sake. I guarantee you. The second she fucking-well gives up the data, she'll be dead—" He stopped speaking and she knew he'd heard her outside the door. Heart hammering, she froze.

"Just a second—Eden?" he called out.

The drinks slipped from her nerveless fingers.

Glass shattered, spraying orange juice over her feet and the stone floor.

She ran.

By the time Gabriel raced out of the library she was already halfway across the entry hall. The little fool was running flat out in high-heeled sandals on the uneven stone floor. "Eden!"

She didn't so much as hesitate as he yelled her name again. She was going to break her damned neck.

He slammed the front doors shut before she could reach them. The sound reverberated through the cavernous room like a pistol shot. Damn it to hell, how much had she heard? He kept advancing on her, but she didn't appear to give a damn.

Using both hands, she grabbed one of the enormous wrought-iron handles, putting her entire body weight into pulling on it.

"It's not going to open," he said quietly, not daring to get any closer. He stopped where he was, torn. The pull he felt for her was profound, even at twenty paces.

Beneath the short sleeves of her T-shirt her muscles flexed, and her knuckles were turning white as she strained to pull the door open using every ounce of strength she had.

"Eden—"

For a moment she stopped, her hands still gripping the handle. Her cheeks were stained, more due to fury, he suspected, than anything else. The sight of tears running unchecked down her face speared him like a knife to the gut.

"Either open this f-fucking door *right now,* Gabriel Edge, or kill me." She punctuated the words with aggressive yanks on the door handle.

"Jesus. This isn't a soap opera, for God's sake. Stop

hauling at that damn handle before you hurt yourself. It's not going to open."

"You killed Theo, you lying son of a bitch." Her voice rose with every word as she spun around, blood in her eye.

Gabriel wasn't prepared for her to charge him like a bull at a red cape. "No, I swear I—"

His heart slammed up into his throat and he attempted to shimmer out. But she got to him a split second before he could get the hell out of her way.

She slapped a hand on his chest as they collided, and a shower of brilliant white sparks like the aurora borealis shot out in an arc around them, temporarily blinding him.

At Eden's touch, a blaze of heat, just this side of pain, surged through Gabriel's body, shocking him with its intensity. The torrent of passion and hunger blindsided him. The pleasure was so sharp he cried out at the same time as she drew in a startled gasp and her eyes went wide.

Ah, Jesus! Too late.

His tenuous hold on his control snapped.

He captured her head in his hands, burying his fingers in her silken curls as he drew her up and in, tight against his body. The fear and anger in her expressive eyes suddenly changed to startled awareness and she parted her lips and arched against him. His entire body burned with undiluted lust.

Savagely Gabriel crushed his mouth down on hers with a raw hunger impossible to deny for one more second. She tasted of sun-warmed oranges, underpinned by tears, and an answering heat that fed his own desire like gasoline on an open flame.

Wrapping her arms about his neck, Eden shivered violently beneath the hot spear of his tongue, denying him nothing. He thrust deeply into her mouth, trembling with the greed in which their mouths joined. He took what she offered with a hunger that was uncontrolled.

He had to stop. Had. To. Stop.

Feeling like he was ripping off his own skin, Gabriel tore his mouth from hers. "No more."

She whimpered in protest, tightening her arms about his neck, holding on. Not waiting for his compliance, Eden stood on her toes, and reclaimed his mouth. She bit at his lower lip, hard enough for the sharp pain to sting. The sensation ratcheted up his lust another impossible notch.

His heart lunged in his chest as he realized that Eden was just as out of control as he was. His body tightened like a drawn bow as he went back to ravaging her willing mouth.

As he kissed her, his arms tightened around her slender body. He raked his hands down her back to grip her bottom. She gave a huff of air as he crushed her hips hard against the painful ridge of his erection. Mouth avaricious and unrelenting in return, Eden tightened her arms around his neck, rubbing her hips in a maddening dance against him. Moaning deep in her throat, she angled his head as it suited her and plunged the slick heat of her tongue over his, returning the bruising force of his kiss with every ounce of her strength.

She wrapped a leg around his, pulling him closer against her heat, body strained against his, her soft breasts crushed against the hard plane of his chest.

The intense pleasure he felt just kissing this woman was like nothing Gabriel had ever experienced before. He needed to touch her skin. Burned to feel the weight and texture of her breast in his hand. Ached to taste her nipples, and drink from a far more intimate moist heat.

Vaguely he was aware that they were still standing in the vast entry hall when he needed for them to be horizontal. *Now.*

Imitating the act he craved with his tongue, Gabriel shimmered them to his bedroom where sunlight was flooding his large unmade bed.

He wanted more than to kiss this woman, but when he tried to drag his lips from her mouth he found himself drawn back for one more taste.

The fragrance of her skin, the silken texture of her hair, the moist clinging heat of her mouth gave him a surge of power he'd never felt before. She was addictive, and he gave up any pretense that he could resist her.

The thought that their clothing was an annoyance barely registered before they were both naked. She gave a small cry of satisfaction without opening her eyes. The smooth brush of Eden's pale skin against his hardness made Gabriel shudder.

Lowering her to the sun-warmed sheets, he linked his fingers with hers, drawing her hands above her head as he settled into the cradle of her thighs.

He couldn't take his eyes off her. She was perfection. She arched her back, presenting him with her creamy breasts, tipped with pale coral nipples.

She opened eyes heavy with passion, and glittering feverishly between her thick dark lashes. "Swear to me that you had nothing to do with Theo's death."

"I swear."

"Thank God," she whispered fervently and kissed him again. They parted, each dragging in a breath. "Magic." Her soft voice was filled with awe, and Gabriel knew she wasn't referring to the mode of transportation or the loss of their clothes. He knew exactly what she meant. It was as though their very DNA knew the other. Loving Eden was as natural as breathing. No wonder she'd been impossible to resist.

"Yeah," he breathed against her warm jasmine-scented skin. "Magic."

God help them both. *Yes.*

Bombarded by intense physical desire, he had to remain perfectly still for a moment or explode. He dropped his forehead to hers, hearing their syncopated breathing as he held her tightly in his arms. "You are so damn beautiful," he whispered brokenly, using his utmost control to remain perfectly still. "And you *smell*—you smell like Heaven. God. The fragrance of your skin drives me insane. Woman drenched in flowers. Doesn't matter which of those perfumes you put on. Any of them, combined with the fragrance of your skin, makes me drunk with wanting you. When you walk into a room, I smell you. And I get so hard I'm in pain."

Her legs moved restlessly against his and she smiled up at him, her face luminous. "I've wanted to touch you. Forever." Her fingers flexed in his hold and he shifted his hips carefully, just enough to anchor her legs with one of his. Gritting his teeth against the sweet agony, he said thickly, "Give me a minute."

He was pressed intimately between her thighs and felt the hot moist center of her pulse against his hardness. Teeth clenched, he struggled for some semblance of control when all he felt was an all-encompassing gnawing hunger.

His craving for her was raw and untamed, and for the first time in his life his control was shot to hell. To be stopped he'd have to be stabbed in the heart a couple of times. Or Eden had to say no.

Her avid mouth said yes. Yes. Yes.

There was no stopping now.

Dragging his mouth from hers, he bit down gently on the sensitive skin where her neck curved into her shoulder. Her body bowed as he knew it would. She was ultrasensitive right there. He'd noticed the night he'd made love to her from a distance. Then he'd thought he'd shatter, he'd been so hard. But it had been nothing, *nothing* like this.

If he slipped inside her now, he'd come in two seconds flat. Would that be so bad? It was a desperate question, and he knew the answer. Even if Eden didn't climax, the damage would still be done. And if he didn't plunge inside her wet heat, soon, he wouldn't shatter. He'd die.

"I want you too much," he admitted, barely recognizing his own voice. Nothing mattered now but the fire consuming his body and mind. He was burning alive, and the small sounds of need Eden was making beneath him ratcheted up his tension, torquing his need.

Control was overrated.

He still had her hands captured above her head, and her nails scored the back of his hand as she drew up her knees on either side of his hips, urging penetration. "Oh, God. Gabriel. Please—"

Silky legs wrapped around his hips, she crossed her ankles, digging her heels into the flexing muscles of his ass, drawing him harder against the heart of her. He'd forgotten how stubborn and determined this woman was.

Gabriel slid his hand beneath her hips, cupping the firm flesh of her bottom, lifting her to receive his first powerful thrust. His entry was hard and fast.

No, he thought dimly as his body immediately convulsed and spasmed.

He didn't last even two seconds.

CHAPTER TWELVE

Eden's hips lifted, and her body shuddered under the impact of his as she climaxed with him. The sensation of her sheath convulsing around him as he continued thrusting took his breath away. If he was wild, so was she, as she dug her nails into his back, her hips hammered back at his as he rode her hard and fast.

He kept thrusting powerfully inside her as a brilliant shower of white-hot sparks lifted their bodies off the bed in a slow spin. Sobbing, Eden bit his shoulder, and Gabriel gave a primal shout as a second climax followed so closely on the heels of the first that they barely had time to catch their breaths.

Drenched in sweat, they moved in a dance as old as time. He tried to say her name, but had to grit his teeth as she convulsed around him in a sensation so sharp, so sweet he forgot to breathe.

He climaxed again, and again their bodies rose several feet above the mattress as they did a slow rotation in direct counterpart to the heat and intensity of their lovemaking. Eden's heels and fingernails dug into his back as they lowered gradually to the twisted sheets where they lay, still joined, their limbs entwined, their skin glued together. Their bodies continued to shudder and the convulsions became smaller and smaller until they lay limp and exhausted in each other's arms.

With his face buried in Eden's damp neck Gabriel inhaled the hot scent of jasmine and the fragrance of her skin.

Jesus. No finesse. No tenderness—"Are you all right? I've never lost control like that." His voice was rough. "Not since I was a teenager, at least." Lifting his head was an effort as he looked down at her.

Eden's slumberous eyes met his. Sunlight brought out amber fire in their depths. Her swollen mouth curved in a satiated, cat-drank-the-cream smile. "It isn't called losing control if it was reciprocal."

He slid his fingers into her damp hair, loving the look of the chocolate strands curling around his fingers. Sunlight bathed her body, lightening her skin to cream and showing him the deep apricot color of her nipples. Looking at her, inhaling the unique scent of her skin and the musky fragrance of sex he felt himself grow hard again. She gave him a sleepy smile as her slim hands, cool as silk, moved down his back.

This time he moved slowly, intending to be more gentle, but as soon as she realized that he was starting to reignite passion she made a wild sound in the back of her throat, and tightened her ankles in the small of his back. Gabriel was lost.

They came again. Together. It wasn't as intense as the other times, but it scared him more for its tenderness.

"Gabriel," she whispered as the tension in their bodies slowly started to release its tight hold and muscles began to relax and unknot. She stroked his cheek with fingers that still trembled slightly. Her eyes were sleepy, but no less expressive. "That was incredible."

An understatement. "Yeah." His voice was thick, his heartbeat loud and heavy in his chest as he carefully separated from her. He saw exhaustion pull at her as her eyelids drooped. He took her hand from his face, tucking it against the heavy beat of his heart.

He wanted to take her in every way he could imagine,

and then invent some more. He wanted to keep them both climaxing for a week. Then he wanted to be able to walk away unscathed.

Wasn't going to happen.

He was so screwed.

"Mmmm." The sound was distinctly drowsy.

He touched her cheek gently. Her flushed skin felt warm and satin smooth beneath his fingers. "Take a nap," he told her gruffly. "I'll be right here."

Fascinated by her determination to keep her eyes open, when it was clear she was spent and completely exhausted, he watched her fight sleep. Finally her lids drifted closed as if her eyelashes were too heavy.

There was a certain amount of trust in her ability to sleep so soundly under the circumstances, Gabriel thought, surprised by that level of trust despite the gymnastics they'd indulged in for hours.

He had, after all, kidnapped her.

Physically he was spent, mentally he was in a sensual fog. He needed several cups of MacBain's coffee. Hell, he needed to be away from the siren call of the woman whose scent and taste were now permanently and indelibly imprinted on his synapses.

On the bedside table the emergency line on the phone blinked red. *An update,* Gabriel thought savagely. *About fucking time.* His gaze went from the phone back to Eden curled trustingly beside him, one hand over his heart.

"I have to go downstairs to take a call," he whispered to her, keeping his voice low. She didn't answer. Her soft, slow breathing told Gabriel she'd be asleep for a while. He slipped from the bed and pulled on his jeans.

He was dressed as he shimmered into the library and picked up the phone. "What do we have?" he asked without preamble, tucking his T-shirt into his jeans and padding barefoot around the island that was his desk.

He could still taste the sweetness of her on his mouth. Still smell the light clean floral scent of her. He could hear the soft sound of longing she made. And wondered how dangerous it would be to kiss her again.

And if he kissed this woman once more, would he ever be able to stop? The situation with Eden Cahill was far more dangerous than he'd ever been led to believe. Not just because he felt drugged after their passionate bout of incredible lovemaking, but because he could feel himself falling under a dangerous spell. A spell that only he could control. And so far he was doing a piss-poor job of it.

He forced himself to concentrate on what Sebastian Tremayne was saying. The sooner this business with the fucking robot was resolved, the sooner he could send her back to Tempe, Arizona, and never see her again. It had only been a couple of days. No harm, no foul.

Sex, no matter how incredible, was still only sex.

"Yo? With me here, Edge?" Tremayne waited for Gabriel's affirmative. "Heard of the Power Elite?"

Gabriel sat down in the big leather chair. A chair bought for a man who'd never sat in it. It had taken him years to realize that *he* fit his father's chair just fine.

"Someone new?" he asked, motioning MacBain, who was carrying a tray, into the room. Not that MacBain needed the invitation.

"Unless it's a splinter group," Tremayne told him. "We're working on it."

MacBain placed the tray on Gabriel's desk. The man had radar where he was concerned, Gabriel thought, as his manservant poured a mug of fragrant coffee from a thermal carafe, placed a coaster on the desk near at hand, then set down the mug, just so. On the tray was another mug, a couple of plates of sandwiches, and two slices of apple pie.

Gabriel picked up his coffee mug and cocked a brow at the duplications. MacBain gave him an innocent look before turning to shuffle off.

"How do we know the Power Elite has the bot?" Gabriel drank some of MacBain's excellent French Roast. He'd need the entire pot to get rid of the sensual fog he was in. Damn it all to hell.

"They were kind enough to tell us," Tremayne said dryly. "A call came into our tip line three minutes ago."

It was a given that the trace had been unsuccessful, otherwise Sebastian would have told him the origination of the call. So all they had was a name. Not the size of the group, not their location, not their intent.

T-FLAC considered every call like this the real deal until it was proven otherwise. Terrorist groups thrived on generating fear early and often. Bragging before and after an act of terror was part and parcel of who they were. Reputations were built on promised threats and payoffs.

How long were they going to have to wait to get enough intel to stop these guys before they started? Or had they started already?

The door closed quietly as MacBain finally made it out of the room. "And did these upstanding citizens tell us what they plan to do with the damn thing?" Gabriel demanded, sitting back.

"Said we'd know soon enough. How's it coming with the good doctor?"

The pun wasn't lost on Gabriel. "I'll keep you posted."

"You need to step up th—"

"Let me know when you've got more." He replaced the receiver. Jesus. He'd been so busy coming himself, that the thought of extracting the data from Eden's mind had completely slipped *his*. He thought of her upstairs in his bed, and felt the answering heat power through him.

* * *

Eden opened her eyes when she felt the cool stroke of Gabriel's hand on her breast. She gave him a sleepy smile. He'd said he'd be right there while she slept and he was.

"Hi," she said, still feeling drowsy and deliciously lethargic. She didn't know how long she'd slept, but the angle of the sun had changed.

"I didn't mean to wake you." His voice was raspy and sexy. His hair looked pretty neat for a man who'd been rolling about for hours; she bet hers looked as though she'd stuck a finger in an electrical outlet. She raised her hand self-consciously, and he pulled her hand to his mouth, kissed her open palm.

"Leave it, you have the sexiest hair I've ever seen. All those wild curls are messy from my hands. Looks sexy. Hot."

He nibbled her fingers until she squirmed on the warm sheets. His broad shoulders were tanned, his skin smooth as satin overlaying rock-hard muscle. Eden ran an appreciative glance down his chest with its light furring of crisp dark hair. Small dark nipples beckoned her mouth and she lifted her head and closed her lips around one flat peak, thrilling to the sound of his harsh, indrawn breath.

She tasted the slightly salty skin on his chest, letting her lips climb to the steady pulse in the base of his throat. Brushing her mouth beneath his stubborn chin she felt the prickle of his beard abrading her lips. She smiled, letting her lips roam over his chin to find the firmness of his mouth.

"Yum," she murmured, nibbling and laving until he moaned and opened for her. He rolled over, taking her with him, so she was on top. Head on his chest, Eden opened her legs to straddle his hips.

He was already hard and ready for her. She lifted her head an inch, and opened her eyes.

"Hmm." She gave the opulent room a vaguely quizzical glance as she sheathed herself over him. "When. Did. This. Oh, God, Gabriel! Happen?"

"You were too busy to notice." He nuzzled her neck, making her shiver deliciously. She closed her eyes again, more interested in what Gabriel was doing than in the heavy masculine decor surrounding them.

She shuddered as ripples of pleasure surged through her as he lifted her body so that he could reach her breasts. Then shivered at the brush of his lips across her nipple as an answering heat twisted through the very core of her. She clung to his shoulders; the very wildness of his hunger called out to everything in her that was female, and ignited her own fire to fever pitch.

He whispered against her skin. Words of admiration, shocking words, soothing words that blurred into the soft sibilant sounds of the ocean tide. Pulling her deeper and deeper into the riptide where her feet would be knocked from under her and she'd be pulled out of her depth with no hope of surviving.

She made a small pleading sound as the tip of his tongue traced a circle around the peak of her nipple. He closed his teeth with admirable restraint over the hard bud, and her body arched against his mouth. He cupped her other breast in his palm, gently massaging it, brushing his thumb over the nipple.

The heat of his breath caressed her skin, and she felt the mounting tension in his body as she ran her hands over the hard sculptured muscles of his upper arms. His skin was sleek and smooth, hard as tensile steel and hot beneath her marauding caresses.

She ran her hand down his body. He shuddered, capturing her hand and bringing it to his lips. He gently bit down on the fleshy pad of her thumb.

His long fingers caressed the soft skin of her inner thigh and then skimmed even higher to find a softer, more tender spot. She started to say something, but the words were lost as his thumb moved again.

She shuddered as the magical sensation shot through her body. His fingers took her to the pinnacle, then held her there, trembling on the brink of release.

Anticipation coiled impossibly higher. She tried to say his name, but coherent speech was impossible. He filled her, every part of her. Leaving room for nothing but pure, sharp, sensation.

It was a long time before the sensual storm passed, leaving them exhausted, their bodies damply entwined.

The sun shone directly over the bed, accentuating the dark stubble on his face that had so deliciously abraded her skin. His eyes shone like indigo crystal. Dark and glittering. Eden caressed his strong jaw, loving the feel of him, and ignored the regret she saw in his eyes.

A shower had gone a long way to waking her up after a long afternoon of lovemaking. While Eden felt lethargic and lazy, Gabriel appeared to be wired. He'd insisted on showering alone. Disappointed, she'd showered in his large, granite shower by herself. He'd been waiting for her when she'd returned to his bedroom. While she'd been in the bathroom he'd retrieved a change of clothes for her, jeans and a pale blue T-shirt, and her gold sandals with very high heels.

He'd also brought in the small blue bottle of Je Reviens perfume. He had specific ideas about where each dab should be applied, and they'd ended up making love again.

The setting sun lanced through the narrow Gothic windows directly opposite the staircase, spilling mellow golden light on the treads as they went downstairs an hour later.

They'd spent the better part of the day making love, and she ached in unexpected places. Under the circumstances, Eden felt ridiculously at peace. And not just because her body had been well loved. She'd never been kissed with such attention to detail by any man in her life. Gabriel Edge's kisses were addictive. She loved the shape of his mouth, she loved the texture of his mouth. God, she loved the *taste* of his mouth.

She felt . . . centered. Centered in a way, she now realized, that she'd never felt before. The man walking so far away from her right now knew her body intimately. More intimately than any man ever had. Yet she knew practically nothing about him. And what she did know should scare her to death, but didn't.

In some strange and mysterious way she felt as though she'd known Gabriel Edge forever.

Her friend Gigi, an artist, insisted on living every moment of every day with gusto. Eden decided she'd take a leaf out of her friend's book. This feeling she had right now shouldn't be wasted on regrets. Sunlight glinted off the metallic straps of her sandals and illuminated the deep gold swirls in the carpet. She smiled, sliding her palm down the smooth mahogany banister as she observed each step she took. She wondered if it would be safe to glance at him again, then realized that looking at Gabriel Edge would never be safe. He was always going to appeal to her. Always going to make her heart kick in her chest. Always make her want to be in his arms.

Gabriel and his Edridge Castle were a long way from a trailer park in Sacramento, California. And this fabulous staircase was a very long way away from the peach box her family had used as a makeshift step.

Gabriel, walking a good ten feet away, turned to look at her. "What are you smiling about?"

"Know what I wanted more than anything in the world when I was thirteen?"

He glanced over at her. "What?"

She shook her head. "You'll think I'm nuts—Okay. Proper *stairs*. We lived in a trailer park outside of Sacramento. Single-wide. My father wasn't too handy. The step was gone long before I was born. As far back as I can remember we had a box—not always the same box mind you, but a box. I didn't care about the inside of the house, but I'd seen *Gone with the Wind,* and I wanted a staircase just like—" her smile widened. "This.

"And now that I come to think of it, I wanted that satisfied morning-after smile that Scarlett wore, too."

"At thirteen? What a precocious child you were." His eyes crinkled and his lips twitched. Oh, it wasn't a full-blown smile, but he *was* amused.

The look in his eyes made her heart thud in her chest. It was more complicated than mere lust. If anything about their relationship could be mere anything. His eyes showed her that he, too, had felt some of the magic they'd made together upstairs, that he found her attractive, and appealing, and at times amusing. He wasn't just attracted to her brain.

The look in his dark blue eyes also told Eden that he knew that what they shared transcended the physical in some mysterious way.

Something inside her shifted and settled and she knew she was lost. She'd been right. Sex with Gabriel had changed her irrevocably. She wondered how she could recognize something she'd never felt before. How this jumble of insane emotions had suddenly gelled into . . . it couldn't be love, for God's sake. Could it? She almost stumbled, tightening her fingers around the handrail just in time.

He was looking at her expectantly. Was what she felt inside showing on her face? God. She hoped not. She marshaled the rational side of her brain and continued the conversation, hoping like hell she sounded halfway rational right now. "I thought Scarlett was so happy because she had such a lovely big bed."

"You were poor."

"Yeah. We were. In every way there was. Dad got my mom pregnant with me when she was fifteen. Lust, not love got them to the altar. They were just kids, and didn't like each other very much. Then I came along, and they liked each other even less, but stuck it out. I think more out of apathy than any real commitment."

"Tough on a kid."

"Tough on the two kids stuck in a single-wide with a baby," she said dryly. "One thing I knew for sure; they both loved *me*. Didn't understand me," she added dryly. "But they did, *do*, love me."

All her life she'd been . . . *apart* from the people around her. All through school she'd been years younger, years less street-smart than the other students in her classes. In college she'd been stared at, never included. Her marriage to Adam had separated her further. She'd always felt somewhat detached from the people around her, a shield against the anticipation of rejection. She'd allowed Adam inside her insular little world because she'd been ripe for attention that had nothing to do with her IQ. She'd been wrong. So wrong.

And look at her now, Eden thought with an inward shudder. Falling in love with a man so far out of her normal world that to compare him to the mistake with Adam was like comparing a minnow to a great white shark.

"Are you close?"

She smiled, because the alternative was to run screaming for the hills. "As close as three people can be who don't understand the first thing about one another. My father lives near Las Vegas; he never remarried after they divorced. My mother's had a succession of boyfriends and two more husbands." Her mother liked her men rich and dumb. The current flame managed the local gas station. Her mother's high aspirations were low.

They stepped down onto the uncarpeted floor of the entry hall. The vast space was warm, filled with the last dying rays of the sun. Eden enjoyed the tap-tap-tap of her heels on the ancient stone floor as they headed toward the library. "MacBain told me a little about your parents. It must have been hard on your mom and you and your brothers to have your father so far away from you."

"We didn't know any different," Gabriel said mildly, shoving open the door to the room. "The marriage was ill-fated from the start. They loved each other, had three kids together, and spent most of their lives apart, just waiting for the Curse to kick in, and for my mother to drop dead. Like your parents, they would've been better off not marrying. Not each other anyway."

"I'm sure *they* didn't feel that way," she added, crossing to one of the dark leather sofas. "They had three children, after all."

"A fact that they appeared to forget most of the time," Gabriel told her. "They were so busy mourning their loss of each other, there wasn't room for anything as prosaic as kids."

Table lamps brightened areas of the room that were already shadowed as the sun set over the mountains. The discreetly-placed large screen TV was on, and the sound of CNN played softly in the background.

"That's pretty cynical," Eden said, not unsympathetically, inhaling the musty fragrance of the thousands of leather-bound books on the shelves, and the sweet, spicy scent of the fresh flowers gracing the stone mantel.

She nodded when he held up a bottle of wine. Eden knew that Magnus and Cait Edge had had a Romeo and

Juliet kind of forbidden love that had kept them apart. Judging from Gabriel's expression right now, he was bored with the subject.

She settled back into the corner of the comfortably squishy sofa. "Tell me about the people you work for."

CHAPTER THIRTEEN

Eden didn't give a damn about the counterterrorist organization he worked for. What she really wanted to know was who Gabriel Edge was. Her body still felt the effects of their lovemaking, which had transcended anything she'd ever experienced.

She wished he'd come and sit beside her. Having him stand halfway across the room, after spending the last several hours in his arms, felt wrong on every level.

He came close enough to hand her a crystal glass of pale wine. A zing of electricity passed from his fingers to hers and her heart started beating faster. God. The attraction she felt for this man was mind-boggling.

"At least you can still manage to walk," she said dryly, and felt her heart trip over the extra beats as his lips curved in a sensual smile. "Talk to me."

"T-FLAC is a private organization to counter terrorism worldwide. We go where we're needed. And God only knows, we're needed often."

Eden sipped the crisp fruity wine, waiting for him to sit down. He didn't. He wasn't drinking either. "And is everyone . . . a wizard?"

Honest to God, as a scientist she knew no such thing existed. She was positive. Yet here she was and here he was and unless this entire surreal experience was a hallucination, he was very much what he said he was. She

looked at him across the vast expanse of the library. Tall
and fit, his body hard—not an ounce of fat anywhere.

She shivered. No matter what magical powers he
professed to possess, bottom line, he was a warrior.

A man far removed from the scientists and mathe-
maticians she was used to dealing with on a daily basis.
A man far removed from her normal life. If not for
Rex, her and Gabriel's paths would never have crossed.

He glanced at the big-screen TV, where they were
covering an uprising in yet another war-torn country.
"No. T-FLAC operatives don't have our skills. I work
for the psi/spec ops paranormal unit."

On the screen a car bomb exploded, shrapnel flew.
People screamed. Was that the sort of thing he did in his
job when he wasn't babysitting scientists?

"And all of you in this special unit are wizards?" Eden
heard how normal her voice sounded asking the abnor-
mal question, and was amazed.

He shook his head, clearly only half listening to her as
he watched the action. "Everyone in the unit has their
own unique talent."

His special talent must be exquisite lovemaking, Eden
decided. "And what's yours?"

"This and that. Transmogrify into a living thing—"

She'd noticed. Didn't believe what she'd seen with her
own two eyes. But she'd definitely noticed. "Can you
transmogrify into someone else?"

"Not a human. Animals only," he told her as absently
as one might mention the ability to play the piano. "Invisibility. Teleporting. Making people see what I want
them to see. For instance, anyone approaching the castle
will see a derelict ranch house. The original house my
mother lived in with her parents." He glanced at her
with a small frown. "More interesting at the moment
are the things I *can't* do."

"Like what?"

"Usually I can extract information from someone's mind very easily." He looked disgruntled. "Everyone's except yours, unfortunately."

The concept that he could do any of the things he claimed to be capable of was as bizarre as it was fascinating. What intrigued Eden even more was the fact that some of them didn't work on *her.* "Why is that?"

"Hell if I know." He was lying. She knew instinctively. But she had no idea why. Despite the absolute impossibility of it, Eden had *witnessed* Gabriel transform himself into a panther. She'd *seen* him teleporting. Been teleported with him, God help her. Wizards didn't exist except in fiction. But here he was.

She gave him a curious look. "You can read my mind when I'm climaxing, though. Isn't that what you told me?"

"Yeah, when your shields are down."

Wasn't going to happen. She needed all her shields up with him around. "Can you really duplicate Rex after reading my mind?"

"Yeah. Ready to give it a shot?"

She shuddered, loathing the idea of anyone, even this man with the dark magnetic eyes and body that had given her so much pleasure, getting into her mind. It gave her the willies. "No, I'm not. I told you, once I've spoken to Homeland Security I'd be willing to rebuild Rex in your lab. I'd need Marshall here to help me."

"I have SA Dixon arriving any minute. Do you remember him?"

"Of course," Eden said dryly. "He interviewed me several times. Does he know who and what you are?"

"I'm a T-FLAC operative," Gabriel said shortly. "Everyone in the business knows T-FLAC."

"Well, excuse me for being so out of the loop." She had a sudden thought. Preposterous, but she asked anyway. "Can you duplicate *people*?" How would she know if Agent Dixon was the real deal or not?

"Jesus, Eden. This isn't *The Stepford Wives*. What the hell do you think I am?"

Her eyes locked with his. "You know what? I've never met a wizard before. I'm not even sure if what I've seen is real or not. And since you appear to be quite capable of turning into a *panther, and* you keep dematerializing m—"

"Teleport."

"*Teleporting* me all over the place, I have a right to know your skills and limitations."

"Christ." He ran his fingers through his hair in an exasperated gesture. "What a mess. You shouldn't even *be* here." His voice was cold, devoid of emotion, his eyes a flat dark blue as he looked at her without expression.

Hurt beyond reason, Eden set the beautiful crystal flute down on a side table very gently, and got to her feet. He'd made love with her for hours—almost all day, in fact. And he *stood* there cool, calm, and collected, telling her this was a *mess*?

That she shouldn't even *be* here?

When he was the one who'd *brought* her here.

When *he* was the one who'd put her in the middle of whatever it was he was manipulating?

Her blood pressure rose. She knew her cheeks were pink with temper. She so rarely lost it that she knew the next step was crying with sheer, unadulterated fury. She'd lost her temper once today. Once was her absolute limit.

"Then *teleport* me back to Tempe and my apartment," she spoke through gritted teeth. "I didn't *ask* to be brought here, I didn't ask for . . ."

Ah, crap, she was going to lose it. It made her *insane* that when she got angry enough she cried.

"Don't cry, for God's sake."

Her eyes stung and she dashed a hand across her cheeks. Dry and hot. But she was close. Damn close. And she refused to shed one tear in front of this insensitive . . . *oaf*. "Go to hell."

"Eden . . ."

She speared him with a heated look as she strode across the carpet in her lucky Marc Jacobs gold leather sandals. The shoes had been lucky when she'd gotten her last, substantial raise wearing them. They'd been lucky when Jason had given her a Mercedes as a bonus.

Apparently they weren't lucky with *wizards*.

Desperate to escape so she could figure out where things had zigged instead of zagged, Eden wanted to get out of his force field and go use her lucky shoes to *kick* something.

Gabriel stepped quickly out of her way as she strode past. He might as well have hit her, she thought, stunned at how his evasive action, layered over his tone of voice, hurt. What did he think after making love to her for hours? That she suddenly had cooties? The son of a bitch.

Suddenly she was back to being a too brainy, too overweight, too *vulnerable* sixteen-year-old. Out of her element. Confused by emotions that had no logical outlet. Damn him. *Damn him.*

"Where are you going?"

"Where *can* I go?" she asked flatly.

She wasn't sixteen anymore, Eden reminded herself. Nor was she fifty pounds overweight. And her emotions did have an outlet. Or they had half an hour ago.

Perhaps her emotions were retarded by the way she'd grown up. She felt as though she were missing an important bit of data here. He'd gone from practically eating her alive to cold disinterest between one breath and the next.

And while it had been a hard lesson learned at the

knee of a master, she knew that she wasn't *always* at fault. She was an adult; she accepted that she made mistakes in the man/woman thing. But in this instance it was *his* attitude that sucked.

"Where can you go?" he repeated. Walking around the back of one of the large leather armchairs, he put the piece of furniture between them like a shield. He gave her a cool look from hot blue eyes. "As soon as I have a bot? Back to your life."

"Right. Like that hasn't changed irrevocably," she said, jaw aching she was clenching her teeth so tightly. "Theo is dead. Someone stole Rex." Silently she added to the list . . . life-altering sex with a *wizard*. "Right. I'll just slip right back into my old life as if none of this ever happened. I wish you'd never brought me here."

"That, Dr. Cahill, makes two of us."

She was vaguely stunned that she was capable of moving, after receiving what felt like a mule kick to the solar plexus. Eden felt numb right down to her core.

Her gaze drifted over him. Black T-shirt, stonewashed jeans showing not only his long, muscular legs, but the evidence that while he might not acknowledge it, he was still powerfully aroused. *So what?* A little voice scoffed. *Healthy males get hard at Victoria's Secret commercials.* And God only knew, she was no model. The way Gabriel was watching her was in direct opposition to what he'd just said, which confused her further. Her pulse raced no matter how hurt she was.

My problem, Eden reminded herself. *This is not a forever kind of guy. No matter how much I want it that way. The second this bot does what he needs it to do, I'll be back in Tempe trying to remember if this was all a dream or the real thing.*

Liar, she scoffed at her own naïveté. She'd have the heartache scars to prove just how real this had been.

Furious with herself for being gullible, Eden headed for the door. She needed some alone time to untangle the mess of her emotions.

Gabriel gritted his teeth as she stalked across the room, her pretty lips held in a straight line as though she were biting her tongue to prevent an outburst. Good. He couldn't afford for her to charge him again. Especially now that he knew exactly what a mere brush of her hand could do to his control.

He walked over to the drinks table and poured himself some wine. That or touch her, which would be a really dumb-ass move. The look in her eyes made him wonder what sex with Eden sprawled on his desk would be like. Unforgettable.

He allowed himself a nanosecond of lunacy, imagining burying his face in the fragrance of her neck, her legs wrapped around his hips as he pushed in deep. He closed his eyes, forcing himself to tamp down the smoldering hunger before he opened them again.

She might not be talking, but she had an entire vocabulary of expressions. Those large brown orbs shot a dangerous message as she kept him in her crosshairs. He figured he was better off thinking about the mundane than trying to analyze the look she was giving him as those sexy high heels ate up the carpet by the yard.

As much as he'd enjoy seeing her walking around in nothing but her sexy shoes, it wasn't practical. But he'd like to see her dressed in something other than baggy jeans and the T-shirts she wore like a uniform. The jeans only hinted at the curve of her bottom. Despite the looseness of the fabric he'd memorized the shape and texture of her ass.

He noticed a fine tremor in his hands, and rested them on the back of the chair in front of him, digging his fingers into the butter-soft leather to keep from grabbing her as she passed. Jesus. He'd lost his frigging mind.

He'd hurt her. Hell. He felt like a fucking bull in a china shop with all these unfamiliar emotions fighting for supremacy inside him.

How the hell could he want her again? Just the fact that he'd been capable of getting it up as many times as he had in the last several hours should be grounds for celebration. Or a fucking casket. It was bad enough that he was addicted to her sexually. But now that he had slept with her, the fires of sexual hunger were being fed by something more insidious.

He firmly pushed *those* thoughts aside before they could take root. Sex was merely physical. No matter how powerful, he could deal with those urges.

Eventually he'd get his fill.

Eventually she'd be gone.

Eventually.

But for now he had to admit, if only to himself, he was obsessed by Eden Cahill.

For the duration he *had* to keep his hands off her.

No more slipups.

But, God help him, he couldn't tear his eyes off her. He should probably say something. But he knew whatever he said now would make the situation worse. So he looked his fill as she walked away, and kept his mouth shut.

Every time he thought of her as no more than an object of his desire, she surprised him. He knew she was brilliant, tops in her field by miles, but together with that first-class brain was a measure of street smarts that an academic such as herself usually lacked. Behind those Bambi brown eyes was a woman who knew her own self-worth. A woman who enjoyed her own sensuality. A woman who didn't take herself, or her accomplishments, too seriously.

A woman with a sense of humor, and a quick temper.

Keep it simple, he reminded himself. The good old KISS principle. Keep It Simple Stupid.

Don't think of her as likable, Gabriel warned himself. Don't think of her as a woman.

Think of her as a walking brain.

Unfortunately the thought was so ludicrous, especially under the circumstances, that he wanted to hit his head against a nice solid wall to knock some sense into himself.

She opened the door, and turned. "I'm going to my room," she said quietly. "You know where to find me if you need me."

Needing her was the whole fucking point, Gabriel thought savagely, not bothering with a verbal response. His blood continued racing, zinging through his veins even after the door closed quietly behind her. The slam was implied.

Hell, he'd had to put the length of the room between them to prevent himself from grabbing her and yanking down those jeans to cup her bottom in both hands. Again. It was an effort to wrench his mind away from the image of Eden naked.

If it had been difficult to keep his hands off her before sleeping with her, now the situation was intensified a hundredfold.

Putting aside the wine he hadn't even tasted, he moved to the table where MacBain always left a tray of drinks and poured himself several fingers of whiskey from the heavy Stuart crystal decanter. Feeling like a caged panther, he paced the room, glass in hand.

Frustrated, antsy. Christ. Scared shitless.

The only two people in the world who could possibly understand what he was going through were his brothers. But Duncan was on an op in the Middle East and unreachable, and Gabriel had no clue where his middle brother was. Caleb had been MIA for several weeks.

Not unusual in their line of work, but Gabriel felt a powerful need to contact both men. He had to forewarn his brothers how strong the attraction to their Lifemate was. Forewarned was forearmed.

Every evasive technique the three of them had come up with over the years was laughable in the face of the strength of the attraction he felt for Eden. Even the word attraction was too mild for the deep-seated hunger clawing at his gut. And for the first time, he understood the ramifications of the Curse.

He got it.

Intellectually, he'd always thought avoiding any woman he could possibly feel anything for, other than sexual, would be a simple issue of mind over matter. Choose not to give in to the attraction. Seemed simple, in theory. That was until now. Until Eden.

He hadn't been capable of evading her; he hadn't been strong enough, wily enough, or resolute enough to keep his hands off her.

That old crone Fate was laughing her ass off at this, Gabriel thought, swigging down the last of his drink, then going back for another. *Laughing her ass off and rubbing her hands with glee.* Because, God help him, not only did he sexually crave Eden Cahill. He was starting to *like* her.

He was screwed. It was bad enough to be attracted to a woman you couldn't have. But that wasn't her only temptation. In a short time, he'd developed a long list of attributes to admire. He found her commitment to her work admirable. Her humor charming. She was thoughtful as well as insightful. Intelligent and smart.

Dangerous and deadly. At least to him.

Worse, he realized they'd made love a dozen times, shared the fire of dozens of climaxes together. *And he still hadn't retrieved the data he needed.*

So now he knew.

When Eden lost control, so did he.

He had to get his libido in check before she returned in a few minutes. He'd heard MacBain opening the front door, followed by the soft susurrus of voices. Dixon had arrived.

The door to the library opened and Sebastian walked in. Alone. He closed the heavy door behind him. "Not that you aren't welcome," Gabriel said flatly, ridiculously disappointed that Eden wasn't with him. "But what are you doing here? I was expecting Special Agent Dixon from Homeland Security."

"He's waiting outside." Sebastian Tremayne walked to the drinks table and grabbed a soda. He pulled the tab, but didn't drink. "We have a situation."

Gabriel motioned to a chair and the men sat opposite each other. "What kind of situation?" Gabriel demanded. "Eden is safe here, I told you—"

"Not the hot doctor." Drink forgotten, Tremayne leaned forward. "Gabriel, Thom Lindley was killed in the early hours this morning. There was barely enough of the body to ID. What the hell does that mean?"

Lindley was another wizard who worked for T-FLAC/psi. Gabriel felt the words land like a sucker punch. "It means I lost a friend."

The small hairs on the back of his neck rose in warning. This was one of the contributing factors to his feeling of unease for the last several weeks. "It also means that there's a rogue wizard out there."

His friend straightened. "Why would you presume that? Lindley was in Barcelona undercover—"

"He's the third of my kind killed in the past month." Gabriel rose and strode over to the phone. Picking up the receiver, he punched in a three-digit number, holding up a hand to halt Sebastian's questions.

"Edge, Gabriel," he said when the phone was answered on the first ring. "Where's Caleb?" He listened with a frown. "Bullshit. He *never* takes vacations. Find him. And have Duncan contact me ASAP. When you've contacted both my brothers, get Stone in Prague." Gabriel glanced at his watch: 1900 hours. "Tell him to be ready for teleportation at 2030. Then convene an emergency, psi/spec ops meeting. Levels one and two only. Here within the hour. No one is excused. I repeat. *No one.*"

"Christ, Edge," Tremayne said when Gabriel replaced the receiver. "You're scaring the shit out of me. What the hell's going on?"

Gabriel crossed the room, looking, he was sure, as grim as he felt. "If the killer is another wizard, he's capable of assimilating the powers of those he's eliminating."

Instead of resuming his seat, Gabriel picked up his glass and started to pace. "We have the potential for some seriously bad shit going down. You've never encountered anything as fucking terrifying as a wizard gone bad." Neither had he. Gabriel had only heard stories. If a tenth of what he'd heard was possible—Jesus.

Out of his element with this kind of danger, Sebastian rose. "What do we do?" He was filling in as control on the robot op while Alexander Stone was in Prague at the antiterrorist summit. Gabriel could sympathize with his friend feeling discombobulated. Thanks to Eden, he knew the feeling well.

He paused, aware by the rapidity of his heartbeat that Eden was approaching. Fear tasted metallic on his tongue. "You want to know what we should do?" he repeated hoarsely as the handle turned on the door across the room. "Anything, *everything* we can, to stop him."

Fucking hell. This new development was going to have to take precedence over the situation with the new group of terrorists having the bot. A rogue wizard on the loose would have far-reaching effects.

But Jesus, so would the bot in the wrong hands.

Both situations were critical.

At least Eden is safe under my roof.

Or, God help them, was the castle the most dangerous place of all? Gabriel wondered with a sense of dread.

The door opened to admit a tall, angular man with military short, graying hair and wearing a badly cut black suit that screamed Fed. He closed the door firmly behind him and walked into the center of the room.

The older man glanced between Gabriel and Tremayne. "Mr. Edge?" At Gabriel's nod, the man stepped forward. He did not extend a hand, and neither did Gabriel; instead, he slid his hand into his inside pocket and withdrew a leather folder. "Walter Dixon, Department of Homeland Security. My credentials." He flipped open the brown leather wallet to display his official shield.

"Your—butler?—has gone to find Dr. Cahill." He glanced briefly at Sebastian. "May I talk freely?"

"Go ahead," Gabriel leaned against the drinks table, not offering the older man either a drink or a chair. This wasn't a social gathering. A T-FLAC jet had brought him directly from Tempe, where he was still investigating the theft of the robot, to a nearby landing strip in short order. Eden needed to talk to someone she trusted. Because he'd interviewed her half a dozen times, Walter Dixon was that man.

There was something about Dixon Gabriel didn't quite like, but he couldn't put his finger on it. Dixon was a typical agent type, bland and unremarkable. Nothing suspect about his behavior in any way. The knife-ironed crease in his pants broke over highly polished black wingtips. His nails were clean and neatly trimmed, his hair short. He smelled slightly of sweat and licorice. So the man was human and had a sweet tooth. Neither was a punishable offense.

He searched Dixon's pale blue eyes, but all he saw was average intelligence, and a dronelike disinterest in the opulent surroundings. But Gabriel trusted his own instincts, and if he didn't like Dixon, eventually he'd know why.

"Anything new on the murder and the theft?" he asked, knowing that T-FLAC would have any solid evidence long before any government agency.

"No, sir. Not yet. But we are hopeful that we will have something very soon."

Yeah, right. "The reason we requested your presence here," Gabriel said easily, "was to allay Dr. Cahill's misgivings about giving T-FLAC all the relevant data to build a second Rx793 robot. Once you've done that I'll have you back on a return flight to resume your investigation in Arizona."

Returning his ID to an inside pocket, Dixon frowned. "Why does T-FLAC want to duplicate Dr. Cahill's robot? We imagine that the prototype is now on the open market. What good will producing yet another do to help that situation? Can it be trained to search for its predecessor? I'm not sure I understand the logic, Mr. Edge. And frankly, I'm not sure I approve of duplicating the Rx793, even if that were possible.

"As I'm sure you are aware, all of Dr. Cahill's notes were taken the night Dr. Kirchner was killed. Are you saying she has access to some of that data now? That she can indeed rebuild the robot from memory?"

"I'm not saying that at all," Gabriel answered easily, sensing her approach although he couldn't hear the tapping of her high heels on the stone floor out in the hallway yet. He imagined her halfway across the entry hall as his heart did calisthenics.

"It's not for you to approve or disapprove," he informed Dixon. "Your sole function here is to dispel any doubts Dr. Cahill might have as to the function and validity of T-FLAC."

"I think I should take the young lady back to Arizona and put her into protective custody, as I've suggested to her before."

What had kept Eden safe in Tempe, Gabriel thought savagely, was *his* safety spell. "She is in protective custody," he said smoothly, pushing himself away from the table. *"Mine."*

He crossed the room, and opened the door just as Eden and MacBain arrived on the other side. He gave her a cool glance. "Come in."

She didn't look happy to see him.

CHAPTER FOURTEEN

The short length of time since she'd left this room had been just long enough for Eden to get a grip on her temper. She didn't object to *losing* her temper. She'd always been good at debate and found a good argument exhilarating. Unfortunately, her loss of temper usually coincided with those blasted tears. And she'd sacrifice the joy of arguing with Gabriel if it meant that she didn't have to show him any vulnerability whatsoever.

She had a feeling he'd see vulnerability as weakness. And while she might be many things, weak wasn't one of them. Gabriel Edge was going to learn that she was no pushover.

No matter how incredible the sex might be.

As soon as she walked into the room he retreated behind a sofa table. She smiled at Special Agent Dixon, extending her hand as he met her halfway. "Thank you for coming on such short notice."

Shaking her hand a little too firmly, he made eye contact, and said meaningfully, "I'm glad you had the foresight to ask for me, Dr. Cahill."

Eden was relieved to see his familiar face. He looked exactly like a government agent was supposed to look. Safe, bland, and unobtrusive. Even if he hadn't been a good fifteen years past the prime of his fitness, he didn't have a chance at being noticed. Not when he was flanked by Gabriel and Sebastian. Gabriel dwarfed him with more than mere size. It was in his attitude; the way Gabriel carried himself practically dripped confidence and assertiveness. Dixon, well, he seemed like a guy hovering right at the midpoint on the success scale.

"I can't tell you how relieved I was when I got the call from Mr. Edge," Dixon said flatly, still holding her gaze. "We've been looking for you since you—ran off yesterday."

"I didn't run exactly." Eden said dryly.

Dixon smoothed the thinning strands of his gray hair back into place in a vaguely familiar gesture. "Mr. Edge explained your concern about the advanced capabilities of the robot, and that he convinced you to—"

"Hold that thought, Agent," Eden said, her eyes locking with Gabriel's. "Mr. Edge, may I have a word with you, please?" She pointed toward the massive wooden doors. "Outside?"

Brushing past the Homeland Security agent, she walked to the door and impatiently waited for Gabriel to step out into the hallway. "You told him that I withheld information on Rex?" she demanded.

"I told him nothing of the sort. He's fishing," Gabriel said almost absently, his expression dark and unreadable. For a moment, Eden saw something. Distraction? Knowing that she didn't have his full attention, especially on something this important, sent a flash of anger through her.

"I won't give you any more information unless, and until, I'm convinced you are who and what you say you are. That doesn't include you coaching Dixon before I have a chance to ask the first question."

"I didn't coach him, I made his flight arrangements." Gabriel glanced down at his watch. "Something's come up. I've got a meeting in about forty-five minutes. Ask Dixon whatever it is you need to ask so we can get on with the mental extraction and get this over with."

Eden shivered. Mental extraction might be run-of-the-mill to Mr. Wizard, but it sounded like a pretty big violation from her vantage point. She tilted her head back in order to look directly into his smoky eyes. The determination was ever-present, but there was more.

New layers hinted at concern, no, it was more than concern darkening his eyes to ink. Her heartbeat skipped. Something ominous spiced the air in an almost tangible way around him. The unspoken danger made the hair on the back of Eden's neck stir.

She put a hand on his forearm. He felt warm and solid. It would have been comforting if he'd put his arm around her. But she didn't suggest it. Just the fact that he didn't move out of reach helped. "Did you hear something about Rex? Has something bad happened?" She used the term "bad" loosely. It covered a multiple of possible sins.

"No, why?" Something in his expressionless face sent a shiver down Eden's spine.

"You look *strange*." She dropped her hand from his arm, because while he hadn't shaken it off, he wasn't exactly encouraging her touch either. She wrapped her arms around herself. "Something's happened, I sense it."

His lips curved. "The powers don't rub off, Eden."

"Not sense as in *supernatural,* I just meant I can tell by your expression that *something's* happened. What?"

"I'm not sure yet. Hence, the meeting. A very important meeting, so could you move this little Nancy Drew thing of yours along?" He started to go back into the library.

"No." She reached out to grab his arm, but he moved quickly to avoid her touch this time. It was a neat, if damned annoying trick. She wished his physical rejection didn't hurt as much as it did. "Not with you in there with us."

Gabriel gave her a mild look. "What do you think I'm going to do? Turn him into a frog?"

"Could you?" she asked, distracted by the notion for a second. "Never mind. I want him to speak freely with me about you. In my experience, people often couch their remarks differently when said subject is looming large a few feet away."

"You have an incredible ability to overcomplicate things. Know that?"

She smiled sweetly. "So I've been told. Humor me, Gabriel. Summon MacBain, please."

"I don't have a lot of time. Definitely not enough to serve high tea to a Feeb. I'll have MacBain make up a picnic basket for the agent. He can take it with him when he leaves."

"I'm not asking either of you to cater my chat with Dixon. I simply want MacBain—whom I trust—to stand watch over you, right here, while I speak with the agent. In private."

"You trust MacBain and not me?" he asked, one dark brow arched for emphasis.

"Yes. MacBain didn't kidnap me. MacBain didn't lock me inside this castle. MacBain didn't—"

"Get to hear those soft little moans you make when you come."

Startled, she took a deep, calming breath. "True, but irrelevant."

She reached out her hand to see how fast he could move. Pretty damn fast, she thought with a glimmer of amusement as he stepped out of reach once again. If she didn't laugh at the absurdity of it, she'd cry.

She knew he wanted her with a hunger as powerful as her own. Why he was resisting her touch now, Eden had no idea.

She exhaled. He couldn't be any plainer about his feelings if he'd rented a sky writer to make his point.

Eden told herself she wasn't in the least little bit disappointed. If feeling as though she'd fallen out of the sky writing plane, *onto her head,* wasn't disappointment. *Idiot.*

"I want you out here, with MacBain at your side while I speak to the agent. Making Rex was foolish and now he's in the wrong hands. I'm not about to fork over instructions to build another one without being completely sure that I can trust you."

Gabriel flicked his fingers and suddenly MacBain was standing in the hallway. He seemed more annoyed than surprised, letting out a loud, disgusted breath as he kept the paring knife poised above the partially carved radish in his other hand.

"Och! What is it ye want now?" he said irritably. "As ye can verra well see, I was in the midst of preparin' a garnish for the canapés. Be a good lad and send me back to the kitchen so I can finish my chores, aye?"

"Sorry, old man, she wants you here."

MacBain turned to Eden. "Do ye have a special request then, Dr. Cahill?"

"Watch him," Eden told him. "Every second."

"Aye. Watch him do what, precisely?"

"Stay right here," Eden pointed to the floor at Gabriel's feet. "I don't want him moving from this spot. Not an inch, not a millimeter. Not an eyelash."

"As ye wish."

"Dr. Cahill?" Dixon called from inside the library.

"Coming," Eden called back, holding MacBain's eyes. "Promise?"

"It will be as if he was glued to the floor, Doctor. Go on about yer business with a clear mind."

Eden knew that wasn't damned likely. Not when she had to tell Homeland Security that she'd been less than honest with them ever since Theo's murder. Oh, yeah, and there was the whole thing about Rex and his capabilities.

She walked back into the library. Sebastian Tremayne was looming over Agent Dixon. "Your presence is requested outside. Close the door firmly on your way out."

Gabriel's friend had very expressive eyebrows, Eden decided as he passed her. "Yes, ma'am," he said dryly. The door closed quietly behind him.

Dixon was running his fingers along the leather volumes lining the library walls. "Impressive collection," he murmured, turning and offering a forced smile.

Indicating a chair, she sat on the end of one of the sofas, waiting until he was seated across from her to begin. Where to start? Lies or robot? Too bad there wasn't a column C among the options.

In the end, she simply decided to suck in a deep breath, and let it all spill out at once. She told him about Rex. About how the robot was indestructible, capable of reasoning, and with the right programming adjustments, the reasoning could include the logical extermination of the human race. Rex had everything in the way of artificial intelligence, advanced sequential reasoning, anticipated optional response, everything any machine would need to respond to any emergency or situation. Everything but humanity.

"While Rex can't factor empathy or redemption into his circuitry," Eden told him, "the right tweak in his memory board could make him the perfect weapon for terrorists. A fearless, conscienceless, indestructible killing machine able to deliver on a massive scale."

Dixon's expression was carefully neutral. "You speak of it as one would a child, Dr. Cahill."

"I worked on Rex for six years, Agent. It's impossible *not* to anthropomorphize something that was such a big part of my life."

"Is that why you made the robot indestructible?"

Eden gave him a startled look. Had she done so subconsciously? Had she wanted Rex in some way to be the one constant in her life? The child she'd never have? Had she, at some point, given up on the idea of ever finding someone to share her life with? God. That was pathetic.

"No," she told him, not sure of anything at the moment. "We manufactured it that way so it could do its job. It cost millions of dollars to fabricate each unit. Having it destruct every time it performed its function wouldn't be cost-effective. There is one way Re—the Rx793 can be destroyed."

Dixon looked surprised. "There is? How?"

"Another bot."

He frowned. "I thought you said the lab was destroyed. Hard drives wiped. Schematics stolen or destroyed."

"True. But that's where Gabriel Edge comes in."

Dixon rose, then started to pace in the small area between the chair and the sofa. "I'm glad he contacted us." He bent to pick up the heavy Bible Gabriel had left on the coffee table. "So was Mr. Verdine."

As he talked he flipped through the pages. He glanced up to find her watching him, and the look in his . . . the *unpleasant* look he gave her made the little hairs on the back of Eden's neck stand up. Why, she couldn't say. He had never given her the willies before.

She'd just told him that there was a way to destroy the bot. Yet he'd segued off the subject without turning a hair. She tried to read his expression. But he had the same knack Gabriel did of keeping his features expressionless. A little shiver skittered across her nerve endings. A goose walking over her grave, as Grandma Rose used to say.

"He's been worried about you," he told her, glancing down as he turned a page. "He went so far as to offer to pay any ransom demanded just to get you back." This time when he looked up at her, Eden knew she'd imagined that look. He was a government agent, with no personal agenda.

Because of the circumstances she was reading things that weren't there.

It was flattering to know that a man like Jason Verdine was willing to use his personal finances to secure her safe return. Okay. Not exactly her safe return. The safe return of her brain and skills. Still—"Tell him thank you for me."

"Tell him yourself," Dixon insisted. "I'm taking you back to Tempe with me."

"It isn't that easy. To repeat what I told you a minute ago. There *is* no way, no *thing*, no device that can destroy this robot. Nothing. If what everyone suspects is true, and terrorists do have Rex, then I have to build another robot with even better capabilities and strengths. And *this* time I'll include a self-destruct device so that once the new bot destroys the first we never have this situation again. Like against like. It's the *only* way to destroy it."

Dixon tossed the heavy Bible down on the coffee table with a thump loud enough to make her wince. "All the more reason to get you back to Tempe as quickly as possible."

Eden shook her head. "I'll do it here. There's a state-of-the-art lab upstairs, and frankly, having Gabriel Edge, and T-FLAC, here to protect me will be considerably safer than going back to a lab that has already been broken into." *Twice.*

"T-FLAC?" Dixon said blankly. "I'm sorry. I'm not familiar with—Is that part of the robot you made?"

Okay. This was wrong. *He* was wrong.

Eden stood. Too fast, apparently, since it made her a little lightheaded. She braced a hand on the arm of the sofa. "*T-FLAC.* I don't remember what it stands for, but Gabriel said you'd know them. Know the group he works for. They do," she paused to swallow, hoping that might alleviate the persistent buzz ringing in her ears. It didn't, and she hurriedly sat down again hoping to hell she wasn't going to pass out.

She moistened her lips. "They're a counterterrorist organization. They're on our side."

Special Agent Dixon gave her a worried look. "Never heard of them, and my dear, if such an organization existed, I can assure you I would know. There is no T-FLAC," he told her. "Look, this Edge guy is well known to us. He's certifiable, Dr. Cahill. Delusional. We've got a file two inches thick on him. He claims to be everything from a master swordsman to a wizard."

The room wasn't spinning so much as it was melting. Eden tried to hold her focus, but it seemed as if she were looking at the world through the bottom of a glass. "He . . . he can . . . be per . . . persuasive."

"That's too bad," Dixon said, his voice suddenly harsh. "I had hoped you wouldn't fall under his spell, but since you have, I'm left with no other alternative."

Than what, she tried to ask as Dixon floated over to her. She flinched as he stroked his fingers almost lovingly up her throat, then leisurely wrapped both hands around her neck. He squeezed, and at the same time pulled her to her feet. God, he was strong. She wanted to fight him, but her body felt incredibly heavy and frighteningly unresponsive.

Gabriel?! Get in here!

Their eyes met as Dixon supported her entire body by his chokehold on her throat. He was mad. Insane. God . . . determined. He held her so tightly that her ears buzzed and her vision went black in undulating waves of darkness.

Gabriel.

"I can't allow you to replicate or destroy the bot, Dr. Cahill," he told her harshly. "Your prototype is already in production."

"No!" She tried to claw at his wrists as his fingers tightened inexorably against her windpipe. Black and silver dots danced sickeningly in her vision and she felt her consciousness drain out of her body.

"You should have died that night with Dr. Kirchner, Eden. Your research should have died with you." His thumbs pressed down hard. She gagged, struggling to drag in a sip of air. "Supply and demand, babe. Supply and demand. Now I'm in control of both."

With her last bit of strength Eden flattened her palms against his chest, tried to push him away.

Her hands went right through him.

"What the hell? Did you hear—" Gabriel slammed open the library doors from ten feet away. They crashed against the inside wall as he burst into the room, Tremayne and MacBain hard on his heels.

He'd heard Eden shout his name.

Heard her inside his head.

He looked around the well-lit room.

Jesus. Empty.

Not possible. He'd cast a protective spell around Eden, *and* sealed all the windows and doors just as a precaution. *Nobody* could have gotten in or out without him knowing it.

"Nobody here," Sebastian said, puzzled.

Gabriel pointed across the room at the faint glimmer of two figures entwined over near the sofa. They were little more than a transparent shimmer.

Eden's feet were dangling a foot off the floor as Dixon, his hands wrapped about her throat, strangled her limp form.

Gabriel's heart slammed into his throat, and for a

nanosecond fear held him immobile. Then fourteen years of T-FLAC training kicked in.

Channeling his anger, he released a powerful electrical current from his fingertips. No warning. No shouts. Just let the son of a bitch have it with all he had.

Jagged shards of lightning-like energy, icy green and serrated, shot from his hands toward the opaque figures. The energy stream hit hard, slamming into the man from the side and making him stagger. He screamed a curse, jerking with the impact from the next bolt, and the next.

"Let her go," Gabriel snarled, advancing even as he fired off yet another salvo. His aim was dead on target, and the man screamed as each flash hit him in the head.

Gabriel wasn't dicking around.

The image was now as faint as a memory.

Fucking bastard was going to shimmer her out. God—

Between one heartbeat and the next Gabriel shimmered between Eden and Dixon, transformed just his right arm to that of a panther, and raked razor sharp claws down Dixon's face.

Without fanfare the man disappeared.

Gabriel spun around, just in time to catch Eden as she rematerialized and fell into his arms.

"Tremayne."

When Sebastian came to his side Gabriel reluctantly handed Eden to him. "Check her out. MacBain?"

"Aye. We have her. Go."

Everything in him wanted to stay to make sure that Eden was unharmed. But neither Tremayne nor MacBain were capable of dealing with this kind of intruder. The fact that a wizard had managed to pierce the shield Gabriel had erected over Eden and the castle was cause for grave concern. He did a lightning-fast recon of every room, every floor of the castle. All one hundred and ninety-five thousand square feet, in under five minutes.

Nothing.

No sign. No residue. No hint that a powerful wizard had been inside Edridge Castle at all.

Returning to the library he saw that the two men had placed Eden on one of the sofas and covered her with a light throw.

Sebastian looked up. "Anything?"

"Not a damn thing." Gabriel had eyes for no one but Eden. "How is she?" He strode across the room, then dropped to one knee beside her to press two fingers to the pulse at her throat. Thready and weak, but there. With his touch her heart rate immediately sped up.

"Better with you around, apparently," Sebastian said from his position sitting on the coffee table facing Eden. "Look at that, you touch her and her cheeks pinked up. Cool trick." He rose. "I'll go make some calls at HQ."

"Yeah. Do that."

"I took the liberty of placing a container on the floor just in case, aye?" MacBain moved out of the way for Tremayne as he left the room. "The lass doesna fare well with reentry."

Gabriel glanced at his watch. She'd been unconscious for a good five minutes. He tapped her cheek lightly. "Wake up, sweetheart. Did she need it?" he asked MacBain. The sensation in his chest was so unfamiliar that for a moment he thought he might be experiencing a heart attack.

It was fear.

A fear that had almost debilitated him earlier.

Not fear for himself. Fear for Eden.

"No, no' yet at any rate. She hasna opened her wee eyes. Something's no' right aboot this havy-cavy business, ye mark my words."

An understatement.

Gabriel peeled aside the throw, and carefully ran his hands over her body to check for injuries. Thank God there didn't appear to be any. He undid the top button on her jeans and eased the zipper down a few inches, then pulled the soft velvet blanket back over her.

"Yer protection spell hasna failed before, has it now?"

It worried the hell out of him that he hadn't felt the presence of the other wizard. And he *should* have. Even the weakest, most inexperienced wizard emitted an energy. Yet he'd felt *nothing*. Not even so much as a damn, fucking glimmer.

"Clearly he's more powerful," Gabriel said grimly, resting his hand on the steady beat of Eden's heart, and willing her to open her eyes. Who was this wizard, and where the hell had he come from? More important right now—why had he tried to take Eden? Or had his intention been to kill her? Or had she just presented the easiest target? Not knowing scared the shit out of him.

"That isna the only reason the spell didna work, aye?"

"He couldn't have bypassed my spell if he wasn't stronger."

MacBain came to stand beside him, and cleared his throat. " 'When a Lifemate is chosen by the heart of a son. No protection can be given, again I have wo—' "

The tight clench in Gabriel's chest intensified. Christ. This was all he needed to complicate things, he thought, wishing he could stick his damn fingers in his ears as he'd done as a kid, and sing lalalala so he couldn't hear MacPain in the ass's theory. "She is *not* my Lifemate."

"Deny it all ye want, lad. It is what it is."

"I haven't even known her a week."

"Aye. Sometimes that's all the time a heart needs."

"I am not in love with the woman, MacPain. Remember that."

"Aye, I'll no' forget," The old man said, droll as always. "I'll be marking the date and time in me diary."

"Don't you have something better to do than breathe down my neck?"

MacBain held up the paring knife and radish, and cocked a hairy white brow.

Eden let out a raspy, painful cough as she came to, and all Gabriel's attention was on her. Her lashes fluttered, then slowly opened, revealing scared, teary, chocolate-colored eyes. "W-what?"

Her fingers curled around his, trusting as a child's. "Don't try to talk," he told her gruffly.

She struggled to get herself up onto her elbows. He should have expected it. The woman had a steely spirit and indomitable determination.

Seeing the red and purple bruises blooming around her throat flooded him with renewed anger. The anger and the fear he was feeling, particularly combined as they were, were something new to him.

He, goddamn it, didn't like the feeling one fucking little bit. Too bad he'd dispatched the wizard so quickly. He would have preferred to explode him bit by painful bit. Preferably with Eden a thousand miles away.

"W-why did Dixon try to kill me?" she croaked, bringing her hand up to her throat. The phone rang and MacBain shuffled over to answer it. "I think he used a topical paralytic on me," she said faintly.

Gabriel gave her a startled look. "Why do you think that?"

"He had to have drugged me or something. One minute we were talking, then everything suddenly got fuzzy and he was strangling me. What the hell was that about?"

"Because it wasna Dixon," MacBain announced. "That was control on the phone. Dixon was in an automobile accident on his way to Sky Harbor Airport in

Tempe. He was pronounced dead an hour ago. A bad business, this," he scowled. "Can I go back to me kitchen now yer back?"

"Yeah." Gabriel absently teleported the old man and his radish back to the kitchen.

"God, it creeps me out when you do that." Eden gingerly rubbed her neck, then frowned. "I've met Special Agent Dixon several times. That was him in here with me. I'm sure of it."

"No," he said on an expelled breath. "I think we have a morpher." A skill only one man he knew about was capable of. That man had been killed in Spain this morning.

"A what?"

"Morpher," Gabriel repeated. "Some wizards can morph. They borrow a body or an identity. It's rare, but it's been known to happen."

"You can do that."

"Animal only. A morpher can replicate *someone*. Borrow a body or identity." He frowned. "I know of only one person with that skill."

"Good. Then you know who this guy is."

"Lindley was killed this morning."

"God. Do you have any idea how freaking *preposterous* that *sounds*? And the fact that I'm lying here, *talking* about it quite normally is—Never mind. Why would he want to kill me?"

A damn good question. And one Gabriel wanted his own answers to. "What did the two of you talk about?"

"Can I have some of that water?" she asked, and he handed her a half-filled glass sitting on the coffee table, then waited while she drained it. She handed him the empty glass. "Thanks.

"He mentioned that Jason Verdine was offering a ransom for my safe return. Then I told him about Rex and what it's capable of doing. I mentioned that I was considering building another one for you as a way to make amends for building Rex in the first place. I asked about you. About T-FLAC."

"And?"

"He said T-FLAC wasn't real. Oh, yeah—and he mentioned you were a nut job, which frankly didn't surprise me much." She shot him a small smile, a smile that in no way mitigated the fear in her eyes. She shivered. "Then I got kind of in and out invisible. And then the son of a bitch *choked* me."

He watched her with brooding eyes and an intensity that he could tell made her even more nervous than she was already. He couldn't help it. He could smell the fear on her, mixed with flowers. An untenable combination, he thought, feeling feral. Rabid.

Her eyes seemed bigger, darker in the paleness of her face. He observed the bruises on her pale, slender throat. A pale slender throat that, if he'd been a second later, would be snapped like a twig right now. He might never have known if she was alive or dead if the wizard had managed to teleport her before he'd come into the room.

In the space of a breath he felt another surge of rage. And fear. Bone deep, primordial terror.

The protective spell he'd placed on her, the one that had protected her so far, suddenly wasn't working. Why the hell not? Was the other wizard so powerful that such a strong protective spell was no deterrent?

He dismissed MacBain's theory out of hand. Falling in love was out of the question. He and his brothers had agreed to avoid *that* affliction years ago.

"For the foreseeable future," Gabriel told her tightly, "I don't want you out of my sight." His tone was grim and implacable. "Understand?"

"Of course I understand," Eden said in the same tone he was using. "You're speaking English."

"Because," he said tightly, as if she'd asked, "the man who was here was sent to kill you."

She shivered. "He almost succeeded."

"He's not going to get that close again."

He saw in her big brown eyes the fear of rejection. The anticipation of wondering if she reached out for him, if he'd stay where he was, or back away even more. "I'm very happy to hear that," she told him.

Turmoil mixed with the fear in her eyes as she watched him. Then the bravado leaked out of her voice. "I'm sorry you were scared," she said softly, reaching up to cup his jaw.

Gabriel lifted his hand to cover hers, pressing her cool fingers against his face. "I wasn't *scared*, I was furious . . . Yeah, okay. Furious *and* terrified." He closed his eyes, struggling for the first time in his life to put intense, very personal emotions in a place where he could analyze and deal with them in a sane, rational way.

The need. The urge. The fucking *urgency* to take her in his arms and hold her tightly. To run his hands over every delectable inch of her body to check for any injury—made him ache. Screw his vow to himself that he wouldn't touch her again.

He wrapped his arms around her, pulling her close, and her arms immediately slid around his waist. "I wasn't the one attacked," he said roughly against her hair, inhaling her sweet familiar floral fragrance as he held her gently against him.

He should be able to protect her. Damn it to hell, he'd believed that he could. Knowing how close he'd been to losing her made all his internal organs cramp, and his heart feel like a small hard rock in his chest.

After a few moments he moved her away from him, feeling the loss of her body's warmth like a rip in his soul.

His eyes raked her face and throat. That goddamned

son of a bitch had left bruises on her creamy skin. "Show me where it hurts." Between one breath and the next more undiluted rage flared. This time rage at himself. She'd been seconds from death while he stood right outside the fucking door.

Eden tilted her head so he could see her neck better. "I'm not sure I want a man quite so murderous-looking checking my injuries. It wasn't my fault, you know."

Teeth gritted, Gabriel ran his palm lightly up her throat again, aware of every part of her as he checked the darkening bruises with meticulous care, wishing his touch could make the marks, and the memory of her attack, disappear. He wasn't that good.

There were no cuts and scrapes, no blood—thank God. "Of course it wasn't. It was mine." She was close enough for him to taste the terror on her lips, but he resisted the urge.

"You thought he was Dixon."

He touched her hair lightly, noticing that his hand shook. He rose to his feet, his gut mirroring the disappointment he saw in her eyes. He wanted to crush her to him and shimmer them back upstairs. He wished like hell he had his brother Caleb's skill for manipulating time. He'd go back . . . to when? An hour ago? Yesterday? Before he met Dr. Eden Cahill?

Would he have felt complete never having known her? He didn't think so.

"I should have known better."

"I don't know how."

"You're still shaking. I'll get you a drink. Whiskey?"

"I don't want a drink, Gabriel." Her dark eyes were somber. "I was terrified, but thank God you came in, just in the nick of time. All I want right now is for you to hold me in your arms again. Can you do that?"

He shook his head regretfully. Wanting it as badly as Eden did. "Can you get up?"

"If I have to."

"I have to take a meeting, and much as I don't want you here, here is where you have to be."

She sat up on her elbow. "A meeting about Rex?"

"No. Something a hell of a lot *worse*."

CHAPTER FIFTEEN

Eden couldn't imagine what could be worse than releasing Rex on the world. She huddled under the luxurious lightweight throw and tried to lip-read as Gabriel and Sebastian talked across the room. It was a skill she'd never cultivated. For all she knew they could be speaking Martian, or perhaps wizards had a secret language all their own.

Walter Dixon had made a wizard believer out of her. *Big time,* she thought, hand protectively held over her sore throat. As a scientist she knew one didn't have to see something to know it existed. Whoever, *whatever* had tried to strangle her had not only existed. It had been pure evil.

"Well, well, well. And who is *this* tasty morsel?" A man said meditatively, appearing three feet from the sofa where Eden lay. One moment there'd been nothing between herself and the two men quietly talking across the room, and now there was a skinny stick of a guy leering at her. His skin was as tanned and weathered as old leather. He wore skintight, worn blue jeans, cowboy boots, and a pearl-buttoned plaid shirt. He was all of five feet tall, even in his heeled boots, and could've been anywhere between thirty and sixty.

"Fitzgerald." Gabriel said by way of greeting. "Pretend she's a piece of furniture."

Raisin eyes glittered as the man looked down at her.

Pushing a straw Stetson off his forehead, he drawled, "A bed?"

"Of thorns," Eden told him sweetly, sitting up.

The man laughed. "Oh, doll-face, I surely hope you're the problem I've come to solve." He held out his hand. "Upton Fitzgerald at your service. How may I be of assist—Shit! Do you *mind*?!" He grumbled as a girl materialized practically in the same spot where he was standing.

The young woman sported an astonishing assortment of face piercings, Eden noticed, and seemed unperturbed at landing almost on top of Fitzgerald. She shot him a mild look from beneath spiked black and fuchsia bangs and half a dozen silver rings in each eyebrow. "Need to move your pointed little ass faster, Uppie, baby."

"Lark Orela. You give wizards a bad name, you really do. Please tell me you didn't come by broom?"

"Nah, flew my Dirt Devil," The young woman gave Eden a curious glance. "Who's she?"

"She," Eden said mildly, "is Dr. Eden Cahill. A guest of Gabriel's." She wasn't sure if the extremely Goth-looking individual had really flown in on a vacuum cleaner, or if she'd been joking. Nobody was smiling.

Lark Orela linked arms with the man she'd almost split in half with her black, spiky, high-heeled—Oh, Lord. She was wearing Jimmy's latest, greatest fall boots, Eden noticed with a little pang of shoe envy. Not that *she'd* ever wear thigh-high black patent boots with the highest FM heels she'd ever seen, but Eden wouldn't mind *owning* a pair.

Lark gave Eden an intensely curious look over her nose ring. "Is she the prob?"

A man, dressed in a well-fitting tuxedo, pleated shirt collar unbuttoned, bow tie dangling loose, materialized beside them. Tall, dark, and ridiculously handsome, he cast a curious glance at Eden, who at this point had both feet on the floor.

The room was starting to get crowded. She wondered if she should be worrying about her sanity when people kept appearing out of thin air and she wasn't even startled, let alone surprised.

"Who is she?" Mr. Tux asked with only the mildest of curiosity.

"Hey, Simon," Lark Orela said cheerfully, linking her other arm through his. "Gabriel's squeeze, apparently. And not the prob—Oh. Hi, Alex." The girl's black-rimmed eyes widened appreciatively. So did Eden's.

Another tall, dark hottie. This one dripping water, and wearing—*almost*—a white hotel towel that he was hastily securing about his lean hips. "The least you could have done was let me finish my freaking shower, Edge."

Gabriel glanced at the clock on the mantel, and then back. His eyes met Eden's on the pass, held, then moved on. As brief as it was, the intensity of his dark blue eyes on her face had been almost palpable, and made her feel as though she were on the receiving end of a visual . . . lick. *Oh, God. I'm really losing it here.*

"Said 2030, Stone."

"So you did." Green eyes checked Eden out. Alex Stone gave her a slow smile, a slow, sexy smile that, forty-eight hours ago, would've accelerated her heart. And all Eden thought now was: *Nice abs.*

His smile widened as if he could read her mind as he said to Gabriel over his shoulder. "Mind if I dress before we get started?"

"Not on *my* account," Lark told him, fluttering mascara-gummed eyelashes at the practically naked man.

Or mine, Eden thought with amusement as Lark did something and Alex was suddenly dressed in skintight black leather pants and biker boots looped with silver chains.

Glancing down, Alex shook his head. "Lark . . ."

"Spoilsport," she pouted. "There. Better?"

The tight jeans and powder-blue V-necked sweater were only marginally less sexy on him. "As long as I can actually *sit* in these jeans, and we can lose the boots—" The biker boots were now athletic shoes. "Thanks, yeah."

She felt the tug of Gabriel's gaze resting on her, and turned her head. Their eyes clashed across the vast room. Hot midnight blue eyes seared her like a physical brand. Her breath caught and then disappeared altogether as her blood stirred.

With a visible effort, Gabriel tore his gaze away from her and shifted it to Sebastian beside him.

"Where's Peter?" Lark asked, moving to sit on the arm of Simon's chair. Drifts of black fabric fluttered around her as she crossed her long legs. "And Duncan? And Yancy—Oh. There *you* are. You're late!"

"Yancy" had his right arm in a black sling, and his left foot in a walking cast. He was struggling to pull a shirt on over his bare, blood-smeared chest. "Want a doctor's note?" he asked, glaring at her with the eye that wasn't swollen shut and colored a deep, painful purple. He hobbled to sit down heavily on the end of the sofa where Eden was watching them all as if she were observing a fast-paced tennis match.

"Hey," he mumbled through a split lip by way of greeting.

"Hey." Eden smiled sympathetically, wondering what the other guy looked like. It was obvious Yancy had been interrupted while he'd been getting medical attention. He smelled faintly of antiseptic and apparently only some of his wounds had been dressed because he

took out a handkerchief and dabbed at a seeping cut on
his jaw.

Absently cataloging the poor guy's numerous wounds,
Eden was distracted by the flash and flair of flames out
of the corner of her eye. She turned her head to see yet
another new arrival. This guy was sitting in the chair opposite the fireplace. Like the others, he'd arrived with no
fanfare.

Wearing black pants and an open-necked white shirt,
he somehow managed to look more elegant than the guy
in the tux. He had a lean, clever face that was vaguely
familiar, and watched everyone with the darkest eyes
Eden had ever seen.

Interestingly enough, while he was indolently seated
fairly near a floor lamp, he was almost completely in
shadow. He was absently juggling three tennis-ball-sized
spheres of fire between lean, nimble fingers.

"Duncan," Gabriel's expression eased when he spotted the guy, and he strode across the room, winding his
way through the knot of people in its center.

Duncan rose, and the two men did that slapping-on-
the-back-hard-enough-to-stagger-a-horse thing.

"Caleb?" Gabriel asked.

Duncan shook his head. "He's gone back. I'm sure
he's fine."

"I'd feel better if I was sure of that."

"Ditto. I'll see what I can find out when we're done
here."

Seeing the two men side by side Eden knew immediately that they were brothers. The same dark hair,
the same lean face, the same sensual mouth, the same
dark, penetrating eyes. They could almost be twins. But
Gabriel was better looking, she decided, fascinated by
the obvious love the two men shared.

Not that their greeting was effusive. Almost immediately Gabriel stepped away from his brother, and went

to stand with his back to the massive stone fireplace. "Blaine can catch up when he gets here." He glanced from one to the other. "In the past thirty-seven days, three wizards have been killed."

"Three?" Simon asked, sitting forward.

"Thom Lindley's body was discovered early this morning. The sweepers confirmed ID. Vaporized. Same MO as Townsend and Jamison." Gabriel searched the faces of the people in the room. "We have a rogue wizard. Either one of ours, or an outsider."

"Man," Alex said softly but with heat. "What we have here, ladies and gentlemen, is a major clusterfuck. And, Jesus. Look at the timing. Isn't the council sitting right now to install a new Master Wizard as leader?"

"They are. I'll go talk to them," Duncan said, now juggling five larger balls of naked flame. They were moving so fast Eden saw only a constantly shifting arc of orange, red, and yellow.

"Can't get anywhere near them until a new leader has been chosen. Caleb first," Gabriel instructed his brother.

Eden caught the look that passed between the two men. Duncan shook his head. Once. Gabriel's jaw locked. "Jesus." He closed his eyes for a second, and when he opened them again, they were as dark as onyx. "Surely to God it doesn't apply to *brothers*?"

Duncan didn't pause his juggling, didn't even glance at Gabriel as he said softly. "Want to test that theory, bro?"

She frowned. What did *that* mean? Was there some wizardly law that prevented them from trying to find their brother?

"One more thing—" Gabriel said grimly. "Tremayne and I are currently working on replicating a robot stolen from Dr. Cahill's lab. Until half an hour ago we didn't connect the deaths of three wizards to our current op.

That changed when a man morphing as the Homeland Security agent tried to kill Eden while shimmering."

"Impossible!" Lark slid off the arm of the chair. "If there'd been anyone but us in this house, palace, castle, *whatever,* in the last twenty-four hours, I would have *felt* him. There's not a particle of residue indicating the presence of an unfamiliar wizard."

Eden was tempted to put up her hand and direct their collective attention to her throat, which felt as though it were black and blue. Like a good piece of furniture, she kept quiet.

"Cloaked," Duncan murmured, adding a gleaming silver dagger to his fireballs; it caught and reflected both the eclectic lights and the orange of the fire as it flipped and wheeled high in the air above his head.

"Impossible," Simon inserted. "Okay. Not impossible with the right device, but pretty damn improbable."

"Improbable or not," Gabriel told him, "it's fact. He was here. Which means he wants what we want. Intel on this bot."

"No," Eden told Gabriel flatly. "He didn't want anything to do with the robot. He wanted me *dead.*"

He searched her face. She would much rather he scoop her up and run like hell. Anywhere would be fine and dandy with her.

"He wanted to frighten you enough to lower your guard so he could extract the data for Rex," he told her as casually as one would remark on the weather.

"Excuse me? *I* was the one struggling to breathe as he squeezed the life out of me. You didn't see his eyes," she rubbed her goose-bumpy upper arms. "He was . . . *shimmering* so *you* couldn't catch him."

"What *kind* of device?" Yancy asked. "What kind of device would be capable of cloaking him from *us*?"

"Something ancient," Lark offered. "An amulet of some sort?" She looked at Eden, and Eden was surprised to see real intelligence beneath the garish makeup and multiple piercings.

"Was he wearing anything out of the ordinary? Jewelry of some kind?"

Eden took a moment to think about it. He'd worn no rings on his hands, she was sure of it. "Nothing I could see."

"Something in his pocket?" A new man moved with unconscious grace to the center of the semicircle. Of medium height and muscle-bound, he was dressed in a slightly too tight dark suit and conservative tie that made the pale skin on his neck roll pink over his pale yellow collar. The late wizard Blaine, Eden thought.

"You're late," Lark snapped, sounding nothing like the Goth young woman she appeared to be.

"Sorry. I've been here long enough to get the gist."

"The *gist,*" Gabriel said in a hard voice, "is that we now know that the missing bot and our mysterious visitor are inextricably linked. We know that this person is capable of cloaking himself and blending right in. We know that he's capable of murder. And we know"— he looked from face to face—"We know, *unequivocally,* that he's assimilating the powers of the wizards he kills."

Eden didn't need the murmur of alarm to feel deeply terrified. If these guys were nervous, she was a hundred times *more* so. "Assimilating?" she repeated, lips dry.

Lark jiggled a boot-clad foot beneath her long black gypsy skirt. "Under the right circumstances, powers transfer. That's how Alex got his. Used to just be telepathic, but now he—"

"I'm . . . more," Alex interrupted, giving Lark a charming smile. How interesting, Eden thought, watching the interplay between Gabriel's coworkers. Alex, apparently, was modest about his . . . skills. Duncan sat there absently showing his ability. Not only to make fire, hell, Gabriel could do *that*. But Duncan seemed more at home with his talents. He was comfortable with them, almost nonchalant as he juggled a combination of unlikely objects. He'd added what looked like a boccie ball to the fire and a kni—*two* knives arcing over his head.

Eden got the distinct impression that Duncan was a little bit different from the others. But she wasn't sure if it was a good different or a bad different.

Then she noticed Gabriel's brother's eyes and realized that far from showing off, far from being inattentive, he was watching everyone in the room with a sharply intelligent black gaze. He was using his juggling act as a blind to distract anyone from looking deeper than the arc of flames in front of him.

Distract them from what?

As if he could hear her, Duncan turned his head slightly and met her eyes through the orange striations. The corner of his mouth lifted in a small smile before he returned to concentrating on what was being said around him.

That powerful glance must be an Edge family trait, Eden decided, rubbing the chill from her upper arms. She wondered what wizardly skill each person in the room possessed, then decided she was probably better off not knowing.

"Lark," Gabriel motioned the young woman forward. "Fill us in on Lindley, Jamison, and Townsend. What precisely were their special talents? We should all know what we're up against."

"Thom Lindley's special skill was morphing into another person for extended lengths of time."

Gabriel moved to sit on the arm of the sofa next to Eden. Her heartbeat went crazy as it always did, increasing its tempo the closer he got to her. As a woman she was powerfully attracted to him, there was no denying it.

She'd done something incredibly stupid, and out of

character. Not only had she slept with him, not only did she crave his body like a drug, but somehow she had managed to fall in love with Gabriel Edge.

She was stunned.

She knew people liked to think of themselves as being in love; but by and large the emotion they interpreted as love was in reality some other emotion—often lust, fear, dependence, or a hunger for approval.

God only knew, at various times in her life she'd experienced most of those.

Despite everything, she wasn't afraid of Gabriel Edge. Nor was she dependent upon him. Nor did she need his approval for anything. She *was* insanely physically attracted to him. But this feeling was more than garden-variety lust. More than the usual chemical release of endorphins. As a scientist she was intrigued with the phenomenon of how powerful compatible pheromones could set off such an intense physical reaction. It was fascinating. Perhaps one day she'd add that component to an AI project.

A watch or some other piece of jewelry that could silently alert one when a compatible person came within a few yards. Market it as The Date Mate 2010. Never approach another loser again.

God. Who was she kidding? She was sitting here, in a medieval castle, surrounded by wizards. Falling in love with her very own wizard kidnapper.

How the hell had *that* happened? *When* had that happened? Yesterday? This morning in the solarium? This afternoon when they'd made love as though if they didn't they'd both die?

Preternaturally aware of him, Eden felt the heat of his body, and smelled the subtle fragrance of his skin as strongly as if they were touching and she had her nose buried in his throat. Yet a foot of space separated them.

He didn't look at her, but she knew he was as conscious of her as she was of him. With a shudder, she felt the weight of his hand on the back of her neck, a sexually possessive gesture only the two of them were aware of. She felt his hand on her, and yet she knew he wasn't really touching her.

Not physically.

Her lashes fluttered as his thumb stroked up and down her nape leaving a trail of heat behind. The same erotic phantom stroke that he'd used in her bedroom what felt like forever ago.

His fingers tunneled up through her hair, sifting the curls as he brushed her scalp with the pads of his fingers. Suspecting that her eyes must be crossing from the sheer bliss, she closed them, feeling the tingle of his secret caress all the way to her toes.

He cupped the back of her head, lightly, so lightly, and exerted just enough pressure for her to lean closer, pressing her upper arm into the rolled arm of the sofa where he sat.

Phantom fingers lingered on her ear, stroking the fleshy pad before tracing the swirls. *This is so freaking unfair,* she thought, twitching her shoulders at the mixed sensation of ticklish and erotic. Then she had to pretend she was covering her shoulders with the velvet throw to hide the telltale movement. She was practically on fire from his touch.

Except he wasn't touching her.

She'd like a few skills of her own, she thought darkly as his hand skimmed down her throat. "How long could Thom sustain?" Gabriel asked, looking at Alex.

"Straight out of the box when he first started? He told me less than an hour. After thirty some odd years? Indefinitely."

"What degree of the assimilated skills would *this* guy have?" Simon demanded. "Beginner or advanced. Alex?" Everyone turned to look at Alex Stone.

"Full bore." His tone was forbidding. "When it happened to me—" Alex cut himself off as he had Lark. He raked his fingers through his dark hair, and his brilliant green eyes glittered. "He'd get everything full strength."

Gabriel's touch disappeared instantly, and Eden felt bereft. He swore under his breath. "What else do we have to look forward to, Lark?"

The young woman started ticking things off on her multiringed fingers with their short, black polished nails. "Invisibility. Levitation. Supernatural strength. Animal cunning. Morphing. Mind control. And flight." She frowned. "I think that about covers it."

Yes, Eden thought, pressing a splayed hand across her bruised throat. That about covers every spectrum of fear she could possibly imagine. And then some.

CHAPTER SIXTEEN

Duncan Edge was the last to leave. Eden, sitting curled up on the sofa, watched the brothers talking on the other side of the room. They were speaking in soft, hushed tones.

She wasn't cold, but she was shivering anyway. Stress. Fear. Nervous energy. It all mixed in her stomach like a toxic slush. Whatever the brothers were discussing obviously didn't make either of them happy.

She desperately wanted to go to Gabriel and slide her arms around his waist. She wanted to rest her head against his heart and listen to the steady beat of life.

And oh, Lord. She wanted him to assure her that this entire situation wasn't as shocking, as *terrifying* as it all sounded.

The men separated.

"Just take care of Caleb," Gabriel's voice carried. "And don't come back until this is over."

"Done." Duncan's tone was as grim and tight as Gabriel's. For a second Eden thought, how silly of Gabriel not to want his brother here with him where it is safe. And then she remembered what MacBain had told her at breakfast.

When the brothers were together they canceled out all but each other's most basic powers.

"I could take her—"

Gabriel cut off his brother. "My responsibility."

"Christ," Duncan said grimly. "To quote Alexander Stone: This *is* a clusterfuck. Watch your back, big brother. I'm out of here. Nice meeting you, Doctor," Duncan called out, lifting an elegant hand in farewell.

What an oddly prosaic comment. Eden collected herself. "Um—sure—"

One minute he was there. Then he wasn't.

She shook her head. "I'm never going to get used to that."

"You don't have to," Gabriel told her shortly, flipping off the lamp on the desk as he passed. Naturally he didn't do anything as mundane as touch the switch. Just a glance did the job.

"Why not?"

He turned off the floor lamp, and another table lamp. "You won't be around us long enough for that to happen."

Eden's heart skipped a beat. And then another. "Are you telling me that you can't protect me?"

His eyebrow lifted. "What gave you that idea?"

"You said I won't be here long enough for that to happen. That means either I'll be dead or somewhere else. Dead is bad. And I don't want to leave. I want to stay here. With you."

"There is nowhere safer for you to be right now than here. With me."

Thank God. "And don't you sound happy about it." Eden kicked the light blanket off her feet and stood. Only the table lamp near the door was on, leaving the large, book-lined room dimly lit and shadowy. And a lot more atmospheric than she'd like. She already had the über heebie-jeebies.

"I don't have to be happy about something to do my job."

She started to fold the blanket, but her hands shook so badly she finally just tossed it back on the sofa in a heap. "Well, you're falling a little short on that count, Gabriel. He got to me once," she said flatly, proud that her voice didn't break with the very real fear that was making her almost hyperventilate. She wrapped her arms about her own waist. "He'll try again. Won't he?"

"There's a protective spell over the castle. Come on."

"Come on—*where*?" she asked blankly. "Wait a minute. There was a protective spell over the castle before. He still got in. He still got his hands around my throat. I'd like some sort of assurance that that can't happen again." Eden started across the room to where he was waiting, impatience in his dark eyes.

"I amped up the protection, and got a little juice from the others. Nobody can get inside unless I let them in. And I'm not letting *you* out of my sight. That's a promise," he told her grimly. "I'm sticking to you like a wet tongue on dry ice for the duration."

The wet tongue statement gave her pause, or was her heart racing again because she was so close to him? Either. Both. "Where are we going?" She looked at her watch. Nine P.M. It felt like midnight.

"Bed."

"Together?"

He glanced at the lamp and the room plunged into semidarkness. "I have a big bed."

She remembered. "I know this isn't the best time to ask this—but would you hold me for a few minutes?" She hated, *hated* being that needy, especially since he hadn't touched her in what felt like hours. But a good solid hug would go a long way in reassuring her that she wasn't as alone as she felt.

His eyes were shadowed and his jaw tightened. With annoyance? With the strength of his restraint? "No. You're a big girl, Doctor. You don't need to be held. You have to be *protected*. To do that we have to stay in close proximity. No physical contact is necessary." He stepped out into the hallway where the lights had been dimmed for the night. "Come on."

"*Doctor?*" She narrowed her eyes, and stopped mid-step. "Excuse me?" she said carefully when he glanced around to see where she was. "Aren't you the man who was fondling my hair not an hour ago?" She didn't feel the need to add what they'd been doing *three* hours ago.

"Jesus, Eden," he said tightly. "What the hell do you want from me?" Looking tortured, he turned and re-sumed walking across the dimly lit entry hall, his shoul-ders stiff. Their steps sounded spooky in the silence of the vast open space.

"Consistent freaking behavior would be nice," she told him coolly, following him across the entry hall toward the sweeping staircase that would lead them to his big bed.

She glared at his broad back. The damn man moved with the stealthy grace of a cat. And he was just as dis-interested, damn him. Would it have killed him to hold her one more damn minute? She shot him a fulminating look. For all the good it did her.

She shouldn't be this emotional. She knew she shouldn't. Worse, she knew she was being unreasonable. She wanted him to . . . pet her when he had enormous responsibilities and concerns.

But just because she knew she was being unreason-able, didn't mean he was right either.

She increased her speed to catch up with him, reach-ing out her hand to grab his arm to get his attention. He moved out of her way like greased lightning.

"No touching." His voice was barely more than a rasp. He took another step back, and Eden thought, *Well, shit. Here we go again.*

"I'm dead serious. Don't touch me right now. Under-stand?"

She opened her mouth to tell the infuriating man that no, she didn't understand. Not him. Not this castle. Not the meeting she'd just witnessed. Instead she snapped her mouth closed, striding ahead of him to start up the stairs.

She didn't understand any of this. And she was a woman who needed to know everything there was to know about her physical surroundings. Knowledge had always been her power. She wanted to know how, and what, made things work and why. It was how she ordered her life and controlled her environment. So this . . . this nonsensical world of his was making her nuts.

The last two days had taken her ordinary world and spun it on its axis.

Nothing was explainable. Nothing was normal.

Least of all could she explain her *own* feelings and behavior.

And everything about Gabriel Edge was a deep, dark *freaking* mystery.

Other than the occasional tap of her heels, the silence was thick and impenetrable, dark and ripe with sexual heat whether he wanted to admit it or not.

"You have interesting co-workers." Eden gripped the banister at the bottom of the stairs.

"Yeah. I do."

She had a hundred questions about what had been said in the meeting she'd just witnessed, but one look at Gabriel's face and she decided to keep them to herself. The carpeted staircase was at least fifteen feet wide. She walked on the far left, he walked on the far right, slightly behind her. Eden took the stairs two at a time, getting more and more irritated as she climbed.

"Do you have any idea," she snarled, realizing that she'd been thinking about this subconsciously for *hours,* "how insulting it is to the woman you've slept with when you won't come near her afterward? Exactly what is your problem?"

"My *problem* is that I get hard just looking at you. And I'm already hard enough to pole vault to Scotland! *That's* my fucking problem."

Well, ask a direct question and get a direct answer. Normally she would have been impressed, but not this time. Not when it hurt to hear the self-loathing in his tone. Heart doing its usual hop, skip, and jump when she was around him, Eden stopped walking, turned to look at him, and tightly gripped the ornate banister.

"You say that as if it's a bad thing."

Three steps below her, he stopped too. He seemed to be gathering himself before turning his head to make eye contact. "If I came any closer," he said thickly, "I'd have your jeans off and your ankles around my shoulders in about thirty seconds flat. Haven't you got it yet that when we touch each other all hell breaks loose?"

She searched his harsh expression even though his admission inspired a surge of white heat inside her. His skin was tightly drawn over his flushed cheekbones. She couldn't miss the turmoil she read in the inky depths of his dark glittering eyes.

Turmoil, but also raw hunger.

That look made her wonder what sex on the stairs would be like. She didn't take the time to talk herself out of it, didn't bother evaluating the pros and cons. She wanted, and so she acted. Holding his gaze, Eden kicked off her sandals. They tumbled down the steps—thump, thump, thump—ignored. She didn't know what she'd do if he turned away from her now. Reaching down, she undid the button on her jeans with fingers that shook.

He closed his eyes. "Don't." His voice was guttural, and he flinched as if struck when she eased the zipper down, the sound loud in the throbbing silence. She could hear her pulse pounding in her ears as it started its manic race through her veins, pausing to throb and pulse strategically.

His eyes opened. Navy black. Hot. Searing. His gaze touched the V of bare skin she'd exposed. "You want me to take you here on the stairs?"

Eden licked her dry lips. "I don't care if you take me here, or I take you. As long as you're inside me in ten seconds or less." She was unprepared for Gabriel's blurring speed as he moved from there to her in a blink.

He gripped her upper arms and brought her body colliding with his. Their faces were level as his mouth came down, hot and ravaging. Blindly Eden freed herself, and reached for him, wrapping her arms about his neck, kissing him back with everything that was in her.

He drew back. "Bedroom," he said thickly.

"Here." She raked her teeth against his lip and thrilled to his shudder. He kissed her again with bruising force, his mouth a furnace. Her heart swelled and expanded. He was out of control. The knowledge that she was capable of making that happen filled her with awe and just a hint of arrogance. She'd unleashed a panther and there was no going back. Not that she wanted to.

He supported her in his arms as he lowered her to the carpeted stairs, still kissing her, and brought his hips into the juncture of her thighs. Heat and longing twisted inside her in a molten river as he ran his fingers across the hollow of her throat, then across her collarbone while he kissed her.

Her hungry mouth clung to his as he bunched her T-shirt and started yanking it up. The feel of his hand on her bare skin made Eden twist for better contact.

"Faster. Faster. Faster. *Do* something! Use magic, damn it. I have. To. Feel. Skin."

"There's more than one kind of magic, Eden. But damn it—I *want* to rip your clothes off you. I want to hear you gasp and see you shudder."

"I'll gasp and shudder—later. After . . . ward." All her internal muscles were tightening unbearably. If she didn't find release soon she'd explode. "Oh, God, Gabriel. Please. Hurry."

He levered his body off hers. Kneeling on a lower step, he shifted so he could draw down her jeans and panties. Eden shuddered. She lifted her hips to help him. He yanked the fabric down her legs and tossed the garments aside. Her breath strangled in her lungs seeing his expression.

She never in her life had a man look at her as Gabriel did now. As if he'd die if he didn't have her.

"This what you want?" His face was taut, primitive, as he positioned himself between her spread knees. With a whimper, she reached for him.

"Y-yes. Now."

But Gabriel had other ideas.

With a low, growling noise in the back of his throat, one of sheer animal arousal, tightly leashed, he bent his head, and pressed his open mouth against her stomach. Her muscles jumped at the contact. She speared her fingers through his hair. The strands felt cool and silky, his scalp hot. She cupped the back of his head, wanting him to return to kissing her mouth. Instead he lifted his head, his breath hot and moist on her skin.

"Take off your shirt," he instructed thickly.

Obediently, willingly, she yanked her T-shirt over her head, then reached for the front closure on her bra. He lifted his head, eyes burning.

"I'll do it." He brushed her hands aside, unfastened the closure of her bra, then dropped his head and drew her nipple deep into the hot wet cavern of his mouth.

Eden's back arched off the step as the suction of his mouth on her breast seemed to have a direct correlation to the pull in her womb. The coiling ache deep inside her was unbearable. She sank her short nails into his broad shoulders as he transferred his mouth to the other nipple and grasped her damp breast, running his thumb back and forth across the ultrahard point.

"Satin," he murmured raggedly before lowering his mouth again. His lips moved south, and he tongued her navel, making Eden's hips arch and twist.

"Please." She begged for relief. For mercy. For less. For more. For everything.

His hand moved down, spreading her legs farther apart. He stroked a finger in her damp curls making her moan in torment. She was swollen and ultrasensitive already, and gasped when he pushed two fingers inside her. Her head tossed restlessly on the step as he worked them deep inside her, pressing upward. God. The man knew his way around her body, Eden thought frantically, as he kept her just this side of mindless release.

He rasped his thumb over her clitoris until she bucked and screamed his name. Liquid heat poured through her and her hips lifted off the stair beneath her. "For God's sake. Gabriel! Do. S-something!"

Slipping his slick fingers out of her, he caught her hips in both large hands, sliding his palms around to grasp each cheek. She gripped his shoulders for purchase. His head lowered, the width of his shoulders spread her knees achingly wide. Exposed. Vulnerable. She squeezed her eyes shut, whimpering as he brought her to his mouth.

The slick heat of his agile tongue opened her, and he hummed his pleasure as he found the hard bud of her clitoris against his tongue, this time closing gentle teeth over it. The throaty vibration made her wetter. More desperate. Her hips arched out of his hands, she needed to be closer to the heat. His heat.

She tried to say his name, but found she had no breath left, it was all dammed in her tight chest as he nuzzled and licked until she shuddered. Biting her lip, she was oblivious to the steps digging into her back. Nothing,

nothing, existed but Gabriel's clever mouth loving her and his hands digging into the taut muscles of her bottom. He hummed against her again.

The sensation was so sharply, so unbearably erotic that she wanted him to stop so she could drag in a lungful of air and center herself. But the tangled desire dragged her down to drown in the dark liquid smoke of mindless desire.

She screamed as the first paroxysm ripped through her. She tried to drag in a breath. Half a breath. But there was no air. No light. Convulsions slammed through her body, making her arch and shudder against Gabriel's avid mouth.

He showed her no mercy while she trembled and her body bowed, nor did she want him to. Eden wanted this man in any way she could get him.

By the time he rolled aside, she was exhausted, drained, and barely conscious. Her cheek brushed against his chest as he gathered her into his arms, pulling her body like a blanket over his.

She couldn't move. She didn't much want to, either. There was a peace, a serenity, and a rightness to being in Gabriel's arms. It was like finding . . . home.

Jesus, Gabriel thought, his own breathing ragged as he buried his face in her damp hair. *I am way too freaking old to be rolling around on the stairs like a teenager in heat.*

Unfortunately, while they'd been rolling around *that* thought hadn't occurred to him. Too horny, too wired to relocate, he trailed his hand down the smooth skin of her back, lightly misted with perspiration, and listened to her uneven breathing.

Aftershocks of completion continued to ripple through her body, ratcheting up his need to a painful degree.

"Now I know why Scarlett O'Hara was smiling,"

Eden murmured raggedly, eyes closed, lips curved. "It wasn't that bed she got off on. It really *was* the stairs."

He felt the rapid flutter of her lashes tickle his chest as he breathed in the floral scent from her hair. This was too comfortable. Not in the physical sense—he was still painfully unsatisfied—but in the emotional danger zone he knew full well he should be doing everything in his power to avoid. He was too aware, too intrigued, too interested in this woman. No good could come of it.

Knowing that and acting on it were apparently two unrelated things. His fingers laced in her curls as he gently massaged her scalp.

Grave fucking tactical error touching her again, he knew, staring broodingly up at the fan-vaulted ceiling soaring forty feet above their heads. But now that he had, he didn't want to let her go. He tightened his arms, and Eden made a small sound of contentment, snuggling closer.

With a lurch in his gut, Gabriel knew that no matter how many times he took her, he'd still want her. There was no end to his desire for this woman. He had always needed her. And he always would.

How many times was he going to have to have sex with her before he got it through his thick head that this wasn't merely a recreational fuck? He wasn't an adolescent who couldn't keep his dick in his pants. He'd never, *never* lost control as he did with Eden. There was no getting away from the reality.

Each time he made love with her tightened the bond between them inexorably. He was skating perilously close to disaster here.

Being near her made every intelligent thought vanish in a vapor trail.

He couldn't let her go.

He couldn't let her stay.

It was imperative he extract the data from her immediately. It couldn't wait. They were out of time. The robot had to be re-created.

Gabriel enjoyed the feel of Eden nestled in his arms for another minute or two, then shimmered them to his bed. Somewhere in that nanosecond, he rashly decided that another hour wouldn't make a difference.

Sheets and blankets were strewn all over the floor from their previous bout of lovemaking earlier in the day—God. A lifetime ago. He brought her to the middle of the mattress, holding most of his weight off her with his elbows.

He settled between her thighs. Brushed his fingers across the dark bruises on her pale throat. The rage and despair he felt inside stayed deep. He ran tender lips along her stubborn jaw, felt her mouth curve in a sleepy smile. Gently he nuzzled her lips, drinking in the warm sweet fragrance of her skin with a soft undertone of a floral fragrance that made a promise he couldn't allow her to keep. "Eden."

"Hmm?"

He was on the knife's edge of arousal, so hard he was in pain. "Just—Eden," he whispered, teeth clenched as he pushed into her slick heat. Her eyes flared open as he entered her with a hard, steady thrust that seated him to the root. Immediately her arms and legs came around him, shackling him to her. Binding him in a way that he could never have imagined.

Need surged through him as he pushed deeper, using the last of his ragged control against the driving demand of his own release. Striving with everything in him, Gabriel kept it slow and deep so that he could savor every liquid pulse of *her* impending release.

He couldn't remember when he'd ever made love without protection, and the sensation of having absolutely nothing between them was exquisite in its intensity.

He held her, steadied her, controlled their frantic

rhythm, his gaze intent on her face as he withdrew a little, then thrust again.

His good intentions flew to hell when she whispered his name on a slow, agonized breath, tightening her limbs around him, then sank her teeth into his shoulder.

An explosion of heat shot from the soles of Gabriel's feet up the nerves and muscles in his spine, and stabbed directly into his brain, demanding he drive into her again and again.

And again.

And again.

Until the world turned white-hot around them and there was no knowing where she began and he ended.

CHAPTER SEVENTEEN

Eden felt like a mass of jigsaw puzzle pieces that had been tossed into the air and landed willy-nilly in a completely random and unfamiliar pattern. She'd loved the picture her life had been BG, Before Gabriel, but somehow now, with him, she was reconfigured. Redefined. Reborn.

She could hear the unsteady thumps of his heart beneath her ear. "You know what's insane?" she asked softly, stroking her palm over the crisp, damp hair on his chest. "When I'm with you I feel . . . safe."

His body stiffened, and the fingers he'd been hypnotically combing through her hair stilled. "I'm not safe, Eden. Far from it. I'm everything a woman like you should be shit scared of."

Not exactly what a well-loved woman wanted to hear when she was still in a postcoital glow snuggled in her lover's arms. "What kind of woman am I?"

"Someone who needs to stay a long way away from a man like me," he told her, shifting out of her arms to slide across the mattress. He threw his long legs over the side to sit on the edge of the bed.

"That's not much of an answer. What's the deal, Gabriel?"

"It's complicated," he answered, his back to her.

"Everything *seems* complicated," she countered. "Just

because something appears convoluted doesn't mean it's inherently bad."

"That may be true in your antiseptic laboratory. Out here in the real world, things are different. The only thing great sex leads to is more great sex. Let's leave it at that."

Her brow furrowed as she pondered the cryptic nonanswers that were at complete odds with his behavior and the slight sadness she sensed in his tone. His powerful body had bucked and arched because of her. The knowledge made Eden feel a power and delight she'd never experienced before in her life. Suppressing the need to go to him, to wrap her arms about those broad shoulders, was overwhelming.

Instead, she stayed where she was, a mile of rumpled sheets between them. She admired the long, lean line of his tanned back, his broad shoulders, and the way his slightly too long, sweat-dampened hair curled at his nape. She admired that he was still trying to warn her off.

"Shouldn't I get a say in where all this leads?" she asked softly.

He turned his head and his eyes were hard and uncompromising. "What do you want from me, Eden? Honesty?"

"Of course."

He held her gaze. "Want a commitment? Not going to happen. Ever."

"I didn't ask for anything that long range, but I certainly appreciate you putting the idea in my head." She shot him a teasing smile that he didn't reciprocate.

God, he was a hard-ass.

She kept eye contact. "But I'm here now . . ." Her voice trailed off and her heart lurched as, naked and still semi-aroused, he rose from the edge of the bed.

Unself-conscious, he turned fully to face her. "Help me

here. This can't be about our physical response to each other. Not right now. No matter how powerful. You have to allow me to extract the data to rebuild Rex. We can't wait. They've had your prototype for weeks. Enough time to figure out what it can do and come up with a creative way to use it."

She bit her lower lip. As much as she would have liked to delve into the pros and cons of their potential, Rex did have to be the priority. Besides, she trusted Gabriel. But, oh God—"What do I have to do?"

He gave a huff of laughter. "You don't have to look so pained. The Joining won't hurt."

"Yeah. Famous last words. Just do whatever you need to do, and get it over with."

He closed his eyes briefly as if he were in pain. When he opened them again Eden felt seared by the heated look he was giving her. "Stay where you are. I'll come around."

His clothing materialized on his body in the short time it took him to circumvent the massive mahogany bed, and he smelled as though he were fresh out of the shower. A neat trick.

She stroked her hand up his forearm. His skin was slightly damp. "Can you do that for me?"

"Sure. Which body wash?"

"Lemon ver—" She gave a little scream when a split second later she was in exactly the same position she'd been lying in moments before, but now her skin felt squeaky clean and smelled of "—bena."

She was dressed in jeans and a pale pink T. Even her hair was wet. "God. That—this is so . . . weird!"

"Welcome to my world," he said dryly, taking her hand to pull her upright.

"How . . ."

Gabriel cupped her face, bringing his lips to hers . . .

Are you going to suck the information out of my b—
"Um—"

His mouth settled on hers, spiking her temperature. They both tasted of minty toothpaste, Eden thought vaguely, as he tunneled the fingers of both hands through her wet hair to frame her skull and her eyes drifted closed.

"Mmm." Her hum of pleasure vibrated pleasantly against her parted lips, and she wrapped her arms about his neck.

His tongue moved, softly teasing, and when she parted her lips a little more, he slipped inside, deep and sure. Eden's body was so attuned to his, that if Gabriel had touched her anywhere else she would have exploded like a rocket.

His thumbs brushed back and forth across her eyelashes as he cradled her head in his large hands and nibbled her upper lip.

God, this man could *kiss.*

He knew how to seduce, tempt, and excite a woman with his mouth, his lips, his tongue, and his teeth.

She wished they were both naked again. She wished—

She felt him inside her head.

It was the most . . . extraordinary sensation.

Part of her was relishing Gabriel's incendiary kiss, but another part of her was letting him in. Feeling the soft probing of his mind reaching for hers. Searching. God. She *felt* him there. Her heart started to flutter, this time in panic.

Easy, sweetheart, easy. You know I won't hurt you.

Abstractedly she felt him iron the pleated frown between her brows with his thumb. *Give me what I need. Help me, Eden. Please.*

I want to open my eyes now, tumbled over—*I don't know how* in his brain.

She heard his soft chuckle. *That's what I like about*

you. He sounded amused. *Your innate curiosity—here?* He probed gently. *Show me the wire frame—that's a girl. Yes. Keep going . . .*

Eden tried to concentrate on what he wanted. And all the while she felt his tongue, warm and slick in her mouth, his damp hair cool between her fingers. Her heartbeat slowed to almost normal as she rapidly walked him through the entire development process. Her nipples were hard and she'd have given just about anything to still be naked. Having Gabriel in her head was like being caressed from the inside.

He groaned. *Working here!*

Her lips curved in a smile. *Take your time. I like it.*

He lifted his head, his eyes dark and glittering. "You would." He combed his fingers one last time through her hair, then took his hands away.

Her brain felt—lonely. But she didn't. Eden struggled with the jumble of thoughts and images that weren't her own. A slide show flashed in her mind and it took her a few seconds to realize what she was seeing. Gabriel. Or more accurately, bits and snippets of Gabriel's life.

The development of Rex had taken her six intense years. With Marshall's help, as well as, at least in the beginning, Theo. Now Gabriel had what he needed. In less than a minute.

Mind boggling. "I'm seeing some—"

"Don't worry about it," Gabriel said dismissively as he rubbed his hands over his face. "Just stragglers from your subconscious because of the extraction."

"But they aren't my—"

"Rest," he cut in, clearly distracted.

It seemed as though the longer she was around him, the more questions she had. And she'd ask them. Eventually. But for now he seemed a little too testy for her to batter him with the full force of her curiosity. "Did you get what you need?"

"Christ. I hope so. No," he said getting up quickly and moving away when she reached out to stroke the lines bracketing his mouth. He walked halfway across the room. "Don't touch me right now."

This time, Eden knew why. Rex 2 had to be built. Now. Tonight. And touching made him burn and forget anything, everything, else. She knew exactly how he felt. She felt the spiraling desire, the heat, the *want*—from both of them.

Sliding off the high mattress she staggered, surprised to find herself already wearing her pink, strappy, peep-toe Miu Mius. "How long will this take?" she asked curiously.

"If I have everything?" Gabriel rubbed his shadowed jaw. "Couple of hours."

She yawned, suddenly realizing just how tired she was. "Can I help?"

"Sure. But I've got to get set up first. That little exercise is going to knock you on your ass for a while. You'll want to sleep for a few hours. I'll wake you when there's something tangible."

Eden plopped back down on the side of the bed and kicked off her shoes. Exhaustion came over her like a bank of dense gray fog.

"Don't fight it," Gabriel told her, the corner of his mouth kicked up as he came toward her. She wanted to lick that small half smile on his lips. The depth of her feelings overwhelmed her. "Sleep's not a bad thing, you know. I promise. You won't miss anything."

As always Eden's pulse raced, and she felt the familiar flush rise to the surface of her skin the closer he came.

He rubbed the back of his neck and came to stand beside the bed, his eyes dark and unreadable.

She *knew* he was trying not to reach for her.

"Lie down."

Holding his gaze, she swung her legs back onto the

mattress and lay down, snuggling the pillow under her cheek. Her lids seemed to weigh ten pounds apiece, and she had to close her eyes. Just for a minute. "If I can help with anything"—she yawned—"wake me u—"

She didn't hear his answer. She was out like a light.

Gabriel was relieved that he'd retrieved the data necessary to reconstruct the bot. But he'd gotten far more in those few seconds that they'd been of one mind. Eden's residual memories would stay with him forever. Part and parcel of the Joining was retaining some of the subject's memories.

Through Eden's viewpoint he'd experienced the pain of her adolescence. The emotional conflicts of her parents' tempestuous marriage. Her love for her grandmother, Rose. And the humiliation of her marriage to Adam Burnett. *The son of a bitch.*

Gabriel gently stroked Eden's warm cheek, then brushed aside the dark curling strands of her hair covering her neck. He didn't have the power to heal like his brother Caleb did, but he sent energy through his fingertips as he stroked the dark bruises on her slender throat.

"Nobody is ever going to hurt you again," he promised. Then knew that for the lie it was. *He* was going to hurt her. He had no choice. Hurt her, or be responsible for her death.

He strengthened the protective spell over the castle, over his bedroom, and over his woman. That, coupled with the magic from the others, would keep her safe.

Nothing, and nobody but himself, could get near her.

Then he left the room to go to the lab and build the robot that had started the whole chain of events.

"Wake up, you stupid bitch."

Eden woke with a vengeance. More from the hand violently shaking her shoulder than from the less-than-loving words. Her eyes flew open to see Gabriel looming over the bed. She'd never seen that expression on his face. Distorted and dark with rage. Her heart kick-started. But not in a good way. With her brain still sleep-fuzzy, she blinked and struggled up on her elbows.

"Gabriel? What—?"

He backhanded her so hard her head bounced on the mattress. So shocked she didn't have the breath to scream, she saw him through the resulting sparkling silver fireworks obscuring her vision. He pulled back his fist and she managed to roll aside and avoid the hit. Not wasting time or energy demanding explanations, she scrambled to the other side of the bed, cheek hot and throbbing, breath coming in painful gasps.

She flung her body over the side of the high poster bed, then screamed because, God help her, he was right *there*. Waiting for her.

"What the hell is *wrong* with you?" she demanded as he grabbed her by the upper arm, yanking her body flush against his. His fingers felt like claws of steel digging into her bicep and she bucked and twisted, struggling to get free. He tightened his grip, holding her hard enough to break bones until she stopped fighting.

Sweet breath fanned her face as he grabbed her other arm, and pulled her up on her toes so their faces were mere inches apart. A twinge of memory struggled to surface, then was gone as fear took precedence over everything else.

"Look into the eyes of the man who's going to kill you."

She looked into his soulless black eyes. Yes. This was a man who could kill her. But he wasn't Gabriel. He looked like Gabriel. But, thank you God, he was not the man she loved.

Gabriel. Wherever the hell you are, help!

Dread, like she'd never felt before, saturated her body as whoever this impersonator was tightened his grip until she gasped with pain. She had a thought, and shuddered with sick fear that this might be her one shot at self-preservation.

She held his eyes. "Then kiss me good-bye first."

It took everything in her not to flinch as he gave her a chilling smile before lowering his head the last few inches separating them. Ice seemed to permeate her body as powerful waves of revulsion buffeted her until she felt physically ill. Eyes open, she stoically parted her lips despite the rising nausea.

Lifting her off her feet by her upper arms, he forced his tongue inside her mouth like an assault weapon. She gagged. He ground his mouth against hers. God, it hurt. She tasted her own blood and the bitter flavor of terror. As he raped her mouth, he grunted his satisfaction.

Keep doing that, you sick bastard. Gabriel? Someone? Anyone?!

Although everything inside her screamed to get this over with, *now!* Eden waited for just the right moment. When she knew she couldn't stand it one more second, when she hoped, *prayed* that he was totally focused on assaulting her, she bit down on his tongue as hard as she could, at the same time bringing up her knee to strike him solidly in the balls.

He reared back with a garbled scream, shoving her away from him with both hands. They both dropped to the floor. Hard. His screams were animalistic, bloodcurdling and terrifying, and made all the hairs on Eden's body stand up as she tucked and rolled out of his way. Clearly he was too preoccupied with his own problems to notice where she'd landed, thank God.

Face contorted, blood smearing his mouth and chin, he clutched his groin with both hands and was curled up tightly on the floor. Oblivious to all but his own agony.

Not taking her eyes off him, she clawed her way up

the velvet bedspread, holding on to the side of the mattress, as she staggered to her feet.

She swiped his blood off her mouth with the back of a shaking hand. *GodohGodohGod.*

He was screaming almost silently now, clearly in such agony he could barely make a sound. *Good.* The horrific and terrifying rasping noises continued as he rocked himself back and forth, both hands cupped between his legs, eyes squeezed tightly shut.

Move it, she told herself. *Move. It! Now!*

When he recovered he was going to kill her. She freaking didn't have time to stand there enjoying her temporary victory.

Gabriel! Damn it, where the freaking hell are *you? MacBain? Wizards? Oh, God—Anybody?*

Frantically she looked around the enormous room for a weapon. Anything she could use to defend herself. The only weapons were the gleaming crossed swords mounted to a shield hanging above the bed. They were almost bigger than she was. God—

How the hell did one defend herself against a *wizard?* How did one kill something that shouldn't even exist?

Scared out of her wits, she blinked back the tears induced by his blow to the side of her face. The room danced and wavered as she tried to clear her vision. No. The effect wasn't just her tear-filled eyes, the figure on the floor was shimmering as well.

Thank God. He was leaving . . .

No.

He was *transforming.*

Now! she thought, light-headed with terror. *Hit him with something now!* He was vulnerable, hurt, distracted.

His guttural moans were music to her ears. While he was doubled up in agony he wasn't getting up. But she was pretty damn sure he wouldn't be incapacitated for long.

Clambering up onto the mattress, she reached up with both hands for one of the enormous swords on the wall. It came off the shield it was affixed to with surprising ease, but the weight of it literally brought her to her knees. The damn thing weighed a ton.

The silver steel glinted gold in the lamplight as she stumbled to her feet. Positioning both hands on the enormous leather hilt, she braced the point on the bed as she adjusted her hands for a better grip.

Years ago, Adam had tried to teach her to play golf. It had been the most boring three afternoons of her life. Now she tried to remember how one was supposed to hold a golf club. Because weight or not, this was all the protection she had. She was going to have to swing at him with all her might.

Gaaaaabriel!

Grimly delighted with the sound of the man still gagging in pain, she hefted the heavy sword, and gave a couple of experimental swings. The sharp point barely lifted from the mattress, but she kept trying. It was all she had.

Now, if she could just figure out how to get herself and the monstrously heavy sword off the bed, and get to him before he got to her, she'd be set.

From her vantage point above him Eden saw that he was gradually uncurling his body.

Stunned, her eyes widened. *Oh. My. God.*

He hadn't finished transforming himself. Perhaps being in so much pain impeded the process. But she knew who he was.

His face shimmered and changed but the vengeful black eyes were filled with rage as he saw her poised high above him.

"I'm going to kill you." The rasp in his voice made the threat even more chilling.

Not daring to blink and terrified out of her mind, Eden adjusted her stance, feet wide apart for balance. He wasn't going to give her enough time to climb off the bed and come after him. His magic was faster than a speeding bullet. Certainly faster than a woman holding a medieval sword.

Pleasepleasepleaseplease. Gabriel!

Tapping the sword on the bed, she heard the tearing sound as its razor-sharp point ripped a hole in the sheet. Her arm muscles burned with the weight as she choked up on the hilt. Lifting her chin, she gave him a thin smile. "Bring it on. *Jason.*"

Mouth smeared with red, black eyes glittered from Gabriel's face. Jason Verdine laughed as he finished morphing back into himself, making Eden dizzy at the speed of the transformation. At the speed, God help her, of his recovery.

He spat blood on the carpet at his feet. "You always were a clever girl. Too fucking clever for your own good. How did you know it was me?"

Talking was good. Talking was *great*. "You're the only man who's ever called me 'babe.' " At least he wasn't turning her into a toad or shimmering her to another location. Or killing her. Yet.

He frowned. "That's it?"

It pleased her enormously to hear that he was lisping as he talked. His tongue must hurt like hell. She'd tried to bite it clean off. She might not have succeeded, but by the way he was talking, and the expression on his face, he was in a hell of a lot of pain.

Tongue and balls.

She was fine with that.

"I smelled the Sen-Sen on your breath." She kept eye contact, even though the look in his eyes froze the marrow in her bones. "Now, and earlier, when you pretended to be Dixon." Her fingers were cramping she was holding the sword so tightly. Her lungs felt constricted. Probably due to the fact that she wasn't breathing. She was on a knife edge of waiting for him to make a move.

He could just zap the sword out of her hands, but right now she still had it. It was sharp enough, heavy enough to do some real damage if she could figure out how to get to him before he fully recovered. Eden realized that the only thing between her and death was the fact that right now he was apparently in too much pain to move. He was standing, but his upper body was still curved protectively over his groin. But that was going to change. Soon.

How did one go about killing a wizard? She'd never been big on violence, but when it came down to her life or his, she wanted hers.

She shifted her fingers around the thick leather hilt, digging her bare toes into the mattress for purchase. If she jumped off the bed, presuming she didn't kill herself in the process, she'd be unarmed, because there was no way she could do it without letting go of the sword. It was too long, too unwieldy to be able to hold on to. And there was no way she could climb down off the ridiculously high mattress carrying a four-foot-long sword that felt as though it weighed as much as she did. And was getting heavier by the second.

But if she didn't take some form of action soon, Jason was going to eventually straighten his hunched body and do . . . whatever it was he planned to do.

Think. Think. Think! Hey! Edge?! Now would be a good time! Get in here. Please. Get the hell back into the bedroom. "Where's Gabriel?" she demanded, measuring the distance between them.

"Dead." Face gray and contorted with both pain and

rage, Jason rubbed the flat of his hand gingerly down his groin.

Perspiration stung her eyes. Every muscle in her body vibrated as she gathered herself for his next assault. Her wrists ached, because she was gripping the hilt of the sword so tightly. "No, he isn't."

Jason brought up a shaking hand to swipe away the blood staining his mouth. "I killed him."

He still wasn't coming any closer, but Eden saw that he was gradually straightening his body as the pain eased. She didn't waste any more mental energy yelling for help. If Gabriel was capable of being here, he'd *be* here. And she had no idea if shouting out a call to all wizards could even be heard.

She remembered in the wizards' meeting that the rogue wizard could assimilate the deceased wizard's powers. But, her analytical mind was quick to point out, just because Jason had morphed himself into *looking* like Gabriel, didn't mean that Gabriel was dead.

She shivered, angry at the thought of any harm coming to her love.

She was on her own.

"You might have tried to kill him," Eden told Jason, watching his eyes, hoping to hell she'd be able to somehow read what he was going to do next. "But you didn't succeed."

He tried to straighten a few more inches, grimaced, and hunched again. "How would you know that?"

Was it possible that he was in too much pain to use his powers? Or was he just playing with her before he did something horrifically unspeakable? Eden had no idea. She was just grateful for the reprieve.

"The same way I knew as soon as you walked into this room and raised your hand to me that you weren't him. If Gabriel was dead, I'd know it."

"Well, he is. Otherwise, gallant Gabriel would have come rushing to your rescue, don't you think?"

She glanced over his shoulder and her lips curved in a satisfied smile. "I think you're a liar, you egotistical jackass. Take a look behind you."

It was the oldest trick in the book, but he turned his head to look over his shoulder, and Eden swung the sword with all her might.

A split second before it connected with his head, he shimmered and was gone. "Kill you, you fucking bitch!" came through the empty air.

The momentum of the swing, coupled with the weight of the long sword sent her flying off the bed. The heavy weapon went one way, she the other.

She screamed as she was caught and held in a pair of arms that clamped around her body like iron bands. She fought like a madwoman, kicking and biting. "You bastard! Let me go!"

CHAPTER EIGHTEEN

"Whoa. It's me." Gabriel tossed her onto the bed, then followed her down, pinning her flailing body with his own, exerting just enough strength to keep her there without hurting her.

His heart was pounding as fast as hers was. Jesus. He'd almost lost her. "Shh. It's okay. I have you, sweetheart, I have you."

Eden started punching him about the head and shoulders, tears streaming down her face as she struck out blindly. "I know it's you, you son of a bitch! Where *were* you? What the hell happened to sticking to me like a w-wet tongue on dry ice?!"

Half-laughing from sheer relief that she was okay enough to fight him, Gabriel buried his face in her tear-soaked hair, hugging her tightly. "Jesus. You scared the fucking hell out of me."

"*I* scared *you*?" She smacked his shoulder weakly. "I s-scared you?! My God. What took you so f-freaking long? Didn't you *hear* me calling you?"

Cradling her in his arms, he rolled to the side, holding her as if she were made of spun glass. "I heard you. I c—"

"Yeah. Yeah. Yeah," Eden grabbed a hank of his hair and pulled his face closer. "I know. You couldn't come into the room when he was in your form."

He gave her a startled look. "How the hell could you know that?"

"Deductive reasoning. You told me you and the others cast a protective spell so that only you could get near me. Ergo he was able to pierce that protection by *being* you. And I'm presuming that two yous couldn't be in the same place at the same time?"

He rested his forehead on hers. "Yeah. We had no idea that the morphing process was so all-encompassing. He's not just a look-alike, he's capable of replicating DNA."

Her eyes went wide at his statement. For a second he thought she was going to start asking questions as that brilliant mind of hers tried to assimilate and make sense of everything that was happening. Instead she held on to him tightly, and her voice cracked. "From now on, Gabriel Edge, make *contingencies* for these k-kinds of emergencies, damn it!"

He cupped her face with both hands, kissing the tears from her cheeks. "I will," he promised raggedly. "I will."

She wrapped her arms around him, pressing her face against his throat. "I knew I was going to die. And God—Gabriel—I was so scared," she whispered hoarsely, her breath hot against his skin. "I've never been so damn scared in my entire freaking life."

For an instant his arms tightened painfully around her in reflex to a terror he shared. He'd honest to God believed the spell he'd cast was invulnerable. A look-alike couldn't have passed through the barrier. But an exact replica of himself could. And had.

This new wizard was unbelievably powerful to have duplicated him so perfectly, right down to his DNA. The knowledge that one man held that level of power scared the shit out of him. Having that evil force close to Eden made him feel feral.

"He was Jason Verdine," she told him, lifting her face from his neck.

"What?"

"From Verdine Industries. My boss? That Jason."

Gabriel levered his body off hers reluctantly. "I know who he is. But—"

"Remember when—Lark, was it?—asked about any kind of amulet or jewelry he might have been wearing? He does. It's some sort of medallion he wears under his shirt," she told him, sitting up and using a corner of the sheet to scrub her damp face. "I felt it when he grabbed me. That and the Sen-Sen he's always eating clued me in as soon as he touched me."

Gabriel shut his eyes for a moment, rubbing a hand across his face. "But until then, you believed that he was me." How could she not. For all intents and purposes the man who had just tried to kill her—again—*had* been Gabriel Edge.

"Hell, no, I didn't." Eden looked at him as though he'd lost his mind. "Of *course* I knew it wasn't you. I knew *that* the second he touched me. If some—*doppelganger* me touched you, wouldn't *you* be able to tell the difference?"

Yeah. He would. With every fiber of his being. When he was close to this woman his heart filled to bursting. His blood pounded through his veins making him feel more alive than he'd ever felt in his life.

No! What the fuck am I doing? Gabriel thought, horrified that he had almost given in to the sweet temptation of loving her.

No fucking way could he allow *any* kind of emotion to creep up on him. Minor detail that caring for her would bite him in the ass.

Eden caring for him would kill her.

"Probably," he said, intentionally offhand. He rolled off the bed, schooling his features, reining in all emotion. Shutting off, and closing down from her. Making sure she believed he didn't care, and trying to convince himself of the same thing.

Several seconds of silence throbbed between them. "Probably?" she asked dangerously, climbing off the mattress on the opposite side. Her hair was a wild, dark nimbus around her flushed face as she glared at him across the rumpled sheets. *"Probably?"*

Gabriel stuffed his shirt into his waistband. He met her eyes. Kept his cool. Impersonal. "I've met Verdine. He isn't a wizard."

"Are you one hundred percent positive of that? Because *I'm* one hundred percent certain that it *was* Jason. He had the same mannerisms, the same smell, the same way of . . . *walking*. It was Jason all right. And looking back, when he impersonated Dixon I *thought* there was something vaguely familiar about him. Again, small mannerisms. His smell . . . His cocky attitude. He even called me *babe*!" She pulled a face, making him want to leap the bed to grab her up and kiss her senseless.

Step away from the table, he reminded himself.

She straightened her shirt, which had twisted around her body, exposing her flat tummy and the dimple of her belly button. Gabriel wanted to kiss her there, where her skin was soft and ultrasensitive. Instead he bent to pick up the ceremonial claymore she'd tried to use on the wizard. How the hell had she managed to lift the damn thing?

"I'm not discounting the possibility," he told her. "God only knows I didn't sense him either time he was here." He propped the sword against the bedside table to replace over the bed later, then straightened. "So the fact that I didn't sense Verdine was a wizard when I saw him in your lab is very possible."

"Let's take it as a given that he's the bad guy. Why would he go to all the trouble of killing Dr. Kirchner, and trashing the lab, and now . . . this?"

She bent to pick up her shoes. "Besides," she said, sitting on the edge of the bed to put them on, "he already owned Rex and all the research that went into it. This isn't logical."

"Terrorism rarely is."

"True. Because he doesn't want anyone to know he's a bad guy? Because he's smarter than the average person? Smarter than all the other wizards in the land? There are other wizards in the land, right?"

"Several thousand," he told her with a small smile. She filled his heart to bursting, this woman with her steady brown eyes and quick mind. This scientist with the springy dark curls and smooth, pale skin and her soft mouth made for kissing.

She shrugged. "Because he *can*?"

Gabriel would have his team run with it. "How badly did he hurt you this time?" he demanded, walking around the foot of the bed. Heading for the door, not for Eden. Or so he convinced himself. *Step away from the banquet.*

"He got one hit in." She smiled faintly as she finished putting on her shoes. "I kneed him in the balls."

That's my girl, he thought with ridiculous pride. "Good for you," he said mildly. "But did he hurt you?" Fury had built inside him until he was ready to tear down the walls in search of this new wizard who could be anyone he damn well wanted to be.

"I'm okay."

"Sure?"

"Yeah."

Gabriel raked her with another all-encompassing glance. Her hair was messy, just the way he liked it. Her eyes were still a little wild, the pupils dilated, and her mouth was pale, but he knew she was tough. She'd have to be for what was coming next.

"Want to see what I've done with your Rex?" he asked, changing the subject.

She ran her fingers through her curls, then dropped her hands to smooth the short pink T-shirt that rode just above the waistband of her jeans. "Sure." She gave him a steady look from dry eyes. "Why the hell not?"

He reached out a hand to touch her, to reassure her, but curled his fingers into a tight fist and dropped his arm instead. This way was better. Instead he shimmered them to the lab.

"Here." He pulled out the duplicate of her ergonomic chair. "Take a look. See if I've missed anything."

Without looking at him, she sat down, scooting the chair closer to the desk, tucking her feet, in those sexy-as-hell high heels, around the base of the chair. Absently she adjusted the height to suit herself, then settled her fingers on the keyboard, scrolling through pages and pages of codes, her eyes moving as she read.

"Hmm. Yeah. That's good. Hmm. Hmm. Okay . . ." She keyed in an adjustment, then continued reading, totally engrossed in what she was doing.

He materialized his phone into his hand. "I'm calling in this new intel."

"Uh-huh."

Sitting on the edge of the desk, he punched in the 911 code for Sebastian at T-FLAC HQ and filled him in.

"Positive ID on Verdine?" Sebastian asked. Gabriel could hear him keying the data into the computers on his end.

"Yeah. Anything?"

"Not a damn parking ticket. Where the hell did this guy come from?"

"Good question." Gabriel observed the muted light from the monitor shining on Eden's face, tipping her long lashes pale blue, and making her lips glisten. The flickering light also showcased the dark fingerprints on her pale throat, and her swollen cheekbone where she'd been struck.

"More important," Gabriel said harshly to Tremayne. "Where's the son of a bitch *going*?"

"Everyone is on the alert. We'll figure it out sooner than later. How's the bot coming?"

"Good." He watched Eden make adjustments on the keyboard, her slender fingers sure and knowledgeable as she scanned and read what he'd done. "Keep me posted on any anomalies worldwide. He wants Eden dead. He's failed twice. He doesn't want the bot replicated, that's clear."

Her shoulder hitched slightly at his words, but she didn't stop scrolling. Gabriel completed the call, then stuck the small phone onto his belt. "How's it coming?"

"Fine."

"Hungry?"

"Three McDonald's cheeseburgers, small fries—no, make that *large* fries, and a chocolate shake. Hell. Super Size me."

"Apple pie?" he asked, lips twitching.

Her fingers flew as she frowned at the screen. "Sure. What were you thinking here? Never mind. If I do this. And this . . . and this. Yeah. There." She held down the scroll button and stared at the monitor narrow-eyed. "Two apple pies."

Gabriel conjured a double order of everything, waiting until her nose twitched before he reached out and unwrapped a burger. He wrapped the bottom half in a napkin and nudged her shoulder. Hating that she jumped when he touched her. "Here, eat while you work."

"Mmm." She took a bite as she read, then used her left hand to key in data. "We need a vehicle for this."

"If you can think it," he bit into his own burger, "I

can build it. I'm going to turn on CNN. If I keep the sound down will it bother you?"

"A sonic boom doesn't bother me when I'm working." She picked up her shake, stuck the straw into it, then took a drink, all on autopilot. Not once did she so much as glance at him.

Addicted to the news, Gabriel turned on the plasma TV hanging on the wall, keeping the sound low, and dragged a chair up closer to his other addiction. Dr. Eden Cahill.

Right now, if she were a caricature, she'd have steam and flames shooting out of the top of her head.

She was as mad as fire, and he admired her restraint. He knew she had a temper. The crying earlier had been just as much fury as it had been hurt at his casual disregard for what she'd wanted him to say. Or so he told himself, keeping his attention fixed on the screen. A car bombing in Cape Town. He read the crawler on the bottom of the screen while they rehashed the event that had occurred the day before.

This situation could be a hell of a lot worse. She could be *dead*. The thought chilled him like an Arctic frost, all the way to his marrow.

"Turn it up!" Eden said sharply, pushing away from her chair to stand facing the TV. "Turn up the sound!"

Gabriel did so. He glanced from the big screen to Eden's white face and rose to stand beside her.

"If anyone recognizes this child"—the attractive blond anchor's face was replaced by a video; a little boy, carrying an oversized backpack, walking away from the camera—"please call the number on your screen. The amateur video, shot by Patty Benson of Idaho, shows a child approximately five years old, dressed in jeans, a royal blue T-shirt, and red baseball cap, walking across the parking lot at three this afternoon in Yellowstone Park."

Eden grabbed Gabriel's forearm. "That's Rex," she whispered through bloodless lips.

"The child was not part of the tour group, pictured here. No other vehicles were in the parking lot, and no one has reported the boy missing. Authorities now suspect foul play as hour seven of the search continues with no sign of the child, and no missing person report filed.

"In further developments in the suicide bombings in London this morning, we turn to our overseas correspondent, Chandler Landry—" Eden's grip on Gabriel's arm tightened. "Rewind it."

The film immediately scrolled backward until she said hoarsely, "Stop." She bit her lower lip, her gaze fixed up at the TV.

Together they watched a group of adults and children leave the large, air-conditioned bus and walk to the guardrail to observe one of the active geysers. From the left of the screen the child in a red baseball cap appeared, and, hanging back a little, joined a small group of kids on the observation platform. CNN had a lighted oval around the child in the red baseball cap.

Gabriel narrowed his eyes as he watched it. At the end of the piece he started it again. He turned to glance at Eden. She looked devastated. He put his arm around her, rubbing her skin beneath her short sleeve. "I didn't see a robot."

She licked her lower lip. "It's the boy in the red cap. The unidentified child *is* Rex."

He rewound again. Looking at the monitor he said grimly, "Jesus. It looks completely human." He turned to her. "You invented a soulless, calculating machine with the capability of doing untold harm to mankind? Jesus fucking Christ, Eden! You made an invincible goddamned killer robot look like an innocent *child*? What the *fuck* were you thinking?"

He couldn't be half as disgusted and appalled at what she'd done as she was herself.

"Don't—" She put a hand up to stop him from speaking again. "You know that *anything* can be made into a deadly weapon in the wrong hands. I'm not defending my actions, Gabriel," she told him quietly. "I believed what I wanted to believe because I wanted to, no, *needed* to, prove to myself that I was just as good as they said. I—" She swallowed the painful lump in her throat. "I let my ego blind my common sense."

"Hell, sweetheart," he said less harshly. "You have a Nobel Prize, and more awards and accolades than twenty people. What in God's name were you trying to prove? You must have known that no good could come of something like this."

"I never intended to make this advanced technology public. You have to believe me. It was just for my own gratification that I went as far as I did. I had no idea—"

"Water under the bridge," Gabriel said grimly. Frowning, he started pacing the small lab. "What is the son of a bitch up to?" Suddenly he stopped in his tracks. "Why steal a robot and let it roam around Yellowstone dressed like a tourist kid on a day trip?"

Eden raked her fingers through her hair. "He was dressed like that before," she said absently, thinking back to the last time she'd seen her creation sitting on the floor of the lab playing ball with Marshall.

"Well, except for the backpack." She watched Gabriel in the dim glow from the television screen.

"Which has nothing to do with its superhuman strength," he murmured as he returned to pacing. "Yellowstone has to have some sort of merit as a target. So far, nothing Verdine has done has been random. I don't think he'd start now."

The silence was heavy between them as they watched the screen.

"Rex just took off the backpack," Gabriel noted. "Not for comfort. I'm assuming he can't feel pain?" He was only being halfway facetious.

"No. When I designed him, I was thinking about the stamina to fight a fire for days on end. Or perform surgery for hours and hours. I was only thinking about the positive aspects of invincibility."

"Why Yellowstone?" he asked himself out loud.

"Rex is strong," Eden answered, eyes fixed on her monitor, fingers flying over the keyboard. "He can dig. He can climb. In. around. Over. Up." She paused, brow furrowed in concentration. "He doesn't really need any equipment to perform. Everything is built in. The only reason for the backpack would be to carry something too unwieldy, or too large for him to hold."

Gabriel jerked his hand away. "My God. The son of a bitch is going for the water supply."

"What?" Eden frowned. "Why? To *poison* it?" When Gabriel nodded, she swiveled around on her chair to fully face him. "What would he hope to gain? Why use a robot to poison people? Couldn't your garden variety suicide killer do that? There are dozens of ways to terrify, even kill people, that don't require a robot. Especially one of Rex's capabilities. It's as if he's showing off for the world to—what?" She demanded when Gabriel had the look of a man having a lightbulb moment.

He held up a hand, and used the other to open his phone and punch in three numbers with his thumb. "The robot is in Yellowstone Park," he said into the phone. "The missing kid report is our bot," his eyes pinning Eden in place.

Not that she needed pinning. She was frozen with fear and overwhelming guilt. Was Rex supposed to drop something into the water supply in the park? And if so, *what*?

God. It could be absolutely anything. Rex could handle chemicals and compounds that not even another robot could handle.

"Verdine is going for the aquifers in the park," Gabriel said into the phone as if he were reading her mind. "He's using Yellowstone as a staging area," he told Sebastian, but his eyes fixed on Eden's horrified gaze. "My guess is he's giving potential buyers a taste of Rex's capabilities to jack up the price.

"He's sending in the bot to taint the water supply. The aquifers in, around, and under Yellowstone National Park feed into virtually all the natural water sources that supply the western United States."

Listening to his side of the conversation, Eden didn't agree. "Overkill," she told him. "That's like killing an ant with an atomic bomb. Dropping poison down a geyser doesn't require an indestructible robot."

Gabriel acknowledged her observation with a wait-a-second lifted finger. "What chemical compounds have been reported missing worldwide in the last thirty days?" he barked into the phone. "No. Stronger than that DZ7 stolen from the Chechnian rebel camp. Stronger than that as well. We're looking for a powerful liquid nerve toxin or bio weapon. Something so powerful it couldn't be handled by a normal robot . . . Look for unlikely components that have this potential when combined. Substances that are out of the norm. Yeah. I'll wait."

"Tell me more about this damn thing," Gabriel demanded flatly, still holding the small phone to his ear.

Eden swallowed nausea. Just because he'd extracted the data from her didn't mean he'd had time to look at it. And even if he had, Eden doubted anyone but an AI scientist could make out anything more than the overview.

"It has a simple and efficient algorithm using configuration space to execute collision-free motions. In other words—nothing is going to stand in his way."

"What else?"

"To perform everyday tasks, Marshall and I had to teach it everyday physics. Rex learned concepts and theories. It can identify and reason about physical objects that break apart, come together, or mix. Rex—Oh, God. *It* knows its chemicals, Gabriel. And it knows what to do with them. It comprehends motive, and—it learns from experience."

She pressed her arm against her midriff where nerves fluttered uncomfortably in her tummy. She'd thought herself so damn clever.

"But not emotion?" Gabriel demanded tightly. "The damn thing can't reason nor does it have common sense. Is that right?"

"Correct."

"Yeah," he muttered into the phone. "You do that. Make it fast." He snapped the phone shut. "You told me nothing can destroy this thing."

"Yes."

"Are you one hundred percent sure?"

She shuddered, remembering all the tests they'd run at each phase. "I'm one hundred percent positive."

"Nothing?"

"Another bot. One that's exactly the same. But stronger. Or magic?"

"Yeah. I have to go," he said grimly.

They couldn't wait for Rex 2 to be finished. They'd run out of time. At least they knew where the first bot was located.

With magic Gabriel could destroy Rex before it did anything. "I know," she told him. Wishing he didn't have to go anywhere *near* whatever was happening at Yellowstone.

"Don't leave this room for any reason. Lark? Simon?"

"As if—" Eden flinched when both Lark and Simon materialized beside Gabriel.

"Hey," Lark said cheerfully.

"The others will meet you there," Simon told Gabriel, walking up to the computer monitor. "Amazing feat of engineering. Glad to have you on our team, Doctor," he told Eden, who was ignoring both of them, her entire attention fixed on Gabriel.

He touched her cheek, then teleported to Yellowstone.

He'd hardly left and he was back again. She looked shocked to see him back so quickly. "I didn't see you there." She pointed at the TV.

"We kept out of range," Gabriel said flatly. He encompassed Lark and Simon in a glance. "Verdine has a protection spell on the damn thing. We couldn't get close enough. We tried our entire bag of tricks. Not a damn, fucking *thing* worked. Couldn't even get the backpack away from it."

Lark went pale. "That's impossible, Gabriel. You know it's impossible. It's a man-made object. It can be destroyed by magic."

"Verdine's imbued the damn thing with his powers."

"Is that *possible*?" Simon demanded sharply.

"I would never have believed so. But yeah. Not only possible. But a done deal. There were four of us, using our considerable combined powers, and nothing made a dent in the shield around it."

Lark glanced at the TV monitor, and then back to Gabriel. "Want us to stay, or get back to the think tank?"

"Go. I'll call if I need you again. Thanks."

Eden blinked as they shimmered and disappeared. "I will *never* get used to that!"

"We duplicate it as planned."

"Fine, but how is the second one going to be able to get through that protective shield, if you guys couldn't?"

"We're working on that. How far are we?"

She glanced over at the blinking cursor on the monitor. "I still have to go through all—" She glanced back at him and took a shuddering breath. She bit her lip. "If magic didn't destroy hi—*it*, what makes you think another one can?"

"We'll give the good guy some magic of its own. But first it needs to be completed, and sent in. Keep working," he told her tightly. "How close?"

"Four hours. Minimum."

"Make it two. Sit down and get the job done."

Eden slid into the chair, and concentrated on focusing. Her hands were shaking. If it wasn't bad enough that her bot had fallen into the wrong hands, it had been snatched by a *wizard*. A wizard who had managed to increase its indestructibility.

There was nothing, not a damn thing that Gabriel could say to her that she hadn't said to herself in the last few days. She'd been stupid and naive to believe that what she'd done was to further science. Instead of being such a vain, egotistical moron, she should have destroyed every scrap of data, and pretended that she'd never gotten as far as she had.

Pandora's box had been opened and there was no way of closing it now.

A headache throbbed at the base of her skull as she speed-read what Gabriel had put together. Joining the threads when she came to gaps. "Damn."

"What?"

"We have a multiple diagnostic disorder problem happening simultaneously here."

"Figure it out," he told her tightly. "Focus on the most plausible solutions."

"Which raises the question: Which hypothesis is more plausible than others?" she asked absently, keying in a string of numbers.

The fix took forty precious minutes.

While she worked she could hear Gabriel in the background, talking softly into the phone. He'd already contacted a dozen people. Sebastian. His brother. T-FLAC, and of course the other wizards who, from his end of the conversation, were in a panic about this new, powerful wizard.

Eden would just add her name to the bottom of a long list. The only thing keeping her marginally less terrified for her physical safety right now was Gabriel's large presence in the room.

She was concentrating so hard she jumped when the sound on the TV came up.

The blond anchor's face became more animated as she spoke. "We're getting additional reports coming from Yellowstone . . ."

"Turn it up," Eden fixed her eyes on the footage being broadcast. The same tour bus from the earlier report was in the center of the frame. Only now, the perimeter of the bus was littered with bodies. Some were obviously tourists, but others appeared to be uniformed: police, firemen, paramedics, and park rangers.

All dead.

The anchor continued her report as the camera lens panned the horrible images. "Sources close to the situation have told CNN that, thus far, all attempts by Hazmat to approach the scene have resulted in death. A small drone was sent in less than an hour ago. Our viewers might recall that similar drones have been used to search rubble following earthquakes.

"In this case, the drone collected items from the dead, including this video camera. In a CNN exclusive, we're about to show you the tape from that home video. A word of caution: these images are graphic."

Eden and Gabriel stood transfixed as gritty, jerky pictures filled the screen. People coughing, choking, crying, and screaming as they panicked and tried to shove their way back onto the bus. The cameraman, whoever he was, had made it to the bottom step of the bus before falling to the ground. The camera had kept shooting.

"That's Rex! What's he doing?"

The anchor seemed just as perplexed, saying, "The unidentified little boy seems to have returned to the group, and is now wandering away again. Authorities are trying to discern why this child was spared the grim fate of everyone else who has come into contact with this busload of tourists.

"However, it is unsafe for any responders to mount a full-scale search for this little boy until the toxin has been identified. The FBI, local authorities, and Homeland Security are treating this as a terrorist incident at this time. We will update you with—Oh!"

They watched with the anchor as the home video blurred and wavered as the camera melted.

Gabriel turned down the sound with a glance, then looked at Eden. She stood with one hand covering her mouth, her face white, her big brown eyes haunted.

"*That's* why Jason wanted Rex's housing to be invincible. Dear God. I'm responsible for the death of all tho—those people."

"Verdine is responsible," Gabriel assured her, resting his hand on her shoulder and giving her a gentle squeeze meant to comfort. "A determined criminal can turn a regular radio into a bomb capable of bringing down an aircraft. We don't hold Marconi responsible for the actions of terrorists. The question now is, can we duplicate it in time?"

He'd been focused on the "brain" of the bot, not what carried it. Now the vehicle was just as important as the new bot's functions.

Eden grabbed his hands. Her slender fingers were like ice as she brought his hands to her head. Her shiny dark hair curled over Gabriel's fingers as he buried them in the silky strands at either side of her temple. Moisture glinted on her long lashes as she squeezed her eyes shut and tilted back her head.

"Suck out what you need. Hurry," she whispered brokenly. "Oh, God. Gabriel. Please. Hurry."

CHAPTER NINETEEN

Gabriel felt her pain and anguish as if they were his own as he began the Joining again. Felt her unimaginable guilt for the deaths she believed she was directly responsible for. He felt her pride and joy turn to something dark and too painful for her to bear. His heart ached empathetically with her pain.

Although it wasn't necessary, he brought his mouth down on hers. Her breath hitched and was ragged, but her lips clung eagerly. Her arms slid around his neck as she held on tightly. Her eagerness wasn't sexual. Not this time.

She craved comfort and reassurance, and Gabriel made sure she had both as he carefully extracted the necessary additional information from her.

The Curse had no provisions for this, he thought, dazed, as he slid his hands free.

He loved her.

The realization went through him like a shock wave. Changing everything in its wake.

Without a word he wrapped his arms around her, drawing her hard against him. She glided her arms around his waist as he rocked them both. Holding her. Holding his heart in his arms.

Gabriel kissed her with gentle passion. Aching with love for this smart, funny, valiant woman who'd turned his life upside down and right way up in such a short time.

God. What a *fool* he was.

A fool for tempting fate and allowing this to happen.

This was why Nairne's Curse was so fucking *diabolically* clever. Their love was meant to be. That was obvious. Two halves of a whole. Nothing half-assed about it.

Blood surged through his veins with impotent fury. He could love Eden from now until eternity. But she could never know it. Because if she knew how much he loved her, she'd never leave him. And staying with him would mean her death.

The warmth slid away, leaving him suspended in a cold reality.

This wasn't a case of making a choice. There *was* no choice. To save her he had to choose duty over love. It was the only option he had: the *no option* option.

> Duty o'er love was the choice you did make
> My love you did spurn, my heart you did break
>
> Your penance to pay, no pride you shall gain
> Three sons on three sons find nothing but pain
>
> I gift you my powers in memory of me
> The joy of love no son shall ever see
>
> When a Lifemate is chosen by the heart of a son
> No protection can be given, again I have won
>
> His pain will be deep, her death will be swift,
> Inside his heart a terrible rift
>
> Only freely given will this curse be done
> To break the spell, three must work as one

What the hell was it that she had to give freely? Her love? No. Three had to work as one.

Something he, Caleb, and Duncan had to do together? At the same time?

Damn it to hell. *What?*

Or was the Curse in three parts? Did each of them have to be given something freely to break the curse?

He had no idea.

Nairne had made that a hurdle as well. His brothers and his sons and their sons would all still be subject to Nairne's wrath. Worse still, he had no one to ask. His brothers were just as baffled as he was. Shit.

Gently he extracted himself from her arms and stepped away. Away from the bruised, dazed look in her eyes. Away from the soft vulnerable downward curve of her pale lips. Away from a future of joy that he'd never imagined possible.

He touched his fingers to her cheek and said softly, "Let's build a robot and kick some ass."

The second robot wasn't as pretty or sophisticated as the Rx793, Eden thought, but it would do the job. It didn't look deceptively like a sweet-faced child. It looked like what it was. A no-frills machine. Its special alloyed steel body was clunky but functional. While the four-foot-tall bot looked as though it would lumber on its short metal legs, its gait was smooth and it moved directionally with ease.

Like Rex, this . . . *one* would be capable of estimating depth and distance by finding the peak in the distribution of velocity-sensitive units lying along the line of sight. In this way, depth and velocity would be simultaneously extracted, sending the information back to them here. Only this bot had a few extras preprogrammed. This bot had an enemy. Rex. Eden had taken great care in making sure that this bot would eliminate Rex by any means necessary.

Which of course, as they both knew, could present a danger in and of itself. Gabriel had already arranged for the area to be cleared within two hundred miles. She'd prefer a thousand.

They both hoped to hell two hundred square miles would be enough.

To achieve what they needed to strengthen the new bot, Eden had ensured it had almost the same metallurgical composition of Rex. This bot would be able to find Rex based on that data alone. But she'd added more tensile strength, and the ability to withstand hundreds more chemical compositions than the original. The new matrix composite materials she'd built in made its strain-to-failure ratio *double* that of Rex. She'd done this, amazingly, astonishingly enough, just by *thinking*.

These complex factors were solely due to Gabriel being able to extract the information directly from Eden's mind, and translate them into something tangible.

The idea was as terrifying as it was fascinating.

Another masterpiece of engineering mastery, she thought bitterly, looking at the ungainly little bot in front of her. She ran her fingers through her hair to press on her aching scalp.

"Headache?" Gabriel asked, replacing her fingers with his own, and gently massaging her scalp. Her tension was palpable. Her stress evident.

How could he *not* touch her?

She groaned. "That feels good enough to be illegal."

"What touching you does to my body should be illegal," he told her gruffly. She rolled her head on her neck to release some of the tension. Then nuzzled her lips to his palm when he cupped her face.

He tipped her head back, moving his lips across hers,

wetting them with a swipe of his tongue, enjoying her small hiss of pleasure. "Like that?"

"Yes." She did it back, mimicking the same seductive sweep of her tongue. Gabriel felt the jolt of desire clear to his toes and pulled her to her feet so he could kiss her properly.

Unfortunately there wasn't time to linger. "Let's test the video feed one more time." He moved back to his position, leaning against the workstation across the room.

Eden bent to make a final adjustment for flexibility on the new robot's flat feet. It was good to go. She joined Gabriel and MacBain. The butler had arrived a few minutes earlier to whisk away the bag of cold fast food and replace it with a selection of fruit, cheeses, crackers, and a large thermos of coffee.

It was a nice thought, but neither she nor Gabriel had the time or inclination to eat, and they were wired enough without consuming a gallon of coffee. No matter how excellent it might be.

Through the bot's impervious eyes, they'd be able to see what was transpiring so that Eden could override and voice manipulate its actions when it was away from the castle if necessary. She'd already given it specific instructions with variables so that it could anticipate, and think for itself.

"Video feed. On," the robot stated in an even voice.

Beside her, MacBain started. "My goodness. It sounds quite—human."

"Dr. Kirchner's findings in voice recognition are— were brilliant. I just . . . tweaked what he'd done and came up with a new tool for specifying and establishing semantic dependencies. Go to the table under the window," Eden told it.

"I integrated syntax and semantics. It understands natural language . . ." Her voice trailed off, the train of thought already forgotten as she placed one knee on her chair, and leaned over to watch the monitor. Through the eyes of the robot she observed its progress as it crossed the room to the window.

It moved well, she thought with satisfaction, and its eye scans were excellent. Earlier she'd laid out seven pens on the table. Five black, two blue. "Pick up the blue pen on the left."

Mechanical fingers deftly lifted the correct pen from the table.

"Shit. That's amazing," Gabriel said behind her.

"So precise," MacBain murmured admiringly. "What an exceptionally clever young woman."

"Hell," Eden said absently, leaning over to tap out a series of numbers on the keyboard beside her. "No. No. No." She sent the new data to the bot, who'd crushed the pen instead of just holding it. "Damn it. This needs more time. I want to—"

"Eden?"

She finished another sequence, glancing up at Gabriel almost absently as she considered adding one more feature.

"We're not going for perfect or even fully functioning," he told her softly, feeling an empty ache opening inside him as he imagined the rest of his life without seeing her every day with just this look of intense concentration on her pretty face. The rest of his life remembering, but not seeing, the way her silky dark hair looked just-out-of-bed mussed all the time.

He drank in the way her big brown eyes resumed focus as she looked at him. *Ah, Eden. What the hell am I going to do without you?* "We're going for getting this done as quickly as possible so we can send it in. Remember?"

She blinked. "Right. Yes. Got it." She straightened from her uncomfortable half-kneeling position to stand beside her chair. Digging her fingers into the back of the seat, her knuckles showed white as she gave him a resolute nod. "We're ready."

While she'd been testing the bot, Gabriel had discussed at length the best coordinates for the drop with Sebastian and the team he'd assembled at T-FLAC HQ. The topographical map of the Yellowstone area was up on the other computer, which he'd set beside her monitor so they were side by side for easy viewing.

"That blinking red circle is the drop zone. Knowing how fast Rex can travel made it pretty easy for Sebastian to calculate his approximate location in Yellowstone. So, now it's just a simple case of zapping this bot into the general area and letting him—*it*, letting *it* do its thing."

Eden turned to look. "Teleport?"

"Yeah."

"Now?"

"Right . . . now." A glowing green dot blinked in the middle of Gabriel's monitor as the robot was teleported in the space of seconds from the castle to the location selected in Yellowstone Park. "Let's see what he can see."

"The tour bus was here, in the lot outside the Old Faithful Visitors Center in the Upper Geyser Basin. Verdine could easily obtain the schedule of when each geyser erupts."

"Don't you think it's a little too coincidental that Jason picked Yellowstone Park for this?" Eden asked.

"The Park has some ten thousand thermal features, according to our geologists. Yellowstone is where the majority of the world's geysers are located. It's not coincidental. It makes sense."

"He could have chosen to contaminate the water supply from the Arctic. Or the Alps, or any other place with substantial mountain runoff and/or glacier melt. But he's practically in *your* backyard."

"Or T-FLAC's backyard. Our headquarters is almost next door." Gabriel watched as the bot navigated a small grouping of bodies on the boardwalk near Old Faithful. Gabriel's gut tightened as the robot weaved through the grim site. Many of the bodies were already bloated from the high concentration of the toxin. And that wasn't the only side effect. Most of the faces showed signs of sudden death with unclotted blood from all orifices. It was a testament to their quick but painful deaths.

If Verdine wanted a graphic and shocking display for his bidders, he'd done a hell of a job.

"Oh God," Eden whispered hoarsely, hand to her throat.

Gabriel expelled a breath as he wrapped his arm around her shoulders and tugged her close. "Verdine is a sick bastard."

Eyes fixed on the screen, she shivered. Gabriel ran his hand up and down her arm. Her skin felt like ice. "I agree," she said quietly. "But I guess my biggest question is *why?*"

"Yeah. Mine, too," he admitted. "The simple answer could be that when dealing with terrorists it doesn't have to *be* personal. But I'm with you on this one. As are my cohorts both at T-FLAC and in T-FLAC/psi—we have a dozen teams working on this one."

"Why Yellowstone?" she demanded, frowning. "Why now? Why would a wizard that nobody's ever even *heard* about, pick a location *this* close to not only Edridge Castle, but also T-FLAC's top secret headquarters? And three hundred miles *is* close."

He put his arms around her waist. "We're working on finding the answer."

She leaned back, and wrapped her cold fingers around his forearms. Her sweet-smelling hair tickled his nose. She tilted her head, resting it against his chest as she watched the horrific video. "I'd say Jason has more on his agenda than a splashy and gory freaking marketing push. He wants *you* to notice him. He wants you to . . . *engage* him."

"Yeah. I agree."

CNN was now exclusively covering the massive deaths in Yellowstone Park and the surrounding area. Thousands of people had already been evacuated. They believed at least three hundred people were already dead. On the TV hanging on the wall above their monitors, Gabriel observed the joint forces gathering at an "undisclosed" location as they tried to figure out who, how, and what.

All T-FLAC operatives had been called in yesterday. Wizards from around the world were standing by to offer assistance.

And Gabriel was waiting for Verdine to return to the castle. It was his logical next move.

"Got you, you bastard!"

"Thank God," Eden whispered as the backpack came into view. They'd watched the bot's progress for the past twenty minutes as it maneuvered past Rex's victims. She wanted to look away from the shocking visuals, but she couldn't, no matter how much the sight sickened her.

Her penance for inventing Rex in the first place.

These graphic images would stay with her forever.

"Where is it?" Eden asked hoarsely as the second bot closed the distance to the little red backpack that was innocently leaning against a rocky outcrop inside a railing separating the wooden boardwalk from the geyser.

"Fifty yards to the left. Verdine must be doing a visual feed as well. He's waiting for the geyser to erupt; when it does the boiling water will hit the chemicals in the bag and disperse them, as well as drawing them back deep beneath the earth to contaminate the aquifer."

"Let's ruin Jason's day," she said determinedly, opening the mic to talk to Bot 2.

"Absorb backpack."

Nothing happened.

She tried again. "Eliminate target."

Thanks to the GPS read on the monitor to her left, she was able to give the bot exact coordinates for the backpack. "Damn it. It's not working! I'm not getting any error messages; why has it stopped responding?"

"Verdine's controlling it. Keep the bot moving, like he's still trying." Gabriel stood directly behind her.

"He *is* still trying, damn it." She closed her eyes briefly in gratitude when she felt the brush of Gabriel's fingers on her nape, and the cool strength of his hand as he left it there in a strangely comforting gesture. She'd desperately needed the human contact. His contact. With him there she could handle anything.

He massaged the knots in her neck as he spoke. "Keep it going a little longer. Jesus," he said roughly. "Verdine is strong. I can feel the son of a bitch pushing at our little guy. Okay, ease off a little. That's it."

He stopped kneading. "I have a few tricks up my sleeve too . . . Watch this—"

The little red backpack imploded. As soon as the bits of canvas and a murky yellow liquid started to drop to the ground they were vaporized and disappeared as if they'd never been. It took seconds. And then there was nothing there.

Eden snapped her mouth closed, and turned to look up at him. "How did—how did you do that from here?"

"Channeled my powers through our bot's eyes. That was the easy part. Now let's issue an invitation. Send good bot over to say howdy to Rex."

"Go to within"—she glanced up at Gabriel. He held up five fingers—"to within five feet of Rx793," Eden instructed. The monitor showed the closing gap as the new bot approached Rex.

Suddenly the screen jumped and blurred to black. "Wait! No. Damn it!" She frantically started a number sequence to get the bot back online so they could see what was happening.

Gabriel clamped his fingers over her wrist. "I have them."

She spun around to look at him. "What do you mean *you* have them? I hadn't finished yet! I haven't instructed—"

"You've done a great job, sweetheart. There's nothing more we can do right now. Verdine's magic is just too powerful to counteract. We'll take care of Rex's destruction later. For now, both bots are safe in suspended animation where Verdine can't find them. He's going to come for a little visit as soon as he realizes—"

Eden, feeling a little sizzle pass through her, shot out of her chair, and grabbed Gabriel by the front of his T-shirt. "Oh, no you don't, Gabriel Edge! Don't you even *think* about zapping me back to Tempe now. I'm here for the duration."

"How the hell did you kn—"

"Do you think I don't know how that devious, wizardly brain of yours works by now? Do something so that I'm safe from whatever's going to happen. But don't send me away. Please, *don't* make me leave you."

"Christ, Eden. Verdine has become one of the most powerful wizards around. There's a good chance—"

She brushed her lips across his. "Don't say it. You do what you have to do, because I'm not done with you."

She hopped on one foot as she bent down to slide her Grandma Rose's lucky ring from her toe. "Here. Put this in your pocket. I know it's silly, but this ring has brought me luck, and kept me safe for twenty-seven years. And it kept me safe from *Jason Verdine*. It'll do the same for you. Take it."

Gabriel took the small ring and stuck it in the front pocket of his jeans. "I'd rather send you back home where I kn—"

"Are you going to meet him here?" Eden cut him off. Even though she wanted to cling to him and not let him go anywhere *near* Jason Verdine, she took a step back. "I'd think one of the bigger rooms downstairs would be better for this meeting, don't you?"

Gabriel touched her cheek and her heartbeat spiked as it always did. No matter what happened after tonight, they would always be hungry for each other.

"Size does matter." He bent to kiss her lightly on the mouth.

When Eden opened her eyes they were in the dining room.

Puzzled by the odd perspective she had of the room, she glanced around, but found that only her eyes could move. If she looked to the side all she saw was a heavy gilded frame. Odd.

What on earth have you done to me, Gabriel Edge?

Startled, Gabriel looked up. *I can hear you.* His lips weren't moving.

After everything that's been going on around here, this comes as a surprise?

You have no idea. "Hang in there, sweetheart. Until this is over, I've put you in a portrait where you can see, but not be seen." He reached up and touched her face.

Not that Eden could feel it. Or anything else for that matter. She was frozen in place. Hiding in plain sight inside one of the paintings hanging on the wall.

His fingers trailed across what were, presumably, her lips and he looked into her eyes as he said softly, "Stay safe."

Clever man, but does it have to be quite this authen-

tic? These stays are digging into me, and I think I have freaking bugs in my wig!

"You look beautiful." He grinned at her disgruntled tone, knowing it hid the nerves she was determined not to show him. She looked as prim and expressionless as all the other portraits, but her big, beautiful brown eyes shone out of the painting like a promise.

Be careful.

"Yeah. I will." He patted his pocket. "I have my lucky charm."

Don't mock it. Grandma Rose had very good karma.

Since he knew he'd need every advantage, even the imaginary good fortune of Eden's lucky ring, he simply nodded his agreement. "Gotta go to work."

Yes. Good plan. Concentrate on what you have to do. You're better than he is. Stronger. More powerful. You're going to do whatever you need to do to beat him, and then you're going to make me . . . round again. Her tone was droll, and his heart expanded in his chest. *Now go. Do whatever you need to do.*

The problem was, Gabriel thought as he rearranged the room to his satisfaction, and as Eden's adorable, telepathic pep talk continued, he *wasn't* stronger or more powerful than Verdine. But he was more determined, and hopefully smarter. It was going to have to be enough.

He had a few tricks up his sleeve, but he suspected Verdine was capable of turning him into a grease spot on the carpet with only marginal effort.

With nothing to do but wait, Gabriel poured himself a drink he didn't want, and went to sit across from Eden's portrait so he could watch her and the door at the same time.

Slouching in an armchair, he swirled a few inches of amber whiskey in the bottom of a crystal glass as he waited. He surveyed the room. He'd shimmered the long table elsewhere, clearing a long, narrow space in the middle of the floor.

Caleb had made arrangements to ensure Eden's continued safety. When this was over, and it would be one way or another, she would go back to her life in Tempe, Arizona. His brothers and MacBain would make sure that she was safe and well cared for, for the rest of her life, if he didn't make it.

And in the event that he did make it, Eden would be safer far, far, far away from him. Once she left the castle he'd make sure she could never find it again. He knew she cared for him. Cared deeply. But she was a woman who deserved to love completely and be loved completely in return.

She was so smart, so funny, so filled with the joy of life that it wouldn't be long before she met a man who could, and would, give her everything she deserved.

Gabriel's chest ached as though someone had kicked him in the solar plexus. He rubbed the flat of his hand over the ache. Damn it to hell.

He wanted everything for her.

He wanted her future to be as filled with joy as his would be empty with loss. He wanted her to find a man to whom she could give her heart and soul. As he knew she would forever hold his. He wanted her to wake with sunlight on her face, while he would forever walk in shadows.

He wanted her never to feel the ache of separation, never to feel a moment of loss, never to experience even a breath of pain.

Because he was destined to live the rest of his life mired in those burdens. He would absorb the loss. The loneliness. The dearth of love.

No matter how short a time he'd had with her, his love for her was going to have to warm him for the rest of his life. And she deserved to be ridiculously, blissfully happy. No matter how he felt.

Jesus. He scrubbed his hand over his bristly jaw, wanting to scream at the fates for allowing this to happen. And yet, he thought morosely, staring into his untouched drink, how could he regret meeting Eden?

God, this was hard. The hardest thing he'd ever done in his life.

He wished that letting Eden go, doing the right thing, would make him at least *feel* like a victorious hero.

He gave a short, mirthless laugh. Because the reality was he was already feeling like a victorious goddamned *martyr*. It wouldn't be called a fucking curse if it was easy.

There hadn't been an Edge in five hundred years who'd managed to elude her powerful curse. No matter how hard they'd tried. No matter how desperately they'd wanted to.

That witch Nairne sure as hell knew her stuff.

CHAPTER TWENTY

Two sets of footsteps sounded in the hallway beyond the closed double doors. Years of experience as a top T-FLAC operative helped him switch gears to focus on the immediate danger.

Gabriel stayed where he was, stretching out his long legs, and resting the glass on his flat belly.

Relaxed, at ease, preternaturally alert.

One hundred percent focused on the now.

The door swung open. "Master Duncan has arrived," MacBain stated formally, and quite unnecessarily, since Duncan was standing right beside him.

"So it would appear," Gabriel gave his younger brother a lazy look. "Thanks, MacPain. Close the door behind you."

MacBain gave an affronted sniff and closed the door with a pissy little snap.

"Drink?" Gabriel asked, rising to cross to the drinks table.

"I'll pass." Duncan strolled into the middle of the room. He glanced at the crossed blades above the fireplace. "Still playing with swords, big brother?"

Gabriel shrugged, lifting the glass to his mouth, watching the other man over the rim. "When I have time."

"Now's good," Duncan said softly, and Gabriel found himself holding his claymore.

* * *

Thank God. Duncan was here to support Gabriel. Eden watched as a long sword appeared in each man's hand. Magic was a wonderful thing.

One-handed, they each easily held the weight of the four-foot-long swords, unlike her struggle when she'd tried to lop off Jason's smarmy head. This was good. Really, really good, she thought, relief washing through her.

Surely with the two of them . . . Her brain froze.

Hadn't MacBain told her that if the brothers were together it canceled out most of their powers? Oh, my God. *Duncan! Get lost. Go. Get out of here!* Shit. Shit. Shit. If Jason showed up now, Gabriel and Duncan will be screwed.

She considered that for a moment. One of them had just used magic to arm them with those swords. Was that considered a basic power? Or—

Oh, God! Not *Duncan.*

Jason.

Gabriel set his glass down on a nearby table. "One round." He toed off his shoes, peeled off his socks, and tossed them aside, hefting the familiar weight of his favorite sword in his hand. "I'm expecting company."

Verdine, posing as Duncan, grinned. "Best of three?"

"I am. Yes." Gabriel sent the man a shark smile as he raised his sword and advanced. So his opponent wanted to toy with him for a while, did he? He executed the proper salute, holding the other wizard's black eyes. "Let's do it." Verdine brought his sword down in a blurringly-fast strike, expertly using pressure against the flat of Gabriel's blade. Gabriel choked up on the leather hilt; he'd foolishly given the other wizard the flat of his sword. Instead of the edge. He frowned, feeling the tremendous strain of the pressure the other blade was exerting on his. He couldn't resist, and let his point drop. Giving Verdine the score.

The man's eyes glittered. "Manage to neutralize the other robot? Yellowstone, wasn't it?"

"I did, yes," Gabriel lied, fighting against Verdine's mental suggestions, knowing, *knowing,* damn it, that it was demonstrably impossible to block a cut with the flat of his sword. But he felt powerless to change what he was doing. *Fuck. Get the hell out of my head, dickhead!*

"But not before over three hundred innocents died," Gabriel finished, sweat beading his forehead as he corrected, by using intense concentration, the angle of his sword against the next blow.

A glittering shower of sparks fell around the two men as their swords connected, slid, caught, as their feet moved across the stone floor. This time Gabriel managed to deflect the blow the right way. And felt the tooth-rattling jar all the way up his arm into his collarbone to prove just how fucking close it had been to the wrong way.

A cardinal principal of defense was to be where the attack wasn't. But Verdine had employed mind control to use him as a puppet. Gabriel didn't spare a nanosecond to glance at the portrait of Eden. But she was there.

She was not going to see him die.

Not today.

Hands traversing up and across to direct Verdine's blade vertical and over, Gabriel directed his point under the incoming blade, and sliced upward using the cutting-through motion, simultaneously sidestepping with the deflection. Even though he knew this man wasn't his brother, it was disconcerting to be determined to kill someone who wore Duncan's face.

"Actually," Verdine said smugly, "it was closer to four hundred. But who's counting. Fuck them if they can't take a joke." He morphed back into himself as he backed up. "Nobody's innocent anymore."

Gabriel halted his opponent's backward motion by sliding his blade down to Verdine's crossguard, jerking the other man in close, bringing them eye to eye. Yeah. This was much better, seeing his enemy's real face. He was going to enjoy killing him. "Children died."

"Yeah? Whatever." Verdine's black eyes glittered as he tried to push away, and found he couldn't. "What did you do with the Rx793?"

Gabriel shoved him away with all his power. The other man flew thirty feet across the room to slam into the antique mahogany paneling with a loud thud. "You didn't think I'd let you keep it did you, Verdine?" Gabriel braced himself for the loss of weight as he teleported both swords back to the wall with a loud clang.

Across the room the master wizard staggered to his feet. "How did you know it was me?" Like the separating tectonic plates in an earthquake, the floor beneath Gabriel's feet shifted and buckled, and it was his turn to stagger and stumble, trying to find his balance as Verdine opened a fissure in the stone floor between them.

Shooting flames and foul-smelling black smoke spewed from the gash separating them, obscuring the other wizard from view.

But Gabriel knew the son of a bitch was still there. He felt his malevolence pulsing through the vast room like a living thing. He extinguished the flames and slammed the fissure closed with a force that rocked the room, shaking the pictures on the walls.

Jesus, MacBain was going to have his head for the mess, Gabriel thought absently as he watched Verdine's eyes for his next move.

"My brothers and I cancel each other's powers when we're together, and somehow I feel stronger with you around. Go figure." As he spoke, Gabriel shot a bolt of jagged, ice-green lightning between them.

Verdine shimmered behind him and the bolt hit the far wall in a shower of rock fragments and arcing balls of white flame.

Gabriel turned on a dime, blasting the man with an even more powerful bolt. The air crackled and jumped, smelling strongly of singed hair and sulfur.

"Go figure," Verdine snarled, levitating over Gabriel's head. He did something that made Gabriel feel as though his body were being eaten by fucking fire ants. The pain was intense enough to make his eyes water, although he could see there wasn't a damn thing on him.

He didn't have the power right then to conjure a nest of fire ants, but one black adder should do it. Teeth clenched against the intense burning pain spreading over his skin, Gabriel wound the length of the snake around Verdine's neck. The snake's yellow mouth opened wide, inches from the other wizard's jugular, its fangs dripping venom—

Verdine cast it against the wall, where it dropped, lifeless. He drifted down from the ceiling to hover several feet over the ash-blackened carpet. Filled with various colors of smoke and falling ash, the room smelled of fire and smoke and unimaginable evil. "Rex can't be destroyed, Edge, so where's my robot? I'll make your life a living hell until you return him to me."

"Go for it, asshole." Sweat ran freely into Gabriel's eyes while the pain of the fire ants swarmed over his body, eating him alive. "Ain't gonna happen." He brought the ten-foot-wide, thousand-pound, wrought-iron chandelier crashing down on top of the other man in a blur of black and a screech of metal.

This time, Verdine wasn't quick enough to move out of the way. He screamed as the sharp curlicues impaled him, pinning him to the blackened carpet. Blood spurted dramatically, and for a moment Verdine went limp.

Suddenly Eden appeared in a heap between them. Gabriel had just released a deadly energy ball in Verdine's direction. He had to draw back the killing power surge he was sending to Verdine before it struck her. It bounced around the room, ricocheting off the walls, and forced Gabriel to sidestep his own life-ending energy ball as it boomeranged back at him.

"Jesus—Eden—" Breath snagged and heart manic, fire ants forgotten, he raced forward to help her to her feet. She was naked and bloody, her hands and feet tied brutally tight by old-fashioned hemp rope that had already cut into her slender wrists and ankles. She was sobbing brokenly, her eyes swollen shut, her face bruised and bleeding. Her lip was cut. Bleeding—God.

"Gabriel." Her bound hands reached out to him, her nails torn at the quick. "Help me, please. Don't let him hurt me anymore. Oh, God, Gabriel. Please." She was sobbing as she stared up at him with helpless, hopeless eyes.

"Just tell him what he wants to kn—" Her words ended on a high agonized shriek as Verdine materialized a long thin leather whip out of nowhere and slashed it down over her creamy shoulders. Her skin split; bright red blood seeped at an alarming rate onto the carpet beneath her.

"If some *doppelganger* me touched you," Eden had demanded crossly, after Verdine had tried to kill her a second time, "wouldn't *you* be able to tell the difference?"

At his feet, Eden curled into the fetal position, covered her head with her arms. Her frantic whimpers tore out his heart, hurting worse than an army of fire ants.

There's nothing in front of you! Do you hear me,

Gabriel Edge? There. Is. Nothing. On. The. Floor. In. Front. Of. You.

The voice in his head was hysterical, but there was no doubting that the sweet voice was Eden's.

Shove Grandma Rose's freaking lucky ring on your pinkie, and kick butt. Now. Do it now!

Forcing himself to drag his attention off the apparition of Eden, Gabriel jammed his fingers into his front pocket, pushing his pinkie through the ring. It clung to the tip of his finger.

Instantly a ripple of sensation, emanating from his hand, spiraled up his arm. Heat and energy buzzed through tissue, muscle and bone, the phenomenon increasing in intensity as it passed through his body.

What the hell?

Suddenly colors appeared brighter. His eyesight seemed sharper. His hearing more acute.

"Trust me," Verdine told him, his voice booming in the room like thunder. "I *will* kill her." He snaked back the thin, black leather whip. It whined as it whirled through the air. "Produce the bot. Now!" The leather screamed an inhuman shriek over his head, then snapped forward over Eden's bowed head.

Gabriel knew how fast that whip was descending, yet to his eyes it moved in slo-mo. Somehow his powers were supercharged. On the downward swing he snatched the whip from the air. In a blindingly fast move he wrapped the leather around Verdine's throat. Over. Around. And over. And around again. Each rotation stripping the thong of Verdine's power, and replacing it with his own.

Their magic battled in little bursts of electricity that buzzed and hummed and danced like fireflies along the length of the whip.

Verdine's hands shot up to grasp the thin cord as he attempted to pull it free of his neck. He tried to suck in air, his eyes wild as his face went red. Then white. Then quite blue.

Eyes bulging, the wizard dropped to his knees, frantically attempting to curl his fingers beneath the coils tightening inextricably around his throat. In an instant he morphed into Gabriel's mother, Cait.

Seeing her beloved face, even though Gabriel knew this *wasn't* his mother, gave him a jolt. She stretched out her hands, fiery hair trapped against her neck by the black cord. "Gabriel, darling, *don't*," she sobbed. "Help me. Please, sweetheart, help me."

Silently Gabriel continued tightening the garrote, grateful when the other wizard morphed back into himself.

"You can't kill me, Edge." Wheezing, he fought for breath, mouth opening and closing frantically, even as he clawed at his throat. "Impossible—you know it. I'm stronger—more—powerful than you—could—ever hope to—be."

"I'll put that on your tombstone." Sweat poured into Gabriel's eyes as he tightened the noose in small increments. Not because he didn't want to get the job done, but because Verdine's magic was fighting him for control every inch of the way.

He knew to the second when Verdine's life force started winking out. The small electrical charges became fewer and fewer as the wizard's power weakened. The fire ants left Gabriel's body so suddenly, he staggered.

Eden's apparition vanished.

Shaken by just how damn close this fight had been, Gabriel walked over to where Verdine had fallen. As he approached he continued to wind the whip around and around his hand, keeping it taut. And watched the life seep out of those evil black eyes.

Holding the garrote in one hand, he held out the other hand, palm up. His sword materialized, and he felt the comfortable weight of it across his palm. He raised it high, then brought it down across Verdine's neck.

The blade made a high-pitched whine as the cold steel severed Verdine's head from his shoulders as cleanly as a hot knife through butter.

Suddenly, the room exploded into brilliant white shooting lights more intense than a lifetime of Chinese New Year fireworks displays. The floor shook and rocked beneath Gabriel's bare feet, until he couldn't keep his balance and staggered before falling to his knees. His heart kicked in like a sledgehammer, and his eyes and nose burned as the pure white light danced around him, and then poured through his body hard enough to knock him back on his ass.

Several minutes, or hours, later he opened his eyes to see Duncan, Tremayne, and Stone surrounding him.

"I should kick your lazy ass for napping on the job," Alex Stone said with a grin, giving Gabriel a hand up. "Jesus. You look like hell."

"You should see the other guy," Duncan muttered. His eyes met Gabriel's. "Scared the crap out of me when nobody could get into the room. You okay?"

"It was an . . . interesting experience. Is he dead?"

"Hell yes," Tremayne assured him. "Simon went off to do some hocus-pocus with the bastard's head. Lark and Upton took the body off for some kind of wizardly cremation."

So it was done then.

Duncan grabbed his arm as he lurched. "You okay?"

Gabriel gave a negligent half shrug. Okay was relative. He felt . . . *different*. Lighter. Heavier. Hell. He didn't know. Just . . . different. He could hear the faint burble of muted voices in his mind, and realized that he was hearing Verdine's past. Jesus. As if he didn't have enough crap going on right now.

Duncan released his arm, but he gave Gabriel a lift of

his eyebrow, a look that demanded explanations. Details. A look most people found hard to resist. Gabriel knew, because he'd taught that look to both of his brothers himself.

He gave a slight not-now shake of his head. Explanations would have to wait.

"I don't know how the hell you pulled that off, big brother," Duncan acknowledged the delay nonverbally, but he was studying him like a bug under a microscope. "The odds were stacked against you. Big time." He gave Gabriel a sharp, penetrating look. "How do you account for that?"

Good question. This was a fight he shouldn't have been able to win. Verdine had been far too strong, his powers considerably more potent than Gabriel's.

Until that last minute when the balance of power had somehow changed.

"He was twice as strong as I was. I shouldn't have been able to get anywhere near the son of a bitch." Eden's ring glinted on his hand as he indicated the room. He narrowed his eyes. The ring . . . ? Nah. Gabriel rubbed the back of his neck as he glanced around the chaos of the dining room. "Shouldn't have been able to best him. Yet here I am."

"You've been holding out on me, bro." Duncan gave him a measured glance.

Gabriel scrubbed a hand over his face. He'd rather face fifty Verdine's than do what he was about to do. "I'm sending her away."

"Not *Eden*," Duncan said impatiently. "Your powers."

He gave his brother a startled look. "What I felt was *visible*?"

"Hell, yeah. You moved faster than the human eye could see. Not your everyday invisible, mind you. Almost faster than the speed of light. Damn cool. That's something new, isn't it?"

Gabriel nodded. "I was . . . supercharged."

"Really?" Intrigued, Duncan's eyes lit up. "Why? How?"

"You were right outside the door for most of it. Maybe our powers *aren't* canceled o—"

"Nope. Not it. Leave it for now. You can give me details later. But we *are* going to have to analyze this business with Verdine. I've never encountered that much power from a wizard before. Where the hell did he come from? Where'd he get *his* powers?"

"There's someone higher than Verdine," Gabriel's blood ran cold as Verdine's memories flooded through his mind in a toxic wash. He'd never felt anything as evil. "A whole fucking lot higher, and more powerful."

"You sure—Yeah. I see that you are. Who is it?"

"Don't know his name, but I'd know him if I saw him."

"You read Verdine's mind?"

"Unfortunately." A vortex of darkness that had almost sucked Gabriel in. As it was he was going to have a few fucking sleepless nights coming to terms with Verdine's recollections of his life.

"Clues as to who or where?"

"I'll have to sort through the swill."

"Make it quick, bro."

"Yeah. I hear you."

"What I don't understand," Duncan glanced around, "is why he didn't kill Eden instead of Dr. Kirchner in the first place. Owning the company she worked for, he had access to the bot from the start. And ample opportunity to kill or kidnap her. Why murder Kirchner and wait until now to try to bend her to his will?"

"Power. Control. The thrill of the hunt." And mixed with those emotions were lust, envy, and greed. In his own sick way, Verdine had loved Eden. "He killed Kirchner to scare her. Believing that in the end, he'd be the only one she trusted. That she'd change her mind about making the bot to his precise specifications, and agree to use her expertise to help him amass the robot army he wanted."

"Instead she trusted you."

Gabriel's jaw hurt from clenching his teeth. "Sometimes," he said bitterly. "Even a genius makes bad choices."

"*You're* going to have his powers now, you know," his brother told him.

"Christ—" He hadn't thought about that. Hadn't had time.

"Don't think about it now," Duncan told him with perfect understanding. "You have another situation to deal with."

"Eden."

His brother smiled. "Actually I meant MacBain. He's on his way. I'll run interference. Go."

Gabriel glanced across the room at the portrait where Eden's eyes glowed proudly back at him. He started walking purposefully toward her.

"Immediate debriefing at HQ," Sebastian said behind him, at the same time that Stone yelled, "Yo! Where are you going? The Council wants to talk to you right a— Where's he going?"

"In the morning," he said without turning.

"What about the bots?" Fitzgerald demanded.

"Safe where they are for now," Gabriel answered, still moving. His chest felt tight with suppressed emotion. He'd rather face, alone and barehanded, fifty heavily armed tangos, than do what he was about to do. "We'll need to run analysis and probability studies before they're destroyed." He had to raise his voice as he crossed to the other end of the long room.

There'd be a debriefing, reports to file, meetings to take, questions to answer.

But first things first.

He stood beneath the painting and brought Eden down to his side. The moment she realized where she was she launched herself into his arms. Standing on her toes she wrapped her arms around his neck in a stranglehold. Nuzzling her face into his throat she managed to choke out, "I was scared to death for you."

That made two of them. He held her just as tightly, burying his face in her floral-scented hair. "I'm okay." Okay, but feeling decidedly shaky. He'd never experienced anything like that last little bit with the fireworks. That would take some processing.

She lifted her face, and Gabriel, ignoring the gathering of men in the room with them, took her mouth like a man taking his last gulp of air before drowning. When they eventually parted they were both breathless. Still holding on, she smiled up at him, her eyes wary. Beneath her almost euphoric happiness was an undercurrent that he was feeling too. It hurt just looking at her. Knowing he had to store each feature in his memory for the long barren years ahead.

Her smile trembled a little before she righted it. "*Told* you Grandma Rose's lucky ring would work."

Gabriel forced himself to return her smile, knowing that like Eden's, it didn't come close to reaching his eyes. "I felt like Dumbo holding the feather."

"But it worked, didn't it?"

He rested his forehead on hers, breathing in her clean, flowery fragrance. For the last time. "Yeah. It did," he told her with forced lightness. "Good for Grandma Rose." But he knew the ring had nothing to do with it. It was Eden who had given him the strength and power to vanquish Jason Verdine. Eden who had made survival essential. Eden whose heart he was about to rip apart and stomp on.

He squeezed his eyes shut, holding her tightly against him, rocking them both as the events of the last hours drifted like smoke around them.

"Take me upstairs and make love to me," she whispered softly, as she combed her fingers lightly through the hair at his temple. He saw the rapid pulse of her heart beating like a trapped bird beneath the thin skin at the base of her throat. Everything she was feeling showed clearly in the dark velvety depths of her eyes. But her gaze was steady.

Gabriel hesitated.

Band-Aid quick?

Or one last time?

Surely a condemned man deserved at least that.

She rose to brush the corner of his mouth with hers. Her lips clung for an extra second, before she broke the contact. "Take me upstairs, my love. Oh, no!" she said on a teasing laugh that ripped open a fresh wound in his heart. "No shimmering. I want you to carry me."

He groaned, willing to pretend, as she was, that they could be lighthearted lovers. Willing to pretend, for just a little longer, that this wasn't their last good-bye. "Up all those stairs?"

"You bet. Come on. You can do it. If you can beat the pants off the most powerful wizard on the planet you can heft my weight up a few hundred stai—" She laughed delightedly as he swung her up in his arms and started striding toward the door.

The men parted to let them through. Ignoring them, Eden looped her arms about his neck and snuggled her head against his chest as if she'd done it all her life.

They met MacBain halfway across the trashed room. "Och! This mess is unconscionable," the old man muttered, seeing the destruction for the first time. He kicked aside a chunk of mahogany paneling in the middle of the carpet with his highly polished black shoe.

Tsking, he picked up Gabriel's whiskey glass from the floor, and placed it, just so, on the heat-buckled silver tray where the drink listed to the side when he lifted it. "This will take me at least a m—Oh, aye. Now *that* is a neat trick. Is it here to stay?"

He'd thought it, and the room was completely back to normal. Nothing broken, nothing awry. No sign that Jason Verdine had ever been there. It was as if nothing had transpired. If only.

Surprised himself, he glanced from MacBain to his brother, and then at Eden, and shrugged. "I have no freaking idea. MacBain? Politely escort our guests to the front door. Then remove the bell. I'm not at home."

As soon as the door shut behind them, Eden touched his jaw with a tenderness that made him ache. "You're going to send me back to Tempe, aren't you?"

Christ. This would be a hell of a fucking lot easier if she weren't so attuned to him. How had this happened so fast? Now that he'd found her, how could he let her go?

Step away from the table.

He stopped walking halfway across the vast entry hall that echoed his footsteps in a way that made him conscious of how lonely one pair of footsteps could sound. He wondered why he'd never noticed that before. "Would you prefer I sent you from here?"

"No. I don't want to leave you until I absolutely have to."

"A farewell fuck?" he asked, going for mocking. Going for insulting. Going for her slapping his face and demanding to be sent anywhere but his arms. He was proud of the cool, matter-of-factness of his tone. Give him a swarm of fire ants any day.

She searched his face, her eyes shadowed. "Call it

whatever the hell you like, Gabriel Edge," she told him with asperity. "*I* know what it is. Don't make a mockery of all that we feel, all that we are, because you feel trapped and not in control."

He started up the sweeping staircase. "This has nothing to do with control." He was lying. Of course it did. Because it took every atom, every particle of control in him not to fall to his knees, Eden in his arms, and beg her to stay.

"Not here," she told him firmly when he hesitated halfway up. "If this is our last time I want to make love in your bed." His jaw tightened, and she ran her fingers through his hair as he climbed. Sunlight streamed through the arched windows at the top of the stairs. "I'll miss you terribly, you know."

"Do you want sex or not? I can send you home in time for dinner."

"Hmm." Head on his chest she listened to the staccato beat of his heart. "A lonely dinner. Boxed mac and cheese. Nasty."

His jaw hurt from grinding his teeth. "Order in."

"I won't have a job."

"You're a genius," he told her shortly, and very unlover-like. "You'll find another job."

She ran a finger around the inside neck seam of his T-shirt as he walked and his body reacted as it always did to her touch. The jasmine scent of her hair as it brushed his chin filled him with a longing he knew was just the tip of the iceberg. This one-tenth of yearning was already almost incapacitating.

"Will you get Jason's powers?"

"Yes." He suspected he didn't have a choice in the matter one way or the other. Duncan was the one who gave a shit about accruing magical powers; Gabriel didn't give a damn, as long as he could do his job. With or without magic.

"Really?" She was silent for a few more steps, then said musingly, "I have a fascinating research project I'd like to sink my teeth into. Private, of course. Not something I'd ever publish. But really, it would take a lifetime to—"

Gabriel stopped dead, letting her body slip down his as if she were contaminated.

Ah, geez. Here we go again. Eden looked up at him with narrowed eyes as they stood halfway up the staircase. Neither all the way at the bottom, not having reached the top. Another handy metaphor, she thought.

The man could teach a mule stubborn, damn it. She almost asked for intervention from his great-great-great-whatever-grandmother, who was glaring out of her portrait at them from the wall at his back. Eden felt about as unhappy as Finola Edridge looked.

She crossed her arms over her chest, and leaned against the banister. "Now what's your problem?"

She knew what his problem was. She just didn't know how to fix it. If he was a computer program she could fix him. But he was a flesh and blood man, and she had no idea how his programming worked. Too bad there wasn't a manual. She noticed a glint of silver as he ran a frustrated hand through his hair.

"Look," he snarled, apparently at the end of his very short rope. "I don't know how to make it any plainer to you than I have already. You're a nice woman. I like you," he bit out. "But we can't have a fucking future, don't you get it?"

He was dead serious and his expression made her heart ache in her chest. God. She was terrible at this man-woman stuff. Terrible, and inept, and so . . . God. She loved him so much. She was said to be a brilliant scientist. Tops in her field. And she didn't have what it took to hold a man.

Not any man. *This* man, with his haunted eyes, and

unshakable belief in a five-hundred-year-old curse. Her academic studies, her scientific background . . . *none* of it was going to make him change his mind. How could she counter what he believed?

She turned and started up the rest of the stairs, her brain going a mile a minute. "No sex in our future? That seems a bit extreme, doesn't it?" she asked lightly. Too lightly? she wondered, watching his face as he came up alongside her. Not that his expression would give her a clue as to his thoughts. He was a hard man to read. No, Eden thought, heart pounding, mouth dry, he was an *impossible* man to read.

Could a heart break? Literally? Intellectually she knew that it couldn't. But it certainly felt like it. They reached the landing and started walking toward his room. Sunlight streamed through the high arched windows, painting swirls in the gold, black, and red carpet in brilliant blocks of light and shadow, all the way down the ridiculously long corridor.

She stopped walking right beside dour Janet Edridge's portrait. "Not talking about the elephant in the room doesn't mean it's not there, Gabriel."

"Jesus, Eden!" His face was in shadow and his eyes burned as he looked at her. "Are you being particularly obtuse? Let me spell it out for you. We *have* no future together. We've had a highly dramatic few days. We've been caught up in the moment. Extreme reactions happen in extreme situations."

"Are you going to insult my intelligence by suggesting what I feel for you is Stockholm syndrome?"

"Of course it is." The finality in his voice ripped out her heart.

There was no point debating the subject, and she didn't even try. It hurt to breathe. She didn't know what to do with her hands because what she wanted to do was grab hold of him and never let go. Her wizard. *Hers,* damn it.

He looked so forbidding standing there in a stripe of shadow, while she stood in a stripe of sunlight.

A man who shouldn't exist, in a place that shouldn't exist.

He loved her. She knew he loved her.

Didn't he?

Could he?

She wrapped her arms about her own waist. Her chest ached just looking at him. From his expression, the drawbridge was up and the battle stations armed. Maybe that was mixing her metaphors, but he looked shut down. Disinterested. Her eyes drifted to Janet's stoic face beyond his left shoulder.

Help me, Janet.

She frowned. There was something different . . . She glanced back at Gabriel, who still looked surly.

"I think it would be better if I sent you back home now," he told her with no inflection. "Why prolong our good-byes?"

She tilted her chin. Nothing ventured, nothing gained. She'd never forgive herself if she didn't at least try to get through his thick skull how she felt. "And *I* think it would be better if we tried starting with the truth and work from there."

"What truth?"

"I love you, Gabriel Edge. I love you with all my heart and soul, from now until eternity. There. Now it's your turn."

He gave a half laugh. "Christ, I love that about you. You cut straight to the chase."

Did he love more than her quick tongue though? "Forget the consequences for a minute. Do you care about me at all?"

"I *can't* forget the consequences. Not even for a minute."

"Answer the question."

"Yes. Hell, yes. I care. With every breath in my body and every beat of my heart. Bu—"

She caught her breath, then stepped closer, and said shakily, "That's all that matters."

"But how we feel is immaterial," he continued, as if she hadn't spoken. He didn't touch her, but he didn't back up as she half expected him to do either. "I'd rather live the rest of my life without you, knowing that you're safe, than risk your life."

Eden's throat closed. "Don't I have a vote?"

"Don't fight me on this. Don't."

"Your parents had eighteen years together."

"They had eighteen years *apart*!"

"Then we have to figure out a way to *break* the damned curse!"

"Five centuries of Edge men have tried and failed. No," he snapped as she reached out to touch his arm. "Don't touch me. I'm about to go off like a fucking rocket as it is."

"Step away from the wizard?"

"Step away from the man who wants to believe that there's even the smallest, vaguest, tiniest hope of making this work, but knows that's impossible."

"What will happen if we try? God, Gabriel. Can't we at least try?"

"You'll die."

"I'm willing to take that chance. Please. I'll die without you if we don't." Eden would never have imagined those words coming out of her own mouth. She wasn't that dramatic, or intense. But she believed them now. Without this man she would die.

"You won't," he told her unequivocally. "You won't die. That's the point. You'll just feel as though your heart's being ripped out. But eventually you'll go on. Eventually you'll forget."

"Will you?" she asked, trying to read anything in his darkly shadowed eyes. "Will you forget me?"

"A man would have to be dead to forget you."

She didn't realize that her body had been braced for a flat out *Yes, I'll forget you,* and she let out the air she'd been holding in her lungs. "Then let's take a chance," she begged softly. "A little time together is better than a lifetime apart."

"Don't you think I want that?" He traced a finger across her upper lip, then the lower, as if memorizing the feel of her mouth, and all the while his gaze played across her face as if storing her features to retrieve later. When she was gone.

"I want more time together more than I've ever wanted anything. But no. The price is too high."

The sun was moving, changing the patterns of sunlight and shadow all the way down the hallway, and Eden blinked as the bright stripe started moving over them, bathing them in warmth and golden yellow light. What a crock. If she was going to have this miserably depressing conversation she'd rather do it in shadow.

"I'm willing to risk it."

"I'm not—" He frowned, brushing her cheek with his knuckle. "Jesus. What's the matter? You've gone ash white."

"Oh, my God! Gabriel! Look at Grandma Rose's ring!"

She grabbed his hand where something glinted in the shifting light. "Look at the ring. Look at the *ring*!"

"Yeah. I was going to give it back to y—"

"*Look* at it," Eden was practically vibrating with excitement, her fingers curled around his as she lifted their joined hands. Gabriel looked at the tiny silver ring on the first knuckle of his left pinkie. He brought his other hand up, and started to pull it off his hand.

"Christ, sweetheart. The last thing I want to do right

n—Okay. Okay." He held his hand up. "Hey. The black wore off. Looks like silver. Couple of hearts—what am I supposed to see exactly?" Gabriel lifted his head to stare at her with puzzlement. "It's similar—" They turned at the same time, hands entwined as they faced Janet's portrait.

"Not similar. It's *exactly* the same." Eden said softly. "Look at her finger, my love."

He turned to look at the portrait of Janet. Where once she'd been bare-fingered, now she wore the twined silver hearts on her pale thin finger. The exact same ring Gabriel was wearing on his hand. "It can't be." But his heart beat wildly enough for him to believe that even this miracle was possible with Eden by his side.

"It *is*. The curse is broken." Her fingers tightened around his. "How does the end go? 'Only freely given will this curse be done. To break the spell, three must work as one'? I gave you Grandma Rose's ring freely. Do you realize what powers were at work to allow my grandmother to find your family ring at a Parisian fair sixty years ago? And strong enough to bring us together in these weird circumstances? Incredible."

"Incredible? How about a *miracle*." He glanced down at the clasped hands where the sunlight bounced off the silver. "It feels warm."

"Look at it! It's glowing."

" 'Three must work as one.' "

"That means your brothers must each be given one of the other pieces of the jewelry to break the spell completely."

He already had his phone in his hand. Eden grabbed his wrist. "What are you doing?"

"Calling Duncan and Caleb—"

"You can't. It has to be given freely, remember?"

"How will they know it's the jewelry that will break

Nairne's Curse? Hell, how will they find the person who's in possession of it? I have t—"

"They won't. You didn't. You can't tell them anything, Gabriel. Not a word. Nairne made sure that all three of you would have to work together to break her Curse." She wrapped her arms about his neck. "I think she means *at the same time*. Let them each find their Lifemate in their own way. Let Nairne have her last word. Let this Curse be over for all time."

"How did you get to be so wise?"

"Desperation?" Her tone was wry. Sunlight streamed over them, illuminating Janet's portrait. It seemed to Eden as though the woman's mouth had curved up—just a little—in a smile. She looked back at Gabriel.

He shimmered them to the bedroom and prone on the bed. With a smug smile, Eden opened her eyes as soon as he made their clothing vanish. Bathed in yellow sunlight she looked about as perfect as a wish. "God," she said happily, snuggling her warm naked body against his. "I love that mode of transportation. I love being naked with you. I love you."

"I love you, Dr. Eden Cahill. I love you more than life itself."

She pulled his head down until he could feel her smile against his lips. Then pulled his mouth to hers and kissed him back with all the love she had in her.

She couldn't breathe and she didn't care. She wanted the kiss to go on and on. She could have been struck by lightning right there and then, and not cared. She was already being incinerated by Gabriel Edge's clever—God, *so* clever—mouth. The sheer pleasure as his tongue touched hers, the slide and glide.

He dragged his mouth off hers, pulling in a deep breath that moved his chest against her aching breasts. Eden hauled him back for another soul shattering kiss. "I wasn't done telling you how I feel."

He touched her face, saw how her glorious brown eyes captured the light as she looked up at him. And knew that nothing, not even magic, could ever come close to the perfection of this woman in his arms. "We have the rest of our lives, sweetheart. We have the rest of our lives."

"I know. How magical is *that*?"

*Read on for an exclusive sneak peek
at the next pulse-pounding novel in the
Edge trilogy by*

CHERRY
ADAIR

EDGE
of
FEAR

Coming in August 2006
from Ballantine Books

"What does it matter what the hell she looks like?" Caleb Edge said into the phone, hoping like hell that the dark, primal lust he felt drumming through his veins didn't bleed into his voice. He frowned absently at his control's odd question as he shifted the compact sat. phone between chin and shoulder, and the binocs an inch left.

A foggy San Francisco street and a shitload of swirling fog separated the two apartment windows. The lights over there were on. The lights here weren't.

His heart, which was normally as steady as a rock, still pounded uncomfortably sixty seconds after he'd lifted the binoculars to his eyes and taken his first look at her.

Bam! Caleb felt as though someone had punched him in the solar plexus, grabbed his heart, and squeezed. *Hard.*

That's what Heather Shaw looks like.

"She looks like a woman with more money than sense," he told Lark absently. His heart was racing; he assured himself it was because his goddamned knee hurt like hell. He leaned a little more of his weight on the shoulder he had propped against the wall.

She'd pushed the sleeves of the thin purple sweater up her creamy forearms while she worked. The fabric draped over her tall slender body as if it had been custom made. Probably had. Heather Shaw had more money than many third-world countries.

"Interesting location for her to hide out." Caleb dragged his gaze from the gentle swell of Miss Shaw's breasts back to the top of her head. *Look up again, honey, let's see those gorgeous eyes again.* "How long's she been there?" Were her eyes green? Brown? Hard to tell from this distance.

"About six months," his control, Lark Orela, told him. "Why?"

Reluctantly Caleb shifted the binocs. "Place's pretty stark. Chair. Bed. Table. Nothing personal that I can see."

"She's been moving around."

"Yeah." And not easy to track down, according to Lark. Finding Heather's father *first* would've expedited this op, and made it a hell of a lot more interesting, Caleb thought. Unfortunately Brian Shaw had been missing for the better part of a year. Interesting, but not surprising, that such a high-profile individual could completely obliterate his trail to disappear like that.

Which left his delectable daughter to the wolves.

Caleb figured he'd been in rehab for too damn long if just *looking* at the tango's daughter gave him a hard-on.

Long, elegant bones. Pale, slender fingers. Silky hair that would feel like sunlight on his skin. He was damn sorry now that he'd begged Lark to send him on a mission. Anywhere. Any damn thing to escape the hospital.

This had been the best Lark had come up with at short notice. Bullshit. She didn't think he was ready.

This wasn't an op. A simple question needed answering. Hell, someone could call it in.

But here he was. Because anything was better than

being stuck in a rehab center for months on end. Surprisingly, Caleb's reaction to the woman he'd been sent to find had been visceral and immediate. He liked women just fine. Hell, he *loved* women. But he'd never had such an instantaneous, energizing, chemical . . . jolt *looking* at a woman before.

Adrenaline junkie that he was, his physical reaction on seeing her—blood pressure up, libido up, temperature up—intrigued him. Pheromones were one thing, but he wasn't even in sniffing distance of her.

His reaction was so immediate. So . . . *primitive* it shocked the hell out of him.

Why her? Why here? Why now?

"Okay, then let me ask you an easy question," Lark said in his ear. Caleb braced himself. Lark was an empath, and he didn't want her picking up any screwy signals. "How's the leg?" she asked, throwing him.

Yeah. Concentrate on something that made sense. The knee was sore. Which annoyed the hell out of him. The only person's injuries he couldn't fix were his own. Pissed him off to no end.

"One hundred percent A-okay."

He'd been pathetically grateful when he'd gotten the call an hour ago during his hopefully final physical therapy session. Hell yeah, he'd check out Shaw's daughter. *Anything* to cut short the boring sessions. He'd been going stir-crazy.

He'd commandeered an apartment across the street, one whose windows looked directly into hers. A typical winter's day in San Francisco. Damp, misty fog eddied in gossamer ribbons between the tall, narrow buildings in an ever-changing screen that challenged a clear view into Heather's apartment, even with her lights on. Caleb had seen enough.

"Liar," Lark told him. "Dr. Long just told me you're still favoring that knee."

"Then why did you ask?" He'd had his knee replaced, but there'd been some nerve and muscle damage. It would heal. Eventually. These things usually did. He had plenty of scars to prove it.

Watching Heather Shaw was more interesting than discussing his knee, which ached like hell. Which in turn made him bad tempered. Which in turn made him even more antsy to get back to work so he could forget about it.

Based on photographs, Shaw's daughter had changed some during the last year.

"To see if you'd lie," Lark informed him.

Lying was the least he'd do to get back to work. He'd been off for three months now. Even one more day with nothing to do but physical therapy would drive him straight up the wall. "I have a medical release from the doctor and the therapist. So, quit torturing me, honey. Find me something. *Anything*. I beg you. This lack of activity has made me a basket case."

"You're a workaholic, Middle Edge."

"You say that like it's a bad thing. Come on, babe, help me out here. Send me to some exotic hellhole to kick some terrorist butt."

"Can you run?"

"Better than most." No. But he didn't want his control to know that his doctors were right. He wasn't fully back up to speed yet. But he'd get back into shape on the job. "And since when does an Edge need to run? We show up, take names and kick ass. There's no heavy lifting and I like the hours."

"That may be, but you should still take some downtime until you're fully recovered. Think of it as a vacation."

"I don't want a vacation. I don't *need* a vacation."

Lark had a pretty laugh, even if it was mocking. "You sound like a truculent five-year-old. But I agree. You can do your job just fine limping. Your trigger finger's just fine. You brain wasn't damaged—*much*—by that beating you took."

"Heartless, Lark. I'm sharp as a tack." Was she going to send him back in? Caleb imagined the young woman who was his control. Lark Orela looked like a cross between a biker chick and a Goth rocker. With spiked black and fuchsia hair, and half a dozen silver rings in each eyebrow, and one in her nose for God's sake. But behind that pale face and scary black eye makeup lived the brain of a brilliant tactician.

The operatives under her control, Caleb included, weren't fully aware of the full scope of Lark's various wizardly talents, which intrigued him. Among other skills, Caleb was damn sure she was clairvoyant. But she never talked about it, and discouraged questions.

"Tell me what you see." She circled back to Heather Shaw.

This was a "look-see." He wanted back to work. Yesterday would have been good. "Are you sending me back into the fiel—"

"Observations, Edge?"

Lark was like a particularly friendly pit bull. Caleb shifted to do a quick scan of Shaw's one-room apartment. "How the mighty have fallen. The walls are bare. No pictures. No knickknacks. Nothing whatsoever to personalize her living space." The covers on the narrow single bed behind her were thrown about haphazardly. Restless night or lover?

His insides clenching at the thought of a lover surprised him. Good thing he would be with Kris-Alice in Germany within the hour. That was one of the benefits of being who he was. What he was. He could teleport with ease.

But to go and talk to Miss Shaw he'd merely stroll across the street and knock at her door. Caleb worked for T-FLAC/psi. T-FLAC was a privately funded counterterrorist organization. Psi was the psychic phenomena offshoot.

This wasn't a psi op. He'd been in Silicon Valley undergoing forced physical therapy on his knee—hell, it had just been a *small* bullet hole—when Shaw's prints had been ID'd. Since he was closest, he'd been requested to get intel from the woman. Intel they sorely needed if they had a hope in hell of tracking down her father, Brian Shaw.

"She live alone?"

"Looks like."

Caleb found downtime redundant. Unlike his laid-back younger brother, Duncan, Caleb liked to be on the go all the time. But they'd insisted. Getting shot in the knee was a pain in his ass. Technically, he was supposed to be off duty for another three weeks. He'd never been real big on technicalities. All he needed was to be sent on an op now, and he'd prove to the team and control that he was in top form. And *this* wasn't an op. It was a frigging *conversation*. And a short one at that.

No hauling ass to prove he could still outrun, out-jump, outshoot the best of them.

Right now even watching a woman through binocs beat lying around on a sun-drenched beach somewhere doing nothing. Give him action and he was a happy man. An op relaxed him. Hell, a fast-paced op made him sleep like a baby at night.

Watching Heather should have been a step in that direction. But instead his body grew even more coiled and tight. He needed to get a grip. *And not,* he thought with a mental bitch slap, *on that perfect body of hers.* Still, the mere thought of running his fingers through her honey-colored hair, allowing his palms to slide over the gentle curve of her hip, either, both, was interfering with his assignment.

Time to focus.

Yeah. That.

He finished checking out Heather's living quarters. The kitchen occupied one corner, an open door led to the bathroom, another door led, he presumed, to the stairwell. The bed, and folding table where she now sat, were the sum total of her furnishings. The small, sterile accommodations, after living the high life, must really cramp the socialite's style.

She was seated at the table, some sort of small tool in her hand, prying a stone out of a piece of jewelry, or putting one in. She made and sold her own jewelry to local jewelers. That's how she'd been found. Her fingerprints had been lifted from a jewelry store after a robbery there yesterday.

From there it had been simple to track "Hannah Smith" to this address. Even simpler to determine that Hannah Smith *was* Heather Shaw.

She'd filled out some. The last photograph they'd had of her—some high-society thing in Hong Kong a year ago—had shown her looking almost skeletal. Now she had more meat on her bones.

Not that Caleb could see much of her, dressed as she was in jeans and a purple sweater. But her face looked softer, more appealing now. His heart, which had started up a peculiar erratic beat when he'd first set eyes on her, picked up more speed as he took in the creamy curve of her cheek, the silky sweep of her hair, the stubborn jut of her chin.

His reaction to her was . . . weird.

The accelerated pounding was the staccato beat of fear. Of excitement? Of premonition? Hell, he didn't know what. Nor did he want to find out. Lark was the one with precognitive powers, not him. But every instinct in him flashed a big neon warning to keep the hell away from Heather Shaw. And in his line of work, Caleb trusted his instincts. They hadn't failed him yet.

"Earth to Middle Edge? Humor me," Lark said smoothly in his ear, snapping him out of his reverie. "Tell me what she looks like."

Touchable. Dangerous. Trouble. "She's not blond any more." All the pictures of Shaw's daughter showed her as a golden California blonde with about fifteen pounds of curls. Now the woman's thick, stick-straight, honey brown hair hung to her shoulders in a shiny curtain. A nice improvement.

"Pretty?"

"Not particularly." No, not pretty, Caleb thought, *stunning.* Appealing as hell. Her even features and lack of makeup made her appear younger, more . . . vulnerable, than her pub shots had. He didn't believe in tarring the offspring with their parent's brush, but the delectable Miss Shaw had run in her father's very fast, very public social circles. Stood to reason that there'd be nothing innocent or vulnerable about her.

"Who cares," he muttered, distracted by the way the lamp over the table brought out caramel highlights in Heather's hair. She was making some sort of necklace, he decided. Something with swirls of silver and purple stones. Pretty and delicate. As pretty and delicate as the slender hands holding it up to the light.

Her hair spilled over her shoulder as she tilted her head to inspect her work. "We have her. Send someone in for the interrogation. My work here is done." He was annoyed that he couldn't seem to take his eyes off Shaw's no-longer-missing only child. Surveilling her was one thing, *ogling,* for God's sake, quite another. Yet, for some weird and completely mysterious reason, he was drawn to this woman in ways he hadn't experienced in years. Years? Hell. *Ever.*

"Not so fast, Hopalong. This is now your op."

He frowned again. While he'd love an op right now—save him from more hydro-treatments, ultrasound tissue massages, and all the other crap—this wasn't it. Too low-key. Too mundane. "Questioning Shaw's daughter doesn't necessitate a psi operative. I found her, now I'm ready to hand her off. Who are they sending? I'll hang around until they get here."

They being T-FLAC proper. His particular talents weren't needed. He'd just happened to be in San Francisco when Heather's fingerprints had popped up on the T-FLAC fingerprint database.

Gotcha.

"I'm assigning Shaw's daughter to you. Use your rakish charm to get that intel ASAP." For an extremely Goth-looking young woman, Lark Orela's no-nonsense tone always came as a surprise. This afternoon it brooked no argument.

It made no sense, but Caleb figured since he was there, he might as well save someone the trip. Fifteen minutes and he'd be done. He'd report in, results in hand, then pursue Lark in person for a mission. A *real* one.

"Yeah. Sure," he told her easily. "I'll give you a shout when I get the father's location."

"Good luck." Lark sounded . . . odd?

Caleb's frown deepened at the strange inflection in her usually well-modulated voice. "What am I missing?"

"Life, love, and the pursuit of happiness?" On that cryptic note the phone went dead.

Caleb stared at it as he snapped it closed. Trust Lark to be enigmatic. She was a cross between a wizard, a mother figure, and a pain in the collective asses of her operatives. But as a control she had no match. Lark could juggle from one to twenty-one operatives simultaneously. Caleb would stake his life on the fact that Lark *could* see the future. She never spoke of it. Ever. But the ability had saved many an operative's ass, no doubt. Her advice and direction were always sound and spot-on. No one argued.

When Lark Orela said jump, intelligent people asked how high.

Caleb didn't bother glancing around the commandeered apartment to make certain he hadn't left anything behind. He hadn't. He'd shimmered in. He'd leave the same way. Sight unseen.

 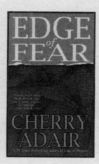 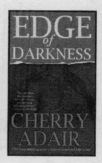